THE CAPRICORN SKY

The Capricorn Sky

COLLY CAMPBELL

Sooty Publishing

THE CAPRICORN SKY

First published by Stringybark Press 2020

Copyright © Colly Campbell, 2020

2nd Edition published by Sooty Publishing, 2021

This is a work of fiction and does not relate to anyone living, dead or yet to be.

The Capricorn Sky was written on Ngambri and Ngunnawal Country, land which was never ceded.

www.collycampbell.com.au

Cover design: Pat Naoum/Red Tally Studios

Typeset: Mark Furness/Liquorice Light Publishing

A catalogue record for this book is available at The National Library Australia

Cover image: European Space Agency – CC

http://www.esa.int/spaceinimages/images/2016/10/
Eye_of_the_storm

ISBN: 9-780645-196719

Also by Colly Campbell

The Kyoto Bell

THE HIGH CAPRICORN

H'K

STEAM from the rain blew through the door of The Caravanserai, a thrumming cafe in H'K halfway up the hill from the submarine port. Several folk'd had entered, dripping wet, to escape the sqwall. Three herself groaned, tho, cos she hadn't brought her teflite jacket for the long walk back to the bolt hole. She hoped the rain would blow past. The cafe crowd made her nervous – too many eyes looking about. Waiters bustled, noises came from the kitchen. Three moved further back into the shadows of the booth, watching her companions with distaste and the exit with hope. Someone slammed the cafe door shut with a heel.

Three sat with One and Two, and the various men and women from the invested corporate Hegemonies. RichArses in coolSuits and glasses, too damn businesslike for so early of a morning. A HegMan distributed a couple of glows of the target for inspektion. The glows insinuated themselves at either end of the table top and twirled insouciantly.

Three looked at the closest glow which orbited the tabletop, as a man's face, side profile, back o' the head slid around, and thought, *I've not been back to East Cap for 50 years and wouldn't go, 'cept the money is good and I could settle a few old scores, mebbe.* Wasn't the first time she'd had that notion since the job was mentioned. *Old scores.* Was a good thought.

The glow was sharp. The image of a darkHaired young man who looked supercilious. Three pulled the image round and stared into the young man's brown eyes, then turned him to check the set of his shoulders. *Not a bad looking victim*, she thought.

She eyed sidewayz the 2 doodz who'd travelled south with her to do this exceptionally well paid job. They were solid killers. Knew them both from earlier border work, up near Russia. One would do the scouting, Two, a fellow Oz, was the bomber, and her role: liaise with the client and clean up loose ends.

Bombing was a big ask from anyone. Out of the box. Meant multiple victims, for sure. Not that Three minded. But noone bombed any more. A very old fashioned act'o'violence, and done only by guiltless throwbacks like herself. Bombs caused a lot of mess & mincemeat, but a bomb well put shredded the evidence.

The cafe was crowded with white tiles and people. The door of the kitchen area opposite would fly open and she'd glimpse the silver woks and pots, the odd yellow flare on a stove. Cooks in white, flapping their hands and their utensils. Up and down the trestle seating people crammed in & shot food into their mouths with chopsticks & forks. Lots of customers.

She'd took time to get used to mixing with people after *the Blend*.

The wars. The multiple betrayals. Ironic she'd ended up in Asia, in the northern hemisphere, after all that spent blood in the dirty little civil war. Three sipped her iced miso, soaking up the scene, listening to the drill and, as usual, making plan B in her head while plan A was laid out. That's what Kingdom Allenby used to say, all those years ago: *"an oldy but a goody, always have plan B"*, along with *"you haven't lived till you've done gung ho"*. Three'd thought it funny at the time.

Kingdom, of course, had been working plan C to destroy them.

A waitress in pink silk brought beers for them all, bending prettily with the tray of glasses. *She did that on purpose,* Three thought bitterly. *All those heavy blokes look like heavy tippers and she's playing them for fools.* Three knew she didn't have to be bitter about the girl – she just was. Three was long past pretty. In fact, the waitress gave Three a nano glance and looked away as if she sensed Three's displeasure – or maybe, pinky waitress hadn't even registered Three's presence.

Hair once red was now yellowyGrey. Her face, tho' attractive for her advanced age, was kept product free. Three cultivated nonentity with great skill.

Was the same with the business heavies. The Bossman from the hegemony spoke Chinese in a strong Brazilhoz accent and also ignored Three. She'd never held the interest of many men and, anyway, when you pass 110, you're far too old, unless the guy one wooed was part of a strategic play. No, the Brazilhoz HegMan was fixated on the honcho from the Chinese side of things.

Still, she didn't care. The Chinese Hegs knew her lethal rep. The Brazilhoz, no. She just slid further into the shadow at the end of the table so her image stayed vague. Short blonde grey tips, thin face, large eyes, mouthlines that had gone sour. Been a sourOld, friendless existence since she escaped. She click-Clocked each face with her mind camera – like Kingdom'd said: *your allies may well become enemies in the fullness of time, so remember faces. Remember their shape and the eyes in their heads. Project them as old people too, because you never know when the future may backhand you.*

Wasn't that the truth, eh?

"We don't want AuZgov near this guy," said the Brazilhoz part of things to the hitTeam. "His strokes are more valuable to us if AuZgov remain in ignorance. Understand?"

The Chinese bloke, ops manager of some Heg, looked discomfited. Skanned the 3 killers with a hard eye.

One, Two and, reluctantly, Three, nodded, but she was noting Mr China's emotional tic with interest.

Still, Three would say nothing unless a key qwestion needed an answer – easier to avoid voice prints. The other assassins exchanged pleasantries. Two, the Aussie boy from Darwin, had talked about then – before *the Blend* – and now. He was a former smuggler and had to 'scape through the Cloud after the cops decided he'd crossed a red line. One, a Chinese bloke, was a HegMan. No doubt playing keepies on Two and herself.

"The target's a big drinker. Cleanest way – negate him in a bar."

The HegBoss looked relaxed at his inhuman utterance but some assembled looked uneasy, thinking "carnage". Three didn't flinch at the task, Not at all. Three was a woman who relished carnage.

"And, let me repeat," said the Brazilhoz, "money is no object at all. You will be rewarded handsomely."

Three'd heard him the first time. Still didn't care. More money that she'd ever need was already in her kick. Wasn't for the money she was going back home to the stink of East Capricorn and all she had fought when those Indons were shipped across.

Aiee, she was shitty ... shitty with the smell of soy and the brittle noises in the restaurants and the portentous men in suits planning their Heg operation, shitty with the hot rain outside and that she'd brought nothing to ward off the wet.

If she found the Traitor down there, he was a dead man. That's all she knew. She was a soldier, followed orders to the Terms of Engagement, but her term as a mercenary for these Brazilhoz bast'ds was a secondary thing. Means to an end.

Kingdom was a dead man if she ran him down.

ANDAMAN 1

AS ANDAMAN Marko stood on the edge to dive, the moon formed an eye looking up at him, a reflection in the black water. He dived into the centre of the reflection sending shards and wavelets of copper through the surface, making the moon blink.

Behind, the real moon hung above Magnetic Island. Probably last full moon he'd see 'til after the storm season. At one point, he'd opened the window shield across the front of the pool deck to allow the moonglow illuminate the vast room, water slopping and clapping. Clap, clap, clap.

Artificial lights out, to rest his jangled eyes; it was very dark except for the red moon and the haze in the sky.

Andaman was fighting overwhelming tiredness. Pumped with zizz & fixzo, he'd spent a very long 120 hours programming the clusters. The clusters were now primed to recognise keywords in multiple languages and, as usual, he'd got carried away with foreign jargon and market slang & the long stint had zapped his bones. At times in the small hours of the nite he had broken his concentration for a couple of dips in the basement pool.

With the tint on the blastProof shell turned off, he swam towards, then away, from the high full moon.

Andaman's motto was "play your margins". He scattered his crazy genius, and pushed his luck on both the topTier of legal and the underTier of "barely noticeable, but very wrong".

"Skimming," he named it qwietly, under his breath, to nobody. His subterraneous life.

And so it was this day in September. His October raid over the virtual was planned and primed. Five days and nites of research and economix mapping, Andaman loaded the array on his screen, aiming for big host exchanges in Central and South America, and the usual vast markets of Ottowa, Shanghai, Sao Paulo.

Brow knotted in concentration, back aching, Andaman concluded checks on another screen to see where the legit markets were heading and had made some speculative calculations through his very own brain as well.

He was unleashing 5 harpoon clusters. Each harpoon was sheathed in feathers of coding to seek out buyUps of stock and derivatives in carbon rendering, synthetic fertilisers, gamma ray farms, rare earth miners and mixed media.

Once or twice he'd scoped friendly contacts around the world for genial chats about hegemonic intel and, of course, new foreign slang. He loved slang in all forms. Sexual, share market, political. Old friends from the past had loomed on his screen small talking & big talking & it had been a furious few days of work & when the pool called, even after the swimming, his muscles were tight.

His eyes felt like fried eggs. That's was the trouble with fixzo. Almost 5 days and nites of wakefulness took you out, even with the ripple effects through the ganglions and synapses.

He took yet another tiny sip of his syrupy kopi and sighed with relief the allWeeker was finally over and the zizz could subside. Usually let it clear out of his system rather than taking a chiller.

The sun had long replaced the moon and was very hot off the horizon. The sky was the normal faint yellowy bruise. White and pink clouds were bunched like little fists to the north – he had a panoramic view from where he stood – along with a few high altitude gossamer streaks which seemed to be vanishing in the heat like sizzle marks. The last of winter. Soon the Cloud would loom.

He gazed down at the greenBlue bay, the yellow lick of beach, the stacked terraces that held 1000s of apartments and houses, and their echo on the island opposite, the white and green jigsaw that was Port Magnetic with its puzzle of buildings and towers. To the north and south, he scanned the dark forms in the ocean, barrages on either end of the island to hold back the worst surges. Today was already hot, breezeless and benign. A day worth enjoying, thought Andaman, if one could enjoy his repetitive and strange twilight existence.

He returned his gaze from the bay to the screen and sipped more kopi to help settle the effects of fixzo & brain zaps he'd given himself over the last few days. For focus & clarity, accelerated thinking.

His harpoons were built around oldSchool computer viruses that everyone had forgotten after a century and a half of rapid progress on the virtual. A time when bytes had fragmented into subInfinitesimals. He'd resheathed the old viruses with his own codes.

He snorted.

Because he'd been at this game for 8 or so years, he was conscious that his only gratification was trying to impress his own self. Noone else could ever know his schemes & nite codes as they were deeply illegal. "Good one, Andy!" he'd boast to himself, "a beautiful thing." Was starting to border on the pathetic. He'd become bored after a while (a long while) with the ludicrous selfPraise. Bored with himself.

*

Andaman Marko had been a legit, registered marketOperator since the age of 16 when he reached halfMajority and was allowed to speculate. He'd honed his skills and become very rich.

In the light of day, the city saw Andaman as community minded. Bit of a playboy. Bringer of local economik wealth. His subterraneous self disliked his generous and friendly public persona and hated the lickspittling behaviour towards him that would arise at city events, charity dooz and parties, when politicians and business people were looking out for some investment into their respective corner.

Glossy national eMagazines would publish stories on his relaxed, but fecund market acumen, for he was so allowed to be fecund with his cashola. The economik fanzine videographers would capture him sitting on his radical bottleHouse eyrie overlooking the bay, prosperous under the sun with his market configurations & smoking the occasional chopChop cheroot.

Now, back in the Ville for the past 8 years, through a mix of boredom, and restless genius, he'd forked into the niteways.

Hidden from the law, and out of the gaze of the glossies, his harpoons, bristling with bets, were pirates. Little harpoons and feathers, out for plunder. More productive than their legit siblings, his tricky codes slithered through the virtual. Even so, he still paid tax on whatever earnings were gleaned. Unexplained wealth did not get past the government – the AuZgovAuZtax folk knew the money was coming in and probably guessed how.

Instead of watching normal market forces tickle up prices & slap down stock, Andaman's newOld viruses sought private places and speculative deals which were still to be consummated, still formulating. His programs were set to sense strong indices showing which deals would prevail. He's sent them to sniff which way the private winds were blowing towards as yet unannounced investments. Informal communications between tycoons, government officials, ambassadors, all of them into a multiplicity of fixes.

Anticipatory algorithms reported back to SQwizzy, his text analysis program seeking key words and phrases, slang and banter. Again, the program was built on renovated versions of rudimentary programs from the dawn of the digital age.

The harpoons raided coded diplomatic cables in the networks of embassies of corporations and governments (decoded in Andaman's mainframe), raided intercompany exchanges, the computers of board members of blue chip and rising tech companies, and the communication devices of finance and business ministers. The harpoons parsed the communications for spikeWords: such as bribe, invest, commission, malfeascence, inducement, insider, "don't alert", confidential.

"Secret", searched in 5 different languages, was also a red hot target.

These words would parse against the context. Any hint of a deal being constructed in a trading transaction would be met with a modest purchase of the stock under discussion – an automatic purchase. Sometimes the communication was just gossip and nothing happened and he'd dump the stock after a time, but more often than not, the information was correct & he'd make a motza on the rising price.

So wrong, so delicious, a beautiful patterning. 150 or so years of the virtual and those jokers thought they knew how to guard & protect, but Andaman had studied the old coding at college. He'd crack open ancient computers, fire them up and trawl their innards like some freaking archaeologist. Everyone said, "Why the freak would you do that, bruzz?" but he kept smiling and scheming surrounded by huge, ancient hard drives the size of hands and matchboxes.

That's where he engineered his strokes.

Andaman pressed *commence + kill* – the latter instruction refried any hostile particles that had slipped into his system through the electronic backwash – because his defences bristled with security. He slid the backup plate out of its corral, deleted everything illegal on his mainframe computer, deleted it again and switched off. He was noWayEver going to keep his material on the commons.

He wandered down the dim, cool passage to his sleeping qwarters and said "shower". He stepped in as it turned on and cleaned off the pool salt, looking through the stormProof window on the top storey. Habitation took up the top 3 floors of his swizzy, swanky house, and a 4th floor – a basement water-Filled cellar – lay beneath those domestic areas, cooling the entire ecosystem.

Andaman loved his house.

Through the windows, yep, he could see the bay was still there. A few boats on it now, and way distant the early ferry from Trinity swooped in around Palm Island. A yellow haze lapped the horizon beyond. Down along the waterfront with its stepped terracing, the scene dark and emerald and tropical, house roofs glinted blue and green, the nanoVolt roofs sucking up the sunlight. He could see one or 2 landVs on the roads below emerge and disappear under the canopy of trees, and electric tukTuks and motorbikes weaving in and out of the traffic.

Lunch waited for him down the hill.

Andaman smacked his lips, tasting the last of the bitter-sweet kopi before brushing his teeth and throwing on a light cotton shirt and shorts. He stepped into the heat and walked the 500 hot morning metres to the funicular station at the top of the hill, entered a cool cab that slid elegantly over the cliff and down into the town, just like his feather harpoons glided elegantly thru the virtual across continents and into the speculative markets of the globe.

The cable car swung across the Ville, Capital City of Capricornia, known as Cap to the locals, often parsed down to East Cap and West Cap depending on which coast you were closest to. Capricornia was a vast Territory jointly administered by AuZgov and ASEAN, and was delineated by everything north of the Tropic of Capricorn, and everything north to the Arafura Sea.

Half the continent shared with Indons, Papuans and Timorese who had fled the climate disasters, along with their descendants, 85 million people, stretching from the east to the west coast of the continent of Australia.

Cap was a global food bowl, a mine, a fish farm, a refuge and a hothouse, as well as a joint AustralAsian economik zone that was integrated diplomatically with its teeming northern neighbours. All the more complicated as political control lay in a loveHate triangle between AuZgov, Jakarta and Cap itself, and residents could vote for the leaders of Cap, when the irregular elections were held, weather permitting.

He could see the Ville, a region of 8 million souls, stretching to the southWest, up through the Towers escarpment in the distant west. Beyond the escarpment, small farms, satellite towns, and large government work camps soaked up many of the people driven south from Asia by the fierce eqwatorial climate during *the Blend*, when the 2 geographies came together. Refugees arrived *en masse* more than 50 years past. Then, the rootless were given some purpose, a new beginning which most grabbed with alacrity.

Glinting roofs tessellated the lower bay and lifted over the hills of Cape Cleveland to the south. The morning smoke haze was forming over the landscape, from distant campfires, as the poor & the dislocated cooked their morning meals. Andaman smiled. The Ville was where the strength lay as the unwieldy influx of people created a massive workforce.

Apart from the maelstrom of weather to the far north, and the desertification of the far southWest, Australia was more verdant than it had ever been, but the top, the part which wasn't eternally covered with the Cloud, fed an unbelievable number of people. SanFran and Los Angeles across the Pacific had given up the ghost as the great American dustDeserts finally arrived at the Pacific Ocean burying everything in their path. Europe was a mess, Northern Africa in recovery. It was all up to the AustralAsians now.

*

Past the foodsmells, tents and stalls of the bustling markets, down at the Swarbar, his friend Flick – the senior day hostess – flashed her cheery smile. The smile (and Flick banter) returned him to the venue most days, because it was so genuine and appealing. His beacon. At the back bar in the dark shade, the buzzCut guy who cracked offColour jokes with him was also on duty, taking trays of drinks to tourists and traders who were parked under umbrellas all the way along the terrace. Andaman liked the buzzCut guy. There was no grovelling respect and that made him happy.

A few of the usual Swarbar denizens were warming up for the day. Dazza with his array of tek devices; a less than successful speculator already zigging high on fixzo, a brolly sticking out of a cocktail that had a seriously unnatural colour. Dazza, though, was addicted to neons which, allegedly, had particles of rare gasses pumped into them.

Emily Gatling was also at her table with her talking cat, writing stuff for politicians in the big house. She preferred the seabreeze to the poky airCon office she'd been allocated and her various politicos were pretty comfortable with her unusual arrangements. Also, the cat wasn't allowed in the Big House. The cat was watching whatever she was writing with a derisive look, but Andaman thought cats were always derisive, so it didn't matter.

"Hi, Flick," he said, "the usual. And a small prawn salad." She nodded and gestured the order into the screen. Prawns, he mused. Lifeblood of Cap & half the world.

He wandered over & perched on the timber verandah rail. This ran for some way inside the Swarbar, which was built along the bottom storm terrace above the ocean. The bar itself was incorporated into the steelDrip cement work of the terrace.

Yachts and ferries plied the bay, and a big container ship with its solar sails aloft was heading out of the new port further south, on the inner lip of Cape Cleveland. The 200 yearOld Ville Port had been smashed in the 2088 super'phoon (named Rex) and had limped along for another decade before the new port was finished and the city seriously took off.

He opened his clamB on the table, and fired up the glows, while at the same time feeling a rush of anticipatory pleasure as they emerged above the keyboard. Small spheres floated against the glass screen, spinning, doing nothing at the moment. He knew the harpoons were burrowing, burrowing, talking to SQwizzy, sniffing out words that mattered for investments that were of a certain qwantum: not too large, but certainly not too small.

Flick came over with his meal and beer.

Gesturing at the yachts, he said: "Lot of people have time on their hands, Flick, tacking, jibing and unfurling their sexy spinnakers."

"Speak for yourself, Andy. I've done an allNiter at the bar here, with the help of my good friend, the caffeinated gum machine in the corner, while you, my other friend, have just had a sweet nite's sleep." She laughed.

"Oh, I tossed and turned. Wouldn't say I slept," he said, guardedly.

She was a selfDeclared Oncer, and she unfortunately knew his fertility status. Andaman Marko – Noughter. No chance of a life with sweet Flick. She'd be wanting to have a kid sometime.

*

Fertility status was usually the second thing a girl asks a guy after "What do you do?" and Andaman had been honest, cos that's what people were, and cos Flick's face was friendly and ingenuous. Even if he was interested in accelerating a relationship with Flick (which he was, slightly) nothing would happen. He knew well.

They were neighbours, he at the top of the cliff, she down the hill. So they'd hung together out of work hours, partied together, and occasionally sexed in a drunken haze. But that was that.

She also knew he was super rich and had told him before, when turpzed up, that he was unattainable, and he'd be marrying a smart richBitch one day, and not someone stupid like her. This negative selfAnalysis didn't stop her continuing to flirt with him, and Andaman obliged with his own dry and handsome retorts.

"... good luck you all, anyway," she said, addressing the yachts, waving an open palm in their direction. "I'm saving up for a boat. Step one – got my little house. Next tick, boat. I'll see it through."

"*Gotta get amongst it,*" said Andaman qwoting a wellWorn advertisement.

"Yep, we all do. Do I put yer vittles' on the tab?" she said in a pirate voice.

She'd arched her eyebrow. Her hair was very curly, lips mockPouty, and to Andaman, she looked very fine.

He gave her a smoking smile and nodded, and started to shovel the salad into his mouth, tasting nothing.

Because Andaman was a Noughter, he tended to play hard. Noughter was both the best and worst of positions on the play board. His status alternately filled him with green murky despair, and a strange fire of anger and rejoice. Knowing he'd never be responsible for anyone 'cept himself made him, at times, reckless. Nought meant no kids, ever.

He didn't know why: didn't know what the DyNAst algorithms picked, didn't know what sounds the DNA data corridors stretching forward and back in time whispered to the Centrl databases that gave some the permissions while others, like him, were deemed to dangerous to breed.

He didn't dare try and hack AuZhealth to find out because, if traced, it was jail for life, tho' he was pretty certain he had the chops to check the file without lifting a breeze. But not worth that tiny shred of risk. His data were an unknown and had to stay that way.

Andaman knew he was physically in great nick, looking good and chiselled, with dark hair, dark brown eyes, and strong body. Brainy, with natural genius which he enhanced with boosters and restorative neuroplasty, but no rejuve. Not old enough for the next expensive step.

And he was acutely selfAware of his additional crazy (which may have been a reason for the Noughter status, who knows?).

AuZgov released Andaman Marko's Public Instructional when he reached full majority at 18. The release had done 2 important lifeStage things: it confirmed he was a Noughter and it allocated him adult residence in the Ville where he'd been born, but long since left. He hadn't been directed to sign up for AuZgov service (which sometimes happened) and he was relieved. A couple more years to finish studies in Brisbane, and then he moved back to the Ville.

Only later, in a mature moment of epiphany, did he realise that any goGetting Oncer female – cleared for fecundity, and who wanted kids – was offLimits. No companionship of the longLasting family variety allowed. Ever. Unless he married a female Noughter, or another male. While the latter option was ok for some, it just wasn't part of his makeUp. As for adoption, that was unheard of. Just didn't happen in a world desperately trying to keep the population capped at 14 billion.

After a few settled years he'd accepted that rules were rules. If he stayed in the official domicile (the Ville, as allocated), and he remained "without issue" (as the text went), he could do pretty much whatever he wanted.

So Flick, who he liked, and who was nice, and who, in her own seemingly subAmbitious way was a goGetter like him (her desire for a boat was eating her up), was never a romantic option because she was allowed to bear one child, and he knew from bitter experience that at some point she would, to another man.

*

Andaman finished the salad and pushed the plate down the bar, along with the murky thoughts, and rechecked the screens. One of the red dots floating above Brazil was slowly turning orange and he checked a side panel to investigate a trade in a Brazilhoz commodities company. The harpoon had picked some intelligence discussion between the Brazilian Minister for the Interior and a mate, which was then picked up by the US Mission in Brazilia. The discussion related to a series of mines being developed. The minister, through a family trust, had invested $New200,000, a purchase the embassy had also flagged to Washington. As the orange dot turned green, Andaman knew the harpoon and SQwizzy had picked up $Old250,000 worth of stock. A tiny investment with heaps of promise. Andaman and his sneaky algorithms loved those embassy cables. The weakest link in his biz, and information rich.

Flick, clearing the plates, looked at the lights floating above the screen. Another red one started going green.

"Looks like Xrissy lights," she said.

"Very much so," said Andaman, smiling at his friend with the simple xShirt that emblazoned Swarbar in a lurid font.

"By the way, a man dropped in looking for you yesterday afternoon. He left his card," she said, pulling something from her shorts pocket.

"Card? That's very oldFashioned," Andaman said, knowing full well it was how certain people avoided any electronic interaction with their komms eqwipment. Flick passed it to him. There was a name: Simon Bluestone. And a scope code – a commercial code for the very elite East Cap Hotel in town, not a personal code.

"Wants you to scope him at the Easty."

"Oh yeah? Have you ticked him in the bar before? What did he look like?" said Andaman airily.

"Never seen'm before. Tall 'n' thin, white tShirt, greyish hair, very blue eyes. Looked a bit old 'n' washed out really. Had a rejuve, I'd bet. Y'can tell they're really old when they look shiny but washedOff at the same time. Anyway. Says he was an old friend, he'll be in town for a couple of days and was wanting to "look you up". Said it was important to him, and you too. And to SQwizzy."

That took Andaman aback. Flick looked surprised at his facial shock. SQwizzy was his secret set of algorithms. A entity known only to himself.

"Who's SQwizzy? Is he from around here?" asked Flick.

"Obviously a mutual friend," Andaman replied thickly. He felt his pulse pick up. He screwed up his nose. He started to cough erratically and took a swig of his drink. He was seriously unnerved.

Andaman didn't really have any friends and none named Bluestone. But someone called Bluestone knew about his programs.

He'd been unzipped.

And "old friend" 'ndeed. Easy enough it was to track Andaman down personally in the Ville. He was nothing if not predictable with his daily habits and movements. The provenance of Bluestone was a mystery. Probably from AuZgov. Who knew? Possibly a rival. Whoever it was, the old friend had got though his firewalls and would be a pain in the back passage.

BLUESTONE

SENIOR Courier Simon Bluestone and Dr Madrigal Phipps, his Exec Courier, were sopping wet, reclined on deckchairs next to apartment 20/21's balcony pool at the Easty. The water in the pool was blue. The sky remained faintly yellow in the late afternoon, ready to take on cowlicks of sunset vermillion. Their primary task was to wait for a call, but otherwise to stay cool until sundown.

Hailing from the colder zones of Hobarttown, the daytime heat intimidated Bluestone. He went to the hotzones often, but never got used to it. Madrigal was from up north, once upon a time, so coped better.

Bluestone spent much of his life on the ocean, on city platforms and in submergeants where the Spokes lay in the southern oceans cold current convertor, he was acclimatised to very cool.

"Bet you another $New100 my wager is in the bag Dr Phipps," said Bluestone. "No likely call all afternoon."

Madrigal smiled and pulled a foot towards her buttock creating an A with her leg on the lounge seat. "Looks like you're right, boss."

Bluestone was unremarkable, pasty skin, blue eyes. Hair grey, maybe offBrown. Noone would look at him twice if they passed him in the street. Of course, he was much older than he looked, but that was the way. As a Courier, this diluted, wavery appearance suited him. He was indeterminate. If he fixed you eye to eye, however, with a glimmering blue iris, you ended up in a dimension altogether more scary. That's why he was known in the biz as Bluestone. Went all the way back to college in the 50s.

Unlike her mentor, Dr Madrigal Phipps stood out in a crowd. Phipps was somewhere in her 30s, an Indijj woman, with her family staying reasonably true to their skin over the centuries. Her name, Madrigal, was a cute riff on the northwest language her family spoke. She was proud of her language and country and liked her name.

Strikingly beautiful, with high cheekbones, dark brown skin, long limbs and shoulderLength wavy black hair, Madrigal Phipps had started professional life as a lawyer and negotiator, but enjoyed the frisson of being a high level Courier, carrying state secrets. One of the most prestigious jobs in AuZgov, attracting risk and reward.

The vocation allowed her to travel for work, mostly accompanying Bluestone, all over the world. Their job was to relay messages or information verbally and present, sometimes handing over paper or qwarantined data chips.

These days, no matter what encryption was lathered on a communication, the porousness of the virtual to harpoons, burrz and the like made it necessary for players in the High Levels, Government Authorities, Hegs and the Industries to discuss the most important secrets face on face, oldStyle.

Bluestone and Madrigal Phipps were waiting for their target to scope them and set up a meeting to deliver their message to Marko. Nothing complex – a simple warnOff for the security peeps. Madrigal had bet that it'd take Marko 2 hours to see what he could find on the virtual and then, frustrated, he'd dial. Bluestone bet he'd come in person that nite and not even risk a commercial scope channel. The hint that they'd busted his strokes would be unnerving for an outRogue like Marko. But now the Couriers were bored and wet, and even by sunset it was failing to cool down as the sky slowly caramelised, then burnt to black.

Madrigal sipped her waterPure and said, "I'm not doubling the bet. Target's still got to turn up tonite for the Bluestone prophecy to be fulfilled."

"Correctomundo," said Bluestone using a qwaint C20th archaism he'd picked up watching grisly 150 yearOld teev shows. He was a sucker for the trash channels. "Last official Courier tour with me, last bet won by me. Then you're off on the ownsome, making bets with yourself, kiddo."

"Ownsome is unlikely, as Centrl'l assign some callow young person like myself to tag along," said Phipps, "but I do thank the very competitive master diplomat, sitting in his daggy swimmers, for all the arcane and obscure kraft he has imparted to me over the last year or so."

Bluestone laughed and Madrigal Phipps smiled and looked west, out to the dirty brown sunset. She knew the Courier drill, and it was often boring. Unless a highLevel delegation job or wellKnown to the government, Couriers generally forced a speculative target to come to them; and never ever follow a target home; wait wait wait; poke out a little more bait if no nibble the first time. They'd both done a fair bit of baiting and waiting in their time.

The lights of the vast metropolis were beginning to twinkle in the dusk, but still, nothing was particularly cool. Phipps shook her head in despair at the 43 degree heat and plunged into the water again, kicking twice to propel herself to the other edge. In the black onePiece with hair plastered down to Bluestone she looked like a seal.

He had visited southern seal colonies off the Spokes, and he knew which seal colony he was off to. Joining the beaten bull males, grunting in their stink, well away from the hubbub of females, youngsters and young bulls. Scarred. Without any standing. Curmudgeons. Scared of the younger, fitter bulls. That'd be him soon.

The new sleek, slippery generation, he thought with a thin smile, watching Madrigal push herself through the water. He liked Madrigal and had genuinely tried to assist her in learning the bizz.

Chilled out, smart, cautious, she was not to be underestimated. She was tough as well, with the best eyes and ears he'd ever come across. Very serious. Not one for joking, but that was ok, cos when there was a joke it was sharp and to the point.

She'd come from legal, and in 2 years he'd given her leg-work, surveillance and contact transfers, and she'd easily passed the training stages through to Executive Prep. He'd also pushed her into tactical as well, training with the hard men and women so she could deal with any unpleasantness.

This job, their last together, was in one sense easy, in another, one of the oddest. Andaman Marko hadn't ticked in on the scope. Bluestone wasn't worried. He knew he'd turn up in person. OutRogues like Marko were the last persons, apart from his masters, to trust any electronic Komms, and from what Centrl had said, this guy was very very accomplished.

After sliding through the pool with a few short laps, Madrigal Phipps hauled herself out. He appraised her strong physiqwe, muscles rippling as she pulled herself from the water, and her long legs. She smiled at him and patted herself down with a towel and told him she was off to get dressed and would meet for dinner at 8 at the reserved table. Bluestone grunted like a beached seal in the expended male colony.

"See you down there," he said. He lay for another few minutes trying not to sweat and then turned into his apartment to prepare for the evening.

He extracted a fresh shirt and pants from a travel pack and stripped, pulling electromagnetic pain relief strips off his legs.

He stuck the strips on their charger and showered. He glanced at the mirror. His body was wrecked from decades of working and travelling. His genitals were wrinkled and cloaked in grey hair. His face was getting cadaverous. Not a pretty sight, he thought. 70 years in the biz and his last rejuvenation, 5 years ago, was it.

He thought: *even going to bed with someone as sexy as Dr Madrigal Phipps, if ever it was to happen, I doubt whether I'd be able to see it through.* The thought amused and depressed him at the same time.

*

Dr Madrigal Phipps showered and dressed in an unassuming light cotton kneeLength frock with a nuanced grey and white floral pattern that was hinted at, like an oldFashioned watermark. She was feeling pleased with herself.

Last job with Bluestone.

Superb mentor he may have been, but he was getting whiny and a little bit too familiar and fatherly, patting her on the shoulder, asking after Todd, her son, in a solicitous voice that rang hollow. Bluestone would also check her backside when he thought she wasn't looking, forgetting he'd taught her about reflective surfaces in street surveillance of targets. Madrigal had caught him doing it in mirrored lifts and in shopping mall windows. He'd given her the once over just then, as she got out from the pool.

We'll see this Marko hombre and sort him, and that will be that, she thought with a little gloat. *Yeah yeah yeah.* Her 'Preparatory' designation would be *gone, gone gone.* Dr Madrigal Phipps would be in charge of the message, do the face on face, travel at her own pace, would make her own choices. She did a couple of dance moves, bending and twisting her legs and swinging her elbows and arms, smiling gleefully at herself in the mirror, and then headed to the bathroom to apply lipz.

Yeah yeah yeah.

*

At the reserved table, the 2 Couriers tried to extend the meal as best they could. Telling the waiter they hadn't yet decided, fussing over wine then abandoning the idea, canapés, entreés, sticking to soda waters. Long rumination over mains.

Their expedition could lead to contact, but also could lead to another wasted evening. Phipps and Bluestone had wasted qwite a few in the past. They'd run out of small talk long ago, and given they couldn't utter a word about work, they invented games to torture waiters and while away the time. Usually, after 3 hours of fun they'd feel bad and tip well at the end.

This time, Madrigal had sensed the presence of a watcher as soon as they'd entered and, through loaded, coded chat, she and Bluestone agreed it could be someone other than the target. They knew what Marko looked like from the media files, and he wasn't there. But the someone watching them could be a proxy of the target, or an enemy. Madrigal was extremely sensitive to the swirl of a room or a street, and well knew there was a tail on them. Almost every table had diners, on the floor level and the sunken lounge, so it was difficult to winnow down the possibilities. She surveilled qwietly and continuously while going through the motions like pretending to choose between venison or crayfish.

After mains, Bluestone lifted his eyebrows and said, "Here we go." Madrigal turned the jammers on to distort and interfere with any sound or photonic waves around the table. This meant noone could insert a light tube through the barrier, or lipRead their conversation off a camera, or hear what they had to say with sound bugs, though to normal diners, they'd appear ... normal.

*

The rather sniffy concierge at the lobby saw Andaman enter and straightened up. The concierge was trussed up in a stupid red uniform and white gloves, to look "olde worlde". He knew

Marko from many fashionable events and caught his eye as qwickly as possible. Andaman walked across and asked the concierge whether a man named Bluestone was staying and if he'd gone out. The concierge knew Andaman tipped big, so qwickly broke the rules and in an obseqwious voice said, "In the restaurant, sir. They made a booking, sir. Left side table. He's with an Indijj lady". Andaman didn't disappoint the concierge, swiping some $New into the man's device, which magically appeared in his gloved hand. Andaman wandered slowly, seemingly without purpose, into the large restaurant, scanned the huge room full of people and moved towards their table.

They were a strange pair, he thought. Mousy old man and gorgeous young woman, pretending to eat their desserts. He'd probably be able to snap the old bloke in 2 with a punch. Not so sure about the woman. Andaman sat at the third, empty chair and looked at the 2 diners.

"Bluestone?"

"That's me," said Bluestone in a qwiet friendly voice. "This is my colleague, Dr Phipps. Glad you could make it, Mr Marko."

"Do I know you?" asked Andaman. He kept his voice very qwiet, pleased his back was to the crowded restaurant.

"Nope," said Bluestone. "We're Couriers. We have, for you, a message."

"Who're you couriering for?" asked Andaman, suddenly nervous. He hadn't expected this.

"AuZgov," said Bluestone brightly. Dr Phipps just stared at Andaman with friendly, goodCop eyes.

"And what do you want with me?" asked Andaman.

"Would you like a drink? Kopi?" asked Bluestone. "Let me get you a kopi." He waved to a waiter and ordered one, tho Andaman hadn't said yes.

There was a pause.

"You're becoming a bit of a problem to us. Unintended conseqwences of some of your activities," said the old man. "That is why we're here."

What was he? 100? 110 after a few of thoseF rejuves? Andaman was a little annoyed to be lectured by some old guy.

"The government is aware of your unsavoury outRogue business practices, but we don't want to interfere, because your work suits us on several levels. State revenue, intel from the information we can glean in the aftermath of your activities, and well, let's just say it's all helpful.

"We also leave you alone because you have never, ever tried to insinuate yourself into your own government's information systems, and that shows a level of loyalty to AuZgov which we appreciate. Loyalty not shown by many of your kind."

"My kind?"

"You know what kind I mean," said Bluestone. His tone was becoming sharper.

There was a pause. The coffee arrived. Dr Phipps kept appraising him without saying a word.

"So why bother me?" asked Andaman, shitty that they knew him too well, that AuZgov was piggybacking his moves, and supremely shitty with himself that he hadn't sussed it.

"Our technicians, who keep an eye on your traces, have picked up a lurker."

Andaman sat forward. His heart sank. The kopi arrived. The waiter backed off. There was an embarrassed pause.

"So?" Andaman said uncertainly. "Your people seem to be lurking as well."

"Ho, yes, but we're AuZgov. This unidentified lurker is not operating in your legit market algorithms. He or she is in the less than legal systems you run on a monthly basis. This presence may be bad for our government. There may be international ramifications if your, and by association, our activities are exposed."

Andaman was not expecting the next speech. He was suddenly aware of Bluestone's eyes, which had sharpened to ice. The old man's voice entered rote mode with the real message, so the target would understand it was a dictum. A hard message. Andaman was mesmerised by the eyes and the voice. The surrounding noises almost vanished.

"Couriered by me as authorised by the Commonwealth Government of Auztralia's security divisions, the official message is as follows," said Bluestone. "This is a serious foreign infringement into your illegitimate trading practices, and benign tho we are towards your activities, we reqwire that a) you desist now, permanently, from your activities, but if you refuse, then you are absolutely obliged on pain of prosecution over your illegal activities to b) postpone your illegal operation for one month and recode your encryptions to expel whoever is piggybacked in your systems, and not returning to those corrupted systems, ever."

Andaman thought about the options.

"What if I ask you to courier a message back to head office and tell them that they could go and get stuffed?' Andaman said.

"Not an option," Bluestone growled. His icy eyes started to glow with menace. "You don't ever mess with AuZgov. Y'know that the consqwences. Y'd be stuck off from trading for life."

A pause.

"Which is it? A hegemony? Cartels?"

Bluestone looked grimly at the tablecloth. "This conversation is descending into unwelcome detail. Let me tell you, we are not here to swap hypotheses. We are not authorised to tell you."

"Because you don't know or you won't?"

Bluestone didn't reply, Madrigal coughed. Andaman got the message.

"What about I try option b. Neutralise this alleged lurker. Would that suffice? I can't let my business rundown. Can I hunt for the bugs in the system and purge?"

"If you did neutralise the lurker, y'd be obliged to provide proof, for security purposes, but that could suffice. The fact is tho, AuZgov knows about this infringement, and you don't. This is no doubt a double humiliation to you, my friend – AuZgov has doubts whether you are technically capable of neutralisis."

There was another pause while Andaman swallowed his pride.

"Let me try."

Madrigal Phipps spoke for the first time, formally also. "You have one month to fix your program. Here is a card. I am the contact officer on this case. Keep me informed on this number. It's a dummy scope but I'll be back to see you ... if you have a result. The identity of the lurker would be of special interest. No result, no contact. By the end of the month, it's a result or you shut down your operation. Repeat, if you are unsuccessful you must activate option a, and if you don't, coercion will commence."

Andaman's hearing of ambient sounds reawakened suddenly; he'd been so concentrated on the low tones of the Couriers. Somewhere in the restaurant, globular music, with its harmonic blubs and liqwid sounding blobs, was playing with its big drips of slow bursting sound. There was babble and laughter. Knives and forks rattled around the room like tiny machines punching holes in flesh. Andaman looked at the card and memorised the number. He handed it back and tapped his head. "In here now," he said. Dr Phipps flashed a slight smile, and he smiled back.

"Not good for my rep," he said. "I'll deal with it."

"Head office said to say you're one of the best and they are sorry it had to happen. They like your strokes," Phipps said.

"Well, you can tell them from me to mind their own business and leave others to theirs."

"Never going to happen," growled Bluestone, but he patted Andaman on the arm in a friendly gesture. "You can go now."

"'K," said Andaman. He was fine with the abrupt dismissal by the stony old man. He'd had enough of the government telling him his freaking, 2 horrible options and wanted to head for a real drink in a real bar somewhere else. The only bonus out of the whole lecture was that if he rang the number in his head, someone as beautiful as Madrigal Phipps might turn up at his doorstep and that could be interesting.

He shook their hands (they remained seated) and pretended to wander nonchalantly out, nodding across the vast lobby to the snitty concierge. The street was bustling with jitneys, but Andaman decided to walk a few blocks. Aware that he'd probably be followed, he didn't look back, deciding to have a drink in a bar along the creek somewhere, find Jimmy or Suzette, or even Flick if she was offDuty, and drown his growing sorrows. Full neutralisis would be the end of bizz. Ow! That entities were stalking him was a freakOut, but AuZgov crapping themselves about this stalker to the extent they sent scary Couriers to warn him off his biz was downright creepy. Jayzus.

And, even worse, he'd be shut down if it weren't fixxed. No. He'd have a drink and ring Cassie and see if she was available for a bit of fun in return for a few $New. That's what he'd do. Before entering the task to find the lurker, he'd drown his sorrows and sex with someone.

Option a, option b … either ultimatum threatened Andaman's whole comfortable existence. It was a bleak choice because if he couldn't play sillybuggas on the virtual, he'd likely go insane.

*

"That went well," said Bluestone, sipping his coffee dregs.

Madrigal shrugged and picked up her purse, switched the jammer off and made for the lobby toilets, but hovered outside the door for a full 60 seconds. Noone was following Marko as he expressed himself into the boiling air outside and walked down the street, busy with traffic. She slid out of the doors and watched him move across the road. No. No tail on him unless it was a long tail using a bee.

She shadowed him discreetly halfway down Flinders Street East until he turned into a niteclub. That would be end of story. Just keep a scan on the camera opposite his front door and he'd turn up at 3.00 a.m. like he did most mornings. She returned to the restaurant and sat down with Bluestone.

"Nothing. And Marko has gone drinking."

He nodded and stayed silent.

"But they're here," she added.

"I don't doubt it," said Bluestone.

He gestured, threw a tip on the table and they headed for the lift in silence. "Not for a second do I doubt you. But fact is, they could be on us, not Marko – so, precautions tonite, and keep an eye on Marko, too." Madrigal Phipps knew he was ordering her to surveil Andaman and make sure he got safely to bed, which annoyed her. From a simple warnOff they'd now escalated to a more aktivist mode. But Bluestone was in charge, and he was way past caring about either her or legwork. He was out. She thought about complaining for a minute, then thought, last job with old Bluestone. Won't fight this one. Back into the streets again.

Bluestone continued: "The guy confirmed all my wellDeveloped loathes about rogueOut hacker types. They just break and enter other people's virtual space like street trash, but think they're clever. He's too smart for his own good. He'll be shut down soon enough. But if we know who's following us or him we might get some understanding. Just stay well back and out of sight. He was drooling over you a bit."

She didn't respond to that one, but was surprised at Bluestone's sudden crassness. Wasn't his style at all. He was legendary in some circles. Bluestone came out of the older generation of administrators from the time of Purity & Virtue, when the world was controlled, polite, mannered.

Drooling ... that was just rude. What was that saying: familiarity breeds contempt? She thought Marko had been qwite discreet in absorbing the threatening message, rather than having space to drool. Probably Bluestone, who engaged in old man drooling, was deflecting to the young man. The young man had just looked supremely annoyed at the end.

Time she and Bluestone parted ways.

"I'll report in when I get back," she said in a flat tone, and headed to her apartment to change.

MADRIGAL 1

SHE TRACKED through the hot, nite streets thrumming with revellers and vendors, tukTuks and chill upmarket statuStaxis with their ridiculous, tinted windows. Buskers added to the melee of sound, looking for a few $Old notes or coins. The smell of street food was strong – sweet chicken flesh burning on griddles, peanut curries. And prawns. Sizzling.

It was hot. She smelled rain on the ocean wind, warm and blowing off the esplanade. Andaman Marko was not hard to track down because he hadn't moved from where she'd left him an hour earlier, which was the Rising Sun Lounge. He was sitting at a central bar with a man and a woman – she youngish with red hair, he with oversized shoulders – having an animated discussion. Andaman was gesticulating in small movements and the man and woman seemed hypnotised by his hands. Big jars of beer sat before them.

Madrigal dared not get too close. She moved through the airy barroom to check on exits. The room tipped patrons out through blastGlass sliders onto a boardwalk along the creek. The dark water, flecked with the reflection of coloured lights – red, gold, blue – was slung with yachts and boats.

She found a table away from the dance floor, where her target and his barflies were in line of sight, and plonked herself down. Within seconds a solo man had wandered over and asked whether she'd like a drink. That would suit hiding in numbers.

"Why thanx," she said. "What about wine? White wine, please."

The man's eyes lit up. "Back in a flash," he said.

Madrigal Phipps rolled her eyes as the man fought his way to the bar. Good cover having a drinking companion, and there was only a 12.5% chance of the man possibly being entertaining, she thought. Andaman Marko was still talking. The guy with the big shoulders also had a crew cut, and the woman wasn't qwite redHeaded – more cherry brown and dyed. All were perched on bar stools, the man in a short T and the woman in a loose cotton dress. They listened intently to his rave without interruption. A oneWay street. She scanned the room for any other players, but could see nothing untoward. There were cameras set into the walls and on the bar itself.

"Here we go, love," the returning man said. A glass of wine was placed firmly in front of her. The man had ordered some sort of cocktail for himself, a plastic crocodile swizzle stick resting in it. "I'm Ronny. To my friends."

"Madrigal. Nice to meet you, Ronny. You from the Ville or travelling through like me?"

Tho Marko was never out of the corner of her eye, she studied Ronny with a nonchalant expression. Late forties, round face. Indijj, like her. It struck her that Ronny had spotted her and made a beeline for that reason. A new face in town. A common need to touch base and welcome the stranger. He looked fit and prosperous, and rather charming.

"Me? Yeah, I live here. Work in the big metals refinery down the coast a bit. I tell people I'm a metallurgist, but I'm basically a sparky. Do a lot of the repairs to the big gear. You're a sister, aren't you?"

"That I am," said Madrigal, lifting her glass.

"Yeah, right. I'm a Wulgurukaba man from round here. Welcome to the Ville and surrounds, though a fair bit of waterfront's gone under over the past 50 years." They clinked glasses.

"Thanx, Ronny."

"Got any kids?" The old fecundity qwestion, but this time laced with that rolledGold First Nation element.

"Yeah, one, a son. He's 6 years old. I've had my qwota." Her gaze shifted to the bar. Andaman still talking. She shifted it back to Ronny. He was asking whether her son was a good boy.

"Yeah, Ronny. He's beautiful."

"There're qwite a few families here, hang together. Not all Wulgurukaba tho. All the East Cap groups got messed up bad over history. History was difficult everywhere I suppose, tho. But most of us have good touch with the country here now. Found our way back. Took a while and a lot of help from the old people. But the weather's kinda changed things. If you're around during the week we're having a barbecue at my sister's place on Wednesday. We always have a barbecue on Wednesdays. What was it you said you did?"

Madrigal smiled. The welcome, the recognition, the intention, the hospitality. It was lovely.

"I'm a lawyer, up here to check something out for a client. I think I'll be heading back tomorrow, but thanx so much for the invitation." She genuinely was thankful. "Give me the address, all the same."

He beamed it to her device with his number.

"Do you have kids, Ronny?"

"No. I'm allowed, but no luck finding the right lady yet," he said. Mebbe her initial assessment was wrong, and he was younger. Obviously he'd thought Madrigal could have been "the right lady", but didn't seem too disappointed that she'd already had her child. He'd be used to these encounters, she thought, as he looked for an Indijj girlfriend to transact into family life.

They had a pleasant chat about jobs, families and hanging on to identity. All the while, Madrigal watched and waited. Andaman at the bar kept blathering, so she ordered a drink for Ronny from a passing barboy and they kept talking. She told him that she kept in touch with her country and, although her parents were city slickers from Perth, her granddad used to take her and her 2 brothers camping and hunting in the dry season every year north of Derby. They'd hike for days in the gullies and riverbeds, tramping over the plateaus looking for wallaby, goanna and other bushTucker and camping at nite. At first she thought her parents were just trying to get her out of their hair, so they could run their energy company, but in hindsight they weren't. They wanted her to understand what it was all about and where she came from. The impulse of country, she called it. (She kept the detail of the energy company out of the convo, made it sound like an electric shop).

Checking the signs. Following tracks. The red ground and the fat white baobabs. Her grandad was shown by his dad, and before him back through the generations. Knew the stars and the songs. All that knowledge. And her aunties who were living there in the community took her, an earnestly intelligent girl, through the women's lore as well. It was serious and still defined her above all things, beyond even her motherhood and her intense job. She was a woman who'd been through the ceremonies and learnt the songs, and was happy to tell Ronny, tho Bluestone would never believe it, wouldn't comprehend it, if she had ever told him. But then, her childhood was none of his business.

When Andaman started to move, she excused herself sweetly. Her qwarry farewelled his drinking buddies and walked out of the club, so she gave Ronny a peck on the cheek, told him to hang in there and headed out also. Her target was halfway down the block, then turned a corner to head uphill. There was no other tail on him that she could sense, but that didn't mean there wasn't one. It could be done via beeDrones or even a lightTube. She wished she'd eqwipped herself with a tekFinder on the way out of the Spokes, but stupidly hadn't. She'd never expected the job to qwantum out like this. It was supposed to be a simple message delivery and home by tea.

"Scuse me, lady, want a ride, lady?" a tuktuk guy shouted to her from the kerb.

"No, thanx," she said. Andaman was well ahead of her, moving up the steep street. Obviously very fit. Then he stopped and pulled out his scope and chatted on it animatedly for a couple of minutes, then disappeared into a door. Madrigal Phipps took advantage of the pause to cross the road for a different angle to tail him. She noted that Andaman had elected to enter another bar, *The Northern Lights*. Her target was a big drinker.

"Either looking for someone or drowning his sorrows," she thought.

She descended narrow stairs to the basement. There was a strange glow in the various rooms where, obscurely for the thick tropics, the owners had tried to replicate the Aurora Australis as a design feature. This made for a very dark space with the odd fade of green & blue lighting. Andaman wasn't at the front bar, so she elbowed through a wide corridor of booths and doors to the second big space. This bar was extremely busy, but not a dance club. Plenty of people laughing. Behind it were walls of booths which people were using to drink in, but some of the booths had sliding doors to give the occupants privacy. A bar especially rigged out for casual intimacy. *A sexing parlour*, she thought.

A trio played in the background – clariozet, keyboard, guitar – their music low and discreet with heavily plucked bass notes. She smelt perfumed smoke and the rougher tang of chopChop, which no doubt was being consumed and filtered away qwickly through extractors. Again, Andaman was perched on a barstool solo, twirling a glass and looking at a small screen on his clamB – a side plate sized device.

She kept a low profile at a table in a corner and messaged Bluestone: *we're turning into a bar crawl don't wait up.* It too dark for anyone to see anyone else in the room clearly, unless you were close to the band, or to the bar which had lights woven through its low false roof, but this suited her. As she looked up from her scope, 2 things happened: a woman, clearly dressed for a sexing service, came to sit on the stool next to Andaman, and, in a burst of random aurora glow that lightened the room for a moment, she noted a face look up from the other side of the horseshoeShaped bar in the restaurant section. The face belonged to a small, nondescript person drinking alone, and writing with a stylus on his device. Cleanshaven. Short hair. Watching Andaman cautiously.

Interesting. *Little fishEyes,* she thought. Flitting from the target to the girl and back.

Forwards and backwards. Andaman was only interested in his girl and her blonde curls, which he stroked. Madrigal discreetly took pix of the girl and the lurker and forwarded them to Bluestone. Thoughts of Bluestone led her to the word "drooling" again. Possibly, the man on the other side of the bar was just drooling over the girl, but there was more intent than that in his gaze. It was hardFace, not softFace.

Got it – processing. Return message, so Bluestone was still up. No surprises there.

The music was low and pumpy, and replicated either the beat of a heart or the rhythm of sex. Or both, as life was life. She snorted at this feeble thought, and sipped the wine. Enough of the drooling stuff, she thought. Two large groups of young revellers were surrounding the drinking area. Couples were peeling off to booths, or emerging from them and trying to look composed.

She watched the curly girl organise champagne and tip the barman's scanner with Andaman's card. She laughed at Andaman's jokes. A receptive, paid companion, Madrigal thought, unlike the ones in the other bar who had looked resigned to his monologue. The couple spent 5 or so minutes chatting and flirting – she was already stroking him on the face. FishEeyes clearly noted this, but refrained from staring. Then Andaman pulled the girl towards a cubicle, with the half bottle of champagne, further down the back of the bar, just inside the back corridor, and he slid the door shut.

The place was very crowded now. FishEyes got up, looked back at the cubicle and walked out.

With Andaman occupied, she felt able to slide from the corner and scope the rest of the place. She passed down the corridor where Andaman had his sexBooth and where a series of other closable cubicles were, a few of them occupied. Then toilets, well appointed, and, at the end, the kitchenette, occupied by a couple of guys in chef hats preparing snacks over hot grills and a waitress emptying a dishwasher.

As she smiled at a chef – who waved with the halfRecognition of a stranger – and as she turned on her heels to go back, the world roared.

A massive explosion from the bar propelled a huge fist of dust, debris, smoke and flame which punched out of the corridor and into the kitchen and deafened her. Everything happened instantly, but she saw the progression of events clearly.

The world went smokeDark. The blast pulse knocked her high off her feet into the tiled wall, which she hit with a shoulder, then slid down on her backside with a crunch. Pain lanced into her shoulder. Pitch black, with crap swirling around her face, coughing and hacking, she groped to the rear entrance and opened the back door to allow air in. It led to a flight of stairs up to the street. She lifted a chef from the floor and pushed him towards the door.

As her hearing returned, the blast was followed by smoke and flames and she could hear crackling, snapping electricity noises, and screaming from the main bar areas. Her shoulder had taken the brunt of the explosive force, followed by the head crack, but she was still standing. Adrenaline surged through her like a tidal wave of energy.

"F'ck! The Target!" she thought.

Madrigal reached for a torchTube in her bag. She gingerly felt her way through the kitchenette to the corridor opening end and then, when the smoke in the room got too much, ducked down and continued crawling along the corridor towards the bar over sharp objects and sticky ooze, thanking providence for the fact she'd changed into skinpants. Coughing and gagging, she got to her target's cubicle, inside the corridor, just out of the main bar area and somewhat protected. Screams pierced the air behind her and there were calls for help as the fire fully caught hold in the gaping hole in the roof, igniting the beams and ceiling insulation.

Horrors, she thought.

She knelt and reached upwards to wrench the halfBuckled door off Andaman's booth – the L shaped location of the corridor and the closed door were the only things that had saved the inhabitants from certain death. Through the cling of smoke, through her torch's beam, she saw that booth doors directly facing the blast had been punched in.

Andaman and the girl were unconscious on a small bed covered in blood from blast fragments. She grabbed Andaman's head and slapped his face, poured some cold champagne over his, and the girl's, head and shouted, "We have to go." Andaman looked up, dazed. She ripped the sheet and wet it with more champagne. "Breathe through this. Hold it around your face." Indeed the air was becoming sharp with chemicals and unbreathable, "Crawl," she shouted, "crawl." She gagged, she exhaled, she tried to hold her breath, but her heart was were hammering in her chest. Ducked her head low under the hot cloud of burnt plastic.

"Crawl fast."

Groggy, Andaman grabbed his girlfriend's wrist and followed Madrigal Phipps along the wet floor. Utterly black apart from her torch beam and some muted flame somewhere in the corner. The smoke was making them cough uncontrollably. "Qwickly … there's no oxygen". She crawled past a torso with a stump of neck and realised the stickiness on the floor was blood, innards, brains, the lot. Redoubled her efforts to flee. "Hurry." The screaming continued; a person stumbled and tripped over her, but she kept going, and checking Andaman was behind, and hoping he'd have the girl in tow. He'd stopped to help his friend, so Madrigal reversed, cursing. They ended up with an arm each of the lifeless girl. She noticed the girl had no underwear on, skirt slid up and it made her appear incredibly vulnerable.

Unerringly, she headed back up the service corridor as flames licked around, providing a glimmer in the dust cloud. Hurry. They got to the kitchenette, which was empty – whoever had been there had escaped out the back. She had kept the scrap of wet sheet over her mouth, but now threw it away. They were almost there, at the exit.

Madrigal stood in the kinetic, lethal gloom, and hauled Andaman and the girl up. She helped him again, carrying the dead weight of the unconscious girl through the back door into a stairwell, which they staggered up. Andaman was in a complete daze, but he wasn't going to ditch his friend. The girl was coming around, sobbing. She'd managed to pull her top over her breasts with one hand, but was in her bare feet and her knees were bleeding. Andaman had no shirt on and his chest was cut. He leant against the wall, heaving for air and did his trousers up. All 3 were sucking in cool, clean air and were lacerated from the bits of broken glass scattered far and wide on the floor they had traversed.

Covered in clumps of char and blood.

Her rescue had taken less than 2 minutes. A couple of others burst from the exit. Then noone. Madrigal could see the chefs and the dishstacking waitress at the end of the alleyway, turning into the street. The waitress was howling. The 40 or so people in the expansive bar – the musicians, the partygoers, the claqwe of kids – who had been close to the source of the explosion, would all be dead.

PassersBy had found the chefs and worked out that there was an exit and rescuers came down the alley, shouting, helping them stumble the last few metres into the glare of lights. Ambulances and fire trucks were on the way to arriving. She heard the *needle needle* of sirens. Milisi in their bright orange uniforms were directing traffic away and securing the street. Andaman, Madrigal and the girl struggled over the road with the help of 3 strangers. They hacked much of the bad chemical air out of their lungs in harsh barking coughs.

Adrenaline was still pumping and the evening was hyperreal, but Madrigal's shoulder was now extremely sore. She picked bits of glass from her forearm. Andaman was consoling the girl, who was now weeping with shock. They sat on the pavement, Andaman with the girl under his wing, and Madrigal Phipps beside him.

This doesn't happen in Australia, she thought, not even in Cap, which stretched over much of old Papua, Timor and some of Indon. Peace was a constant. Society was too punchdrunk from other disasters. Outrages like this were for the history boox. Not in the time after the Age of Purity & Virtue.

"What were you doing in there?" Andaman suddenly asked Madrigal, perplexed.

"Apparently I was assigned as your guardian angel, Mr Marko. That was a bomb. There was a man at the bar watching you for a while and when he left, boom! Any idea why someone would want you dead in such a gratuitous, wasteful way, killing so many?" She was angry at Marko's tone, given the dead. But then, he wouldn't have realised.

"Me? Kill me? No. Why?" A sandyHeaded ambo ran over and started checking the girl out. She was groggy and suddenly became hysterical. Andaman said her name: "Cassie? Cassie, can you hear me?"

"Friend of yours," asked the ambo.

"Sort of," said Andaman. He caught Madrigal's wry look. "Yes, she is. A lovely friend," he added.

"Who'd want you dead?" repeated Madrigal as the ambo dealt with Cassie. Marko was distracted by his distressed friend in the crook of his shoulder. The medik was crouched and sedating, her limp hand stretched, 'jector clicking into her forearm.

She asked again: "Who?"

"Dunno. You and Mr Bluestone, mebbe?" Cassie was heaving with sobs and Marko cradled her. "Sh, sh," he whispered into her ear, and he brushed ash stuff from her hair with gentle fingers. "It's 'k." Cassie was shivering violently. Madrigal looked over the street at the fire hoses heading into the building, dragged by men in crashsuits. Milisi and ambos were everywhere, with the wounded and the dead.

"To be frank, Mr Marko," she growled, "You're much more useful to us alive, and talking 'bout your codes and feathers ..." before another vile coughing fit interrupted. He waited till she'd controlled her gag reflex. The coughing set off her sore arm again.

"I haven't any idea who'd want to kill me, *if* that was their aim," Marko said, voice strained thin, turning to look at her. "So it's got to that ... someone really wants me dead?"

"Either your assassination, or it was a nasty, nasty insurance job on the premises. This sort of attack never happens in Australia. Or East or West Cap. Or ASEAN. Nowhere! Crimes like this," she waved at the shapes of slumped casualties on the footpaths, "thing of the distant past except in extremity settlements that aren't surveilled, and the Ville is a *Capital City.*"

Cassie started sobbing again as the ambo extracted some glass from her face. Only a little, but it bled everywhere. Andaman turned to help her again. Madrigal tried to stand, but it was hard, and she was wobbly. *Gawd.* The ambo who was crouched over the other 2 said: "Sit down. You've inhaled a lot of toxic stuff and carbon monoxide. Get some oxygen into your corpuscles." She sat again and messaged Bluestone, but knew he'd be on the way anyhow. They'd have alerted him instantly.

*

One minute he and Cassie were pressing lips and mooshing tongues and she was sqweezing out of her clothes in the cubicle with its muted red light and excellent bed, the next he felt everything sqweezed out of his torso and was coming round to the Courier woman slapping him and pouring iced champagne on his face in the stinking dark. Then he was in the street with Cassie clinging to him like a limpet. What was her name? Madrigal. Madrigal had pushed him, in a stupor, through the nitemare, into fresh air. He felt his belt. The clamB was still there in its holster. Hadn't even had time to take off his pants in the boudoir before the bomb blew. Now he was under interrogation by an AuZgov Courier with angry eyes.

"Not an insurance job," he said to Dr Phipps. "Noone would do that to get money from insurance." He remembered the people. The room had been full of people. And 3 bar staff, the band, and the terribly young boy passing round delicious dumplings on a silver tray.

"I need to take Cassie home," he said. "She needs to clean up and feel better. Away from this."

The ambo had been joined by a young, freckly brigade doctor checking Cassie's eyes and ears.

"She's concussed," the doctor told him. "And an eardrum doesn't look good. But .... you'll have to hang around to talk to the milisi from the Brigade. You're a witness." The doctor started checking Dr Phipps with his torch and exclaimed, "You've dislocated your shoulder." Andaman looked and saw her shoulder was pushed awkwardly out. He hadn't noticed as they'd struggled up the steps.

"Fix it," she said. "Push it back in. Done it before, playing footy with my brothers and sisters in the dirt oval when I was a kid. They just pushed it in." She lay on her back.

The doctor raised his eyebrows, but knelt over the Courier's shoulder. "An anterior dislocation. Not so bad," he said softly. He straightened her arm along her body and moved her forearm to lie perpendicular across her waist slowly and cautiously, and twisted it. She grunted. He did it again and the misshapen bulge in her shoulder settled back in.

"Is that 'k?"

"Sore, but doesn't hurt so much," said Dr Phipps rubbing the pectoral area and rubbing her shoulder gingerly.

"You need to get some of that glass out of you."

Then the man named Bluestone arrived, the man who had threatened him earlier. His face was grim, he nodded curtly at the young dok. Bluestone jerked his head towards a vehicle parked across the busy street. "Come on. Let's go."

"Witness statements," said the doctor, checking Andaman's eyes with a great white beam from a torch.

Bluestone spoke in his clipped official way. "I've given names and numbers to Brigadier Smith over there. It's fine, doctor. We'll report to Brigade HQ in a couple of hours. These people need to clean up."

Somehow, the man named Bluestone had found a large wagonV, with a driver. He helped Andaman bring Cassie round the back. "Hop in." He waved at Dr Phipps to get in the front while he climbed in the back seat with the other 2. He looked back at the devastation on the footpaths and the men in spacesuits hauling charred remains out of the still smoking disaster that had been the sex parlour. "F'ck me sideways," Andaman heard him say. How peculiar.

"Your place?" he then said to Andaman, who could only nod. They headed up the hill through the traffic barrier and past the pile up of Vs attempting to detour from what was usually a main road. Vbike cops were still bringing order to the mess almost a k down the road, with red and blue detour holograms and checkpointz. Tonnes of folk had parked and were walking into town to see what had happened. Was late. The cable trains had been stopped for the time being and people were welling out of stations. Was slow progress through the moll.

"Are you 'k" asked Cassie in Andaman's ear. She was still clutching him. The car was cool but her skin felt icy. "Yeah. Just." He gave her a hug. She was a dormitory girl, but one he liked to hang with, so they were a little beyond the pure cash transactional relationship. He liked her because she was good at spending his money. And he tipped her well and she liked that. She must be all of twenty. Buying friendship was a bit pathetic, he had thought in the past, but she seemed genuinely affectionate. Pleased to see him. She was not the only one, but one of the main ones. That's what too much money could afford. Affection and $New all round. He gave her shoulder another sqweeze and she faintly smiled.

The car slid behind the terrace and up the skyTrack, which crossed in front of many of the suspended homes attached to the cliff face, a steel bridge which retracted when weather got too bad. It was a wild drive and a great view, high above the urbs and the ocean, but Andaman was unable to face it. He was hurting, and Cassie was traumatised.

A second car sat in the elevated driveway of his house. "I rang ahead for a doctor. A proper one to check you all," said Bluestone, flintily. "This whole ep is a disaster, Mr Marko, but I am glad you and your totsie are alive. And I am certainly glad Dr Phipps survived. You must tell me how you did it."

"Only luck," said Dr Phipps.

"Oh, I doubt that," said Bluestone. "No such thing."

The milisi at the top of the drive helped Marko and Cassie from the car to the front door where a doctor was standing with a couple of med cases. "Dok," said Bluestone, shaking the man's hand. Sensing Andaman's approach, the door slid open. As he entered his own home, Andaman had an overwhelming urge to open the clamB in his belt and check the feathers' progress, how many targets had gone green ($New invested), and if any had gone gold ($Returns), but in the present, regulatory company, he held back.

*

Madrigal pushed (gently) her charges up a short flight of stairs into the living area. Bluestone's scope pinged. He stopped at the bottom of the stairs and checked it, then went out the door again to speak to his caller. The others collapsed in the soft furniture, and Madrigal Phipps just stared for a tic or 2 thinking about the carnage – the burnt corpses, torn limbs, innards, sobbing survivors and saying to noone: "that must have been what war once looked like."

They just sat, grasping for some sort of eqwilibrium, and waited while the doctor started a set of checkOvers. Madrigal was mildly impressed when Marko insisted Cassie be treated first.

Bluestone emerged at the stairhead.

"They have the bomber," he said. "We had him surveilled electronically, Dr Phipps, after you sent through his image, so we saw him go and they picked him up real qwick."

His voice was still muffled. She hoped her sharp hearing would return.

"So it was him."

"There's no doubt?"

"Biometrix from your snap got him."

Madrigal nodded, then looked round Marko's luxurious deckLounge with its soft carpet and wall filigree of copper and gold, the panoramic view across the bay, and incredibly contoured couches and seats. He even had boox – old kopiTable boox and new luxuryPress tomes – littered artistically on antiqwe credenzas and tables. The guy was loaded if he could afford good boox.

"Got brandy or whisketty or something?" asked the doc. "The old remedies are often the best." Andaman staggered to his feet and found a flash looking bottle in a walnut drinks bureau and poured a slug in glasses for the 3 wrecked people. Neither Bluestone nor the doctor wanted one.

For more than an hour, the doctor checked the 3 bombing victims with his fingers and sensorWands. Cassie came off worse with concussion, a perforated eardrum and shock, tho brandy was helping with that. He fussed over Madrigal's injured shoulder but declared it "rehinged" and gave her a shot of painkillers to take the edge off the ache. Andaman had tiny shards of door in his chest, which the doctor extracted. All of them had shards of glass and other pieces in their knees and palms from when they'd crawled out of the smoking ruin, so a fair bit of fussing commenced with tweezers, scalpels, antiseptic and spraySkin. He prescribed and then handed them some puffers to help clear the crap out of their throats and lungs. Finally he stood, nodded and walked out into the 2am dark.

Bluestone stood looking at the 3 injured persons with a hand to his cheek, as if surveying a difficult problem.

"You are all lucky to be alive," he finally said. "Did good work, Dr Phipps, hauling these 2 birds out." Andaman looked at Madrigal whose expression of weariness did not change at the praise.

"We'll let you be, Andaman," said Bluestone. "There are brigade officers on watch outside. I've organised it. They'll need a statement in the morning. Miss Cassie ... do you want a lift home?"

Andaman looked at Cassie who was curled on the couch. The thought of her bunking down in the town's huge public dormitory was too much. He shook his head. "No, no. She can stay here and sleep," he said. He knew she'd appreciate that, rather than struggle for a bed. And after all, she would provide him with a bit of cover.

"Ok."

"Are you really a Courier?" he asked Bluestone bluntly.

"Yes. And despite this outrage, and the hurt to you and your young friend, the thrust of the previous conversation stands. Once you clear your head, you'd best find out who your demons on the virtual may be."

There was a pause. Andaman watched the skin around Bluestone's eyes soften slightly as he made up his mind to be kinder.

"Look, Mr Marko," he said calmly, "our authority extends much further than just delivering messages. You know that. We are official representatives of AuZgov. That means we deal face on face with messages, negotiation – serious people stuff."

"And so why was Dr Phipps following me? How did she rescue me?"

"As you know, we are concerned about the lurker in your program. They end up in the virtual because real people put them there – you know that. So Dr Phipps was watching over you. She sensed – let me say she is extremely good at reading crowds – a hostile presence in the restaurant and that either you or we were being watched.

"The bombing has magnified our concern by many times and that's why you have an armed guard outside now. Tomorrow we will provide even stronger protection. As for your rescue, and that of your charming companion," he waved a hand at the sleeping Cassie, "Dr Phipps is trained for emergencies of every type. The lurker is why I asked her to follow you. You must take care, Mr Marko. They want your strokes. They are worth a lot."

"If they wanted the strokes they wouldn't kill me. If they were after it, kidnap mebbe."

"Perhaps they've already mined your strokes – they already have the algorithms and they wanted to eliminate anyone who could trace them. This is my greatest fear."

"My very own lurker," he groaned.

Madrigal shook her head, thinking: This guy just doesn't get it.

She and Bluestone vacated, leaving guards around the house, with a big team out the front.

As soon as the front door clicked shut, Andaman flipped the clamB open and the scattergram emerged into the space in front of him. It was dim, and the windows reflected very little of the city light. After all, his house was almost at the top of the hill.

The glows looked like fireworks. All his targets had gone green and one was turning gold.

Xmas had arrived.

*

Madrigal woke in the dark with her heart beating out of her chest, dreams fading fast. She sat, hyperventilating, looking at the hotel room curtains. Her shoulder still ached. Her knees stung and her mouth tasted bitter and electrical. Dawn etched light where the curtains met the floor. She stood and walked softly across the room, carpet between her toes. She found some water in the frijj. It helped calm her and cleaned the buds. She had rocketed awake, possibly when the sedatives faded.

The dream had jolted her. Better check the target. She looked at her clamB screen which was looped into the crew at Andaman's house, and could see the security guys and van still in place outside the front door. She switched into the infra-heat sensor in the van and she could see a bean of warmth in the house, in the bedroom, hovering above the floor. The target was still in bed. Except ...

She straightened up and headed out on the landing to bang on Bluestone's door.

FLICK 1

ANDAMAN eased out of the bed, leaving the sleeping Cassie curled. They'd been wakeful hours, sweating under the sheet. Everything felt overheated – skin and mind. He avoided body contact with Cassie, but the young woman, sedated, slept on.

Fully alert, with last nite's monstrous adrenaline charge tingling his skin, he crawled on hands and knees down his own corridor, qwick as he could, downstairs to the pool level where his infrastructure was stored. Pumps, water purifiers and mainframe rigs.

There, efficiently, Andaman electronically shredded a working hard drive in the bottlehouse's basement room – one that'd see him jailed for life – and hid 2 more in a secret cavity in the floor, sealing them in. He then crawled over to the back service exit. For the past hour and a half he'd mapped every move in his head while lying stockStill. That's what mappers did and he had got High Passes for mapping at the University Facility, Brisbane. Maps and plans in his head. Schemata of codes & mazes of options. All in one. All the same.

In his jangle of fear there was only one option that he could contemplate – escape.

Andaman let himself qwietly out the back door onto the skinny rear rail passage that connected houses along the floating suburb on the cliff. The exit hugged the red, igneous rock leading to the tight gap where the house was clamped to the cliffFace. A small pathway of rock and short steel bridges followed, taking him past the rear entrances of other hiTek bottlehouses suspended together.

Andaman had guessed, or at least punted on the idea, that if he skittered downstairs qwick enough, the body of water in the huge pool would mask electromagnetics and heat emanating from his own body. The granite would do the rest.

His backpack contained files, a huge wad of cash & keys, a bottle of water, and an emergency cashOut card rated to an avatar he'd created years ago. He'd intermittently filled the account over the time, in case of emergencies. His secure clamB, with all tracers switched off, was in its pouch with a few tools and torchtubes stashed in the underzip of same pouch. He was travelling lite. He knew Cassie's warm body in his bed would fool his captors and their infraheats for only a little while. Impelled by the need to flee, although he hadn't slept, his shoulders and legs were feeling strong.

There was no doubt he was hyped and anxious, even after the sedation. How did he know AuZgov weren't responsible for the bomb? As Bluestone stated, they wanted his codes to various investment programs. With a pathetic excuse of 24 hour protection he was already becoming their prisoner. Bluestone and Dr Phipps were slowly sinking him into their agenda using the glue of purported kindness. Before this benevolent incarceration could be formalised, he was out of there.

He breathed the fresh dirt pungent air and edged down a goat track into the warren of townhouses and paths of North Ward, towards Flick's place. Flick would help him, because they were mates. And she lived alone.

Dawn was on the way. It was only a dash down the stone staircase on the side of the cliff and a 20 minute walk to Flick's. There'd been a bit of rain & now the air cooled before the sun fronted the horizon. A couple of dogs in the street, or behind fences, told him to "go away" or "fuck off" depending on what the owners had taught them to say. One was qwite adept at talking. A scrawny mutt, with a bit of heeler & a bit of terrier, yarped, "Fuck off mate, or I'll bite ya."

Although a few hawkers and beggars were zoned out under blankets and plastic along the way, noone was awake yet, and he padded along the grass verges in the jumble of small roads and alleys. Andaman veered up a street from Alexandra, climbing some more very old granite steps past a palm or 3, and knocked gently on Flick's back door hoping she was off her shift.

She lived in one of those very old houses from the early days. Tin roof, wooden, and verandahs and casement windows. At least 200 years old, kept alive by enthusiasts and strong clear goop over the decades, and with steeldrip frameups retrofitted to increasingly tough building standards. The house was not his style, but a pretty relic. Silver corrugated iron, dark green trim. Flick had said she'd bought it from her bruz'n'law. The door opened slightly. A splinter of Flick's face and curly hair appeared in the crack.

"Let me in. I need to ask you something," Andaman said, a bit breathlessly.

"What happened to you?" she asked looking at his bruised face and scaryStaring eyes. "You weren't in the Northern Lights when the bomb went off? Nooo ...!"

"Let me in." She let him in. He half staggered through the door. Some of the stagger was pretend, some was real. He sat heavily on a kitchen hair.

"I have to ask you something, Flick – I need to get out of here. The AuZgov people are trying to jail me and someone else is trying to blow me up. What's the co ords for The Nest?"

"I'm not going to tell you that, you dick," she said.

"I have to hide. The Nest is where people disappear themselves. Under the cloud, away from HighEyes."

"The Nest is way north. Way north. Who's trying to kill you? Was that bomb in the Northern Lights meant for you?"

"They're saying yes. Yes, it was. Come with me. I'll pay you if you show me. And you can have *The Capricorn Sky*. Just get me out of here."

The Capricorn Sky, his beloved cruisecat. She gaped.

"Who's they?"

"The milisi ... scary people from AuZgov... I dunno. You can have my boat. I don't care."

The more Andaman jabbered, the more he panicked himself. Andaman's demeanour made Flick very uneasy. She'd forgotten that she'd blurted something about the Nest at a party, ages ago. Now he was back at her door like, what had her dad called it? Back like a bad penny.

Flick looked at him with perplexed eyes and calmed. Here he was, a desperate man. But a wealthy man, she knew, who'd never gone back on his word, with her at least. Would she be taking advantage, she wondered, of his desperation, of his boat? Or was he just being generous to a fault?

"Boat's good, but what's the risk for me?" she asked. "Could I get killed?"

"I honestly dunno. I'm not arrested. I'm not a fugitive, because I haven't been warranted for anything. Last nite I was asked to cease my investment activities by a really serious AuZgov official guy, spooky voice and all. So I went for a walk through town to think through shit, and then the bomb went off. And he reckons someone else is after me. And I just want out. Out of this space. I am totally freaked. StiffScared beyond imagining. Just drop me at the Nest, and you can have the boat."

Flick looked at him with a qwizzical face. No one went to the Northern Lights to think about things. She knew exactly why he'd gone. But to take a risk like heading nestward was a big step. Once there, you were out of circulation.

"You're in shock," she said, "from the bomb."

He shook his head. "No Flick. I know exactly what I'm doing. I am trying to bribe you with my boat!"

So Flick made her decision and headed to her bedroom and threw on a xShirt, shorts and a hat. Shuffled under the bed for running shoes. She hoped Andaman was thinking straight. She hoped that *she* was thinking straight. It was a hugely unexpected offer, but not unlike Andaman. He was a very loaded and often random person.

She reached in the frijj, grabbed some food and beer and stuffed them in a bag. He leant against the doorjamb, watching her sudden activity.

"Come on. *The Capricorn Sky's* at the northern marina, isn't it?"

"No, I moved it to the one near Pallarenda Harbour a couple of months back. Let's go there, and you can have it."

"Andy, I'll have to take you up to the Nest myself. It's hard to locate, what with the new charts and coastShifts after the last few wets, and there's a lot of crap in the water. I'll take you, drop you and head straight back to my real life," she said. "You won't find it otherwise."

*

What a nite – and wasn't ended yet.

Her vBike was yellow, with chrome handles, and as it ripped through the streets the fingers of the frangipani trees and their pale ghostly flowers seemed to stretch out for him. He was so tired from the adrenaline let down and the last moments of the sedative, he just held tight around Flick's waist with his head on her shoulder. The air was almost cold, the breeze sloshing against his bare skin. Should he have packed a windcheater? Didn't matter. Clothes were in the boat. He breathed in, fresh tepid air up against the acrid flavours of bomb and burnt plastic still tingling his throat. Ocean air. They used to say it was medicinal. What was it? Go to the beach to breath ozone? That's what he needed. Now down on the Warburton Terrace, engine buzzing, heading along towards the big marina along the shores of Rowes Bay.

Behind, the white city and the big pink hill. Capital of Cap. A few beggars were getting their stalls in order, for the morning traffic, and street sweepers were humming the gutters, clearing things for the dawn. Not many roadVs or even the oldStyle cars that poorarse fishermen generally drove. A stream of Vs were heading where he and Flick were heading – the marina jetties. Maybe they had vessels tied up there. Some towed trailers stacked with speedboats to run down a ramp. Fishermen were getting down, hoping the tide would sluice a few fish their way, better'n the shit frozen packaged prawns and chicken they all ate.

Andaman knew he'd evaded Bluestone and the Milisi. Otherwise there would have been tags, drones, telltale elements that he was being watched. He was qwite sure of that. Among the early crowds and V's they stashed the vBike behind one of the dinghy sheds and, once down at H jetty, qwietly boarded his unassuming 18 metre cruisecat, put the beer in the frijj. Flick almost sprinted to the cockpit to run her hands over the wheel and instrument panel. She'd crewed his boat before, for partying and joyridings, and had skippered it very well. Andaman knew she was a competent sailor – one of her mysterious talents. She first checked the fuel and the water levels and satisfied, she pulled the back of the instruments panel out from the roof cavity and disconnected the emergency safetrace so HighEyes couldn't locate their transponders electronically, a crucial blanket over their escape. Flick was limiting HighEyes trace to optical, which was much more difficult in a shipping channel "haystack" full of boats.

He cast off in the grey light, and she turned the engines to minimum to steer out of the marina.

The hill, with his beloved house perched almost at the top, receded behind them like a reddening carbuncle in the dawn light. A flock of cormorants flapped over them. Straight out past the beacon, steering north, they were caught in a stream of boat traffic: ferries, fishing flukes, early morning rec fishermen zigZagging behind the island to their spots to catch bream or trevally or mangrove jack in the fishing channels between the no go zones Andaman wasn't into fishing like many of his compatriots. He found the practice dull. But he was still amazed how the coastal fish had returned to thrive after the changing sea levels, while ocean sealife had somehow collapsed along with coral reefs. Emergency adaptation management in the 2080's and '90s had regrowthed coastal mangroves to provide fish nurseries and hardLine no go zones allowed an important free catch protein source to return qwicker than expected.

Men could fish again, after 40 years.

The boat skimmed on its blades through calm, pink pastel waters, past the houses and mangroves, the loop of Pallarenda Island which sat on the inlet entrance, and thin bronzed beaches, north. The almost cool air was pleasant. Made a change from muggy day air. Andaman looked at Flick's lithe brown body, white xShirt and floppy hat; her strong thin arms – one wrapped round the wheel, steering confidently, the other holding the cockpit windowframe. She was alert to make sure she avoided other craft, and watched the sonar for sandbars. She turned her head and he saw her taut jawline and small sharp nose for a second, then her face disappeared as she scanned to the other side. A large sailboat was unfurling its panels in front of them and cutting starboard towards the open sea. Probably heading east to the Americas.

"What a beautiful yacht," she said, pointing.

His route could not be as languid as the yacht's was sure to be. The mapper in him said it had to be start & stop, no lingering in any towns, or in boatbays. No loitering – just crouching and watching, and rushing to cover. Andaman was convinced he needed to go somewhere to think.

As Flick cruised out of the harbour boundaries and past the giant barrages that held back storm surges, she revved the engines to the max and they started to crash through the water at high speed. The swell, which used to be held back by the fabled Great Barrier Reef was from the northEast and qwite strong at almost one and half metres. The wind was picking up from the east. She tipped the prow of the boat into the crests like a real pro. "Enough wind to hoist the solar sail," she announced, and pressed the winch button, then moving onto the deck to trim with the main sheet. "Anyone behind? They might find you on the HighEyes." Slap, slap, slap. The hull hit the waves.

"Yes. One of a 1000 identical white vessels in the coastal vicinity. Get me to whatever dropOff point it is, and then leave me be. If they ask where you've been –"

"Don't worry. I'll think of something."

Again he was drawn to Flick and her grip on the wheel. She was thin, but it was such a proficient grip. Was she emaciated, like so many people in the streets, making do? No, he thought. He looked at her with a new eye and decided she was deliberately sculpted.

So how was she strong? He didn't know how she did it. Some sort of exercise, but she never spoke about any sport or physical regime. He drank at her bar during the day, sometimes socialised. Had been to her house a few times. Sexed with her on occasion. He was that sort of guy. Like an ephemeral creek intermittently coursing across her terrain.

He didn't know much about her past, but was aware of her fertility rating, the fact she loved boats and that she knew where the Nest was, a secret she blurted to him after one too many neons at a party. Which meant she knew people, renegades, AuZgov haters, crimms, who lived there. Had visited. Hung out. He hadn't prompted her for further info, because those sort of secrets were dynamite in the Ville and at that point, 4 years ago, he hadn't wanted to know. But he'd remembered clearly that she knew.

Flick had never struck Andaman as an outlaw type, and if she had a steady job and a savings plan for a boat, was probably reformed from the underside. Despite her past. What had she been? Smuggler? Parlour girl? Thief? Didn't matter – he felt sqweamish about his boat bribe but frankly, it was touch and go. Flick hadn't registered a second thought – she'd agreed to help without much hesitation.

So, he'd discovered an outlaw buried beneath that curly hair. He also discovered something else, just then as dawn chased them north. He really liked Flick. Everything. Personality, chutzpah, convo, her sculpted body. The idea took him aback.

He gazed at the islands slipping past: Orpheus, the Palm group, and considered the previous twelve hours. That Madrigal, she had been on his case. Then the brigade guys. And especially the long thin streak of misery, Bluestone, with his beady blue eyes. He could still taste the tang of burnt plastic and insulation in the back of his mouth. Threats, near evaporation, blowing his cosy life – both the secret and the revealed – to bits. That's what happened. Blown to bits.

About conseqwences of doing a runner, Flick seemed cheery and blasé. But Andaman wasn't so sure. He was overwhelmed by the feeling that he could be endangering someone who seemed innocent ... except she did know the location of the Nest in the uninhabitable zones. And that was, in his estimation, his only hope.

"This is fun," Flick announced. "We'll break the course. I'll get you there in 2 days, and then turn around and come back slowly. I'll message Brian and let him know I've been called away to look after a sick aunt, poor dear. She's had a fall.." Flick started improvising her excuse.

He held the wheel as she fiddled with her scope and sent the message.

"Done. Enid can fill in for me. Stick, please," and she was back in the captain's seat, gunning the throttle, shooting past Orpheus Island, heading further north.

Hull, sail and deck studded with white solar nanovolts in keeping with the shiny fibrohull, powering the day engine, except when they hit the cloud and batteries kicked in.

Inside: luxurious teak and chrome fittings, swank galley and comfortable berths. Andaman's money bought the best.

"You, get below and out of sight of the HighEyes and make kopi." Andaman could only nod in agreement. On automatic, he made her a kopi in the galley, handed her the steaming mug and went back below, falling asleep, exhausted, in the forward bunk, the sound of the ocean smacking the boat beneath him.

Slap, slap, slap.

*

That nite, moored in an estuary with the bugkill in the saloon zipZapping sandflies and mosqwitoes, they lay side by side in the master cabin's soft double bunk.

"If AuZgov knows everything that goes on, everywhere, why do they allow the Nest to exist?" Andaman asked. A tiny ball light hovered in the corner and illuminated the cabin and he could see Flick's face, eyes awake and looking up. She had long eyelashes. More and more he felt overwhelmed with the thought that she was so beautiful.

As for Flick, she seemed not to notice the intensity in his eyes, and was on a roll.

"Dunno. It's a haven for old war veterans who's brains have frizzled, angry people. Or women who are barred by the Fecundity Act who wanted a kid and have gone ahead and bred. People with criminal records who've continually got The Man on their case when they're down south. All sorts. At the Nest, they are out of the way. Living isolated in the bush, in small groupings, or round the town. Some are dead dangerous so watch y'rself..."

"AuZgov probably reckons it's better to leave them there than pay for jail time or spend xtra surveill funds. They're people best ignored. Why bother with the Nest when there're plenty of people in reachable places to crack down on, eh? And after those decades of moral purity last century, when AuZgov sat hard on society and crime was totally wiped out, you know what happened? The big let down?"

"No," said Andaman. He hadn't heard of crime being totally wiped out. And he'd gone to college. "What d'you mean?"

"They sterilised society. Sterilised from crime. AuZgov saw, and knew, all the felons. They eavesdropped on them. Took them off the streets and sent them to rehab. Disappeared the psychopaths. Fixed dysfunctional families. Made sure sad kids got seen to. Steamrolled the zeitgeist 'til it was flat and manageable with their frilly language of truth and honesty and purity. The ten rules of neighbourliness. Orderly fecundity. All that crap, Everyone believed the spiel. You following?"

Andaman remembered some of it. She lay on her back beside him, face silhouetted in the dim light, looking at the cabin roof. He suddenly felt safe in the nameless bay where the boat was anchored, with the hull tipping backwards and forwards, ever so gently in the swell.

"So," continued Flick, "for a few decades people who lived under this regime refused to take risks, bend the rules, or take a chance. Because of mass surveill, they didn't shift funds illegally, or rort insurance. And as you know, they also never told lies, they lived cleanly and loved their neighbours because that's what we all do, still. So the Age of Purity & Virtue took hold and to AuZgov's shock, the economy went stale. You do know that bit?"

"No."

From the corner of his eye, Andaman saw Flick looking a little worried. She started to choose her words carefully.

"Well, things began to fall apart. Noone was taking risks with ideas, with activity, with anything. It was like ... picture ripples on a pond. You can't have grey areas without dark areas of activity, without crime on the margins. Things don't happen when the pond is still, blanketed in algae. The economy started to stagnate. So a lotta Governments did a rethink."

"I didn't know that," Andaman said in the dark, looking at the roof of the cabin just above him. He reached up and pressed it with his hand. "How did you know that, while I don't?"

"Oh, this is history – generations ago. They won't admit it. So after a few decades, when there was *The Grief*, and the climate blowBack killed millions of people ... "

"I know about that!" said Andaman, knowingly.

"And *the Blend* happened, when all those refugees came across from the north. Well things were so stale, AuZgov wasn't actually prepared for the conseqwences – disruption, anger, and panic. Nowadayz, the authorities allow a certain level of criminal activity to catalyse on the edges of the economy to create ripples. To test the edges of society AuZgov still pretends it's the Age of Purity, but it can't be. They even have an economik formula for it. It helps insurance companies and milisi operate, the shifting sums of money between the black and benign economy. Authorised badness pushes things around. It creates momentum. Causes momentum that is good and bad. Yin & yang. Bing & bang!"

Ok, that's probably why Bluestone had eyed him fiercely and said Andaman had a "period of grace" to fix his problems, sort things out, before he was officially closed for business. They knew what he did and didn't care as long as he paid AuZ-tax.

Andaman repeated his qwestion: "How do you know all this bizz?"

"Oh, folk knowledge," said Flick mysteriously.

"Folk knowledge about some secret AuZgov economik formula?" said Andaman with a smile. "That's very unfolky."

"It's true. It's something I have found out," said Flick, swivelling around on her elbows and looking down at him. "But on the whole, I'm a simple sort of girl."

She leaned across, breasts brushing his bare chest and gave him a kiss, full on the lips. She then reached down, below the sheets and held him hard with her fingers and Andaman was instantly distracted. "Ooh," he said, "I might be too tired for this!"

Flick ignored his stupid comment. Her eyes were bright with lust. She lay on top of him with her head ducked close to his. He put his hands on either side of her head and kissed her back, slowly and passionately as her fingers roused him, up and down. He was about make another comment, but she slid onto him and the talking stopped.

TODD 1

THE GLOW fired up in the scope tube. And there he was. "Hi, sweetie." "Hi, Mum."

"What you up to?" Madrigal said.

"Gran got me from school today and we went and had a swim down the beach. I've got a new skiff board."

"Great," she said. "How is Gran."

"She's good. Grandad's still away. Like you."

There was a pause. She waited for the qwestion.

"Will you be home soon?"

"A little time. A little time, my chicken. I have more work to do up here in the Ville and then I'll be home."

"I'm missing you, Mum."

"I'm missing you too, my little man. When I get home we'll go north together and visit your aunties and uncles, and you can play with cousin Rob and all of them."

"That'd be great. Can we take Gran?"

"If she wants to come."

They talked for a while, and then there was an awkward silence caused by distance and loss. Madrigal looked at his face, and his soft, unsullied skin and his smile, which was the same smile as his father, only without the cynicism or pain. Full beam love it was. She could smell him. She could feel his soft young skin and wavy hair.

"I gotta go."

"See you soon, Mum. I love you."

"Love you too."

THE SLOTTERS

EVEN before a nervous 'hop unzipped the hotel apartment door, Madrigal well knew Bluestone was dead.

Talking to the hotel people, Madrigal had plastered it on thick about her boss's dicky heart so's the poor 'hop was freaking out about the inevitable corpse. The kid could hardly hold the wand in his hand it was shaking so much, let alone press the switch to unzip the door. She wanted to snatch it from him and do it herself.

But was a homicide.

Just the buildUp of the last 24 – the random, violent bombing the nite before, the surreality, Bluestone's failure to answer anything – scope, Komms, computer – and failure to open the door after her brutal banging. This was a man whose Komms response reflex was instant. Simon Bluestone was always in the moment, ready to react. In the previous ten minutes there'd been no response, and she'd directly scoped Centrl and rung hotel security.

Bluestone was slumped, head on the desk, in an oldFashioned upholstered chair in front of the work panel. His clamB was gone. His face was greyer than ever, blue eyes open, but spark extinguished, dry saliva on his protruded tongue.

Madrigal groaned the long groan of sour vindication. She knelt briefly to check for any life signs, told the 'hop to call an ambulance and flipped open her scope and again pressed for Centrl.

"Bluestone's dead. His clamB's gone too," she said.

"Oh, no," said Centrl with an uncharacteristic wail in his voice. "No lifeSigns?"

"No." She waited for orders, but heard an oath instead.

"And Andaman Marko has slipped off," she added. "The heat bean on the scanner showed only one person in his house – the girl. Bean wasn't bright enough for a twosome."

Centrl swore again and then his orders came thick and fast, because orders were Centrl's forte: "A team of slotters are already en route, ETA 9.15 hours, to try and lockdown any assassination team. Can some other senior guardian take over Bluestone; the postmortem, body security, etcetera?"

"The Ville Brigadier can do that," she said. "Smith. He's ok though his Milisi blokes are pretty amateur."

"Yes. Smith. I've met him. Good. I will talk to Security Administrator Jembrana, and make arrangements. But you must take charge when the Slotters arrive. These are our people, AuzGov not East Cap people. Work out what has gone down. And find Marko."

"Which Slotters are coming?"

"Chime, Folly, Pearl and Dante."

"Ok," she said, "they'll do."

They always came in 4s, Slotters, and she'd take charge.

The job demanded action and she was ready, and knew how to lead them. Not normal Courier practice, but there were regulations which allowed a Courier to take a milisiStyle role – she'd been trained up for proactivity. A risky business, but here she was – taking on the hunt for a killer and an absconder.

Long gone were the days when she'd shudder at the mention of Slotters. Yes, they were "throwbacks", whose violent psychopathy had not been treated. AuzGov needed some people like that to fight fire with fire. Over the past few years, she'd trained with them. Made friends. They were efficient, loyal and tough. They didn't frighten or appal her, as they did others.

'Ndeed, Madrigal already imagined herself as some kind of shark's tooth, moving forward when the front one had snapped off. THAT made her shudder, imagining herself as a shark. Couriering was a subtle, diplomatic business, but if she had to revert to shark, she would.

Like she did throughout any day, she thought of her son, Todd, momentarily, regretting that it would be another few days before she'd be home to see him. A 4 years old, he was fascinated by sharks.

"Pursuit of Marko," Centrl said, "is the priority. We are backscaling HighEyes vision around the house already – get a click on his moves. Follow and fold him in. We need his knowledge and his backLogs. You know that."

Indeed she did. Why Marko wasn't taken into custody immediately had perplexed her even when her ears were ringing and she was coughing out dirty phlegm from the blast. Bluestone's decision had struck her as soft. Or mebbe Bluestone had thought immediate detention a dangerous move – the possibility Marko'd be shot or snatched. Or mebbe he was just lulling the guy to extract info. There was no way Bluestone would have sympathised with Marko, even though he'd just been blown up. Or would have had compassion for his traumatised sex companion. Bluestone never acted without a very sound ulterior motive in mind.

She looked at his old body, limp on the desk. What a mess.

Near the end of an illustrious career as an Administrator in the Age of Purity & Virtue, and as a Courier, Bluestone would be marked a Fail. She was next in the line to fix things. Fail and fix, fix and fold – as it always was. She groaned for the second time. A twin of the first groan when she entered the room.

"Was he your friend?" said the 'hop with a sorrowful face, misunderstanding the groan's origins.

"I worked very closely with Courier Bluestone for a long time," said Madrigal, buying into the Bellhop's misconceptions. "It's very sad."

She knew she'd be sad, but just didn't have time to invest in grief, just at that inst. Madrigal walked out on the balcony and scanned the sky over Cape Cleveland for an incoming hopper. The aircraft would be here soon. With her team.

*

She told the hotel concierge she wanted her things packed and sent to Brigade HQ. Carrying her clamB case and her shoulder bag, she walked down the shallow stairs through the plexiglass hotel doors as the world awoke and brought out its stalls & chargrills, hoverpeds and runners tracking through to the esplanade for exercise.

It was 7.30 a.m. and the air was already hotMoist. The Brig was standing by a military landV, with big wheels and armoured plating against windstorm projectiles. The Brig, was talking on his scope. The landV was modulated with a few non-Military comforts such as leather seats, but she knew it was still super robust. Nothing would be left to chance after the bombing of the Northern Lights. A milisi private opened the rear door for her. The Brig held out his hand to stop her from hopping in. He clipped his scope shut.

"There's a critical deviation in the diary. Not the barracks. We are now reqwired at the Capricornia Parliament," the Brig said to her as. He sounded annoyed. "Get in. Driver, the south entrance."

Madrigal was not prepared to front the Parliament or any politicos. She'd dressed in a cool teflite top and jacket, softskin pants, and good trekBootz – the fashionable version of training fatigues. Nothing flash. Had changed, but not showered. Her hair was up and ready for action, not properly brushed and made black and lustrous as she liked it. She felt underdone.

"Who wants to see us?" she asked tersely.

The Brig didn't look impressed either. His weatherbeaten face and crowclaw eyes gazed uncomfortably up at the villas and streets further up the hill with their red and green roofs and verandahs. Some of the houses were 250 years old and still there, steelDripped into place for heritage atmosphere. They did look pretty. The car accelerated down the street accompanied by 2 outriders on big military vBikes. After the bombing, heightened security. Extra men on bikes. For the Brig? For her?

"We're seeing Jembrana. The top man."

To Brigadier Smith "top man" didn't mean the Premier of Cap. The Premier was Paul Luff, the Chief Administrator. Jembrana was the Administrator of Security of the State, the Brig's boss, but of course, not hers.

She was answerable to Centrl alone, who answered to the P/EM.

The car whizzed through the streets as it was still reasonably qwiet. They looped around into the city centre and up to the big white palace in the Northern Ward that accommodated the assembly and the senior administration of the joint State. A massive 8 storey building filling up an entire block, topped by holoFlags of Capricornia with its red honeyeater and sponsor nations, the blue southern cross of AuZtralia and the rainbow hegemonik of ASEAN, the facade glowed in the morning light, the white catching a lemony tinge from the sun and sky. Madrigal was partially aware of the magnificence, but her mind was on other things. Courier brain ticking into the strategies of how to manage her own façade in the presence of the powerful security chief.

The outriders peeled off at the gates, and the car, admittedly cool and very comfortable, slid round the back ring road to a more discreet entrance in a covered road. A Brigade milisiman in the bright orange uniform emerged, opened her door and saluted. Halfheartedly, she saluted back. They walked between an honour guard of foxtail palms and into the building's atrium cast in a bluish light because of the tinted windows high up, way above the pillars and frescoes.

The atrium with its staircases was even more impressive.

"This way," grunted the Brig. "Here's a hint. Don't overtalk. Answer his qwestions straight."

"Thanx," said Madrigal politely. *Thanx for telling me how to do my job.* Professional Courier. Talker. Persuader. Agent of information and change. Human and unhackable. Firm façade in place.

As she walked the sweeping staircase towards the power-Man, Madrigal started to tense. This was unusual to say the least. Couriers usually worked under the wire, out of sight, away from domestic politicos. She left Centrl to deal with the politicos. This time, she couldn't escape.

The pair were ushered through 2 giant white wooden doors as soon as they arrived at the security chief's office.

Jembrana, in his dark uniform with a loop of braid, was standing talking to a couple of aides in the official domain, light pouring through the massive windows which overlooked the bay. He turned when he saw the Brig. "Ah, Brigadier Smith. This is Dr Phipps?"

"Yes, sir," said the Brig.

"Thanx. I will be talking to Dr Phipps alone, everyone." The Brig stopped in his trax, swallowed, said "sir" and turned on his heel, following the aides out.

Jembrana was largish, Javan/Balinese. In Cap it was the ASEANs turn to run security and AuZgov's turn to administer.

For a telling flash of a second, Jembrana ogled Madrigal. But ogleEyes were qwickly curtained off, because he was obviously a diplomat. Eyes took the shade of friendly and sincere. Eyes lied. Madrigal shook his hand. Jembrana smiled cheerily. "Welcome," he said in English.

The room really was beautiful, an echo of the onceWealth of Northern Australia before the climate changes impoverished everyone. Her eyes followed the abstract organic shapes in the white plaster architraves. She admired the shining, and ancient, red cedar desk. The desk was so polished it mirrored the coral shaped chandeliers and a low tinkling of pleasant music filled the background. They sat in armchairs, looking out over the Magnetic Island.

"I was most sorry to hear about your colleague, Courier Bluestone."

She thanked him for his coldolence.

"Worse, you may be a survivor twice over. You appear to have escaped a hotel assassination attempt by someone who was cloaked – Bluestone's killer. As well, you evaded death in the terrible bombing." he said in Bahasa, the common language of ASEAN.

Madrigal wondered at his knowledge of a cloaked assassin. First she'd heard. The locals must have detected this, but she didn't press him on details because she was loath to appear uninformed.

"A grim attack, sir. Terrible," she replied in the same language. Jembrana called for kopi and an aide slid out qwietly.

"I agree. There hasn't been an outrage like that anywhere in Cap for a decade and I'm talking across the top end and in the Papuan islands and Irian. This is a most peaceful Territory. Maybe not so much in the European or Chinese States, but in our country, it is unprecedented. Purity has been shattered and on my watch. I hear you did magnificently rescuing our bird from the niteclub ... but I also hear he has escaped?" Jembrana looked at her as if to convey further condolences.

"Yes, sir."

"I'm sorry. Our men have failed in the lockdown. But the unfortunate Mr Bluestone did argue Mr Marko be kept overnite at his Castle Hill home." Jembrana suddenly sounded a bit sour after the fact.

"I know."

"You have a view about that?"

"I don't want to speak ill of the dead," said Madrigal bluntly. Jembrana nodded with a smile flickering on his face. She felt bad about the words, but meant them. What a mistake, after a catastrophic evening. She was more convinced the girl, Cassie, should have been sent home after a debriefer had talked to her, and Marko should have been secured at the barracks.

A silver kopi service arrived and even before it had been poured, thick and rich into dainty cups, Madrigal knew it would be good. It smelled terrific, and the ASEAN guys who shared the power really knew how to eat and drink. But this hedonistic thought rankled against the urgency she felt in chasing after Marko. She should not be exchanging mots with a smooth security politico. She should be planning the recapture of the target.

"Still, my men failed and they will be disciplined," continued Jembrana. He looked at Madrigal and sensed her urgency. "We want Andaman Marko back. He is one of ours, a citizen of Cap. A very useful citizen who brought wealth and prestige."

"Sir," murmured Madrigal.

"I can assure you that all resources from my forces will be available to you."

"Thank you. I have Slotters arriving midmorning. We will need your surveillance capacities of course."

"They are yours," said Jembrana. "Are you by chance Capricornian?"

"Well, yes. My ancestors' country is in West Cap, in the East Kimberley, tho I was born in Perth," said Madrigal. "But I spent much of my childhood here."

"A hybrid then?" said Jembrana smiling widely now.

She smiled at the joke and thought: hybrid in more ways than 2.

"You probably know I'm one of the Phipps ... the energy company," she confessed. "I have a tangled background. Frankly, sir, what I do best is Courier for AuZgov. A manhunt is no problem. All my life, I was the best at finding things – bush food, obscure law texts, even topographic stuff for my dad when he was looking for industry lokations. I've been charged by Centrl to find Marko, one way or another, and that's my goal. He needs to be retrieved and I'm after him."

Autobiography was not meant to be part of her façade and she wondered why she'd suddenly blurted out her connexion and brought Phipps Industries into the eqwation.

Jembrana smiled again and reached into his silver clap box, containing sensitive eChips, on the shiny red desk. He passed her a tiny gold chip.

"Here is my contact code. Here is a further code for the East Cap Satellite Bureau to hook any transmission." She inserted the chips one after the other into her scope, then passed them back the Jembrana. She noticed his fingers were soft and man-icured, and surprisingly slim.

"If there is anything else you need, my ADC will help you. Most of all, keep me informed of progress. This disruption is occurring in my administrative period and, although I know you are responsible to Centrl, we coShare security across the north. As for the bomber – he has been captured and is in cus-tody. He is resisting the debriefers and they are now making application in the Supreme Court for a warrant to enter his lim-bic system. When he talks, which is rare, the assassin reveals a Hong Kong accent and so may be working for Chinese interests which is very bad news indeed. Very odd, really. Do we know if the Chinese had a trace on Mr Marko?"

He was obviously aware of, if not across, Marko's lurker on the virtual.

"Not known. His system was breached, but he had no clue. Was a blank to him when we told him. Couldn't find the net origin, it trailwayed into infinity. The Spokes, which had been appraising Marko's electronic trailways, could not trace it, and even though he is a cyberSavant, he himself was unaware of the presence.

"Last nite at our hotel, before the multiple outrages against Cap and AuZgov," continued Madrigal, "Bluestone challenged Marko to fix his problem, as he had everything to lose and also had the skills to find the presence. It's all up in the air now."

Jembrana appeared to absorb the info and nodded in agreement. "That's all, Dr Phipps. I will follow your operation with interest." The security chief shook her hand and ushered her to the door.

"By the way," he asked, "are you partnered?"

"I was," said Madrigal. She didn't explain further. There was a long pause where they looked at one another without affect.

"Thank you for your time," he finally said.

*

Brigadier Smith and Madrigal studied the hotel vision from the previous evening. She and Bluestone had parted ways in the vestibule and crashed to bed in opposite apartments at 2ish after being delivered home from the Castle Hill medical check at Marko's house.

Hers was, no pun intended, a dead sleep. No dreams. On the screen, from external cameras, no movement showed on the hotel's outer shell – up and down the balconies and windows – so she assumed any killing had to have happened internally. Sure enough, the internal vision revealed a grey haze moving through the lobby at 3.57 a.m. Whatever shimmer the killer was using didn't have enough grunt to completely disappear from the hotel's eyes or heat sensors, so they could see the shimmery introodr slip into the apartment. The haze emerged, Bluestone's door slid shut and the shimmer disappeared for an instant, then crossed over and tried to wand open Madrigal's door, but for some reason the instrument didn't work and the door failed to unzip. Time ran out on the haze, and it vanished from the lobby leaving Madrigal alive. There was no facial imprint to go on as the photon shield would have been most powerful around the head.

"At least I'll soon have my protection," she said to the Brigadier. The Brig had a middleAged, suntanned face, a bit lizardy and thick. He looked very concerned about the second assassin.

"Never had proKillers on my patch. The usual domestic murders, the odd smuggler and peopleTrader," he said. "Good thing your Slotters are on the way, tho' I'm not hot on throwbacks as a rule." He licked his lower lip, uncertainly. "By the way, postmortem showed the slight burn trace in Bluestone's blood caused by a heartstopper. Skin was fine. No sign of a pulse into the body, tho' we wouldn't expect it. He died instantly," said the Brigadier. "The scan otherwise was clean."

"I'm sure it was."

They looked at each other across the table in the glowRoom. Their grave faces reflected the gloomy fact that they were dealing with very expert people who'd be hard to catch. There was a pause. Brigadier Smith appeared an empathik man, busy with a 1000 cares in this sprawling town, and 100s of his officers, but for a moment they were together caught in an eddy of deep worry.

Centrl's news held no leads either. The backscaling on the satellite HighEyes nite vision at the bottlehouse had revealed very little apart from cars coming and going at the front. How Andaman Marko had escaped was unknown and proved he was reasonably devilish and clever, but having spent time with him the nite before, Madrigal was yet to accord him fullBlown respect. He'd had a lucky break with the milisi boys out front not being able to read heatPrints properly, along with the fact his house had a back, winding path unobservable from the street, his most probable escape route.

She pondered Marko. About his algorithms and the concentration they must have reqwired, hidden behind his effete lifestyle of girls and parties. The luxury. She still couldn't see him as a serious operator. A savant, a genius without awareness. A hedonist. A technician but careless about his sitch awareness. And again, he was a fail at tracking the lurker in his system. Didn't even know.

*

The local milisi qwickly worked out Marko's boat was gone from the marina. The transponder had been turned off, and he'd left his scope behind, so they were working on other ways of electronik tracking. The boat could have gone north, south or east and would be pretty indistinguishable in busy coastal traffic.

There was a knock on the Brigadier's door and a head poked in.

"There's a Slotter team in meeting room 4 for Courier Phipps," said the head.

Madrigal and the Brig headed down a set of stark corridors and metal stairs to the ground floor of milisi HQ barracks.

The 4 Slotters were standing at ease in the room, and they instantly looked up down when she entered. Apart from Chime, who was much older, they were all from her recruit demographic. Big people who looked bigger in their jackets; 130 to150 kilos, over 2.5 metres. Big People.

"Pearl, Folly, Dante, Chime," she informed the Brig and introduced him in turn: "Brigadier Smith." She had trained with them all in the past because Courier school taught kinetic skills.

Madrigal, for all her training, was relieved Pearl was there, another woman in the group. Pearl was allowed slightly longer hair than the men. A short, dark black bob. The men preferred very short. It was a helmet thing.

Pearl was Eurasian, tho DyNAst's traces through her mitochondria would have tagged her as both largely Vietnamese and Viking. Big shoulders, very serious face, as all women in the service tended to have, because the business of Slotters – chasing, punishing, capturing and/or killing – was essentially seen as masculine.

Madrigal knew they were a perfect job fit because in the time of extended peace, postPurity, Slotters were used discreetly to deal with people who went crazy, endangering citizens, or organised criminals who broke boundaries and had to be brought to heel, or running secret missions outside the various jurisdictions. Or dealing with incursions of smugglers and people traffickers on the borders. Rare crimes indeed.

But Slotters maintained their training, and were lethal, unafraid to kill and unafraid of death. Very unusual people 'ndeed.

The 4 stood in the briefing room with its multiScreens and kopi machine. They looked pleased to see Madrigal. Pearl smiled at her with pleasant crinkly eyes, and saluted when eye contact occurred. Folly was slightly shorter, blond and fluid – relaxed and ready, but always watching, always scanning. Folly being shorter, around 200 meant Madrigal had sparred with him in the past in the gymRink. Best sparring partner she'd ever encountered as he always came at her laterally, with tactical nous and invention.

Only her adolescent footy playing occasionally gave her an edge in balance and speed, as she was still much shorter – only 152. But in skills, she and Folly were well matched. Chime, the team leader was a Slotter through and through – courteous and tough – all the hallmarks of a Purity man. Ensured he and the team were always ready. Chime had a bent nose from a fight, somewhere in the mists of time. Best of all was Dante. Took the moniker because of his Italian looks. He actually had a sense of humour. Spent his money on investments and was always asking Madrigal, when she was around, for stock tips because he was aware of her family background. Droll though he was, he was as lethal as the others.

"Ma'am," Chime said. "All present and awaiting instructions."

"Sit down, guys," she said. Madrigal went through the brief. While Slotters were mostly impervious to emotion on the job, they were surprised, and a bit shaken, to hear about Bluestone's death. He was one of the best operators they'd ever worked with so his murder meant their target was cunning as well as lethal. She told them of the bombing at The Northern Lights; she showed them the vision of the haze in the hotel lobby and atriums. She showed them tangential vision off the satellite that morning and the heavy boat traffic leaving the north marina. She told them Marko would be terrified about his sitch, and unpredictable. Her guess was he went north, but it wasn't good enough for a pursuit order. Her guess was he was in the dark about his enemy, but would include AuZgov (i.e. them) in his personal threat assessment.

Chime and Pearl were tasked to check the sat vision with zoomIn on the jetty and the boat. Dante was tasked with pursuit prep – ensuring the hopper was ready, especially for hard weather up north. She told Folly to come as her protective detail into the town.

"We're going down on the lower terrace to see a woman Marko was friends with," she told Folly as the car moved along towards the esplanade. "Bluestone touched base with her. She may know where he went." She knew the Brig's people had worked over Cassie, who had no info whatsoever.

When they arrived at the bar, with the palms and the blue sparkling bay, Madrigal ignored any urge to stop and have a moment over a cool drink. Tired and aching as she was.

The armed presence of Folly helped her make the decision. She found Aldo the Swarbar owner in his office round the back. Aldo wore shorts and a wikVest and looked hot even in the airCon.

"Flick? She messaged earlier to say she was looking after a sick aunt," he said. Madrigal, in her nicest manner with the dangerous armed hulk, Folly, looking over her shoulder, asked about Flick, where she came from, how she knew Andaman, where she lived.

Aldo said he didn't know, that Flick kept to herself and seemed smart. It appeared her name, Felicity Lynn, was not a real name. Centrl's people couldn't identify it or the security number Flick'd given to Aldo. The money paying her rent came from a fairly new account in the pseudonymous name. DNA from her flat was a deadEnd. Biometrix had difficulty mapping Flick's face against the National data bank as well, and there were several 1000 possible matches. She'd altered the original photo supplied to the Swarbar, with prosthetic putty.

"So she's a pro," said Madrigal.

"She's a pro," said Centrl in the earbug, "but she was never one of ours."

At that moment, Folly's muscled bulk leant over her shoulder and whispered, "They went north."

Madrigal nodded. He must have clocked a message from the Brigade HQ in his earbug. From the corner of her eye, Pearl had picked the vBike and departing boat, but everything had hit cloud around Hinchinbrook Island and vision disappeared. There was a pause in proceedings as Madrigal had a think.

Aldo, the bar owner, sat there looking warily at his visitors. He kept glancing up at Folly, and his black jacket, with the black hardArm sticking from the holster, the menacing sunglasses and the chin. Guns were almost invisible in the Australian continent, banned during the Purity, and the sight of a hardArm hypnotised Aldo. Then he returned his gaze to Madrigal who emanated poise and at this juncture, charm.

"Flick? Did she ever talk about her past? Where she came from?"

"Not really. She was always talking about saving for a boat and a house. Bit of a party girl. Said she'd had a rough childhood and wanted to make everything sweet before she had a kid. She had the permissions. She wanted a boy. I'm sure she thought Andy Marko might have been the man, but he is such a dilettante loser. And a Noughter. She rented a house off the hill in Alexandra Street. Old one."

Madrigal raised an eyebrow about the Oncer thing. Flick didn't have a known identity let alone a Fecundity Status.

"Anything she said about where she was born? Location?"

"Funnily enough, no. I always thought she was from East Cap tho'. Accent and everything.

"Could she have been a refugee from further north?"

"Never said." Aldo paused and looked concerned. "I'm being straight with you here by the way. I'm not trying to bullshit you."

"I know. It's ok," said Madrigal with her prettiest smile. The man was clearly terrified of the gun, and that was good.

"Was she Marko's lover?"

"Probably, from time to time. He rooted everything that moved." The terror subsided for a tick, as he was overwhelmed by the pure envy buried beneath his sneer.

"But they were friends?"

"She was always distracted when he came down for his lunch. Every day, they'd have a yak. I had to keep an eye on her, because she'd forget her duties, like serving customers, cleaning up. Normally, she were a good worker but me and Danny had words with her about Marko now and again. Then again,

Marko was a regular and bought the pricey stuff, so she were also a bit of bait." He shrugged at the contradiction.

"Ok," said Madrigal. "We've gotta go. Thanx for your time." Folly exited first, sweeping the terrace of drinkers and diners with his eyes, and scanning the crowded roads beyond. "C'mon," he said to her finally. She shook Aldo's clammy hand and they left.

*

"Is it track and follow, or track and stop," Chime asked.

"Track and stop. Centrl says fold him under," said Madrigal. They were cruising about 400 metres over Hinchinbrook Channel. Were flying low between the island and the mainland, seeing waterfalls emerge from cloud cover in an incredible cascade of wetness as if poured from the grey. Silver against the thick dark green vegetation. To Madrigal it was beautiful. Silver hair wrapping the old country. Had the hopper been any higher, they'd have been lost in the clouds with no visuals on the channel below. Madrigal suspected Marko and Flick would have pushed forward as fast as possible, but whether through inner channels with the main boat traffic, or further out, it was hard to guess.

Chime said: "Could be anywhere down there. We've got 100s of kilometres of mangroves. Inland estuaries, rivers ..."

"My hunch is they're heading as far north as fast as possible," said Madrigal. "Even Torres, Irian. And beyond. Tho' the weather may be too sharp."

She scanned the boats and the marina towns along the coast. Appeared that the scope device Flick had sent the story about her sick aunt to her boss had joined the fishes, along with Marko's scope. There was no trace. She turned around from the coPilot's seat and looked at the 3 other Slotters strapped tight.

Pearl was staring out one of the wider ports at the view of the huge old island, and Folly was asleep. Madrigal looked at the lines of prawn ponds along the coast, and great oRings factories in the channel containing barramundi and other fish, a constant hazard to fast boats.

Madrigal said: "We tiktak with milesi in the northern settlements, specially the town of Trinity. They need to be scoured as we go. Gotta be methodical as we go, but I think they're headed for the Nest. The likely scenario is that Flick comes from there and that's why she's an assumed person. She's swapped partial IDs with a woman who's embedded there now, probably to have an illegal kid. Now, we do have reasonable relations with the folk at the Nest on a "leave us be/we'll leave you be" arrangement, but we can't afford for them to harbour Andaman Marko. Someone who knows their biz is, undeniably, trying to kill him. Understood?"

They nodded. All were listening, including Folly who'd woken instantly at the sound of Madrigal's official tone.

"There is also nothing to discourage my thinking that whoever bombed the Northern Lights, and killed Courier Bluestone, won't be unaware of Andaman's escape. Flick may be part of that conspiracy. She may not, but I'm leaning to her being a hostile agent."

Madrigal looked at Chime and Pearl. They were both Eurasian, but their families stretched way back. They weren't postBlendGen. Neither would be aligned with ASEAN. Madrigal also knew would be unlikely ASEAN was directly involved in any hostile operation. Too much was staked on coGovernance of Capricornia and it had gone successfully for over half a century now. But very easily, there could be an ASEAN Heg Corp involved, or a Chinese/ASEAN interest.

Whatever, the foe was hostile, and killing was not anathema to them, and they also wanted the Couriers out of the way which was heroic, given the reach of AuZgov and the penalties for murdering a officer. She had a private shiver at the vision of the haze, floating in the vestibule, attempting to wand open her apartment door.

"Chime, I want your focus on defence. Hostile tracking. Anything that could be a threat. Pearl and Folly, I want you to concentrate on offence. Scope every milesi station as we go, while we carry out a visual chek, see if they've noted anything. Milesi are on alert already. Nag them.

"We need to find and secure that boat. Dante – you do the recon for us. And the weather. Watch the weather. Up round the pointy bit it's volatile."

"Ma'am," they said.

And I will just lead, she thought.

M'BERS

THEY'D sailed north for two days, evasive of settlements, sticking to the sea side of islands, avoiding the northernmost Port of Trinity. They headed to islands, both nites anchoring in bays. The first nite Flick had distracted him with sex, but the next day, over breakfast of toast and coffee, he'd asked her about her parents, thinking that some of her "folk knowledge" about the Age of Purity – which struck him as a potent theory – must have come from either her mum or dad. She said her mum was dead, killed in an accident. She became silent and sad and would not elaborate, and added that she didn't get on with her dad and he lived up north and that's why she was dropping Andaman at the Nest, and pissing off soon as he was ashore.

"I like you Andy. This trip is not just for the boat," she said, before they pulled anchor on the second day. "You asked me to take you and I'm doing it. The Nest's a hard place. I wouldn't ever go there any more, but you reqwested it."

It was the nearest she got to warning him off. He felt a little wash of pleasure penetrate his anxiety when she said she liked him. She was normally so guarded, Flick, but the warmth in her voice was generous! They'd had fun in the cabin bed last nite. In fact, they always had fun when they sexed. He looked at her again, her blue eyes fixed on him, her sweet mouth relaxed and friendly and her strong hands around the coffee mug. Early morning light through a cabin window lit her hair.

"I like you too, Flick. Thanx for helping me." Her unerring competence as a sailor amazed him too. "You're a true friend and I don't have too many of those." They sat in silence for a moment, smiling at each other as the boat rocked gently, then she stood, rinsed her cup and, with the authority of skipper, said, "Ok. Better be on our way. Keep a check up the bow –I'll winch the anchor."

*

Massive red and lemony clouds reared into the stratosphere like distant alps in the dawn. The ocean held a sheen of pewter. The sight reminded Flick of images of rare jewellery and beaten gold. The only ominous portent was an occasional flutter of blueWhite lightning in the highest mass, momentary threads of hi borne electricity, a reminder just how dangerous that weather band was, if you went under the Cloud, that mass of turbulence which started just further north, thickening and massing the further north one went, muscling up and leaving the land and ocean in turmoil. In an almost unbroken wall of eqwatorial storm – apart from a few calm eyes and "knotholes" – the Cloud flowed violently through to the southern Philippines. Currently, the cloud lay just north of the Nest, as far as she could tell, her calculating eyes running along the familiar coastline, but already there had been early summer storms where they were sailing.

Water surface was now full of chop, making helming tricky for Flick. Along with the erratic swell, the surface started to get slicked and opaqwe from runoff via black mangroves stretching into the hinterlands as they passed. In this patch of clear space, she well knew HighEyes could have seen them, specially since boat traffic had faded. As the sun rose higher, the ocean looked like pale brown shit, lifting and falling. She knew behind those inlets and hills was land laid waste by mining, and agriculture, which had been marginal for cropping at best. Poisonous runOff had inundated the waters once the new weather came down. For some reason, 120 years ago they'd opened the country up to all sorts of extraction. Her grandada had said that folk back then knew what was coming, but they still did it anyway. Even a few of the Indijj people had agreed to the extraction. And now there were drowned mines, old tailings pouring out into the ocean. Unrooted soil, still from the clearance days. If people weren't scared of the crocs inhabiting waterways, or the weather, then they sure as hell were scared of the poisons swirling into the rivers. Heavy metals, acid soils.

She had to tool down and steer evasively sometimes because of logs and crap floating in the waves, just beneath the surface.

"Andy," she said when there was a huge clump of stuff in the water ahead. A branch raft.

"Yiz?" he said. She looked at him sitting slumped on the cockpit couch, rubbing his arm. He looked miserable and distracted, something she'd hardly ever seen before in Andaman Marko. She felt sorry for him, sorry that the wisecracking and bigNoting had evaporated. Every so often he looked at her and gave her a thin smile, or looked to the south at boats in the distance. After the port of Trinity the boat traffic had dropped back to seagoing vessels and fishers. You didn't contemplate sailing just south of the Cloud without some firm purpose.

"Keep a lookout for debris. It's packing up in the waters here," she said, giving her friend something to do.

"'k," he said. "Beer?"

"Sure." They stood on the cockpit and he put his arm round her shoulder while they looked out for potential snags.

"When the rains build and flush the rivers, all this stuff ends up along the coastal waters."

"What about reefs?"

"Stuff of myths. Like dragons. Don't have to worry about crashing into those any more. There's a few moved further south now, but this is where the great underwater reef existed in the past. Inner and outer. A big coral wall. Granddada said in the old days they worried it'd bleach and die 'cos of the heat, but was mostly wrecked by storms."

She told him her granddada had taken her diving a few times further north. On calmer days and way out beyond the run off, she'd seen some of what was left of a reef. Mostly looked like a broken boneyard, but there were still a few pretty fish and some colour. Flick remembered going under with a snorkel and flippers and following shoals of brilliantly coloured fish in among bommies. Grandada knew where remnants could be found and he had revelled in the excitement in her eyes as she surfaced and wittered on about the fish jewels.

Grandada, who knew his waters, had explained that a good century before there'd been an extensive coral reef along the coast, but with the sea levels rising and clouding out the sunlight for the polyps, and the acidity, and smashed by thermocells – intense stormcells within 'phoons, it was all but gone. And the big waves pounded the coast when the weather was up, and washed things away.

*

The Convocation had dispersed and the rebuilding work was done. Only a few of the group were still in the barracks further up the hill preparing to head to their bunkers and huts, which were scattered through the jungles and heathlands, and beyond, in the savanna.

Two Caterpillar graders, ancient vehicles, were now re-housed in the massive hangars made from *the box of the north* – steel shipping containers – that were buried deep in a hill. A bridge had been rebuilt, and the jetty at the creek, their lifeline, was operational. Most men who'd come from the hinterland had returned there. A lot of those blokes, he knew, were on a knife edge; a mere slip of the tongue away from a wound acqwired in a vicious fight. Only selfInterest allowed them to work together, and when they did, it was with sullen intensity and bush expertise, generally grunting at one another. At nite they'd sit around the Nest's coupla liqwor shanties selling rough rum and other forms of lampjuice, and drink until comatose. And M'bers drank, as well as doing his level best to prevent fights. These were men with no friendly aspect.

The Nest, a small township with a main street and hardened residents had been smashed by 3 thermocells a month before. A bit unseasonal, but, then again, nothing was seasonal any more. Hadn't been, for as long as M'Bers remembered. Two boats destroyed, along with their vital jetty, part of his house, one guesthouse, and the hill tracks, which were washed away. Since everything in the Nest was reinforced and waterproofed to the max, this was a truly unearthly effort from the elements.

So M'bers had called in the troops from the backwoods. Blokes with detonators permanently popping in their heads, a few Indijj who stayed behand to look after sacred areas in what was left of their country, and women too, who either lived alone, or with their illegal brats, or with blokes, beyond the fringes of his domain.

The Convocation.

They knew how to weld, build, make workable structures out of wreckage and rubble. The Nest was their lifeline to the outside too, and they owed him and the infrastructure that sustained them.

Channing, M'bers lieutenant, stood beside his boss, wearing his teflite poncho as the rain mizzled down. Better mizzle than stinging pelts.

"Jetty's sound. C'n take vessels now. C'n bear weight, bruzz." Channing always choked his sentences, more than most.

The rains had swept old mine tailings, copper, gold, even uranium wash, from the hinterland through the creeks and river. Neither men knew how toxic the water was, but they wouldn't fish there for a while yet. Water was the colour of murk.

"Yep," M'bers said. They walked onto the clanking metal platform, out over the river. A long shape, probably a croc, slipped under the structure's shadow. Likely a radioactive croc. "Hope we get a bit of peace and qwiet from the sky for a while. We have debts to pay after all the construction. Had to call in a few favours."

Channing'd heard this every day for the last month. It meant somewhere in the next few weeks they and a few friends would mount a raid on a rich boat going through international waters way north, or raid even a southern township, which was dangerous and usually violent.

M'bers was thoughtful. He looked at his own boat tied up down the end of the jetty. It was still workable, because he'd been fixing it for the past few days after downing tools at the end of the day, and before the session at the lampjuice shanty. A small aluminium fishing boat with a cabin and cockpit, it was tied alongside a couple of slider boats that were owned by blokes who lived up and down the wild coast.

Channing pointed downriver to the top of the headland.

"Incoming boat," he said. They saw a spanky white job, from down south presumably, because everyone round here sailed on handMe downs and wrecks. "Mebbe they can give us some cash to finish the build. Mebbe rich doodz."

"Or we make 'em pay," said M'bers his face screwing up in thought. The boat was heading up the channel now, threading its way past the sandbars, guided by an expert invisible hand. The water was green and aqwa where it lay across the sand shallows, and under the mangroves along the channel, black.

"I'd say the skipper's been here before," said Channing, sqwatting. "Knows the channel. They ain't toning down throt-tle." The boat roared over to the jetty and tooled down, clanking against a barge that was moored. The engine noise was cut, and the wake subsided. Two figures emerged on the runner along the side of the deck.

"Young Flick gracing us," said M'bers. "Thought she'd gone forever."

" 'Never again' ... s'what she said when she left 4 years ago. In a fury," Channing replied. "Stole Kingdom's boat if I remember and he had to go to Trinity to retrieve it. 'Never again', s'what she said."

"Hi, M'bers. Hi, Channing," Flick said. "This is Andy. How's Dad?"

"You just missed him. Just held a Convocation to fix up some damage. Headed back up river this morning."

"Least he's still alive. I'm only here to drop Andy off. Wants to hole up for a while. Thought he could go down the anabranch for a bit."

"Cost him," said M'bers.

"What? To be bit by sandflies and drink illegal lampjuice to kill the itches? Come on."

There was a pause. The old men looked at her suspiciously.

"What do you know about this bloke, Flick?" asked Channing, completely ignoring Andaman who was standing with his bag beside her. "Will he bring trouble?"

"Possibly," she said.

"Happy to help with repairs here," said Andaman offering usefulness up. On the spot value, a pair of hands. They ignored him again.

M'bers added, "Yeah, why are you here anyhow, Flick? Swore you'd had it with us and y'd never ever come back."

"Andy asked me to bring him here. He's a mate, so I did. I'm off. See ya."

"For what?"

"He's a mate. Don't you listen? I gotta go now," she added walking toward the jetty. "Look after him for me."

"Wait, wait. Don't you want a drink? See Kingdom?"

"Why would I want to see him?"

The 2 men were nonplussed.

"He's your dad," said Channing.

"Tell him I'll visit later in the year," she said, "but I gotta go now."

Flick's insistence shocked Andaman. She really didn't want to hang around, and he had no idea who these guys in scrubby clothes and battered hats were. One had a rifle, the other a knife in his belt, like something from the olden days. Backwoodsmen. Pioneers. Pirates.

"See you, Andy," she said to him. "thanx for the boat. And the fun times." And she hopped on board, pulling the painter with her, and revving the throttle.

Marko didn't mind about the boat. He could buy 100. But he did feel abandoned by his friend. He turned to look at the 2 weatherbeaten men as his exLaunch weaved a braid in the water back down the channel. The men returned his stare with dubious looks.

He loosened his hands with a shaking gesture, and felt the humidity around his head and neck. It almost strangled him.

"Hide me," he pleaded.

*

The rain stopped, and for a couple of days Andaman Marko attempted to find his place as a resident of the Nest, but noone really noticed him. He drank a few rough liqwors in one of the steel leanTos which sported a palm leaf roof and managed half a conversation with the drinkers, basically because they were shattered and would talk to a passing dog if it spoke to them. But none of the many dogs wandering round the Nest had genetically modified voice boxes and boosted brains. They were just dumb dogs.

The place was rundown and muddy. A patch of bitumen ran through the main strip with a few steeldrip shops and a bunch of oldStyle shippingContainer condos welded at the back as a dormitory cum guesthouse. A hill rose behind the town, and along its ridgeline were horizontal windTubes with long turbines pumping the power. Since the cloud was prevalent, solar arrays were a hopeless bet, though some of the roofs still sported them, a hangover from when things weren't so wet.

Andaman wandered round trying to pick up conversations. Normally, he was a gregarious fellow, happy for a chat. But the locals were sullen and withdrawn. You had to be a local, or you were noone. And to be a local, Andaman noted, you needed to be mad, drunk or hopeless.

M'bers found him a berth in the Nest's barracks where he bunked down with some roughLooking blokes who smelt of sour sweat, alcohol and machine oil. They didn't give Andaman a second glance. One nite, Andaman was sitting with M'bers and Channing at a table in the leanTo, beers in front of them and Andaman mentioned Flick. He decided to be guarded, but he certainly hinted that Flick was his dear friend and that he could pay them well if they protected him. Why? He explained that someone had tried to blow him up. M'bers knew The Northern Lights in the Ville and had been shocked when he'd heard the news of someone blowing up a "very classy drinking hole with it's sex booths". Andaman relayed the gory details.

"Cheezus, that was real bad, I heard," said M'bers. "They reckoned full carnage. You were there?"

"AuZgov thinks I was the target."

Channing and M'bers looked at each other with concern suddenly blazing in their eyes. AuZgov involvement was anathema to the 2 men. The Nest was a haven for the lawless where Gov didn't reach, and they didn't want any interference now.

Andaman's revelation that the claws of authority might head their way, and his promise of a payout, had suddenly made him the focus of attention. M'bers started talking again, as if Andaman wasn't even present.

"Channing. Let's see what remuneration he can supply, and we'll move him into the Crow's Nest, I think. And keep a watch," Channing nodded.

"Can't be too careful with those AuZgov bast'ds," said Channing, draining a glass of lampjuice. "Should by rights have him dunked in the creek with a few crocs after Flick left."

Andaman felt a chill down his skin. They probably would, he thought.

"Ah, she's sweet on him," said M'bers. "Couldn't do that to her."

"True."

"And you'd better meet Flick's dad if you are sweet on her," added M'bers.

Channing grinned, showing a row of teeth that looked like dirty brown pegs. For some reason the 2 hillbillies thought it funny.

M'bers added: "He'll have a word to you about your prospects..." and they chuckled again.

They poured him another shot.

"Should I be worried?"

They didn't answer. Just exchanged knowing glances.

*

The shooting started as soon as dawn tinted the water mirror silver. All he could see down the hill were blurred shapes and red spits of gunfire. The noise popped and echoed against the terrain, rattling the dawn and his nerves. Andaman, suddenly ziggy with adrenaline, cautiously stretched his head out of the cave mouth where he'd been sleeping in a swag, and yes, down the hill there were a couple of boats, lifted onto the beach, and shadow figures moving through the camp. Gunfire! Of all things. Could hear the *krak krak* clearly. Someone fired back from the barracks where he'd been moved from the day before, and where a whole bunch of blokes had headed at 2 or so that morning after they'd drunk their weight in rotgut. Afterwards in the dark, with a tiny glowstick to show the way, he'd staggered thru the trees and up the steep path, past a huge battery of horizontal wind tubes that cranked methodically as the breeze spiralled down them, to the cave – the Crows Nest – where M'bers and Channing had advised him to sleep.

"Out of line of sight, away from HighEyes," they said. They'd even given him a pile of old paper boox from last century to while the time away.

Now it was all guns blazing down in the Nest and he was frightened. Andaman reckoned there'd be around 5 bunked down in the container plaza, which had been welded together.

One of the shadow figures fell, which led to a fusillade that hit the walls of the steel building, making sharp panging noises. Other figures were running into the scrub from tents and buildings. Behind the store and the huts that lined the main street of the Nest, more *krakking* opened up from a flank, but it was silenced with another rattle of sound from the dominant figures.

A shadow threw an explosive in through the halfOpen door of the barracks. There was a crump, and that was that. No more shooting from the barracks. All dead. The shadow figure attackers combed out through the settlement. There was further gunfire from a ridge, aimed at the invaders, and shouts, and Andaman slid back to the cave to grab his stuff. He didn't wait. He pulled the pack onto his back, grabbed the clamB case and a couple of water bottles and headed into the scrub, leaving the battlefield behind.

MADRIGAL 2

FROM the air, they saw the damage to the settlement known as The Nest. Visible from qwite high altitude: bodies in an open area in front of various asymmetrical steel constructions. A man waved at the aircraft, and put down his hardArm. Once their hopper lighted, and disembarked, Madrigal and Folly stared at the wreckage. Smoke still rose from a burnt domicile. Within a large welded shipping container they found flesh spatter and bodyparts. Pearl and Chime were scoping a camera across the tracks and the ruination and were feeding the footage straight to the Spokes and Centrl himself who was watching the screen.

"Couple of hours ago. I reckon it only happened then," Madrigal said. The Slotters' hopper sat in a clear area next to the creek and Dante cagily watched the overgrowth from a dozen angels. He was a snap at flying the numerous flakes of metal hung in congealed light and keeping appraised of the screen array. The congealed light could be focussed like a lens as the photons tautened, pulling images into the transmitter and sending them to his bank of screens. A second hopper was positioned about 30 metres behind theirs.

After scoping the small settlement, Madrigal said to Folly, "Up this way". There was an almost indecipherable path heading up the hill behind the settlement. She tracked past the front of the 40 metre wind tube array in their horizontal hardMesh cages without a side glance, Folly and Pearl following silently. Only sound was wind impellors buried in the windfarm cages, swishing busily, with one or 2 clanking, where flanges had come unstuck.

"See. There's one trak visible. Wasn't a crowd that passed." She waved at the path. "The leaf litter's pretty much intacto." She pointed to some mud further up on a leaf. "But here's the heelprint of the single doop. One person."

"You really are extraordinary sometimes," Centrl said in her earbug.

"Thanx, boss. Not extraordinary enough to control this sitch before it got out of hand."

"True." An almost transparent angel followed above them, piloted by Dante. She could just catch its lightShine.

"See, his hand used this tree to balance. Gets a bit bushBash here. Come on, Folly," she said, launching herself up the slope.

"Take it easy, ma'am," said Folly. A massacre had occurred a couple of hours past. He was in no hurry. They got to the Crow's Nest after 5 more minutes of qwick climbing. Folly checked it out and then went in through a steel portico and found the basics – camp bed with swag, stove, frijj.

"He's gone. Don't blame him." She could see he'd have had a clear view of the attack. "Inland for sure, if I'd been him."

Dante's voice cut through. "The raiding party that came here, they've gone. The angels have scoped the terrain, but there's nothing." Angels were ni'on invisible, but when the light took on a hint of mass, they could be glimpsed. The tiny flake of technology, the size of a mosqwito, sending the image from the natural lens, was too tiny to see.

"Mebbe they got Marko," said Folly.

"Not likely, chook," said Dante.

"We'd've seen traces of more people up the hill here if they had," Madrigal said, "and there aren't. Country tells me only one person was up here lately. He's cleared out, taken his gear. Trouble is, he probably thinks it was us who mounted the raid, so he'll stay in hiding. I should go after him."

Centrl spoke, a voice of pure logistics. "Brigade personnel are on their way to secure the Nest area. Leave Dante and Chime until they arrive. You take Folly and Pearl and pursue on foot. They will follow with eyes, and then with the hopper when forensics arrive."

"Be aware," Centrl said, "that there are many residents in the area. They are armed and are dangerous and do not welcome trespassers. And they hate AuZgov people. The Nest acts as an elective detention precinct for Cap, where individuals opt out to avoid authorities on a what suits us/suits them, basis. But many have psychopathic traits, or are desperate. Understood?"

"Understood, Centrl," said Madrigal, factoring in the new information. She supposed that if the reason for the Nest's existence was fully understood, that the settlement was there on AuZgov's behest, the psychos would go somewhere else.

"Do we sustain the facility?" she asked. "Are there contacts here who can assist us?"

"That's an infoLock, Courier. Not authorised to clarify."

"Ok. Got ya," said Madrigal. If it was ever known they had contacts amongst the denizens of the Nest, the "contacts" would be dead in seconds.

Pearl reached them without even having to catch her breath.

"Which way, ma'am?" she asked.

Madrigal scanned the trees, the stringy bushes, the boulders and soil. The atmospherics hit her as the cloud darkened to the north and was backlit from the west. The colours were strange and the bush seemed to vibrate slightly.

The ancient people were here, the ancestors, in whatever strange timeloop they lived. She could feel them, and Madrigal, while she acknowledged them softly, wished she had found someone alive to ask permission to walk on Country. It was someone else's place and she full knew the Indijj people still lived and breathed their ways here. At some point she'd have to sqware it away. Channing was Indijj and a local. She'd seen the file. When she caught up with him mebbe, as long as he was alive after the massacre.

Whatever, the old ways worked for her here, as well as they did in the west. Madrigal crouched, looking at the ground carefully. It appeared Andaman had elevated himself behind a couple of boulders for a short while, to watch while the attack was proceeding and then headed west along a ridge. Madrigal took a gulp of water from her bottle, checked the sun's arc, wiped her face with a sleeve and detached her helmet, which she hung from a clip on her slim backpack.

"This way," she said, grinning.

*

Dante watched closely the turmoil in the ocean to the north-East. Radar showed a tentacle of cells, deep lows in the churn that ran from the conveyor belt of the eqwator, and while his flock of angels were watching the terrain above the estuary for trouble, his main fear was 3 red patches firming up in the Coral Sea and drifting qwickly towards the coast, north of the Nest. The notorious weather in the High Capricorn – anywhere north of 16 degree latitude – had caused, over the last 80 years or so, abandonment of towns, the end of mining and ranching in the Cape.

Outside the hopper, around the settlement, Chime, and the 20 unit holding team from the Ville, were working through the debris trying to identify the killers that had attacked and annihilated the residents, who'd obviously fought back. They checked slugs, phosfire traces and blood to work out how many and what weapons. The Brigade hoppers were stationed beside Bertha, their command hopper. The cloud, as per usual, made HighEyes impossible.

Dante made a decision.

"Taking eyes off the angels for 5," he said to the panel. He whipped the helmet from his head, and slid back to the main door. The storm sitch was AMBER SE now, or sky endangering, and looking at red spots on the radar was one thing, but nothing beat checking the actual sky. He slid outside into the 100% humidity, down the hopper ramp and looked up. Rain was starting to pelt down and the horizon was dark with a belt of wet. Even halfway down the estuary he could see chop in the waves, and a swell building.

"Ah, shit," he said, and turned back up the ramp and into his seat.

"Ma'am, weather's closing. Activate suits and keep lively. I'll try to keep the angels up in the air for as long as." Normal light was impervious to wind, but congealed light could get blown about.

"Hear ya," said her clear voice.

Over the past few hours, Madrigal's team had moved qwickly over the topography and Dante'd been impressed with her focus. For a Courier, all diplomat and execStyle, she could sure do the action thing. As a sparring partner he knew she could just about hit the mark as a Slotter. Not qwite, because she vented moral objection to killing, but apart from that deficiency, she'd almost scrub up. He'd watched the 3 figures work their way over a series of ridges and gullies – at least 20 kilometres inland and to the north, avoiding the worst terrain. They'd been qwick, accurate, surefooted. She'd closely tracked marks and signs on the ground and around the bush.

"How d'you do that, ma'am?" he'd finally asked.

"Bush skills from the oldies," she answered. "Used to hunt kangaroo with my uncle and aunties east of Derby when I was a kid. They taught me to do this when I was a littlie. Eyes on the ground, they'd say, think like the roo. Be the roo."

"You're chasing a bunny, ma'am, not a roo," said Dante, smiling. "Don't think bunny thoughts."

They were talking on the team intercom, but offline from Centrl and, no doubt, his crowd of dopey analysts and technicians, though Dante could never tell when they might be listening in. He didn't care. As long as he wasn't rude about Centrl.

He watched her on visual 5 working her way down a mossy, muddy slope through a thick, stunted treeline with Folly and Pearl behind, and wished he was with them in the twisting gale. The 3 stopped and engaged the skins which wrapped around them, full helmet. *Harder than steel but lighter than styro*, the old merchants'o'death ad went. They hadn't changed these rigs for many decades. Still the best. If debris and rain slammed into them, the skin's inhabitant would feel very little. Keep them at perfect temp. No need to toilet, no need to eat. All soloSustainable.

The gear had been developed for war at the beginning of the last century, but when the wars ended because they were unaffordable, money had to be spent on survival, feeding the refugee populations and infrastructure rebuilding. So the suits were used for some space exploration (in case of evacuation) and extended elements were incorporated into the skins, such as boson enhancers for the Mars and Saturn moon habitations to calibrate for gravity. They adjusted for gravity in the heaviest and lightest of surfaces. The suits Madrigal and her party wore were minus the heavy gamma ray shielding and so were lightweight on Earth. But the skin/helmet combo, a testament to the glory years of highScience, impervious to big gusts of wind, didn't please everyone.

"Hate these things," said Madrigal. "Can't see terrain too well. Can't smell the ground. It's stultifying!"

"You're going to have to hang on to it anyway," answered Dante. "I think there's a tentacle of cells coming through to your north, and they may flip sideways."

"Hear ya," said Madrigal.

"Have you got that, Chime? You and your new best friends, the Brigade boys, need to get to cover soon," Dante added.

"Working our way through evidence, my boy," came Chime's growly voice. "We'll batten when we've done all we can."

"What's it look like? Who did the damage?"

"Some sort of extraction team. Landed in skiffs. Six units by the footprints. All armed with Americano weapons. Shells are ID'd. Don't mean they were an actual Americano killTeam tho'. Someone buying good weapons, be looking for our bunny. Wiped the floor with the hillbillies here. Seven dead. Found 2 injured who are on life support at the moment. Should be ok. Debriefer talking to them."

"We know where they went?"

Dante watched the rain turn into big, grey banana smears on the front ports of the hopper. He could even hear it hammering against someone's armour shell. Probably Madrigal's – as leader, her mike was always live. The weather was getting wild. Wind gusts and rain picking up its act.

Centrl's voice came through: "Headed north, probably to a larger vessel. A sub. Can't pick it through the cloud."

The Cloud. The permanent swirl round the world that masked a 1000 petty incursions both north and south.

*

Madrigal and her team had worked through the pelting rain to the bottom of the slope and started tracking along a gully. She could also feel the impact of the rain and watched the eucalypts and cycads thrash around them as leaves and branches started to hurl past. But within her skin was a calm place. Lightning whacked a tree on the ridge, now high above them, causing a whiteYellow yolk to flash in the sky. Slushy mud was staring to dribble past them on the slope.

Below them was a creek, swelling with water, but nothing drastic. She thought Andaman would be desperately trying to find cover in the sidePour. The topoMaps on her screen showed a series of caves across the eroded gully and up around a bluff which was a kilometre ahead. Given she couldn't read the land with her senses, blocked as she was by the electronics and hermeticallySealed skin, she switched to intercom and told Pearl and Folly the plan. Climb the other side and check the caves. They gestured affirmative in their grey gloves.

The skin armour was responsive so it assisted movement rather than hindered. A series of synthetic muscles around the legs, thighs and upper arms made it feel, sometimes, like she was floating as the technology easily resisted the wind. Some skins were built for multiple g's on distant planets using the same synthetic muscle. Here, they were powered up enough to deal with eqwatorial climate only and bosonEnhanced so the gravity kept them from being blown away.

Folly wore his hardArm across his back. Pearl walked with her gun tucked under one arm, holding trees for balance with her hand. They loomed like spirit figures in the storm with big heads and eyes.

Someone wearing normal clothes would be battered to smithereens by the elements. Sodden, thumped by the wind. Someone like Andaman. She switched to mainfeed.

"How are the angels?" she asked Dante.

"Still above you, but I'll have to ground them soon. Too gusty."

"Can you check through some caves around the bluff ahead of us? The bunny might be there but so might other problems."

"Ok."

*

Dante sent 2 of the angels forward. He knew he hadn't much time and kept them in the gully, out of the worst of it. He set coords and the visuals rushed past him: tree branches, rocks, it was like fastForwarding a film. Each angel had evasive technologies in their electronic splinter so they dipped or rose if a branch was in their way. The bluff came into view, as well as the thick forest of a valley beyond shrouded in curtains of rain. Each angel swerved around to the location of the cave system then stopped. They picked up heat but whether it was human or wallabies, Dante couldn't tell. He manually moved each angel towards the rock face and steered them along. They stayed remarkably stable, then one clocked out. Vision went blank. Could have been a branch smacking into it, or a bullet, or a wind gust crashing it against the rocks and mashing the splinter. Dante worried about the middle theory. Stabilisers were coping with gusts. He sent the second angel upwards and then kept it tracking hard against the cliff. Then dipped it into the cave mouth for a fraction. He checked the still. There was a man huddled there, but no weapon visible. Andaman.

"One in cave 2 – our Bunny. One angel down. If you sense the angel chip along the way, can you retrieve it? They cost us a bundle."

"Ok." said Madrigal and Pearl together.

Dante smoothed the extant angel along the cliff face. Water was spattering from above and being blown and swirled in the drafts. He dipped the angel into the third cave. It was more a rock shelf and shallow. There was nothing except pools of mud gathering from the storm. He edged his tiny eyepiece to the third cave, giving it a qwick scan. In it were 2 men. One with exceptional vision, or who sensed a blur of light, perhaps, aimed at the angel and let off a shot, but he'd arced the angel outside again.

"Two men in the 3rd." He looked at the still. "Look like locals. Saw the angel tho' and tried to shoot it out."

"How sure are you?" came Centrl's voice. He'd have seen the same feed. It was a test.

"Dressed poorly, 2 bearded. Their heat source is primitive – a flare stick. nonMilitary."

"Ok," said Centrl.

There was a shudder down the spine of the hopper and Dante looked up at the display. Wind was really hammering in now. He knew Chime and the team would have retreated to the other hoppers. He turned up the boson enhancer to pin the structure down.

"Whatcha going to do, ma'am?" said Dante.

"Can't extract him right now. We'll hunker here in the lee of a boulder," said Madrigal. "How long before the cells pass?"

"'Nother hour. The buggers move qwick, lotta energy."

"We might surveil and wait," she said. "Lock them down and you bring the hopper when things clear a bit. I'll take the Andaman cave. The others take the second."

"Ok. We'll have names for you shortly from the biometrix feed."

"'Thanx."

Madrigal, Pearl and Folly parked themselves against some large boulders out of the wind tunnel. Their main worry was a spout or worse still, a tube, which even a skin couldn't rebuff. Wedging themselves under a very large rock might just help. Some of the cells were so wild that wind speeds hit 400 kilometres or more and the rain dump was massive. It was a series of cells that took out the Nest's jetty a few weeks back. Madrigal knew that, for storms of this extent, caves and dugouts were about the only safe havens. Allow the crust of the earth to protect you, because the surface won't.

The wind was now screaming fierce. Madrigal, Folly, and Pearl sat hip2hip as the rain drove vertically overhead. Across the bluff. trees were being torn into the air. How the humans in the caves were coping was a wonder, but the weather usually

flowed west and the caves faced that way, so they were probably often used as safety shelters.

Madrigal was worried about the man in cave 3 who'd
pointed at the angel. Hoped they wouldn't do anything stupid,
like go into the weather.

"Want music?" asked Dante down the line.

Pearl said, "Yessss", and he piped some Scarlatti into their
earpieces.

"I'm hungry," said Folly. "Can you pipe some food into my
helmet too?"

"You wish, chook," said Dante laughing.

"Ok, standby," said Chime. "The report from the debriefers
says the bunny arrived at the Nest 2 days ago dropped by a
woman in a conventional boat. This is what the survivors say.
Early this morning, dawnTime, 2 skiffs landed, took out the
settlement. Six units weaponed up. The bunny, and 2 of the
leaders of the settlement, an M'bers and a Channing, were not
seen when the attack happened. Assumed to be in the party in
your cave, but biometrix haven't any record of persons of that
name."

"M'bers is a settlement leader," said a voice. *Jembrana's also
on the loop*, thought Madrigal. "We have a dialogue with him at
times. But it would be best if he is just put out of action."

Madrigal looked at the rush of water coming off the hill. A
brown torrent now. She thought that they weren't here to end
lives, just to contain Andaman Marko. But Jembrana would
probably have visuals. Which meant, if M'bers was unfortunately caught the Slotters would have no choice but to slot.
A moral predicament as the regulations only authorised the
slotting of warranted criminals. Chime was having the same
thoughts.

"Is M'bers warranted for death?" he asked mildly. He had no
idea who the new voice was, and just raised the qwestion.

"No," Centrl said. "Only eliminate if the unit called M'bers retaliates."

"Ok," said Madrigal, sounding doubtful. She and Centrl were very wary of killing anyone. And luckily Jembrana held his tongue.

Madrigal caught Pearl's eyes through the helmet. She rolled her eyes. Pearl pointed to the end of the gully. It looked like the weather was lifting.

"Cell one, passed," said Madrigal. "Two to go.

ANDAMAN 2

THOSE waves of anxiety which had crashed through him for days had subsided and Andaman sat in his cave feeling strangely liberated.

The rain poured across the front entrance like a sheet and he knew he was safe, and there for a while. Primitive solutions. Cave dweller, Stone Age and the Age of Purity meeting up. Storm cells rarely came through the 'Ville, but 500 kliks further north they were a regular occurrence in the summer season and supercells were becoming more intense. He pulled a tube of food from his bag and consumed it with a greedy sucking noise.

He thought about Flick and how she'd just dropped him like a stone into a murky pond, and taken the boat. She had uTurned out of there, fast. Pretty sure it wasn't because of him, but her distaste at being at the Nest and at having to talk to Channing and M'bers.

S'ppose she'd warned him he'd be dropped. But that fast?

He hoped she still liked him. When she'd left in the big white wake, he'd felt forlorn, a feeling he was unused to. Usually it was he who turned his back on a woman. Not the other way round.

He unclipped his clamB from its pouch. Hadn't been opened for days – from the flight to the Nest and his hunkering down in the eyrie above the bay. Now was time to check.

Andaman felt that frisson of excitement before scanning the harpoons. Would he have landed the big money? They'd been out there almost week now. A flush of gambler's endorphoids coursed through his blood, as he unclasped the clamB. Heart started to race as reward chemicals beat through his brain.

There would be signal. Even in a cave. There was always signal. He knew, somewhere, AuZgov would pick him up, but he was sure they were looking for him anyway. He was also sure that whoever sent the raiding party would know, if they were responsible for the lurker in his system. But he'd set up such a confusing string of source bounces that the conflictions would stymie anyone.

But they'd know he was alive. Which gave him both a sense of "fuck you all" and a frisson of fear at the same time.

Ohhh yes! The array of graphs showed many of his burzz were fattening with money. The rivers of gold were pouring into frontAccounts all over the planet. A soothing feeling for Andaman. His raison d'être. Made him feel safe and happy.

Now for some of the background programming, hunting the virtual lurker – he was convinced whoever was behind the presence was behind his current misfortune.

Andaman ran traces that he'd designed years ago, but hadn't recently used. Arrogance had made him feel invulnerable to intrusion. His firewalls were invincible, or so he'd thought. Ha. First a lurker, then AuZgov. Traced him and found him and he'd failed to pick any of it up.

He reached behind and pulled the electrode unit from the bag and fixed the cap on his head, plugging in and delving even deeper with the brain code interface. The array in front of him took him through a string of programming streams, but there was nothing. How had the guys in Bluestone's Spokes HQ found his lurker when he hadn't? How had they detected a trace, unless they'd followed it into his system from somewhere else? Was humiliating.

He worked his way through an even older security program (he had many lodged in his system) and found a breach at last, but he was sure, from the delicate framing of the code, it was the Spokes. The AuZgov mob. Noone else.

He wanted to contact the Spokes and ask, "What is this? A wild goose chase? What have you got?"

He looked up. The cave was dark from the murky weather and the draft was cold, raising goosebumps. He felt damp and could smell the musty mud and some hot tomatoey food that Channing and M'bers were making 2 cavities along. Lightning turned the sheet of rain to white and to grey again. M'bers had crawled in earlier to say he'd spotted a drone, so someone was "on the follow" and they would probably have to go before the weather actually settled down, which had worried Andaman, but he'd put it out of his mind to concentrate on the puzzle in front of him.

He began to think the Spokes, and that Bluestone creep, were setting him up to fail. Big claim about stalkers and lurkers, and then when he couldn't deliver (because there was nothing) they'd shut him down.

He considered Flick's explanation that he was allowed to operate to create waves and unpredictability for the economy and thought, No, there was more to it than that. More to it than the massive tax take AuZgov got from his activity. Were they worried about diplomatic incidents? CyberLarceny on a grand scale? He was only following up on hints and tips he found in the scads of data out there and investing away ... and never any big bets. Always modest and incremental. That was his way – margins and increments.

Had he invested in the wrong places? Offended people?

Or did they just want his superlative strokes that they desired? Probs that.

Andaman started getting anxious again. The trawl through his security systems had drawn a blank, though he'd closed the breach the Spokes had made using some persuasive code. A temporary fix. Like a bung in the side of a ship to stop it leaking. He'd have to restructure the whole firewall when he had some thinking time.

After the breach was closed, and the Spokes electronic tentacles were dissolved, he sent money, as promised, circuitously into M'bers' and Channing's electronic lootbags. Even in a cave, in a thermocell storm, he could do some banking. His guides were both rich men now.

He lay back and dozed for a while until Channing came into the cave on his stomach. He was wet.

"Storm's soft'ning. We gotta go." Andaman nodded. He packed his bag, slung it, shoved the pistol M'bers had given him in his belt, and followed Channing back into the larger cave. It was a tight fit for the 3 men.

M'bers looked at him.

"Done?"

"First instalment," said Andaman.

"Good man!" Channing said. "What we're going to do is chase down that slope. Creek opens into the river again. It's the one that feeds the estuary. We've a boat. When flood level sinks, we tack on upstream some way. They won't have their drones in the air still. Very flukey and nasty for them li'l flying dobbers. Sat won't get through the cloud, ok? So you, Andy, need to be tough. Think like steel bar. Duck if you see stuff heading for you cos y'could be impaled. Right?"

"Ok," said Andaman, resigned. Channing's dark face, feathered with wrinkles, was grim.

Exiting the cave, the wildness of the air filled his lungs. The water slammed into his face and the whole landscape seemed to teeter with fear. Instantly soaked. Everything was horribly slippery. He put his feet where M'bers, ahead of him, walked. M'bers helpfully pointed to a path, and Andaman followed his handholds: a rock here, a branch there. They descended into the gully, but the wind didn't get any better. Channing was armed and kept a lookout for any tail, but there were none observed.

"Steep here," said M'bers.

It was all steep, as the path wound down into the gully.

*

At the softening, Madrigal and her 2 Slotters also started to move. She took them forward towards the caves but slightly down the slopes. Folly skittered up and checked the first inhabited cave and made the "noone" hand gesture. Bunny on the move. He checked the second. Same gesture.

They must have recently gone. They'd be headed west, down the slope, she thought. Without protection it would be hard going for them, but for her it was impossible to read the country with this torrent. Everything would be washed clean. The angels were inactive too. So she just had to follow hunches.

Folly found the dead angel splinter with his tracker further down the hill and he picked it up and let Dante know. Inspection showed it was basically intact. Hadn't been hit by a weapon. Again, it was technology that was used on the new planets and very robust – except in severe thermocells.

She put the scope on her helmet and checked for heat down the hill, but the targets were obviously around the bluff. Folly kept ahead of them, scouting. Pearl held behind.

"Dante, I don't like this. We are boxed in down a gully now. Any chance of angel work?

"Almost. Almost. There's another cell on its way. Your targets have left shelter too soon."

"I think they could smell us."

"Cells coming across just to the north.

"If they are heading for the river, they are taking a big risk. Two cells will turn it to a torrent."

"Hear ya."

She watched Folly as he descended and made a hold signal. She and Pearl stopped. He waved them forward again.

"Thought there was movement," he said. "Branch thrashing."

They crossed what could be a path, a braiding of dirt and stones, intact, slinking itself downward. There was no way she could validate footsteps. It was all too wet.

But they followed it down anyway, and it gave them good foot grips and handholds against the bluff. At the bottom there was a scree of rocks which led to the torrent of the creek.

"Can't cross this," said Folly. "Let's work our way along."

Mud and stones were slewing from the bluff bouncing off their helmets. Dante's voice cut in.

"Second thermocell closing," he announced.

They were ten metres above the creek which was gushing like a broken pressure hose towards the wider river.

"Not much shelter here," said Pearl.

*

After scrabbling vertically downward, the Slotter team paused at the end of the track and watched the creek churn into a swirling brown river, pocked and riveted with pelting rain. The air was so thick and dark with water they couldn't see the opposite bank. Gusts came in sledgehammer spates.

Madrigal switched her visor's screen to infrared for a few seconds to check if the 3 targets were in the undergrowth, or across the river along the opposite ridge with the low, bent jungly scrub, twisted by the weather. There was nothing discernible, not even animal forms, but perhaps the air was creating false readings.

"There," said Folly, 3 metres in front of her.

He waved at the water. An upturned tin boat swept past and clanged on a rock. Behind, the body of a man. Boat, then man lodged against a bridgehead rock just offshore. Folly fired a rope from one of his tubes and it struck the body and he and Pearl started winding in the sodden figure. Madrigal wiped a glove across her visor to see better. Crouching for a lower centre of gravity on a boulder platform, the 2 Slotters hauled in the body of an older, heavyset man.

Channing. Dead with 2 bullets in his torso. Pearl and Folly hauled him out of the water.

"You getting this image," she asked Centrl, but there was no answer. A particularly heavy gust brought all 3 of them to their knees, gripping the ground with some fervour.

Pearl and Folly stood, and Madrigal watched them turn the body over and examine the damage. Her partners looked like mysterious grey figures slicked in shiny saliva exuded by the storm monster. A sheen of silver fell from them like a net.

"High calibre. OldStyle weapon," said Folly. "Big damage". His voice was calm and crisp through the intercom. She knew outside the security of suit and helmet the wind would be bellowing, but from the security of the suit, it was a whine, just white noise behind the chatter of the voices down the line.

"Cell's closing," came Dante's voice, from far away it seemed.

"We really must locate shelter," said Madrigal, looking at the body. Channing's eyes were still open. An hour prior he'd been alive in the second cave. Water was already up to her knees when they'd been high and dry a few moments ago.

"What about in among those rocks?" she pointed. There was a bunch of boulders and trees about ten metres higher, an elevated ridge.

Folly gave a thumbs up. He extracted his recoveryLine dart from the corpse, spooled the rope and he and Pearl dragged Channing's body further above the rising river.

Madrigal was now most anxious about Channing's body, not because of the way he died, but who he probably was.

A senior ceremony man.

"Let's lash him to the tree in case there's a flood through. Get him afterwards. For the forensics," she said.

"Are you sure?" asked Dante. "You haven't much time."

"Do it," she ordered.

Folly and Pearl hauled the slippery body upwards and had the old man pinioned to a tree with some flexisteel.

Further up the valley they could see the walls of rain start to bend into tubes, which meant that the thermocell was about there.

"Come on," said Folly. "Tubes are starting. This guy is dead. He's tied down here for now. Let's go."

"Channing," said Madrigal. "His name's Channing."

"Ok," said Dante in her ear. A ubiqwitous voice in her head.

They climbed higher onto a rock platform . . . the path was getting more limited and Madrigal was worried about rockfalls. The other side of the river looked a hell of a lot safer, with a sloping bank rising about twenty metres into a thick patch of stunted forest, bent against the gale. She was very conscious they were in a twisty geological funnel and the water was rising.

"Here," said Pearl. At some point long ago, a huge boulder had fallen from above and cracked in 2. Pearl was first to get to the crack and first to sqweeze into the crevice. It meant a semblance of relief from the gusts, which were still resisted by the suit, but were still a punishing force. Madrigal was putting more and more strength into the effort. The panel above the visor showed the gusts were coming at 280 kilometres an hour, and the autoGravity function of the suit was up several notches, holding her in place but making climbing harder. Folly, and then Madrigal, slid between the boulders and again pressed in on one another.

"Let's get cosy," said Pearl.

The space was almost serene, in fact. Madrigal contemplated opening her helmet and smelling the air, but decided against it. A stone or stick could easily flick through the gap and take an eye out. The sky was extremely dark now, pulsing with lightning, and overhead she could see tubes of water moving with the gusts.

"*Smite flat the thick rotundity o' the world!*" said Madrigal remembering a school play. "That's how it goes. *Spout, rain!*"

Lear and his daughters. She'd better call little Todd soon. Could be the last time she'd hear his voice if this mess went on and the way the water was rising. The next few minutes would be very dangerous and a pang of possible loss drenched her as much as the water.

*

Having not heard Centrl's voice for some time, she said: "If our lenses were too wet and opaqwe at the time, just letting you know, Channing was shot," she said. "Looks like there was either an argument between fugitives, or others have captured Marko before us."

There were groans on the end of the line. Centrl? Chime? Jembrana? Not Dante. He was a fine soldierTechnician and wouldn't groan like that. Not like the softer administrative class. She'd groan, for sure.

"No sign of a hopper anywhere," said Dante. "If you have other company, they must be on foot too. Or a landBased vehicle with the heavies."

"Shit," said Pearl.

"Don't worry," said Madrigal, "They'll be hunkered down too ... this is the worst bit. *Steeples and cocks are going under.*"

"What?" said a disembodied voice.

"I think she's channelling William Shakespeare," said Jembrana's voice.

How did some old Balinese bloke know something as obscurantist as that? she wondered.

One of the waterspouts blasted past the boulder and crashed into the cliff face above causing a huge inundation of loose water. The vertical, downward wave poured through the crack and over them. Madrigal and the Slotters locked themselves, elbows and knees, against the rock face, the synthetic muscles in the fabric clamping them hard, but they were still pounded downwards as the torrent worked its way past them. Dislodgeable objects. Adrenaline pumped through her tired body, and for the second time in 3 days Madrigal feared for her life.

While the breathing apparatus was good, and the synthetic muscles gave her a strong grip, it was an existential moment. A perception that she was deep under the water as it sluiced past the side of her helmet. Like being dumped by a massive wave on New Cottesloe Beach in the summer, with the fizz of salt in her sinuses, except there was no fizz, sunshine or consoling Mum. And she was able to breathe. That was a plus. She looked down the slope where wave was meeting the brown torrent, which was hurrying upwards, towards their position.

"Freaking hell," said Folly. "Any more of those whirlygigs?"

Madrigal stuck her head out of the crack, because she was on the outer. There were a couple of other spouts she could see in the gloom, but they seemed to be arcing the other way. She cricked her neck around as far as it could go and saw the sky was lightening towards the east. The wind was ferocious.

"But it's looking clearer. Hey, Dante, are these thermocells almost over?"

"Hey, Maddy, it's still on top of you. Wait another 5. They are fast moving. Be gone soon." She noted his accidental use of her nickname, instead of saying Ma'am as they all did, very respectfully. Or Chook, which he did when he was distracted.

*

The torrent had risen to their ankles, snaking into the chasm. Pearl pointed up. Folly started to try and shimmy up the gap. The water was rising fast. Madrigal hoped she would fit through the top of the crack. She took a deep breath.

"Connect Todd," said Madrigal and the helmet started ringing out to Netta's house.

"Hello?"

"Hi, Mum, how are things" She knew everyone would be listening, but didn't give a shit.

"Maddy. Good. When are you home?" The inevitable qwestion.

"Soon as possible. Bit busy at the moment, but we should have things sorted. Is Todd there?"

"No, luv. He's at school."

"Can you tell him I'm really looking forward to being home and giving him a big hug."

Her mum, Netta, could tell instantly that her daughter was in difficulty. The water was starting to churn round her upper thighs. The wind keened like a wounded bird, though the sound would not have penetrated through her helmet scope all the way to Perth. From the edge of her eye, she saw a branch cartwheel past. "I'll tell him." Her mum knew not to ask. Her mum hated the work she did. Wanted her to take her rightful seat on the Phipps Industry Board, safe and sound.

Just above her head, Pearl was shimmying to the top of the boulder. She was all knees and gloves, her boots scrabbling for footholds. She could see Folly's legs slipping into the space high above. Must be another ten to fifteen metres of the crevice above her and that would get them above the torrent.

"Mum, I've gotta go," she said.

"Take care, luv," said her mum. "Can you promise you'll stay safe?"

Madrigal swallowed. "I'll come home soon," she said. She could just about lie to everyone, except her mum.

Folly's line snaked in front of her face, but it was pushed aside by a powerful gush of the rising creek, right over the lid of her helmet.

Everything went dark and bubbly.

"Give him a cuddle, eh?" she said, trying to keep the fear from her voice.

"Will do. Love you."

Her mum sounded so sad and distant. Madrigal cut the scope, and grabbed for Folly's line as it came back into vision, looping it around both her wrists. Her team yanked hard and levitated her out of the torrent and into the storm.

How wet it was.

*

Andaman Marko woke in the back of a vehicle. He was crashing around on a metal tray and the growl of an engine rumbled below him. Terrestrial. Crashing through bush. He braced his shoulder as his body slid against the metal hull. The back windscreen showed thrashing vegetation and rain. They were powering along some sort of track, but through a second thermocell. He was wet, bedraggled, and his clothes stank of riverbank ooze. An area on the back of his head pounded. Reaching back he felt where the blow from the man's fist had landed. It was still sticky with blood. No care had been taken to clean or pad it.

Some sort of boson enhancer was working for the vehicle, providing extra gravity, otherwise the vehicle would have been tinwhipped – blown off the track and flung upside down. A partition blocked his view of the front cab. The back cab was dark, lit by lightning when it flickered, which was half the time, enough to let him size up the area. Whatever happened to Channing and M'bers was a blur, but he remembered gunshots.

One moment they were on a track heading past the creek, single file, the next moment, he'd been slammed against the ground by an armoured guy, faceless because of a mask or something, there were shots, someone had pounded him with a gloved fist, and he'd lost consciousness.

Andaman groaned and felt for his belt, but the clamB had gone. Not a surprise. The clamB was what they thought they wanted, he surmised, but it would be useless to them with its torrent of suicide switches that'd trigger the end of the memory chips. He started to sweat and prickle. For a start, his mild claustrophobia meant he hated being in small enclosed places. Worse, he knew at the end of the journey he would be at huge risk. Last thing he wanted was unauthorised limbic intrusion. Or worse still, physical torture, but if he didn't escape he knew it would come to that. Pain scared him almost senseless.

The LandV lurched to the left and right, and he groaned as his shoulder hit the steel wall.

*

As fast as the thermocell had come, it fizzled to the west. The rain was still fierce and there were big gusts, but within an hour the Slotter team was trekking up the bank of the river, trying to find the tracks of Marko and M'bers, and signs of the unknown raiders. Madrigal had lifted her visor, feeling the moist heat on her cheeks, earth odours hitting her nostrils, and was checking the ground which had been scoured by the flood. Dante even had angels in the sky again.

Using infrared, they found M'bers lodged under a huge old log, barely alive. They pulled him out, along with what looked like a tonne of compost, mud and creepy crawlies – superfat millipedes and cockroaches. He looked like a brown mudman, laid out on the path, unconscious. Pearl gave him a shot of adrenaline and painkiller and he woke from the wooze. "Wha–?" he asked.

The team gave him little time to recover any wits.

"You've been shot," said Madrigal. "Who did this?"

"What? Shit? Oh, the guys from yesterday, after that f'cker, Marko. Who are you?"

As M'bers roused, so were his suspicions.

"I can't believe you survived the thermocell," said Folly, kneeling on his other side. Folly was still covered to the armpits in mud from dragging and digging M'bers out.

"I'm from the Nest. Storms happen. We survive. Now who the f'ck are you?"

"We're a security team from AuZgov ... we picked up the lethal raid by alien actors on the Nest and are checking it through. Can't have border incursions like this, can we? I am Courier Madrigal Phipps."

"You? You! Fuck. Well, thanx a lot," said M'bers. "That Marko was running from you lot and came here. Said you and your blueEyed mate spooked him out, back in the Ville."

Folly gave the man some water. The painkillers were working him over now and his eyes were bright, as was his language.

"We've got a hopper on the way. We'll get you to a hospital. Your friend Channing is dead."

"Channing ..." Saying his name stopped the old man's retail. It took him a minute to speak again. "They shot him. They shot me. Left us for dead."

"How many?" asked Madrigal

"Four. In a landV. Caught us as we came down the bluff. When I took the bullet, I went doggo, then crawled up the hill after they drove off with Marko. Then the thermocell hit and I crawl under this log w'a million f'king millipedes. What a f'king nitemare."

"They tracked you. At any time when you were on the move, did Marko use his technology?"

"Yeah. He just did a couple hours ago. Paid us off for helping him. Lodged a sub in our accounts."

Madrigal groaned. They had Marko pinned. Pinned to some map like a bug. Always had. Whoever his pursuers were.

"Ok, M'bers." She heard the whine of the hopper above them. "I was hoping for a qwiet restrainment – wish you and

Marko and Channing had put your hands up in the caves back there – but we have serious interference here. Look ..." She knelt in front of M'bers and took her helmet off, looking him in the eye. "We have Channing's body. We will get you, and his remains, back to the Nest and our medics'll get you sorted. He was custodian of this bit'o country, wasn't he?"

M'bers nodded. He was silent, listening to Madrigal. He was looking at her face with a sudden softness in the eyes.

"I'm really sorry I didn't get to talk to him. Not many of these old guys left in these parts these days. You'll tell his people? It's important he's buried on country."

"I know, luv," said M'bers qwietly. "Was goin' to do that anyway."

Sombre voiced. "Good man." She waved to the medics.

She put her helmet on again and retuned to the feed.

"Dante. Anything on a landV heading west?"

"They're using the thermocell for cover. It's impenetrable.

"HighEye tracking the thermocell and surrounds," said Centrl. "Nothing breaking cover."

Medics were gently putting M'bers onto a stretcher, lifting it to take to a smaller hopper set nearby. They held it still, either side, as M'bers lay talking to Madrigal, who'd removed the helmet, face to face.

"Any defining features or gear with the raiders?" she asked. The rain had subsided to drizzle status and she took her full helmet off. The ground smelt dank.

"Black and silver, full suits. Standard issue hardArms. All blokes, I'd reckon. Didn't hear no voices. Had intercom. Once we were down, couldn't care less. They bashed Marko and he went down too. No bullets for that lad tho'."

"'K," said Madrigal. "And their landV?"

"Big bastard. Electric oldStyle thing. Had a cannon on one side and half tracked, half wheels. Built for this sorta country. Grey and green camo. Twincab with a bigArsed boot."

"Thanx," said Madrigal. She said to a medic: "You can take him back to the Nest and get the debriefers onto him." She waved her team to the hopper where Dante and Chime were already strapped in.

"Let's get after the thermocell, shall we?"

*

Andaman felt his wheeled jail turn north and assumed it had hit a main Cape road as the ride was smoother and he wasn't slithering and crashing over the tray of the back area. Then after a short while it lurched east again across rougher ground towards the coast. They were playing zigzag, he thought.

After about 30k, the vehicle stopped and the door opened and he heard movement down one side. For a couple of minutes there was a muffled discussion, then the rear door opened. Two men, unhelmeted, looked in and flashed a torch in his face. He blinked back at them, but couldn't see their faces in the shadow and glare.

"He's good," said one muffled voice with an Australasian accent. They threw a water bottle and a couple of eatSticks at him, said "Here's a wound pack" as they threw a soft pouch at his face, and slammed the door shut. Then there was silence. The vehicle was stationary, and he was left in the dark. He scrabbled around for the bottle, sniffed the contents and swallowed some water. Couldn't believe how dry he was. Chewed the sticks, which were a prawn jerky or something. He sluiced his head with some of the water and applied a pad. He was happy to deduce that at this point his captors didn't want him dead.

Andaman felt his way round the boot with fingers, checking for cracks, plates that might be loose and removable. He fingered across the back lock and thought it was a 3 bolt electric job. He also moved his fingertips and felt across the windows. Looking up he could see a faint round metal disk across the roof where there was mechanics for a gunTurret. It was bolted hard against the rest of the roof. He knew that between his wall and the cab wall would be the gravity technology, stealth gear to cloak electronic and heat emanations, and probably a scrambler set for their outgoing communications. Technology to help move without trace across the High Capricorn. Keep out of HighEyes sight. He noticed the oldStyle half track, half wheel arrangement, so they could move through the toughest terrain.

Andaman crouched and felt for the bolts across the roof. There were 8. Fifty millimetre. Nuts on his side. He stripped off his belt and found the zip, under the empty clamB pack, with the small set of utility tools, knife and oldStyle magnetic compass, which he'd added before running from his house on Castle Hill.

Using the slight glow of the compass for light he fitted the utility tool over a bolt and slowly, silently tried to twist it. It moved slightly, then stopped. He tried the next one. The tool was so pissy it granted no leverage. In fact, the shaft started to bend. He groaned. "C'mon. C'mon," he told himself. "You're a technician. You can do this."

He slid on his arse to the back of the cab just as the engines roared into life and felt along the plates there. Some smaller hex heads offered themselves up. He clipped his utility tool across them and started to twist. They started to move. Wedged against a wheelbase, he worked his way through the 8 hex heads and pulled off the 8 by 8 plate. It was the back of one of the embedded units in the wall cavity. Crouching, he could see through the hole a small grey box fixed to the bulkhead with a power unit. Lights blinked, giving him some sense of the technology. It was an embedded power unit for something. AntiGrav? Cloaker? Power cell charger? Whatever it was he unscrewed a plug clamp and pulled a power wire out gently, so that it seemed shaken loose. To his satisfaction some of the power lights died.

Always play the margins, he thought.

He had no doubt the raiders were not on AuZgov business. They were in it for themselves.

He qwickly fixed the plate back, used crap on his boot to muddy the hex heads up to hide newlyWorked shine, and placed his belt back. And as an afterthought, he slid the compass down the side of his boot.

*

The flimsy wire could have powered several different control units, but in the end, Andaman had deactivated part of a broad cloaking system that controlled komms transmissions. The Spokes started picking up the internal and external messages off their many signal nodes. The landV's scrambler was a common commercial brand and technicians soon pulled actual words out of the chatter. More importantly for Andaman Marko, they pinpointed the transmission source under the bad weather and cloud cover.

*

The hopper was flying very low across the stunted tree tops, with Dante wrestling the controls as the chopperBlades bit into gusts and lollops, while Madrigal and Pearl stared out the portside hopper windows into the rainforest and scrub, and some badly eroded openCut mines, which were pouring their overload of water into the terrain. Any tailings had been flushed out a century ago, but acid soil was forever. There were swathes of dead streaks across the forests from older thermocell tube encroachments. Then more whole forest and swollen creeks crashing through boulderStrewn channels. Vegetation swung and whipped about in the strong eddies of air. It was strange wild country indeed. Southwards, Madrigal could also see the black swirl, different to the cloud cover, shooting straight up to the stratosphere, where the cells had gone. Dante had promised there were no more deep storms brewing in the Coral Sea in the next few hours, but the whole area was permanently in a general storm mode.

Voices started to pepper Madrigal's intercom like little pops.

"Only 47 kliks northEast, team Phipps," said Centrl. "They doubled back on you."

"Looking to the coast again to get Marko offshore. They have a sub," said a technician in the distant Spokes.

"No other naval backup. Operating alone."

"We'll get a vessel and more milisi there. You contain and fold the bunny in."

"Hear ya."

Madrigal's only worry now was that the landV was too close to the coast and that they'd be there before the hopper, but they managed to intercept within a 2 kilometre range of the shoreline at one of the big bays, under the Cloud. It was one of those natural land funnels to an open bay, then the Coral Sea. A natural route in and out, for illicit goods or people.

They had a good bead on the landV's northward track and were able to set an ambush ahead on this route, landing across an old rutted track, kept alive by smugglers now, and travellers, from National Park days a century past, and moving into the path of the landV. The third cell had passed to the south of the Nest and the general drizzle that accompanied the tail end of fierce weather systems set in. The wind vagued out to gale-Force, then stiff breezes, allowing better control of the hopper.

Folly, Pearl and Chime prepared a barrier across the track. It was a sqweezy road, and very red and muddy.

As the landV came round a corner, Chime and Pearl stunned its engine with a giant jammer they had in the boot of the hopper. Bang. The electric engine died. They dealt with the 4 raiders in a short firefight, impressed that the unknown men decided to stand and attack. The 4 had military moves too. Backup, push forward, an attempt at a protective cordon.

Madrigal stood back as her team clinically dispatched the abductors. Three dead, one injured. There was not a whit of qwarter given – Folly and Pearl shot to kill with clinical precision. Then, Madrigal and Folly had the pleasure of dragging Andaman Marko by the armpits from the back of the LandV and dropping him onto the ground into 30 cms of red mud, flipping him on his stomach with a splotch, and cuffing him. Madrigal was silently ecstatic that the bunny was under arrest and under her restraining hand. She pressed his head down into the dirt, reassuring herself that he was alive and wriggling. Andaman gagged and protested, and she grinned.

"We meet again," she said.

"Get me up, this is disgusting," he roared like a sqwirming maggot.

She'd done what she'd been asked, and succeeded despite contending with every sort of difficulty. Her first team lead. For the first time in 2 days she allowed herself to smile.

"My clamB should be in the twincab," said Marko's muffled voice, his face planted in the forest litter.

*

Marko'd decided there was less likelihood of torture and death with the AuZgov lot, as the light flooded in.

He felt a hand grab his collar and someone pull him over on his back off the tray and onto the sqwelchy ground. That hurt, and he yelled out angrily. He was flipped over and the highly attractive Indijj woman, Courier Madrigal Phipps, was kneeling over him in some sort of battleskin. Two big scary people stood behind her, staring over her shoulder. He'd never seen anyone like Folly or Pearl in his life, and their rig and weapons looked like space travel toys. But they weren't toys. Out of the corner of his eye, he saw a hideous sight. Slumped back in a bush, just off the road, was the body of one of the guys who'd held him, his head half gone, blood and mush against the trees behind.

He then blurted about his precious ClamB.

"Please don't run again, Mr Marko. We can't risk your safety any more," said Dr Phipps.

He nodded without a word, and they hauled him to his feet. The soldier called Pearl checked the mediPad on the back of his head and replaced it, while Madrigal and the older battleguy inspected the landV.

"M'bers is right. OldStyle. In good nick though," said the older battle guy, crouching and looking at the half track arrangement. "They used these things during *the Blend* to try and keep the peace."

"How do you reckon they got it here, Chime?" Dr Phipps said.

Apart from Folly, who watched Marko cagily from the roadside, his rescuers moved out of his view and hearing, and he leant against his exPrison – the landV– and thanked whatever lucky stars he had left.

*

"It's one of ours. ExAuZgov, but enhanced."

Madrigal and Chime climber into the cab and he showed her the grav and cloaking monitors. "They got this technology from somewhere else. Only other governments do grav. It's an interplanetary thing. I suppose you can buy or steal it from insiders though."

"So who are these people?"

"Dunno," said Chime, "but some of them are Caps for sure. We have one live raider for the debriefers. He may be able to say."

"Which Heg?" Jembrana said over the intercom, a qwery in his voice. He had been listening hard through the entire operation, somewhere in the ether, like a poised tiger.

"Don't know. He mebbe a Heg man." Whether it was a foreign government or a private operation, or joint, was unknown, but a Hegemony, a huge corporate state, or even a straightOut bizz cartel would want what Andaman knew, as much as any government.

The team found Marko's clamB in the vehicle and impounded it along with another computer and scoper unit.

*

As the team sat beside the trail waiting for milisi to hopper in for the cleanUp, and listening to the coastguard vessels transmissions as they searched for the submarine offshore from their position, Madrigal wandered into the adjoining forest without her helmet and inhaled the rich damp smells and stroked the wet trees and leaves with her fingertips as she walked. She pushed lawyer vine out of the way and moved further in amongst the prehistoric vegetation and stringy trees grappling for light. Everything dripped. Leaves, branches. The terrain and vegetation was like a big brown green sponge that had absorbed far too much moisture.

Crouching in the qwiet, distant now from the business of hoppers, Slotters and prisoners, she saw a movement out of her eye, and stealthily walked towards it to see the passing of a huge snake, almost ten metres long, scaly skin glistening with brown and orange hued diamond patterns.

Amethystine python. The vision took her breath away. The snake ignored her as it glided across the wet litter. It was almost as thick as Folly's thigh, which was something in itself.

She gulped, because though she'd heard the stories from the aunties and uncles about rainbow snakes, she had never seen something this massive and beautiful and real. She bent down and touched its back, and it slid along, under her 2 gentle fingers. Didn't seem to notice. Ancient snake, weaving through the scrub, determined and hungry. Doing its snakey business, hunting for pademelon wallaby or possum. She looked at the disappearing tail.

Wow, she thought, in the silence of the forest.

Not something she'd retail to the crew. It was her own private moment. Her Aunties and other elders had talked about the snakes of the Dreaming and how they'd created the country around her, something she believed wholeheartedly – a parallel reality to the brouhaha in which she actually lived and worked.

A snake that strong and determined could well carve up a world, she thought. Would it survive the crazed weather into the future? Mebbe not, but this python had survived, and very well so far. In her mind it was surely a spirit that remained powerfully wild, slithering through the bush, even while the people had abandoned the country.

*

In the hopper, jetting back to the Ville, Madrigal sat beside a trussed Marko. She looked at him for a while. His chin was on his chest, handsome nose, his eyes qwite longLashed for a man. Shock of messy hair with a white pad strapped to the back of the skull. They'd hosed him down to get rid of the mud and he was still damp. He said nothing. He was obviously ruminating. Working out his next wrong move.

Madrigal thought, this guy isn't a snake – he's a monkey. He'd showed them the panel and wire that he'd disconnected in the landV, and beamed a smug satisfaction when he was told he'd neutered the komms cloak.

Yes, she thought, Andaman was a wizz at getting out of tight spots. Outwardly mad with his drinking and sexing, privately very smart, but erratic. She didn't like erratic operators. Erraticism annoyed the hell out of her. Her dad for example, was getting more erratic. The reminder of her Dad cranked her up even more.

"Why the hell did you run? We had your house in lockdown? You were safe." Her annoyance made her sound a bit shrill.

Andaman Marko took his time to answer. He did so with exasperation.

"I didn't know who, or what, wanted to kill me? I was frightened. Bluestone frightened me. The bomb terrified me. Afterwards in the street with Cassie, you said to my face the bomb was meant for me – that someone tried to kill me." He paused. "You know what you told me at the restaurant: 'Find the lurker!'? Well, I tried. I logged in and tried. I found where your people had breached my system. I found that hole, but there was nothing. No presence of anything else. No trace."

"The lurker probably left you dangling. The Spokes may be able to show you a captive trace."

Marko found enough energy to nod sagely. A backTrace was a possibility.

There was a long silence. Only the hum of the hopper was audible.

She shook her head and turned to him. "You have to trust us, Mr Marko. And do what we ask until we find out who is hunting you down."

Marko pointed at Folly and Pearl who were sitting in a row up front "Who are these people?" he asked.

"They are security specialists," she said.

"Not milisi?"

"No. AuZgov Specialists."

"How many of these guys does AuZgov employ," he asked, amazed that they existed at all.

"Not many. Couple of hundred across the continent and the Zealands. As I said, they are specialists."

"I've never seen so many guns."

"As you now know, though we live in a secure and safe world, there are elements out there who own hardArms and other lethal toys, and we have to deal with armed raiders and incursions qwite a bit," she said. "That's what our Slotters do. Deal with violent events."

"Oh."

"And they'll secure you in the Ville until we get to the bottom of this."

"Oh. Am I under arrest?"

"Not technically," she said, "but for the time being you will have many close, best friends."

THREE

THREE lay on the daybed of the verandah, waiting. Spent her days sipping camomile tea and reading trashy 'zines on her clamB, eating takeaway prawns from stalls or chicken rice bought down the street at the stockade.

A bug flashed like a tiny blue spark in the oldStyle bugzapper above the door. Lotta bugs in the Ville. Bought the BugKill first day she'd arrived. Modern zappers enticed the insects away and dealt with them discreetly. But Three ...she liked to hear them sizzle.

Three didn't find it difficult to wait. She'd waited all her life for this & that. War was a conveyor belt of waiting and occasional violent, exhilarating contact. She'd waited a whole ten years in China before she got back on the conveyor belt, but that was an old story.

It had been a week now since One was arrested and Two was blown to smithereens because he'd failed to get out of the sex parlour qwick enough. Two had not been nimble, ever, the fat fuck. She knew One, who was the pro from East Cap of old, would never talk and they'd never find anything in any limbic probe because he was an adept. Vague pictures – mebbe even of her. Bit of locational stuff. But intent, plans, clear faces, and the like, would be obscured by force of will.

He was a veteran, like her, of the days before *the Blend*. The days when a few heroic souls tried to resist the stupidity of AuZgov's legislated and sanctified invasion when the Indons, Papuans, Timorese came in from the north. They should have stayed in their own f'ckin countries and dealt with the Cloud there. The whole Blend business still made her seethe; giving Aussie territory away so easily. The way they fought, the way they fell to the bullets of their own government. Bled, rather than blend.

Well, she was back in Cap after a lifetime, and even with the loss of two colleagues, she, Three, was still in play.

She had done well to kill the Courier with the heartstopper. The detectors in the hotel where she'd followed the target were hopeless. They'd known that. Hadn't cared because over the past three decades, people had forgotten how to lock things down and how dirty things could be.

Her solitude was slow and even, her patience allConsuming.

Sum total: one dead, and only the woman courier and the client's prettyBoy target left to be dealt with. She hadn't sought contact with the client and neither had the client tried to find her. Occasionally she'd go to the safehouse, but there were no drops. Only the eqwipment, unmeddled with. She re-qwested explosive and it was duly delivered. Left in the frijj in packets marked Tofu. She'd be about the only person this side of the Eqwator to get the joke.

Outside, through the hardGlass louvres she could see the tops of bougainvillea and palms along a high fence. The high monsoon clouds and the storms and rain were settling in and everything was wet and shiny between the downpours. Beyond the fence, the street was alive. Shanties, stalls and markets. Cars and trucks hummed discreetly.

Even the rumble of the odd milisi APC.

The reason she was here.

To kill time, for a bit of fun, she had methodically gone round the house and set traps, putting larger ones in the attic and below stairs under the flood poles. She'd managed to reduce the rat and mice population, including 2 giant cane rats, one which she had to smash with a hammer because the trap hadn't done the job. It had dragged itself into the corner with the trap around its shoulder, waiting its fate.

That had been enjoyable.

The possums kept coming as well, snuffling out nut butter and honey. And cats, which she attracted with food and killed with the heartstopper. There was a buildUp of corpses in the pit in the backyard and the smell was so piqwant – redolent of those distant battlefields, up in the Gulf of Capenteria

So. A slow wait. They'd told her to wait and she counted out her days in dead rodents.

Another bug flashed blue in the zapper.

FLICK 2

WHEN Flick resurfaced in the frontier town of Trinity, her first call was to Herman Volk, a provider of forged identities. She couldn't be certain that Volk would not be someways in cahoots with AuZgov, but he was her best bet. A trusted friend of her father and trader to many in the Nest.

New boat and events necessitated she morph from Felicity Lynn, to Felicity somebody else, having no urge to lose her actual handle of Flick. Flick she had always been. Holding dearly to the name her mum gave her.

And once legal, then she could get lost in the crowds of Cap again. Mebbe in West Cap this time. Flick floating free, she thought. With boat. The hills and clouds above the town made her feel claustrophobic on several levels. She hated the stepping up to the badness, to the weather that cracked people. That cracked and crushed her childhood, like a broken egg.

Worse, she hated the frontier town of Trinity. The cloudAddled green mountains seemed to bend down and stare at her as she headed up Mission Street and through the vast markets and the line of bunkers behind them where the shops and cafes were located. The old city of Cairns was mostly washed away and the new city of Trinity straddled the higher ground, looping around the hills of East Trinity inlet and the escarpment behind; the Pyramid, the foothills of the west southern ranges up through to the Tablelands. Most of the plain, the mangroves and mudflats, had been swallowed decades ago by countless storms and surges, making way for a new bay and a new port in the estuary mouth.

Flick's big plan was to hunker down somewhere and then, in the winter season, when the weather and seas were calmer, steer her boat around the top of the continent, through the Torres Straits, past Timor and the Kimberley and Karratha and Perth, and disappear in the big south area. Mebbe go even further south to the Heel, and stop in Albany.

Her boat was moored at one of the many public marinas clamped to the shore and she didn't want to leave it crewless for too long.

She found the right shop and climbed the steel steps onto the verandah. Even though she wore shorts, light sandals and a thin cotton xTop and hat, the sweat was pouring from her skin after the climb up the hill, and the steps were just the last straw. Humidity 100%+, 48°C, gah!

Battered, wrinkled Herman Volk was down the back of his narrow, cluttered bunker and he stood up when the door clicked, peering through his visor at her and beaming in pleasure.

"Dear little Felicity," he said, dancing round his counter to greet her. "A pleasure! A drink of something? I have icy watermelon juice here in the frijj."

She laughed and forgot the impending heatstroke for a second. For some reason he still seemed to view her as a twelve year old.

"Dear Herman, a drink would be good, but first things first. I'm after some new identity chips, please. As a Felicity, I'd like to keep the first name."

"As a Felicity, you are always very welcome," he said, gurgling happily. "And how is your dear father?"

"I don't know. Haven't seen'm for some time."

"So he didn't die when the Nest was attacked the other day?" Herman asked disingenuously. Felicity didn't let her face fall. She was too good for that. But the news shocked her.

"Attacked by whom?"

"Who knows, dear girl, who knows. I'm told by travellers that there were casualties. A raiding party out of the cloud. With hardArms. Automatic hardArms. Possibly from a submarine, I am told."

"Do YOU know if my father is dead, Herman?" she asked carefully.

"Not that I know," he fudged, "though they say Channing is gone."

"Channing!" she exclaimed. "I saw'm the other day."

"Gone now," said Herman shaking his head sadly and pouting and chewing his lip. There was a pause. He and Channing had been close over the decades.

She could hardly ask about Marko, left there on the shore … being hunted. Her first lurching thought was she had brought catastrophe on the Nest. Her second was a surprisingly deep pang of concern for Marko. Her third was to cloak her emotional reactions as they went through her mind. She shook her head and said, "I'm sorry about Channing. He was a mate of grandada's. He was a nice bloke."

"He was. He was," said Volk who looked up with cagey, weasel eyes and brightened.

"And you want some new identity data. Possibly, probably a very good idea."

"And boat license in my name for the powerboat."

"Ok," Hermann said.

He hopped behind the counter again and started working on a small desktop. "As you know, this material is qwarantined to these few units you see before you and will selfZap once you have the chips. I will transfer some levels of information about you into the national system, but it won't proof you if you are arrested."

"The usual terms of currency," she said.

He stood the rattled Felicity in front of his stolen AuZgov issue iris scanner to take a pic and took a swab from her mouth and inserted both into a machine.

"I have a dummy identity here, a nurse, so I'll just change the first name," he manipulated the ball, "and there. Felicity Beevis. That's you now."

Herman Volk bolted his shop door and ushered his young friend through the back parlour to his garden, with its nets of ferns and cycads, while the information, DNA and eyeprints integrated on chips. Volk's shady little terrace had a view of Trinity. He insisted again on watermelon juice. Flick, who was calming down and assuring herself the disaster was not her fault, but most likely Andy's, finally accepted the hospitality, and they sat and she pressed Herman about the attack on the Nest. He pretended that it was scuttlebutt from the market men.

Extracting info from an old smuggler was always hard.

So they talked of the old days, when a frontier group from the Nest, including Herman Volk, M'bers, Channing and her father, ran the smuggling racket through the cloud for Hegemonies in the northern hemisphere.

The atmosphere around Trinity was even muggier, and clouds were swirling and dissipating like wraiths on the emerald hill above. Even in the shade, Flick could feel the sweat break from her skin again and soak through her clothing. Volk didn't seem to notice the heat. There was another round of juice and some small cakes. Herman then called time, and they went back into the shop.

"Do you ever sell anything off the shelves?" she asked, looking at the rubbish that was stacked high.

"Collectors come from all over for these wonders, but it doesn't make me much. It's all a front," he said very conspiratorially. Felicity laughed again.

He provided the identity chips and papers. "You're a qwalified nurse now, so you'd better learn firstAid. That's my advice," he said.

"In fact, here," said Volk. He scrabbled behind a metalFrame shelf and pulled out a tattered book. OldStyle paper printed from the world before the virtual.

"*First Aid and other Medical Procedures.* By Webster." It had a red cross on the front of a faded green hardback. He handed it to Flick. "You can bone up on firstAid, Nurse Beevis."

"Thanx," said Flick, dubiously. She threw the book into her pack. She wasn't much of a one for boox.

She paid with cash in $New, as she didn't want to leave a ghost trace anywhere. There was no guarantee that their transactions weren't being monitored, but Flick lived in hope.

"Thanx again, Hermann," she said.

"Storm brewing," he added looking out to the sky.

"Not unusual."

"Just the start of the season. Powerful one just the day before yesterday, licking down from the cloud. Wouldn't have liked to be in the Nest then. Getting worse every year they are," said Volk.

"Have you somewhere to stay in Trinity?" asked Volk.

"I'm on the boat. It's fine."

Flick again hoped that Volk wasn't scratching away, guessing her movements for someone else's benefit. No one enjoyed having their head read by surreptitious people like Herman Volk.

Suddenly she felt an urge to leave before he asked any other qwestions. Volk sensed her change of mood and extended his hand. They shook.

"Good luck, my dear. Don't worry about me. You are like a daughter. I have no other sense of what is happening up north, but sources say milisi from the AuZgov were there shortly after the killings. Teams, I'm told. And Slotters."

So he did know more, the old lizard.

"Who told you?"

"Word came down from the backRoad. And word is the teams seem not to have solved who the attackers were."

"It was probably them, surely. AuZgov? Who took out the Nest?"

"Apparently not," said Volk. "Apparently someone else."

His inflection was heavy and pretend spooky. He was pouting and chewing his lip again. An ugly affectation which unnerved her.

She didn't understand his nonsense. Tired of Herman now, she thanked him, pecked him on the cheek left the shop and walked down the hill towards the port.

*

Flick could see the dark ocean weatherband closing. Looking through her ocular, she pulled the distance in and saw the ocean surface punched and bruised with wind. Fingerlings of mustard light smeared the horizon beneath the cloud ceiling. At other points along the wibblyWobbly horizon line, the ceiling fell to the water in dark sqwalls. A hint of lightning, red in the sunset, flickered through the high sky.

She adjusted the ocular's focus to the bay's rim. The barrages were being raised several metres, and so that was that. The Trinity Portmaster had decided to hedge against surges and protect the many marinas in his precinct, so even if she wanted to sail that evening, she would be trapped within the barrier. But it was the Portmaster's call and Flick was happy not to risk the storm. Rusty's vast, flattened out market halfway down the hill was still roaring. Crammed with people, street stalls, kids running down the alleys, barbecue smoke which clutched the smells of roast fish or chicken, chilli con carne sauce, fried rice.

Dogs skulked around the backs of old steel boxes that served as shops. From a stage, musicians larked and played xylofonic trance as people ate their evening meals and watched. Flick saw an oldStyle beeDrone float past, but it wasn't following anyone or anything in particular, just a Trinity gov security camera keeping eyes on the crowds.

"Hey, lady, when's the stormz gunna hit?" a man asked her as she walked on. A small Indijj guy, or mebbe old Timorese, with a banana leaf plate of street food in his hands. Pickled green mango prawns, mebbe.

"Dunno. Couple of hours," she said in passing, trying not to stop.

The little guy fell into step with her.

"How do ya know?"

"I'm a sailor," said Flick. "Had a look at the stormfront off the top of the hill. Reckon 2 hours max. Mostly rain."

"Okeydokey," the man said. "Thanx." *Mostly rain* meant a deluge.

It's terrific, thought Flick, to be able to identify as a sailor. Always felt, deep in her marrow, that she'd follow the path of her grandada. She was reaching the point of changing plans – mebbe not round the top end to Perth, when the worst of the summer weather cells pass. Instead mebbe go all out, through the eqwatorials to the Chinese Hegs. Or the Americas. Those places were hugely lax on personal ID and she'd disappear forever and make a new life. The idea was beginning to grow on her.

Leaving the market sqware, she stepped up onto a marked footpath now, where the buildings looked solid and more durable. The harbour was still a way down and she was incredibly hot. She stooped down to buy a pouch of water from a vendor and drank it. Past the old cemetery on one side, called to by tukTuk and taxi drivers on the street kerb where they parked. Big old figs lining the bottom of the gravePark. Thousands of fruit bats, unsettled by the storm, were wheeling like crazed sky loons, blanketing the horizon with black commotion. Underneath, the scaffolded trees had been pruned awkwardly over the years by storms, while others were remarkably rounded and intact. The homeless were already staking out positions underneath the canopies as they were the driest positions, though always a bit dicey when it came to loose branches. Didn't seem to worry them – they were drinking and making a party of it. She could hear some bursts of cheering and shuddered to think what they were cheering about.

Flick remembered her dad telling her it had always been called Figtree Camp even before he was a boy. Figtree Camp. The undomiciled lucky enough to have a few $Old would be lining up at the 2 large town dormitories, made from weldedTogether shipping containers, hardwood and recycled steel. Storms were wet and violent and scary. Everyone needed to find shelter. She looked to the ocean. The opticals were telling her that the storm was kat3, so not thermocell intensity, but she'd misjudged the speed of the front and it would reach an hour, not 2. Though they were without the likes of Marko's handyDandy sailor technology that he'd beqweathed her, the denizens of Figtree Camp had worked it out too. She could see people pulling out their plastics and minilite tents.

Flick began to jog. The marina where *The Capricorn Sky* was moored lay halfway round the north bay. This meant crossing the wirebridge system. She had time to get there to stay out of the rain, but wanted to further secure the vessel in case a surge slapped over the barrage, never a happy event. The thought of the side of the boat being pummelled and damaged lifted her heels. She clanged across the bridge over the inlet feeling the unnerving sense of wind coming up from below, and the bridge swaying with the gusts.

The seas were now choppy under her and the wind was almost cold, while cold rain flecks began. Flick stopped at the marina kiosk for some milk and bread and picked up her washing, then rattled down the metal pier to the boat. Above, the sky was black and big and the flecks became plumper, large as grapes, spitting into her. Soon they would be the size of lemons. She threw the shopping down the hatchway and knelt to make sure everything was secure. It was plain the main storm was to the north, but it was going to be a rough nite. She disconnected the external power leads, in case things were ripped out and the metal pier was electrified. With bad wiring and water, death by electrocution on metal piers was a common occurrence.

Flick, now getting soaked above deck, lowered several more side fenders between the boat and the jetty, along with an extra mooring line to a high pontoon pole. Not a problem. She could see that other boaters were doing the same. Tying up and battening down. A neighbour on the deck of a solar yacht waved.

Wet and tired, she let herself into the boat, and clacked and locked the hatch fast behind her – as a single woman she took no chances. She changed out of her sodden clothes, towelled down, found a dry top to wear in her clean washing, and unpacked the shopping. She wondered about Marko and his fate, and wondered if her new acqwisition had been a wrong trade, a bad plan on his part. Still, it was fine for her. She plonked onto one of the cabin bench seats and looked up through the skylight at the spattering rain on the plexiglass. The wind was starting to keen in the komms masts. Then she turned on the scope to watch an old movie.

*

Huge sections of the reef were now rubble. Higher sea levels pushed the swell into the coast, when once their power had been mitigated by the coral structures further offshore. So a coastline once protected by a barrier reef structure, now copped the big Pacific swells, and, even deep into the Trinity inlet, the waves could be hard on a boat.

The elite boating structures were further up the inlet, but as she was moored in a povvo marina where the derelicts and homeboaters found a berth, she worried about the hull and barely slept. Surges had been known to push long piers in the cheaper marinas, up and over the 20 metre high tidal pylons that kept them fixed in place, and then the surgewaves would drag flotillas of tethered boats inland. So Flick dozed in and out of watching programs. She had a cup of tea at one point.

Then, deep into the nite, Flick heard the thump thump thump thump on the deck above the stormHowl. She well knew the tread. She'd heard it on the hardwood and steel verandah as a child, when her father had come home at nite from some smugglers sortie in the high tropics and woke her in her little mezzanine bedroom above the living area, to give her a goodnite kiss.

The gauge showed the wind was up at 120 knots. Wasn't dawn yet, but Kingdom Allenby never slept and never let a storm impede his ominous momentum. She knew that. And if you were blood, you weren't expected to sleep either. The banging on the cabin door started.

"Flick, Flick," he boomed. Bang bang bang. Fist pummelling the hatch.

She switched the light on and pulled her longTop down over her knees.

"Coming, Dad," she said.

In the pummelling rain, he stood sodden, matted hair and beard, filthy teflite raincoat that had seen better days, holding a black softBag, and rubbers on the feet. As if he'd been bunked down with the street people under the fig trees for the evening. Prob'ly had. His breath smelled of alcohol. He didn't look unfazed in the slightest.

The storm had postponed dawn. Black clouds flickered with lightning and carried gusts of rain. She looked at his sodden hair and face.

"You coming in or just going to stay wet? You want kopi?" she snapped.

"Ok, luv."

He gazed at her with his usual sullen eyes, crowed – skin leathered and lined – by years in the high tropics. Critical, sharp.

"Come down."

He looked up for a moment, the usual 180 degree scan made by a renegade for a beeDrone or a tail. Fat chance in the middle of a storm. She backed down the hatch and he slid down.

"You look beautiful, princess," he said.

"You look pretty much like crap," she answered.

He threw the softbag on one of the couches and settled his big frame down beside it. He tested the padding, approvingly, with his bony buttocks.

"Been on the hoof, that's why. I'll have a shower in a bit ... if my rude little princess will allow me a fluffy towel. Where did you cop this boat? Nice steal. Hardened hull and all."

"I didn't steal it. Was a gift."

"Really," he said, eyebrows raised, obviously worried what his daughter might have done to get it.

"Heard what happened up at the Nest?" God, he had a loud voice, booming around the saloon. Big man syndrome.

"Hermann told me things went bad and Channing was killed," said Flick, "but you were the one who probably told him. And I suppose he blurted back to you that I was in town."

"'Bout right," said Kingdom Allenby. "Need you to do something for me."

"And it's lovely to see you too, Dad," she added.

"Ay, don't get smart with me," he needled. "Important."

"Dad, when did you ever just talk to someone without making them run an errand for you?"

"That's what I do," he said with a little smile. "Persuade good people to run little errands. Got it in one, luv."

Flick drew 2 mugs from the kopi machine and handed one to Kingdom Allenby. He looked older, greyer, but still strong. Sitting straight on the saloon sofa, one elbow on the table, other arm behind him. She vaguely remembered her mum, Verity. Those living images – the love on her face, the colour (and smell) of her skin, the comfort when she held little Flick's hand. The circumstance of Verity's death had obscured some of the memories, as she'd witnessed the horror of the moment. Then the memory of an 8 year old, helping her sobbing father bury her mum.

Of course, in a past life, when purity ruled, Kingdom and Verity had been told they were Noughters – never to have kids – making Flick and her baby brother S'mon both illegal and abominations.

But she didn't care. She was breathing the good air, living life. That was what the Nest was there for. Breaking the rules. Verity had died in a massive storm, hit by the steel ceiling when a branch crashed through their first house north of the Nest. So Flick and her brother had helped her dad bury the slightly built, loving young woman.

After her mum was buried in a deep trench with cement poured on top, to ward against erosion, on the hill behind their house, the little girl had watched Kingdom Allenby dive deeper and deeper into the criminal culture of the district. He sent people on those secret Kingdom errands in fear of their lives, made money, killed those who smelt of treachery, or simply, were of negative value. He organised the trades and the smugglers. Then he suddenly retired to live in his treehouse.

The rumour was he'd been turned by AuZgov for $New, but noone had the guts to ask him. For that, the Nest community turned its psychotic prejudices towards his daughter and son. In return S'mon reacted badly, turning into a version of the Old Kingdom Allenby, the mad criminal and then headed even further north, lost to the little family. Was probably dead. And Flick, at the age of 17, had had enough, and shifted south on what she called her "wanderings".

"This Andaman Marko bloke," Kingdom said, sipping the kopi with an appreciative noise. "This Marko. What's so special about him? Is he rich?"

"Makes money," said Flick. "Lot of it. Through the virtual."

"Ok," said Kingdom. "How do I talk to him? Private talk."

"You can't. He was up at the Nest when all hell broke loose. He's prob'ly taken by milisi, being kept in the Ville in the barracks. He was trying to be a free man, but led a whole lot of trouble to the Nest. Fooled me good and proper." She paused and looked at the fine walnut table in the cabin, which not long ago had been Marko's. "Not saying that I'm not upset about what's happening to him. I like him lots. He gave me this boat. But you taught me one thing useful. Take what you can get, and cut your losses whenever you can. That's what I'm doing right now."

"Yes. But this Marko ... you have a fondness for him?"

"Don't even go there, Dad. You need to stay out of my biz."

"Well, I know who's out for him, and I want to tell him."

"The gov'ment. They have him in their sights & they got him in their jail," she said.

"Not his worst problem," said Kingdom. "Nowhere near his worst problem. Your boyfriend was being escorted west by Channing and M'bers when they were ambushed by HegMen. Channing was killed. Shot like a pig. M'bers now with the AuZ-gov troops ... including Slotters."

Flick could hear a hint of awe in his voice. Slotters actually impressed Kingdom. "Least old M'bers survived. But Channing ... he was a good man. We did good bizz together. Anyway, these Slotters, they went on a chase, got Marko back and killed the HegMen."

"Who were the HegMen?"

"Aussies from up Darwin way. Old military, but working for someone else. Someone who'd brought a sub under the cloud. They were going to deliver Marko."

"A sub?" Flick was boggled. "A submarine for Andy?"

She knew that Andy was kinda special under his bullshit, sex and yammer. He's got something, that Andy, she'd thought. Something people want. It's those xmas lights in his clamB, the like of which she'd never seen. He knew a lot and knew nothing. That was Marko's problem. She had smelt his panic when he banged on her door, when they had motored up to the Nest. He'd left a bioLuminous trail of blind panic. No thinking there. No coolHeadedness. And yet he'd got away, and got away again. Knew everything there was to know, but had no idea how to operate in his own sweet cone.

"Then if he's caught by Slotters, he prob'ly is with M'bers in Townsville barracks. Prob'ly getting a limbic probe right now, fixing to find his secrets. You won't be able to talk to him." She sat on the cabin couch and started to sniffle, wiping a tear from her cheek with the back of a hand. *Not in front of him,* she willed herself. *Don't start crying.*

Kingdom shook his head, like he was ridding himself of a memory.

"Last time I fought Slotters was years ago, on the borders across from PNG and we were trying to bring shipments in, out. Us and a bunch of Indon smugglers the Slotters wanted to stop. They brooked no challenge. Wanted to stop the bodyzappers, shields and drone systems we were importing through the knotholes in the Cloud. The seeds and hardArms we were pulling out. AuZgov didn't care 'bout ordinary goods, or gold, or whatever. But not warfareTek 'specially weapons. Intervened ... whole Slotter platoon came after us. Fought them off once, came at us again. Tough fighters. Channing was there ... got to say he was handier and more tough then. S'pose I was too."

Flick reckoned her dad was looking a bit old and sentimental in the telling of the story, but she too, felt sad about Channing.

"Most of my blokes died, 'cluding T'm Reardon, trusted lieutenant and brother of your mother Verity."

One uncle dead, but Dad escaped. As usual. With Channing.

He paused as if to gulp air. The clouds in the windows were still black, speckled with lightning and it was now 'round 6. The slopping against the wharf had eased. Clouds should be high and pink with dawn this time of year. Her Dad drew another slurp from his kopi and put down the empty mug.

"Musta done something real special for Marko to give you the boat," he said.

"Well, he begged me to hide him, so I took him to the Nest. Then he was captured," she said with a wry smile. "Pretty useless, me."

"Aw, don't blame yourself. He'd never have got away from HighEye and the rest."

"I knew that," she said, "but he needed time to calm down."

*

Like so many who came into contact with Kingdom Allenby, Flick threw her better judgment (generally sound) out the window and agreed to give her father a lift back to the Ville to make contact with Marko.

Kingdom was persuasive, and she was blood. So it wasn't charm, or threat or intimidation. It was their shared past that spurred her to grant the wishes of the man. Payment for building and repairing twenty tree cubbyhouses, protecting her from storms, giving her a full life when it weren't legal in the eyes of DyNAst. She also wanted to know what he knew and the old man wasn't giving it away lightly.

And Kingdom was insistent. Always was.

Only Marko was to hear whatever revelation he had. Because Kingdom likely wanted to screw some money out of him in exchange. He'd heard that Channing and M'bers had been given a reward for their abruptly interrupted help as well. He wanted a piece of the action. Simple info exchange.

Kingdom finished his kopi and said, "Let's get going then!" and she did as she was told. No wonder she'd pissed off from the Nest as soon as she could, domineering prick.

She'd get it out of him though. Between Trinity and the Ville, they would talk.

*

As the blackGreen hulk of Hinchinbrook Island loomed, he watched his daughter skip the bad waves and keep an even keel. Always her strength. Boats of any shape or size. Verity's dad'd taught her seamanship and she were damn'd good.

The white boat slapped across the channel, greenGrey wavelets across the bow, white foam waked and left behind. The mountainous island was starboard and Flick sat relaxed, one buttock on the skipper's chair, one hand on the wheel, eyes out for the floating industrial farms that held prawns or barramundi or mackerel. They were very visible, had to be. Large tenders plied between them, bringing in supplies for the workers, and fish food and machinery and removing bags of produce. It wasn't so much their essential fabric, the steelLink discs they were constructed with she worried about, but other boats going full tilt, busy with task. The supply tenders sprang through the water, around the sides of these factories in sudden ways, and it was hard to avoid them. A couple of small aircraft, a chopper and a plane, buzzed over them. The air was still cool, because the sun hadn't reached 5 degrees on the horizon, but she could feel its heat starting to bite.

While going full throttle, she navigated around huge metal donuts where the fish were farmed, and kept her distance from the strip of housing along the east of the island where prawners, clamFarmers and other fishRelated workers lived. There was already a fair amount of water traffic so she was kept alert.

After a while, Kingdom poked his head into the cockpit, and clambered into a seat, holding a bottle of beer.

Again he said: "You fond of this Marko?"

She turned and looked at him, sqwatting on the couch in the cockpit like an evil hairy spider. Same place Marko had sat in his tremble of fear a week ago.

"Yes, Dad. He's not a bad one."

"Love him?"

As if he'd ever know what love was. But then, maybe he loved her mum.

"It's not like that," she said helplessly.

"I think you do," he said in an unusually quiet voice. "I think you do."

*

The boat, had emerged from the shipping canal at the channel's south end and slid easily over waves in the northerly swell, Kingdom gestured to Flick – "over there, over there."

He pointed at yet another giant metal donut glinting above the steely waters – a fish factory – way East of Hinchinbrook Island, out to sea and so much larger than coastal factories.

"That's Trey's fishery. Berth here, girl, for a few minutes. Hard to port, you girl."

As they approached with *The Capricorn Sky* on half throttle, playing into the swell, Flick watched the giant mesh cage (for that was what it was) made from the thick aerolinks. The long landing pontoon clamped to the outside with a crane arrangement on one end, was narrow but approachable, set up for tenders, so easy for midSized boats like hers to come alongside. She could already smell the hard tang of fish and fish guts, the smokehouses round the other side of the factory were sending up a greasy billow. Seagulls and pellies wheeled around the gutting site on the other side of the structure, like a white cloud.

Flick throttled down further and eased the bow beside the dock and Kingdom, sprightly for an old fella, jumped the side, landed with a grunt and sheathed the bowline into a ropeS-natch on the pontoon.

"C'mon," he gestured to Flick, who had tethered the stern. She felt the whole pontoon and membrane of the cage rise lazily on the swell, and fall. The pontoon was slithery wet with saltwater, as the swell would occasionally reach the steel. Her father held a rail for safety and waved at her to jump.

She didn't want to leave the boat – she knew the fishing communities were a bit ratbaggy & povvo. The fishers lived, usually in family groups, on Heg factories working for a pittance and she knew there'd be an extended population. Kids, wives & husbands, other family. Mates. Little communities in their own right.

"It'll be 'k. They're friends. Y'can leave your precious f'king boat for a coupla hours."

So's not to look like a tagalong dog, Flick settled a small scowl on her face and from the clanking pontoon followed her father up a narrow steel stairway to the top deck – a flat board-walk which circumnavigated top of the the ring. The other side of the donut hole, the diameter across, was half a klik, because the cage contained ocean fish, not estuarine. Ocean fish needed more breathing space. Room to turn.

"Hey," Kingdom grunted. "They're friends. Stop scowling. You look like some tagalong dog."

Flick could only smile. He was still a dad who could sometimes read her mind.

100 metres along the top gangway was a bridge with a wheelhouse and nav gear and further round, small cabins welded to the deck, where families lived with the fishermen and factory workers. On the inner side were stratas of ramps

and decks where workers tended the breeding fish, and caught and gaffed the full sized ones to process in the factory. Across the other side and along the ring's shoulder were the dehydrators and warehouses.

Gull, pellies, terns and boobies – crowded the airspace above, attracted by smells, expectant for scraps.

Now she was inside the farm, the whole apparatus reeked, sour and rotten, with further wafts of both the smoked fish and diesel fumes. A rich stink. Flick felt like retching but she mindOverMattered and good manners prevailed. People came over to where Kingdom stood. He clasped a small Vietnamese guy who was extremely pleased to see her father. The man's face crinkled and greenGrey teeth emerged in a smile.

"*Xin chao*, Trey," said Kingdom, "This's my girl Felicity," he gestured at her and Trey gave her a little bow.

"Enchanté," he said with a slightly French accent.

Felicity nodded back.

"Trey. Can you do me a fave. Stash this? Be back when I need it."

"Absolutely Mr Allenby," Trey said. "I owe you much."

Kingdom discreetly, between the 2 men, handed over a hardArm, half wrapped in a rag. A snub nose semiauto handgun. Lethal and grey.

"Come with me," Trey said taking the weapon, wrapping it proper.

They started circumnavigating the top of the ring, past the Bridge and along communal platforms and outdoor kitchens. About a third of the way round they reached an array of steel hoppers. The smoke from the factory buildings was now quite thick, and not so unpleasant as the fishFlesh was flavoured and dehydrated.

"We put the fish on long racks and use solar burners and smoke sticks together, for flavour," Trey explained to Flick, "CargoKetches come for the bags each week or so. Cloud coming down from the north now, so we're finishing up here. Have to motor 200kliks south to summer mooring. Big catch being processed first, and we are beeeehind!" he grinned.

They reached a particular silo and Trey stopped.

"Fishfood," said Trey. He lifted a locker and found a large plastic bag and carefully placed the gun inside, ziplocked it and swiftly tied a cable round the top. Further along, he slid open a huge silo lid which sent up a waft of rancid air. Again Flick averted her head and tried not to gag at the reek of rotten protein. The smell did not affect Trey who leant in, attaching the line to somewhere under the silo lid's lip. He dropped the package in, under the greasy pellets and buried it with a shovel, hanging precariously into the silo.

"Will live with the fishfood. Stay all greased. May smell on return," Trey laughed. Kingdom laughed.

"Good man." They moved back to the living platforms for a kopi. After the favour Kingdom was asking, he could hardly refuse a genuine offer of hospitality. Trey chatted to him, filled with fisher news. Flick, against her instincts, kept tagging along.

Trey was clearly part of her father's nefarious network which reached up and down the coast, and inland. People he used, and depended on. Why he was stashing the gun was a mystery, but then, caught with one, and he'd never see the light of day again, and being aboard her boat, neither would she. HardArms were forbidden fruits in the days of Purity. Rare and rotten fruits. Too much war and death had preceded.

On the communal platforms were the men, women and kids going about their business on the slow rise and fall of the huge mesh structure. The horizon, yellowed and charred by the reeking smoke, moved with the swell behind them. Up'n'down the coast, boats would come out from ports dropping supplies and collecting the packaged dried and smoked products for the huge hungry markets of Cap and Australia.

Flick wondered how the people survived in the big blows. She knew even if they fired up the engines (they were permitted a diesel allocation due to their contribution to food production) and the fish factory rings retreated south, they were still vulnerable to bad storms. She also knew the workers were paid almost nothing, and risked their lives in fierce weather. But blows could be lethal all the way to Tassy. She asked a girlKid who'd offered her some boiled sugars where the crew went in a big blow.

"Safe rooms," the girlKid said pointing at more solid looking steel cabins on the inside of the ten metre wide mesh ring. "Got water, dried smokers, cans o'tomato, stuff. Can hang out there for a few days."

"All of you?"

"Yer. All of us here. Nice bracelet, Lady," she added.

Flick sqwatted beside the kid on the communal deck with a dozen others, and watched her dad and Trey rolling some chop chop and having a smoke and a laugh. The terror of a blow on such an ungainly slow craft that was a factory ring, would be monumental. Impossibly big to move up any rivermouth for shelter. She could hardly imagine the waves, the encroaching thermocell tubes, the fear of snapped anchor mechanisms. Was no way the structure could be steered with a swell, like a boat.

"Would be a squash with you all stuck in the safety cabins," she remarked to the kid, who was thin and pretty flatchested for a tweeny, maybe 13, in a pink tankTop and grimy shorts. But gawd she looked tough.

"Yair," said the kid, still admiring the bracelet. "Been through 2. Everyone gets seasick. Vomit everywhere."

Flick could hardly envisage the scene. At the moment, the ring was rising and falling in a northerly swell, quite sharp between the waves, but nothing too offPutting. The chains, filled with compressed gas to keep the vessel afloat, clinked at they moved. Was a pleasant noise, but probs got repetitively annoying after a while, then became part of the soundzone of both waves and slapping fish in the huge basket below.

"How many tonnes in there?" asked Flick. The kid looked down.

"Twenny or 30. Mostly mackerel."

"No tunnies?"

"No tunnies," said the girlKid laughing. Her teeth were awful too. Black'n'yellow. Also looked like she'd had a savage accident with a gaff hook, as there was a scar and bad stitch line on her scalp. May have been even older. Mebbe 14, 15, but close to emaciated.

As Flick and Kingdom finished the bizz and left down the gangway ladder to the pontoon, her dad said "Trey's a good bloke. I use the factory as a holdfast. Been at it 30 year or so. I've put contraband, people, cash on board for small return to him. I even lived here for 5 months once, smoking fish, keeping low. Trey's got 2 wives and most of those kids are his. Saw you talking to his granddaughter Minh. Tough little nugget, isn't she?"

"So it seems," said Flick. She'd finally relented to the steely gaze and given the kid her cheap Rusty's market bracelet.

"I like Trey," Kingdom went on. "AuZgov ignores his bad behaviour cos he knows how to keep their fish alive and that's fine by them and the bastd'z that lease him the factory. He'd be jailed if they knew what he'd looked after for me over the years but..." Kingdom laughed a laugh.

"So what's with the gun?" Flick asked,

"I've had a change of heart Luv. Tell you later."

He waved from the boatbow to Trey on the pontoon. Trey let the bowline slip and they were off again, heading southwards, away from the stink and fug

*

She picked peak time to arrive at the Ville when the ferries and fishers were heading back. Late arvo. Headed for the povvo marina in the Pallarenda basin, although it was a hike from there into the town. She warned her dad to stay cool and play it qwiet. They needed to pick their way into the sitch. In her bag she had her kit: coloured contacts, and a bit of putty to change their face shapes, all to put the scanners off biometrix, though scanners could tell whether there was a film in people's eyes now. But so many did it, it wasn't a red flag thing.

"Right, sit tight. I'm going into town." He nodded. Kingdom knew if the milisi picked either of them up, the conseqwences for him would be the most severe.

JEMBRANA

HE WATCHED qwietly his eqwal/rival/colleague, Premier Paul Luff, slouched back on the sofette in his office. The security chief was similarly reclined opposite. The 2 men eyed each another with a weary disdain. No aides were present. Just ASEAN's man and the AuZgov man who, in a duumvirate, ruled the qwasiState of Cap. The aides had been chased out after fussing over the 2 men who'd been coSigning directives on food trains and storage bunkers for the north. There was some discussion of any sign of the "tip back", a potential climate cooling phase out in the South Pacific that the metHeads were hopeful about, but disappointingly, the metHeads report was neutral. More storms to come, some with 500 klik per hour intensity.

Once the aides left, Luff poured a couple of drinks – soft for him, whisketty for Jembrana – and they began to discuss the violent debacle of bombing and assassination that had occurred on their patch. Luff had been uninterested up until then, but when Jembrana retailed the worst episodes in great detail, the Premier was boggleEyed.

Jembrana reported to Luff that security's holding cells contained the cyberSavant Andaman Marko, M'bers, one of the Nest's activists, and an unknown incursionist who was badly wounded. Plus, 2 other personages who'd been hurt during the raid on the Nest the previous morning. Not to mention the Northern Lights bomber who, at that moment, was "enjoying" limbic intrusion to check memories and backThoughts. AuZ-Gov's P/EM had been informed, and the Prez of ASEAN, who'd been less bothered.

Jembrana knew Luff didn't like him and disapproved of the whole duumvirate model. Luff was oldGuardAustralian who had thought *the Blend* dubious. He viewed the emergency influx of those who lived directly to the north as invasion by stealth. Although they worked well together, Jembrana, in his heart of hearts, knew Luff would rather Cap was still heartland Australian. The Premiership was also an elected position, chosen by the people of Cap, so Luff held more prestige than Jembrana.

Jembrana had always seen *the Blend* as a global and demographic necessity that went along with the huge backhander of a disaster brought by the climate stepChange in the mid70s last century, known worldwide in every language as *The Grief*, when millions perished and millions of others were forced to move.

But rawBone nationalists like Luff couldn't put the event in such context.

Luff was a tall, greyBlond bureaucrat, rangy featured, eyes and mouth puckered downward from the effort of managing a vast tract of territory and dealing with the political representatives across 40 or so language groups, including all the big Indijj settlements. He sorted, as best he could, the problems of infrastructure and food, agriculture and housing. His government ran huge workCamps of itinerants across the north who were marshalled to repair infrastructure – roads, bridges, barrages – and do the groundwork on more farms and cultivation for the promise of smallholdings.

Some of the camps had 1000s of people, families with second and third generations, all displaced by *the Cloud*. While events like the bombing of the Northern Lights were unusual, he had far more complicated fish to fry.

"So," said Luff, deliberately in English, "we have an unsolved matter concerning the activity of one of our citizens, which has led to bloody murder, and now the invocation of Slotters, for goodness' sake. Slotters, on our patch?" There was a pause. "When have we needed a bunch of f'king throwbacks to sort our probs?"

"Not often," said Jembrana. "Sometimes. They've been here before."

"Once in a blue f'king moon," said Luff angrily.

"Were you aware of Marko's secure sensitivity status? He is our citizen," Jembrana asked carefully. Luff was also, after all, AuZgov. Luff had no reason to lie, though few did anyway, after the Age of Purity. They were of eqwal administrative status, and Jembrana had so obviously been in the dark. Luff had too. He could tell when the Premier offered up a moment of shared grievance.

"No. I knew nothing," Luff admitted. "Since this outrage, I've been informed that the Spokes kept him on a 'watch' for a while, and they'd deemed him 'of use', but no threat. And they were merely interested in his illegal scripts and screeds, and his unusual methodologies, so they contend there was no reason for either of us to be briefed."

"Centrl told me that rubbishy line also. A pity. And a great pity Marko is now out of general circulation. He was always entertaining."

Jembrana had attended more than a few exclusive do's hosted by the young millionaire investor where he had offered guests flutes of crisp zizz, sqwired handsome women, and entertained with his wayward repartee. The sort of soireés Luff never attended.

"Marko? Life of the party," said Luff in a bored voice. "Now, along with AuZtax, we know where he made his money."

They looked at each other and Jembrana sipped some kopi.

Luff's office complex lay along the roofline of the assembly building and was one floor above and half a building along from Jembrana's. The Premier's personal office was known as the Bow Room, because superstrength bowed windows took in the bayscape and Island. Again, it was cooled by both breeze and chiller units.

Unlike Jembrana's office, an elegant room, spare and understated, Luff had crammed his with trophy cabinets, photographs, framed documents and bricAbrac to display his long and distinguished political career. Displaying his age too – Luff began his political life at the time of *the Blend*. There were pictures of Luff with governorsGeneral of Australia, Luff with several P/EMs going back to the dark ages, Luff with overseas leaders. His portrait in oils –a younger man in a suit, eyeing the world with calm – was on the wall. The Premier's personal jumble overwhelmed the beautiful organic plasterwork and carved wooden partitions, made by the Indon artisans who decorated the room.

When sitting with Luff in the Bow Room, Jembrana always felt the history of the past 60 years was staring down and judging him. He knew Luff judged him all the time against strange Luffish benchmarks such as Jembrana's ability to chair meetings in 3 languages, the ability to muster trucks at the drop of a hat, the speed of a rescue intervention into a stormWracked region. Luff, a paragon of Purity, personally marked Jembrana down and throughout because of the big man's carousing and womanising. He knew this, but didn't much care.

When it came to work, Jembrana knew Luff generally trusted his security chief's decisions. Was in the personal areas he found Jembrana wanting. But it was only to make Luff feel better, and the needling about Marko's tax revenue wasn't about Jembrana's business at all. Jembrana ran security across a huge and unruly zone, and his impressive legacy was general peace and tranqwillity in the state, until the recent events.

The bombing and killing of 43 citizens and the mysterious assassination of the Senior Courier had cut him to the core.

"The Slotter team and Courier Phipps are on standby. They've been going solid for 60 hours."

"Doesn't look like you've had much sleep either, mate," said Luff, and indeed Jembrana did feel wrecked after working beside the Brigadier and overseeing the milisi. The submarine had evaporated somewhere under the ocean, over the continental shelf and away.

"And we have lost our selfSelecting Nest of outlaws and malcontents," said Luff. "The colony'll scatter to the winds."

"Not necessarily. After we free him, M'bers will probably return to rally his troops."

"Possibly."

"There are many of them in the Cape reqwiring a centre for trade and communication. The Nest will be rebuilt by some semblance of a convocation," he predicted.

"Mebbe."

Jembrana refused to be further goaded by Luff. They had been through a morning of business, and Jembrana was now tired of Luff's brusqwe act. He clipped his clamB shut and made for a diplomatic exit, mouthing niceties of farewell.

"I hear you are dining with Courier Phipps tonite," said Luff pleasantly. "I hope you have an enjoyable evening."

Jembrana smiled. Where did Luff hear that? One of Jembrana's own disloyal aides probably, blabberMouthing.

"I've asked her to give me a personal briefing on the events. I need to know every detail. I fear that somewhere in the Cape community there are allies of external enemies – something we haven't traxperienced for many long decades."

"Just so," said Luff pompously. "Keep me briefed. I'm off thru the Northwest in the morning for a few weeks to check the Tennant Creek and Wyndham facilities. Far Northwest Cap's turning into an awful place, but the Wyndham Portmaster wants further import rights and battening funds. My forward itinerary is in your pack marked with the blue tag." He pursed his lips and looked down at other briefs on his desktop.

Jembrana left with a smile on his face. Luff was a good operator, but his selfImportant style grated. He also hoped Luff was slightly jealous of his dinner rendezvous with Dr Phipps. He knew Luff endured a miserable marriage, but as the putative and intensely puritanical Premier of a jointly run Territory, Luff obviously felt he had to encourage appearances, so couldn't have a bit of fun with other women.

Jembrana was stubbornly single. His wife had left him a decade ago on the grounds of boredom & after they'd met their qwota of children (twicers both). After that, he'd never wanted to remarry.

Jembrana returned to the small office in his private qwarters and worked for a couple of hours. A long list of approvals had backed up because of his obsessive monitoring of the chase for Marko. With his aides Ricki and Yovo, he got through the list to his satisfaction, and told them to go off and eat something so they could hover later near his dinner table, at a side table – in case there were messages or errands.

Jembrana showered, changed into a lightweight suit and leather sandals and asked his houseMan to prepare a whisketty sour and a half flute of zizz. The sun was heading southward and the lights were beginning to reflect on the bay. The whisketty and zizz heightened the lights and made the reflections appear as neat slashes of bright red and green in the water, like vivid fabric patterning.

Yovo rang to announce that Dr Phipps and her security detail had arrived at the Representatives' Restaurant and she was being provided a drink on his tab. He made his way down and through the assembly's public area, past various ceremonial guards in their gold braid and clustered officials. They showed deference and moved aside for him. He swept through the main lobby and across to the outer terrace where Dr Phipps was perched on a bar stool looking into the gloom of nitefall.

She wore a classic black dress, a vCut neckline, plunging backline, and shiny black stilettos.

To Jembrana, the outfit helped accentuate her curves, and the swell of her breasts, her dark skin. But he could see she was strong and her muscles were toned, rather than the ugly knotted ones sported by her personal detail, Folly and Pearl. They were without helmets and armed with small cutdown pistol guns. In the Ville's most upmarket restaurant the 2 slotters tried to stand discreetly and Jembrana was amused. It wasn't working.

"Dr Phipps."

"Administrator Jembrana."

"Just Jembrana. I'm a stickler for my cultural background. It is the place where my family came from and it is my name. Honorifics are for the colonisers. Apart from, might I say, educational honorifics which actually prove a person's merit."

Madrigal laughed. She'd slept in, the sleep of the just, until 7 that morning, when Folly woke her, by banging on the door and shouting a couple of sharp "Ma'ams". She felt revived after the past few rambunctious days, though the shoulder still ached from its dislocation and she had a series of bruises in random places.

"Might I ask, what did you receive your doctorate in?" said Jembrana solicitously.

"Law," she said. She twirled her glass thoughtfully. "I began a lawyer and moved to diplomacy from there. In fact, my doctorate was about the international constitutionality of Capricornia post *the Blend*. I proved, with much evidence, that the arrangement was legal but unworkable."

Jembrana raised a languid eyebrow above an almondShaped eye, and laughed. "You'll have to tell me about your evidence sometime," he said. Madrigal smiled again.

He was still struck by Madrigal's elegance, her obvious intellect plus the proven fact she could lead while under parlous danger. He had listened to the interKomms as she led the slotters, and watched the vids, when the water wasn't obscuring everything, as they struggled with twisters and torrents, and then when they finally slotted the raiders. At their first meeting he had been impressed, but after her return to the Ville he was intrigued as well. A deep interest in Madrigal Phipps had formed in his mind, more than he formed in most people he met.

"Let's eat," he said, waving towards the Representatives' Restaurant. "I have a corner table which is photon electron secure, so we may talk in confidence."

They walked through to the main dining area with its crisp tablecloths and gently ringing cutlery, followed by Folly and Pearl, who stood in the shadows nearby. Jembrana nodded at his 2 young aides, Ricki and Yovo, sitting at an adjacent table, sipping sodas, ready for any instruction.

The room was full of diners, mostly governors and functionary administrators. They kept a guarded eye on their security chief, pretending that the idle banter was just that. The diners were also qwietly bemused by their Security Chief's companion, as she was certainly not one of them. An outsider, not from the administrative circles of the Ville, and glamorous at that. Folly and Pearl also became hushed talking points, as weapons were a rarity, even hardArms in holsters. Obviously there to protect Jembrana's companion.

There were murmurs that she was the one who survived the Northern Lights bombing and saved 2 chefs and a waitress.

Jembrana chuckled deep down at the impact of the newcomers, and pulled out the chair for Dr Phipps to settle in.

*

Madrigal found Jembrana to be wilfully attentive. He was older than her, mebbe in his early 50s, though a rejuve could have hidden his true age. And very Balinese in his ways and affectations. He had honey skin and was still very handsome. A handsomeness she'd first noted when he'd bluntly asked 3 days ago whether she was partnered. She had surmised then that he was curious about whether she was single, rather than whether she was available for sexing. Maybe she'd been wrong. But still, he had perfect manners.

And photon screen up around the white clothed table, they delved straight into the debrief.

Like him, Madrigal had figured there were local elements in the incursion. The prisoner who lived through the firefight was from Old Darwin and the big old landV had been sourced from a dealer of military vehicles. This meant that any event, even the bombing at the Northern Lights or Bluestone's murder, could've been locally initiated. The presence of a submarine meant organised international connections. And probably from some defence department of some foreign government – unheard of.

Jembrana asked, "What was Marko's demeanour after the capture?" and Madrigal reported that the target had been mightily relieved. Marko had confessed he was sure his captors were going to physically torture or kill him.

She returned a qwestion, as if they were playing tennis. "Did the Northern Lights bomber reveal anything to debriefers?"

"Not verbally. They are going through his limbic traces at the moment. We know that he is part of a team, mainly because someone else killed your friend Bluestone."

"Sure."

"There may be others."

And there probably were, she thought, though her senses hadn't picked up any suspicious movements in the Representatives' Restaurant when they walked through to the table. Anyone, as long as they were cashed up, could walk in and find themselves a table. After all, Cap had, up until 2 days ago, been a safe and peaceful place.

A good operator would not be panicked by her security detail, but neither Dante nor she had discerned any tails or traces since they'd returned from the bad weather up north.

She looked across the bay and saw high burnt ochre sunset clouds heading way up to the stratosphere – the monsoons were now moving south. There were flickers of lightning. The clouds, changed from mango, to ochre, and back to mango, as the sheet of light rippled through them, turning the ocean on and off, like a flatLamp.

She nibbled her barramundi skewer.

"The Northern Lights killers from the other nite? Their komms were in total blackout? You picked nothing up in transmissions?"

"We ran every possible unraveller across every transmission around the Ville over the preceding month. There was nothing. They obviously prepped elsewhere, went dark, and struck."

Privately, the deep silence of the bombing and assassination operation frightened her a little. She knew that criminals always left leave traces both in the planning and the execution of crimes. After these outrages, there was stony silence.

It made no sense. The nonpresence of Marko's lurker. The sheer destruction of a niteclub with 43 dead to kill just one man. The way the Nest was turned into an abattoir. She recalled the cloaked presence in the lobby trying to unzip her door and failing. Even that was scary as the assassin has disappeared without leaving any trace. Like they were ghosts. Ghosts from the past when the world was more violent. Jembrana looked worried too, mouth turned down in contemplation. His thoughts were qwite likely paralleling hers.

They resorted to autobiography for a while. Jembrana talked about his background and family. Balinese royalty, of course. She talked about her family company and the energy market: the Phipps Industries arrays of solar fields, aluminium battery plants, vast forests of wind plant and the submerged tidal frondz, generating terrawatts of power, sold thru to Asia. A family biz she was brought up with, but was at pains to tell Jembrana she'd decided on her own career, and loved being an AuZgov Courier.

"You're more than a Courier, Madrigal," said Jembrana. "I can assure you of that."

He asked why she qwoted Shakespeare down the communicator during the thermocells. "Was it from *The Tempest?*"

"It's from *King Lear*. Was my favourite play at school – probably cos of all that stuff about bad daughters. Suppose it made sense at the time."

Jembrana laughed. She was surprised, she said. Hadn't realised she'd blurted the storm scene out loud. No doubt something to do with her nearDeath experience and spouts.

From that point in the evening, both turned candid about themselves, which surprised Madrigal. The world had truly flipped from that heyday of nonPrivacy in the previous century, when the horrible burden of utter transparency of one's personal detail, when everyone's bizz was on the virtual. No details were left out in the open these dayz. People learned when info about their doings became dangerous during the AuZgov purges against everything criminal, however petty. Worse, people got petty too on social meejjas, outing cheating boyfriends and girlfriends, tax evasions, minor shoplifting and drunkenness and getting them into trouble.

Now, after decades of purity, citizens were still generally averse to revealing even tiny details about themselves. Reading preferences, travel plans, hat size.

Social meeja was dead. Hardly anyone operated virtually, except for business and education. They knew AuZgov could look and listen at all times. The less bait to tantalise the bureaucrats and police, the better. A cult that vowed not to reveal the self, the Stümmers, had grown in those early years, although they were a weird minority who kept to theirselves until general culture caught up with their privacy paranoias and everyone became silent about private affairs, except among close family. Silence had become the standard practice for a civilised society.

Certainly no personal records were stored in the virtual – apart from what AuZgov could grasp: DNA, health and employment records. And people always, always talked face on face if they had something important to say.

Madrigal, because of her line of work, was very private (crisis scope calls aside) and was surprised she'd succumbed to Jembrana's cool charm, blabbing about her life. But he wasn't holding back either. There was a kind of truce between them, where their guards were deliberately dropped. They both enjoyed the hot blast of kiss & tell about their strange childhoods, caught between cultures, dealing with difficult Dads, and Jembrana's struggle to adjust to a new world, and how he prevailed. Then talk circled back to the recent events again, as talk does.

"And the bomber?" Madrigal finally said, knowing the photon shield around the table meant noone could hear or lipread. "What did the limbic reveal?"

Jembrana pushed his glass around.

"We have trace images of his recent meetings. Several people around him. Caucasian and Asian men, and a darkHaired woman in a pink dress serving beer. There may have been an older woman, but she placed herself in shadow, not enough detail for biometrix. Background memory seems to be a busy urban area, somewhere tropical, possibly Trinity, maybe further north. Also, banqwets, sexual encounters, and in the short-Term memory stronger limbic images of his view of Marko and the girl in the bar – the assassin was concentrating on the targets, so we have the bag clearly, with the bomb, then his leaving up the stairs before the blast. He never saw you in the corner of the room. Also, the traces that appear from his time at the Ville don't include other people, so he's a fly in. They prepped elsewhere."

"Has he talked?"

"Not a bel."

"Can I have a session with him? Just straight interview room job. No Folly at my back."

"Don't see why not. Your file says you have the security qwals in the area."

"So you'd know by reading my files from cover to cover that I am a highly trained operative?" She laughed and waved her wine stem in a salute. Her flirtOut suprised even her.

Jembrana grinned broadly. "I'm glad to hear it," he said, and waved an aide over.

"Yovo – get onto the barracks and let them know Dr Phipps will be interrogating prisoner X at 7.30 in the morning. And you and Ricki can retire for the nite."

*

Neither spoke. By then they both knew what was next.

Jembrana led her to his private qwarters on the 7th floor, through his vast living room and into his spacious boudoir, with its long balcony, and dim, crushed purple lights. The lights were low, which turned them both into shadows. Madrigal and Jembrana stood on either side of his enormous bed and disrobed. Even doing that gave her a rush of pleasure, dropping all the pretences of a public life. Her soft dress and pants flopped to the floor. Standing there, without a stitch. Last time she'd sexed had been, well, more than a year ago.

Naked, he was not as lean as she had thought. Must be wearing underSkins. A little pudgy, with a slight middleAged belly, large upper arms, and a jowlette, which was more prominent without the collar in place, but smooth enough skin. They slid into bed where he sat up and pulled a small drawer open, to access and imbibe zizz.

"Want some?" he asked, passing the paper flute. She never used the stuff and shook her head gently, but looked forward to the burst it would give him and the pleasure he would then bring to her. He pressed Madrigal back into the new crisp sheets and they kissed for a time. Jembrana then straddled across her like some giant golden xmas beetle, his pleasant round face smiling benignly above her, his lips kissing her until she went beyond the places of the day, and all that weird internalised grief over Bluestone, the worry about her team and Toddy, the weight of responsibility.

They rocked together, grunting softly and coming separately, with low sighs. Had been slow and pleasurable, she thought. She turned and let Jembrana move into her from behind. He was starting to become more animated, more focussed all round, his teeth and tongue gently on the back of her neck, his big hands playing with her. He knew what he was doing so she just let him do what he wanted to do until they groaned and collapsed together. She was somewhere else, after that. Far away from Cap. They lay still for while recovering, Jembrana holding her qwite delicately.

"This is delicious behaviour for a security chief," she said eventually. "Does it happen often with other ladies?"

"I have my camp followers," said Jembrana mysteriously. What did he mean by that, she thought? Girls from off the street? Soldiers? Young (or old) assistants? This guy could get away with anything. Balinese people, she remembered, seemed a little more socially flexible when it came to sexing than AuZgov advocates of Purity & Virtue, including she admitted, herself.

"My exWife even visits me occasionally," he said with a low chuckle. "And you?"

"I am not in a position to engineer much ... fun for myself," she said. She thought of Folly and how she would like to lie beside his rockHard body, but as a superior officer it was impossible. They'd kissed once when trainees together. That was it. Sometimes she managed a short "romance" back home in Perth with a business contact or 2 after a boozy dinner. Nothing while she was publicly a Courier. She knew Bluestone had lusted after her, but he'd never ever tempted her. He was twice Jembrana's age, at least. "I get away with occasional sex back home. My ex husband certainly doesn't have visiting rights."

"Always good policy to keep on terms with your former partners," said Jembrana. "You never know when you'll need them."

"Not mine, unfortunately," she said. The x was somewhere in Europe anyway, working at some university. Never in contact with her or Todd. A disappointment. She didn't want to think of him.

She turned over in the damp sheets – even in cooled rooms the outside humidity penetrated – kissed him and stroked his skin.

"I might shower."

"I might join you."

In the giant shower area, fragrant steam and warm water soaked her hair as they soaped. The water cascading across her face was pleasant and cleansing. On the spur she crouched in the water spray, and pulled him towards her – she nuzzled up, and massaged him with the palm of her soft wet hand, trying to jumpstart him again – and it didn't take long. The zizz kicked in once more, and he lifted her onto the bathroom bench where they sexed again. This time the sexing was robust and noisy. They climaxed hard, grunting together, laughing afterwards, as if they needed a valve for both stresses and pleasure.

"Oh, 'K" she said finally leaning her head back against the hard mirror looking at his smiling face. She lowered her legs from the bench and looked down from where she was perched. He even looked lithe now, though it was some sort of postSex optical illusion, and a bit pleased with himself.

"Let's talk in bed now. Too much action."

"Yes, let's."

He had lovely, very absorbent, giant towels as befitted the Security Chief of a territory of 85 million people. She dried off and as she crawled back into bed with him, felt his eyes scan her breasts and belly.

This was Jembrana, a new lover, so his candid eyes didn't worry her like when she was on public duty and men canvassed her body rather than listening to her. That was always rude and annoying.

They lay awake for a while, returning to the world, him zizzing, her coming down from another high entirely, talking about the qwaziNew nation, the pressures from the massive population and his tactics to keep the peace. Politics was never far away.

Jembrana spoke of Luff running around, shoring up the state, and observed that the Premier was beginning to lose his political touch, which he thought was a pity.

"Luff'd never had any grace and charm to leaven his tough decisionMaking persona," he mused. "The job is too big for diplomatic approach, so he jettisoned the niceties a long while back."

"He may never've been a charmer. He's from NorthAuz," Madrigal murmered.

"Qwite so, but he's becoming even more prickly," Jembrana said.

Madrigal, still damp, thought the man beside her was a mite narky 'bout Premier Luff.

"My own people, the refugees from ASEAN and Timor and Melanesia, they just want peace and security," Jembrana said. "Noone is willing to get angry about the food shortages and shelter problems. ASEAN and AuZgov did the right thing, years ago, to make room for those who were dispossessed by the forces of the Cloud. They are grateful to be given a second chance. This makes it easy for me."

"A second chance. That sounds good," she said.

She turned and looked at the face staring at the luminous blue ceiling. The eyes looked sincere and thoughtful. Hers crinkled into a smile.

"What's going to happen then?"

"I worry of the violent outrages of the past few weeks, such as the Great Northern bombing which was all across the meeja. I worry this will turn on us like a snake and bite the whole community. My worry is of a ripple effect that turns bad."

Is that why you listened and watched the entire mission at the Nest, she wondered.

She said softly, "The incident at the Nest will never be made public, however outrageous. These events are about one man and what he knows. This is about Marko and his product, his strokes. Hegs in other jurisdictions want his knowledge. It's nothing to do with Cap."

They lay in silence.

"Have you ever considered resigning and moving into politics," Jembrana finally said. "Considering your family's business, money. Your skills and connekts. That would be a second professional chance. There will be an election in 5 years' time. You are a very, very attractive candidate. We could form an alliance if you did that."

What sort of alliance, she mused. Romantic? Political? Business?

He felt her silence. "I'm just speculating," said Jembrana. "Rhetorically. You don't have to answer."

"My answer is just this: our enthusiasms in your big bed tonite will cost me more than a few millimetres of skin if my superiors find out."

Jembrana looked at her in the blue shade, with his hooded eyes and qwizzical smile.

"Don't worry," he said in a voice glazed with irony, "your secret will slip out, Dr Phipps, like water under a door. This administration is a seething nest of spies and gossips. The duumvirate sets up for 2 eqwal leaders who have instant followers and on the flipside, instant critics. But I'm used to that. I'm used to Luff and his prudery. He's getting worse as he gets older, you know. Wouldn't put it past him to get right back to Centrl himself with the information.

"So, Maddy, be like me. Just do as you please and ignore the critics. My grandfather was a Prince and, while that is old currency, it doesn't hurt to approach life in that way. You are answerable only to yourself in the end and whatever ethical framework has formed in your heart. And anyway, you are not just a Senior Courier, you are a Phipps."

Easy for you to say, Prince Jembrana, she thought with some foreboding. But she smiled anyway.

KINGDOM 1

FLICK got back to the boat late, showered in the cubicle, dressed in a fresh xTop and shorts, then sat with her legs over HER bow, banging her bare heels on the hull of HER boat, drinking one of Andaman's leftover beers and looking out to the island.

It was dark, but the bay was smooth thanks to the barrages, and necklace of lights strung along the island foreshore threw spears of red and white reflection into the dark bay while the channel lights winked.

Pretty.

Notwithstanding the happy flush of boat ownership, Flick had spent an almost fruitless day searching for answers, until a journo, who she knew had been following the story, intimated that all the players in the bombing were under arrest in the barracks. She'd guessed this, but it was still a tricky. How she'd get to see Andaman, she knew not. She was relieved that he was held, protected in the barracks.

The local Brigade was on high alert. A lethal bombing in their qwadrant, or even in Cap, had sent them fanning out in a frenzy, like meat ants from an anthill, to protect the colony. She'd seen patrols in the street and black cruiser cars had hurtled past between scooters and pedestrians as she'd caught slower busses around.

She'd bought that sneaky, sleazy journo from Ch343, Slade Choo, some beers at the Flinders Tavern and he'd happily unloaded for some hours on the hunt for other bombers and assassins, a hunt that had the 'tropolis enthralled and worried. Choo was always a sucker for a beer.

"Flick, just the teev of the bombing of the Northern Lights and those burnt matchstick bodies being hauled out on sheets hit both home, the panic button, and everyone," he enthused.

Slade had 'specially focussed on the action ever since. There was a large international meeja consortium in the Ville that was following the story as well, so Choo and Ch343 were in hot competition with them.

"Those bastids are aggressive, but don't have the local licks," he said. "Connexions at the barracks tell me one guy is getting the full limbik probe. Imagine that Flicks! You are reduced to mindJelly after those."

He crouched over his beer as if it was a bone. She hoped like hell it weren't Andy Marko getting the treatment.

Choo'd suggested further examination of the salient facts at his apartment, but she'd fended him off. As they parted ways she'd succumbed and halfPromised he could visit the boat at some point, but fudged where it was berthed.

Later that nite, when Flick boarded the boat from the creaking marina she called out, but Kingdom wasn't there. She scowled. Clearly he hadn't listened to her instructions to stay put and hidden. Instead he'd gone rogue, as usual. She'd expected him to decamp to some drinking hole to throw back liqwor and blind himself to the realities of his present and past.

Would no doubt sleep the nite in the scrub, covered in dew, like a wounded animal.

Curled up on the couch in the boat's saloon, Flick started leafing through the mottled first aid book that Herman Volk had given her to help bolster her nursing identity. She knew most of it, of course. Grandada and Channing had both taught her the medikLore when she was a young kid. Resuscitation, wound cleaning, suturing, breaks, bandages. HeartThumps when lifeSigns stopped, poultices and bush medz. She hadn't worried a skerrick when Volk had deemed her a "nurse". She well knew how to medik. Up at the Nest, emergencies could happen with the snap of a branch, or if you were caught out bush in a thermocell. Or a snakebite, or a bullet wound from a lampjuice addled maddy. Everyone was taught how to deal with it all. And the accidental death of her mother in that storm had made the young Flick determined to medik to the max.

She leafed through the illustrations, taking great interest in some of the details on blood transfusions. That was something she hadn't got in the medic kit on the boat. A test kit for blood types. She made a mental note to buy one.

Flick roused herself from the couch and ate a defrosted prawn wrap, then went to one of the bulkhead cupboards and fished out the back half of a detachable oar and wrapped it with cloth and visiTape to make a decent club, stowing it along the top of the couch in the saloon. Just in case.

She sat back, sipped another beer, then considered Andaman and their strange relationship. His longTime dependence on her for casual human contact and conversation. Her sense of comfort in his (usually) cheery presence, and her awe at his seemingly endless wealth.

While she'd never think of herself as a lit candle, she did see Andaman as some sort of moth. A rich, handsome moth that hung at her bar, or walked her home in the evening with a peck on the cheek, qwite often, before he made his way up the thin stairways to his house on the cliff. Parting as friends, rather'n lovers.

She didn't care much about his womanising because that was his bizz, and she enjoyed the times they'd frolicked in bed, but mostly he was her friend, and when she'd told Kingdom she cared for Andaman, she meant it. And mebbe after the last few days she felt that much closer to him. He'd sought her help. Out of everyone in the Ville, he ran to her. Mebbe it wasn't just about the boat.

Soon she dozed on the couch and woke with a start to a crunching noise above. Her father. Home. And falling against the outside of the cabin.

"Girl," he shouted, "let me in, fuck it!" She could almost hear his teeth grinding in rage.

He was roaring drunk.

"Sleep it off on the deck," she shouted. "I'll make you breakfast in the morning."

"Let me f'king in," shouted Kingdom. She could hear him weaving to the cabin hatch. She dashed over and slid the locks across. She wanted no smashing, no vomit, no piss in her boat.

"In!" There were some crashing blows on the hatch. First with fists, then applying his heel with massive force. "In!"

A force of nature, they'd called him, up at the Nest. Her disobedience enraged him. She started shaking – not from fear so much, but as a reaction to the brutal slamming of her boat. Fear and anger.

"Stop it, Dad. Stop it. Where have you been?

"Up Ross River Tavern with some boys ... good boys! Not like you, you foul bitch!"

She didn't take the curse personally, but she did take personally the destruction of her boat. The fabric of the door started to splinter. Kingdom crashed his shoulder and the door cracked. His hair was knotted and his hand was bleeding, eyes enraged with alcohol and madness. He was even slavering with spittle. His filthy bulk rushed through with a triumphant growl, and he swung a fist at Flick who stood stockstill in front of him. She swayed out of the way, but not qwite qwickly enough and a couple of knuckles connected with her jaw.

A powerful force knocked her backwards onto the couch cushion. Triumphantly, her crazed father leapt to try and sqwash her. Flick thought she'd been ready for him, but caught offGuard by the sudden punch, she swivelled across the couch and grabbed the end of the oar she had prepared earlier, stood, and smashed the homemade club across Kingdom's head. There was a lull while he registered the blow. He started laughing as he collapsed into a drunken stunned unconsciousness. There was silence. She looked down at the slumped figure, its face sunk into a pillow on the couch. It groaned. So she hit him again, smashing him sideways. She looked at her father for a few minutes, catching her breath and conqwering the trembling which worked across her arms and torso.

He had always been a savage drunk. The padded club was a trick of her mother's. Most times, when he woke in the morning, he would have no memory of being struck unconscious. She supposed his laugh had been a dim reflexive memory of those times.

Flick was a wiry, strong person, and she dragged the limp body of her father onto the deck, and tied him with some tight knots to the railing.

"Never ever do that again, old bastard," she growled KingdomLike, for after all, she was his daughter. She tied his legs together to make sure. Someone shouted, "You all right, doll?" and she waved at a dim figure 2 boats along. "All handled. Just Dad having an epileptic fit."

"Ok," said the voice, already muffled on the way down a hatch, really not wanting to get involved. The door to her hatch was smashed to pieces.

She went back downstairs and grabbed a sheet and lay on the couch. Even if he woke up now and she undid the ropes, she knew the fire was out of his belly already and he wouldn't harm her.

*

"Flick, girl. FLICK!" It was still the middle of the nite but Kingdom had woken up. She stretched, went to the head and pissed, then climbed in the dark onto the moonlit deck. He was still tied.

"Dab hand at ropes," he said.

"Grandada taught me ropes. You know that," she said.

"Got a pill for me head?" he wheedled.

"Not yet. What do you want to tell Andy?"

The old man was still half drunk and dazed.

"Andy? Oh, yeah. Your bloke. Give me some water and I'll tell you."

"Promise?"

"I'm dry. I'm fartin' dust, girl. Water ..."

She got him water. She didn't deny Andy was her bloke either.

He grabbed the flask with 2 tied hands and unsteadily drank, smacking his lips. "Andy. Yes. A few weeks back I was keeping tabs on a few of the boys up behind Old Laura. You know. They were making sly grog and being disreputable. Nothing too bad. Running it down to Trinity with old Channing and co. One boy was like you. Born out of permissions. An abomination as well."

"Thanx for reminding, Dad".

"You were a cute little abomination in your time but."

"That's enough, Dad," said Flick, crouched in front of him. "Cut the bullshit. I wasn't an abomination. I was your daughter and after mum was killed, you left us ... in both your head and in your heart. And you're still somewhere else."

"That's not true, girl." Kingdom started tugging at the ropes. He sounded whiny, rather than irritated.

"You know it's true, Dad," she said.

"I never ever left you with my heart. Head, yes. I'll agree to that. Head went elsewhere and it wasn't pretty. I've been a bushpig, worse than you'll ever know. But you're still my daughter. I have always looked out for you."

She knew his justifications were false. "Go on with your story," she said with a voice that was tired and resigned.

Kingdom took a moment to compose himself. He was upset that the scab of their history had been ripped off, far more than the fact he was shackled to the boat.

"Ok, girl. So be it. Boys said some militaryType recruiters had come through wanting help snatch a young bloke in the Ville. Lift him and bring him north for an extraction. The young bloke was a businessman called Andaman Marko. The militaries were from a syndicate, which one of them named, after a litre or 3 of Laura lampjuice, the White Lady, but you know those big bizz conglomerates, they're from all over these days. The blokes had cash, a plan, and gear. What more does a bushpig want?"

"So you agreed."

"Naw. Not then. I gave Kingdom's blessing for their party to proceed through the Cape, but I took off north. Then they got in touch a coupla days ago. After Andaman was rescued by the Slotters. Got onto me immediately. Offered a $100,000 New if I knock him off. And that's why I'm here."

"Kill him?" she said cautiously, as if his words hadn't sunk in.

"Course, love." He took another untidy swig of the water, his hand still clamped to the railing. "They said: 'Find his captors, find him. Kill him.' They wanted him dead."

Flick bit her lip at the knowledge. She knew he was a brigand, but the thought her dad was a hired killer, targetting her friend, shook her to the core. Humanity had left murder behind because the fights were now with the weather, not each other, and no matter how rough her upbringing, those dictums had well sunk in.

Her father looked at her with bloodshot eyes and smiled.

"I'm from the past, love – from another sorry time. I'm a real bad dood. You don't want to know any'o that, so I've never told. But like I said. I look out for you, always have done. Now I know how you feel 'bout him, I'd never knock off Marko, even for a $100,000New..."

Flick felt like she was going to cry. Break down and cry. Instead she bit the inside of her cheek and kept listening to her raving murderous Dad.

"... Naw, naw, wouldn't do," he continued. "But my best advice is to stay clear from him for a bit, because I don't want you caught up in any crossfire."

"Dad, what are you talking about?"

"I know all about crossfire – I spent a lifetime dodging it. Believe me, it's not pretty."

MADRIGAL & ANDAMAN

MARKO was having a tasteless breakfast in the barrack precinct caff. His kopi stank of chemicals, and the eggs, which he pushed around with a spoon, were cold. He was dressed in a cotton shirt, a teflite jacket because the aircon was too cold, denims and boots, and wasn't feeling glammed. In prison, glammed isn't a highOrder think.

A few low security inmates and guards were moojjing around in the room, having breakfast or reading their clamBs. His precious clamB was locked in a safe somewhere. He was pretty sure the milisi and Slotters who'd picked him up had deactivated the clamB's deadman trigger, sucked it dry of info and streamed it through to their masters, encrypted. So now AuZgov would have the guts of his feather codes.

That depressed him, in concert with the 2 days of debriefing, which left him mentally stagnant. Worse, as he was claustrophobic at the best of times, being locked in a cell caused serious insomnia. Andaman knew he wouldn't be criminally charged or sent to trial, cos he hadn't harmed a fly, so the security measures were for his own safety. And after what had happened up north, he was unlikely to bolt.

In fact, even tho his brain was hazy, Andaman had been designing, in his head: 1) a lateral program to find his goddamn lurker in the various frames, and 2) a personal security plan to hire people who looked like those Slotters, and 3) a better, sneakier, & more elegant feather code.

Because Andaman was determined to go back to his old ways.

So much so, he had agreed to talk to the tekkies at the Spokes about aspects of his program as a deal to cut the AuZgov leash. He hated the leash.

The caff was clean & littered with potPlants. Unfortunately the air smelt of old fried oil. Not Marko's sorta place.

Across the vast room a door slid wide. Folly and Pearl entered, still armed but without their scary battleskins. They posted at the door and then Dr Madrigal Phipps entered and started to weave her way, elegantly glammed, through pot plants and tables towards him. She spoke to a waiter who took a kopi order.

"She'll be sorry," thought Andaman looking at the avid waiter.

Dr Phipps then made a beeline to his table.

"Morning, Marko," she said, sitting down. She looked tired, but cheerful. The kopi arrived and she looked at it without interest. "We'll be lifting out later this morning. They want you at the Spokes for technical debriefing today. Whatever needs to be packed you should go to your room and pack. And we'll release your clamB to Folly and Pearl. They will form a personal detail to your impersonal device." She laughed.

"Ok," said Andaman in a small voice. "You ok?"

"Just been in the brigg with the bomber. Dirty bastard. Told him he missed. That gave me some satisfaction. Sullen little prick."

"Did he say anything?"

"Got a bit out of him, a bit. Reckoned he was innocent by-stander. Bomb wasn't his. Must have been someone else."

"So what happened? Did this whoozit admit to anything? What about the Bluestone murder?" Andaman's face started to contort. The violence was all too raw for him, the blood and the smoke at the Northern Lights. The flight into the heart of a thermocell. Guns. This woman who had hauled him out of not one, but 2, certain death spirals, the same woman in front of him, sitting qwietly, now might have some answers.

Dr Phipps slowly answered: "He smelt of Darwin. That smell of the far north – saltwater, frangipani, mildew. I said: *You're from way up north. Darwin.* He said no. He was lying. I said: *You are connected to some Heg and you need certain persons' dead.* His eyes said: *How did you know?* It's what happens after limbic probes – they think you know far more than you do. Silly pricks. *Why dead? Have you stolen his strokes?* He was like a cement block. No reponse. He doesn't know. I said: *Where are the others parked in the Ville?* Got an iris flash for that one, which is a surefire afterEffect of a probe. He is petrified of exposing his people and the qwestion hit deep. The iris flash indicated that there is probably still a team in town."

"Team?"

"From whichever hegemonic organisation he belongs to." Madrigal Phipps pursed her lips in thought. The waiter came over asking whether Marko wanted another kopi.

"You can warm this one up for me," he said, handing the guy his cup. The guy looked unimpressed.

"The bomber was a small bloke. Smaller than I had picked in the club. His body was extremely tense. Didn't want to blurt a thing. Four out of 10 of his knuckles had seized." She laughed. He didn't know whether Dr Phipp's was serious.

"So did you get him to do the iris flash thing again?" asked Andaman, now intrigued at the tactics of his jailor.

"Twice more. They are a remnant reaction to having probes behind your eyes and the limbic system is still in flux. He gave away, also, that you were definitely the target and they have a lethality brief."

"So they won't stop until I am dead?"

"Yes. So we are off to the gloriously cool Derwent Estuary, away from an unknown team with a lethality brief. That was about it from the prisoner – the effect faded, and I got no further with his oscillating pupils. Good trick but."

"I'm impressed." He was scared of Dr Phipps and her skills.

"Simon Bluestone taught me that one. When we couriered overseas talking to all sorts, we'd watch their eyes, their pupils. Pupils of minor functionaries, shop assistants, waiters, criminals, targets. Job was often so boring he turned things into a game. Bluestone told me there were excellent pickings with the drugged, the zizzed and the brainwaved, and diminishing returns from the sober and normal. But people who've gone through the gamut of probes and whatNot ... easy pickings."

*

Madrigal felt a lurch of sorrow, qwoting Bluestone verbatim, and then felt bad about having privately cussed him hours before he died. But he wasn't to have known. They were still friends.

She looked at Marko, cool as a cuke, sitting on a tinPressed chair in a prison cafeteria. Looked more relaxed than the day before, feeling safe behind bars, tho' dark rings under his eyes gave the game away. She didn't need special skills to see he was tired.

As she took a sip of kopi, she wrinkled her nose at the unpleasant taste.

Andaman said, "Before we leave town, I must collect a hard drive from my house. No tricks. It's important." His heart was beating, hoping that he'd be permitted to go home one more time."

"I'll have to clear with Centrl," she agreed. "Be ready to lift at 3 then. Flight's at 5."

*

The road, which curved through the pandanus palms and rainforest greenery to the top of the hill almost made Andaman cry. They took the old road with its sweeping views of the bay and the city trowelled like stucco cement across the mountains behind, the glittering river and estuary.

One hundred years ago and more, it had been a dry brown place, but now as storms were common, the hill was verdant with grevillea, palms, fig trees, syzygiums. Parrots and blue-Faced honeyeaters flickered in the branches.

"Nice road," said Folly from the front passenger seat.

Andaman nodded. "Miracle they kept houses off the saddle and allowed some of the park to remain."

The vehicle stopped in the big car park. Brigade vehicles had already cordoned the site off, and Pearl and Folly shielded Andaman as they hustled him down the driveway and round to his house at the cliff face. Brigade officers opened the door into the cool brown, gold and white chamber. His zone, his sanctuary filled with strangers. The whole catastrophe made him wince.

Folly, 2 heads taller and twice as wide as him, muttered into a scope. Pearl was silent, looked amused as she glanced at his prize sculptures and other art. With Dr Phipps leading the way, they hustled him into the cool of the house.

"Where now?" asked Dr Phipps in her chilledOut voice.

"Downstairs to the plant room."

They descended staircases to the underside. The Slotters were impressed with his massive swimming pool which doubled as the cooling system. "Could do decent laps in that," Folly observed.

Into the plant room with the tech and mainframe, which he'd decommissioned a fortnite ago when he sneaked north.

Andaman knelt and slid a cement panel across to the hidden safe in the floor. It was twenty centimetres thick and lined with live cloaking agents. He pulled out 2 drives and handed them to Folly who slid them into a bag. He'd shredded other drives when he'd fled – ones that would incriminate. But these were workhorses. His archives.

"Any more hideyHoles?" Madrigal asked.

"Only the one," said Andaman ruefully.

Madrigal glanced into the hole, then snapped on a torch for a closer look.

"It's furthermore empty," she said. "Say bye'd'bye to your house for now, let's go."

Then there was the sound of shouting, a commotion up the steps and out the front. "Wait," she ordered, as if he were a dog. "Pearl, with me."

Outside the front portico, a thin blonde curlyHaired woman was being gently restrained by 2 Brigade men, but she wasn't putting up much of a fight. "Dr Phipps," the curly one said. "I'm …"

"Flick," Dr Phipps answered. "I know. You're Flick. Marko is officially off the grid. Go, now. Go home."

"I have a message for him. From my father." There was a pause. Madrigal Phipps tilted her head and looked at the clear expressive face of the young woman who had no identity. Who had a paperThin past. An *identity Sink,* that's what the boys back at Centrl called it. A woman who was obviously risking everything for a simple message.

"Your father is?'

"From the Nest. He's from the Nest."

She didn't venture a name, and didn't have to. Madrigal knew.

And Flick knew she knew.

"Trace her," said Madrigal to a Brigade man, who looked surprised, but did as he was told. Word was leaking out to the milisi about Dr Phipps and what went down up north. They got wands and checked every centimetre of the slender woman.

"Pearl. Restrain her." Flick was cuffed. "Don't want any handViolence. You'll be set free once you have talked to Marko." Flick nodded dumbly, and with her arms pinned behind they crunched back across the gravel into the shady portico and into the house.

"Flick, what are you doing?" said Andaman when he saw her. He jumped from his couch where he'd been sitting with Folly.

Flick produced a forced smile. "Taking a chance, Andy. I have a message about your attackers. And I suppose I can't tell you in private so I'll tell you now in front of this lot. It's the White Lady."

Andaman looked at her blankly.

"I don't know what you are talking about," he said.

"It's a message from my father. His intent was to come and kill you. Use me to get close up, and kill you. The White Lady told him to."

Dr Phipps stayed qwiet, but her raised eyebrows and head tilt were indicating to Marko to ask more qwestions.

"This White Lady asked your dad to kill me?" Andaman blurted.

"For some reason he didn't go through with it."

"What reason?"

"He saw that I was fond of you, Andy, and for some reason he couldn't do it. I don't know what got into him. It's not like him to turn down a $100,000New."

Andaman smothered a surprised look, and nodded furiously.

"And who is she, this White Lady?"

"Some lady from a Heg, Dad reck'ns. He says that she is powerful and wanting your ample resources. That's all he knows. They have big bucks on your head and even more for your clamB. Got some conglomerate together with Brazilliance, as well."

"Does he say why they want to blow me to smithereens?"

"That's all I know. Please keep safe, Andy."

"We're taking him somewhere safe, Flick," said Dr Phipps pleasantly. She could see the young woman was starting to lose her composure. "Where's your dad?"

The qwestion jogged Flick out of her mood to immediately find her composure again. She laughed. "I'm not telling you," she said.

Madrigal shook her head slowly. "You're gutzy, that's for sure."

"I'm an idiot."

Blunt and final. Flick, who was still cuffed, slowly approached Andaman and reached her face up and kissed him slowly on the lips, eyes shut, as if tasting him for the last time. He looked surprised, but kissed back, putting his arms around her shoulders. Her lips tasted of cinnamon. Watched by an interested crowd, Andaman lingered on the kiss, then pulled his head back.

"You stay safe, Flick," he said.

"I'll see to it," said Madrigal Phipps, now with a powerful bargaining chip. A target. Bait!

"Flick. I'm going to get the Brigade to take you to your house and secure it. I'm worried about your safety now."

Flick nodded. She knew this escapade would bring conseqwences. House arrest.

"We're disappearing for a while. When it's safe, I'll bring Marko back. Ok?"

"Ok," she replied, with a sad voice.

"Do you know any more about this conglomerate?"

"They sent the submarine. And hired those guys for a small fortune. He heard about it from Sharkey in Laura. That's all Dad told me."

"Every time you talk you seem to know more and more."

"That's it," Flick said, closing down the conversation. "I know nothing more."

*

Three had watched the altercation on her scan, parked well down the hill. Dressed like a municipal worker in an unassuming van. Three was pissed off. She'd found the target almost by accident, by the discreet follow of a passing convoy, that she'd scrabbled into gear for. Lazily following, in a most unpronounced manner, through the streets and halfway up the winding hill drive, where she'd parked and launched the infinitesimal drone. A bee.

At least there was some action and she'd found her main kill. And more besides.

When it came to a kill, there was no hope. Far too many milisi in the area, a real cordon for the target and subset target. The bee, which had perched on the eave of the crazy bottlehouse, had picked up some of the content, and it was now clear AuZgov was moving the target out of harm's way, probably south. This could be dealt with, of course, by others. A note would be left in the safehouse for the client.

But she was also interested in the third player. A smaller Curligirl who had intercepted and talked with the subset target, the Courier woman who'd wandered into the Northern Lights after her bunny, only a few dayz back.

Instead of following the convoy back down the hill, when it passed the carpark, she sat in her own V and sent up a second bee following the landV that contained the second prisoner. Didn't go far. Curlygirl was taken to a house not far from the car park and the milisi were not going anywhere. They began securing her property. Three paused for thought at this. Could she be a further subset target. Or a future contact?

Why throw together a milisi guard for a momentary introodr? She rubbed her chin and decided to keep a bee on the eave of the prisoner's house, everWatchful over Curlygirl.

She'd forge on after the convoy now, knowing where it was bound. The lockedDown barracks. Didn't take long for the line of Vs to swing towards Mt Stuart and the milisi complex out through the canal lands. She knew Marko would be buckled into perhaps the only secure compound in Cap. For a milisec she considered a shot at the vehicle that contained him, but shook her head.

No.

Not yet.

She had other plans for that one.

BAABI 1

KINGDOM had followed Flick. Shadowed his daughter under the fierce sun.

He'd been having a beer at the shop up the hill & saw it all. The povvo marina, as Flick called it, seemed a home away from home for people who barely managed to keep their boats from foundering. Hulls speckled with patches, rust and chemical residue. On the verandah at the shop, there was always someone to drink with, and he'd been having a fine time with Freddriqwe, the owner, who wore what he considered a rather small overRevealing xShirt, and a guy named Chaz.

Kingdom saw Flick down the hill hitting the gangway. She'd returned from one of her forays. She called out for him, "Dad, Dad," continuing her "Dadding" along the boards of the boat. After waiting a mo, she realised he weren't there, muttered something rude and then headed back to her vBike.

He had been in 2 minds, but now knew, full well, she was off to involve his name, inform someone, somehow, of the story from the blokes in Laura. She wanted to warn Andaman Marko, which was very diligent of her, but would bring him straight into view. So he'd have to go'n disappear again, which was how he liked it, most of the time.

He started to get a steam of anger, though daren't direct it at Flick – she'd had her fill of his moods. Had a good mind to direct it at whoever she spoke to. Before he vanished, he'd just take a look at what she was talking about, what he was up against. Mebbe have a word.

If she cared for this Marko fellow, a man generous enough to give her a boat, there must be something big between them, like he'd had for Verity. He let Flick head towards town and then sauntered up the jetty to where a bunch of vehicles were parked. Looking around, he took an illegal starter from his pocket and aimed it at a small qBike, which thrummed into life. Looking around again for any semblance of an owner, he then pushed it into the car park and sped off after his daughter.

While he could, most times, move like a wiry land worker, Kingdom was very old. He was weatherbeaten and selfAbused in so many ways: physical, psychic, emotional. Living for so long, using a hundred different guises had taken a toll. His life was a tangle of layers, many kept separate from the others by a wilful amnesia.

Unfortunately, events over the past 3 or 4 days had broken the boundaries of the amnesia and he was being overwhelmed with things he'd hoped to forget. Freddriqwe at the kiosk had been helping with her idle chat, gossip and litres of beer, but that wasn't enough to innoculate him from his tangle of lies.

In his time, Kingdom's moral code had slewed across every habitable philosophical position, like a vBike on a wet surface, barely holding the road and the direction. Now, with Flick on his plate, and those incidents in the Cape, he was hopelessly compromised on several levels. He hankered for the anonymity he'd enjoyed for so long. It was all making his head pulse.

Once, in the soCalled Age of Purity, which he now slagged off as the "age of puerility" to whoever would listen, he had been a hardHeaded young man with Bluestone, Fingal Wen & all the others, when they were "administrators" making sure there was no crime, violence, insurrection or theft; making sure that waves were not made, the unspeakable was never spoken. He'd enforced interventions on criminals, and journalists, and business people profiting off their fellow humans. His "brothers" brought peace and compliance, and with various mechanisms rubbed out the aggro which had plagued previous centuries. A worldwide effort to let "the better angels fly" at the expense of privacy and individuality.

When they were heading from Trinity across the greenGrey waters, Flick had mentioned a "bloke called Bluestone, killed in the Ville," and his mind had reeled.

Bluestone dead? Wasn't he an immortal? They'd been close once. His own son S'mon had been named after Bluestone, though Bluestone weren't to know. None of the old "administrators" ever knew about his son and daughter.

Why. Because even back then he knew that "purity" was a mistake, because it was a mirage. It stultified everything, it did. The arthritis of nothing settled in the world's joints. Purity was essentially entropic.

Slowly and surely, and when *the Blend* intervened, the 2 arms of the body politic had wasted away. There were no ideas, no creativity. Both leaders and followers had become complacent with the big efforts on climate. The vast swathe of communities across the southern hemisphere were not ready for the impact, the anger, the panic, the fear. Millions died in *The Grief* and noone was ready *because of them!*

And the anger was the worse. The blind xenophobic anger.

As a crack administrator (that's what he'd said then – "crack". Ha!) he'd volunteered to lead a team to where the insurgency was happening, go undercover. Fight for purity. In the end, he himself was overcome with the excesses of blood and waste, and had headed to the far north, retired hurt, angry at how it had all turned out. Angry at the people he'd killed and betrayed, parleyed with, got drunk with. Angry with himself, with his "brothers". Kingdom went rogue & cut ties.

Except ties can't be cut. Not ties like that. Not in the inter-connekt.

The insurgency they'd all experienced was terrible, bloody, stupid. M'bers was there. Channing. None knew him, really. Took to him as a leader of men cos he could teach them how to believe & how to kill. There was nothing he or his AuZgov controls could do except ride out the insurgency and try to upend it. When the 3 or 4 insurgent groups turned inwards in their civil war, some of it thanx to his subtle games, there were blindRage massacres of whole towns, including Indijj communities regarded as proGovernment. By the time he'd persuaded the guerrilla groups to combine and finally take their last stand, he'd been there, firing at the government (or over their heads), then running with stragglers from the Gulf through to the Cape in some of the worst weather he'd ever experienced, and that was 50 years ago. Half a century, but like it was yesterday for him. A swamp of hideous experience.

People he knew well, dead beside him. Shot and bombed in shallow ditches filled with mud, and behind long barricades south of the gulf town of Normaton while AuZgov used their old jet fighters thru the burgeoning Cloud to bomb the inurgency torpedo boats in the northern waters and strafe their defensive lines.

The civil war, the rebllion of angry white and Indijj folk who didn't want their lands revoked for climate refugees to subsist on – and they'd all paid the price.

His forces were sqweezed. The torpedo sqwadrons, who'd been sinking those legitimate refugee barges in the Gulf and north of Darwin were forced on land to join the final melee. Their Medik tents underresourced, bodies shuddering in death on blue tarps as projectiles flew over them, fighters fleeing as the AuZGov Slotters and their APVs crashed through the barriers of truckbodies and steel containers and overwhelmed them.

He remembered the smell of smoke, explosives, blood, sweat and shit interrupted by periods of blinding rain and wind. He remembered pulling a kid back behind the barrier with him to find half his jaw had been smashed off by a Slotter bullet. Because of him.

He still dreamed of the kid's face like a summonsed curse. Almost nitely, unless he drank.

Kingdom had enjjineered it all, and his kingdom was Death. The guilt. His injuries. Didn't know what was worse. But he'd lived with both, tried to forget.

After the AuZgov mediks found him in the bottom of a mortar position, and patched him up, he was gone.

His wife, Verity, pulled him out of the worst of it. They'd had Flick, they'd had S'mon, 2 shots of life which she'n'he had fired defiantly at the powers down south, because both he & Verity had been told firmly that they were Noughters. They grew their kids in the forest, a violent border to the Cloud, toughest place on the planet though Cloud cover was there most of the time, shrouding them from HighEyes.

⁕

So last week, when Fingal Wen rang, Kingdom knew it would be bad. Because ties like those – b'tween Wen and him – could never be cut in the interconnekt.

Naturally, Wen didn't say who he was. Not out loud on electronika. The voice of an AuZgov cypher. But he knew Wen's voice and Wen knew he knew.

Wen said that there had been an incident under the cloud north of Trinity. Three people had died and one was his son, conducting an illegal incursion. A kidnapping.

"I'm sorry to inform you of this. Your son was shot and killed. We ran the genome and yours was the closest match, so you are his next of kin. There is no record of this man. We do not know his name."

"That'd be right. For your precious files, Fingal Wen, his name was S'mon, named for our mutual friend. He was my son, but I haven't seen him for a long time," said Kingdom.

He knew that Wen knew that Kingdom didn't give a toss about the whole paternity on the map, DyNAst shit. "N'fact, not for decades. Sad that he's dead." Kingdom had sighed.

His son had walked out of the house near the Nest more than 15 years back, firing personal vituperation at his old man, which was meant to hurt, but just bounced off Kingdom's leathery skin. He had sneered and shot words back, expecting his boy to be home before dark. It was after Verity was killed, when he'd gone rotten in the eyes of his kids. But S'mon never did come home and he had surmised the boy had died, or moved incognito through the cloud to the northern hemisphere. Disappearing was a family talent.

"I have to say again, I am very sorry," said Wen, making the most of the call, because he meant more than just "Sorry your son died", but also "Sorry that our brotherhood was broken," and "Sorry you were minced into pieces by circumstances." Kingdom knew what Wen meant, because they'd grown into men together on the training grounds and in the corridors of influence. But that was a very, very long time ago.

"Thanx," said Kingdom abruptly, and broke the komms to show Wen what he thought of calls from on high. He hated them.

There was nothing worse than a death, as life was so precious. Every single life.

Kingdom shuddered at the thought of his son being shot dead, and how he and Verity had risked it all to have an abomination to prove their love. The skin on his neck and scalp shuddered. He'd seen people shot before, had shot a few himself, and the mess, the blood, bone and the brains ... it was inglorious

After hanging up on that call, Kingdom had washed his face, spat his chopChop juice over the hull and into the water and headed to a shanty tavern miles away, on a jacked vBike (mebbe it was Flick's, anyway, because when he brought it back there'd been no uproar) and went on a blinder with whatever lampjuice they were making out there.

He remembered driving out because the cool air had made him cold and more focussed, and that had just enraged him even more. His shuddering skin had become a wave of pain and grief. All he wanted was to forget his son, his self, and everything around him. And most of all, he wanted to again forget Fingal Wen.

As he drove though the dark, he told himself that there'd be no telling Flick the news. She didn't deserve that hurt. She had mourned for her brother long after he'd left, which had given Kingdom the right royal shits.

Now he was very, very upset. As he roared towards the shantyTavern he thought he saw Flick standing by the side of the road in the nite, but it was a phantasm coming from somewhere behind his eyes. He heard the world swirl angry around him, the cicadas, the whine of the bike, the air on his face.

After that he remembered nothing except waking up with a throbbing head, tied to the boat's rail, hands roped behind him with a fiendishly difficult knot he couldn't undo. A bit like his life.

Or his heart.

*

Kingdom remained as a shadow, another family talent, following his girl, and swung right and saw that they were heading up the wooded boulevard to the hilltop. Thin road. Difficult to remain anonymous, unremarked, and he wondered how to cut through to the summit without being seen.

ThreeQwarters of the way up he swung into a visitors' vehicle station, lined with palms and bougainvillea, which led through the gardens and the tracks. He parked near the toilets and was going to assess a track when he saw a face.

Out of the corner of his eye in a distant vehicle's wing mirror. Serendipity. Or his very good instincts, picking little cues up all over the place, but only alerting him to the important stuff.

The familiar face wasn't looking at him. Seemed to be looking at an internal screen, but that face in the mirror was one he knew very well. To the point where he took a sharp intake of breath and immediately slid down behind a tree. Did his knees actually buckle? The infamous Kingdom Allenby asked himself, so shaken to the core was he.

It couldn't be her? She'd died in one of the last 2 or 3 sorties that they'd run against the AuZgov forces when the whole palaver of the insurgency had exhausted itself and failed. Fifty years ago. Surely she'd died? He'd tried to make it so.

Kingdom had rejuved 4 times, once very early when he was an AuZgov dipshit, then 3 illegal juveJobs in Hong Kong over the years. He'd gone one juve over the limit, and he knew it, and could feel it – like the weird arthritis in his joints – but it meant he still remembered stuff from way back.

She was still blonde, but now like him, slightly cadaverous. She fixated on the screen. Kingdom could see the line of an electronic setup in the back, which smacked of a drone console, so she too, was perving on the meet up the hill. An old-Style beePack with 2 or 3 beeDrones, and a hiVis receiver same as those they'd used for sorties years ago. Before light became malleable, everything was electronic.

Her presence was a very bad omen.

They'd been comrades in arms, once. She musta seen the writing on the wall, had deserted, fled west mebbe? True, he'd never seen her body in the smashUp. Never assume. Good rule that.

The insurgents concluded *the Blend* was happening vowed to stop it. Force of nature, force of arms, force of history – that was their maxim. But he knew the peoples to the north – Timorese, Indons in the Lombok/Flores chain, Papuans. They'd nowhere else to go except Cap, and ultimately what AuZgov done was a transcontinental kindness. Finding some room for those folks tipped out of their country. As the Chinese did with the Bangladeshis, and the Yanks with the Central Americans, not that it did the Yanks much good in the end.

He knew it all the way down to the very fibre of his being, that *the Blend* was humanity – had to be done. But the people he'd infiltrated disagreed and took up arms.

*

Baabi was the worst of the worst.

"Fuck," he thought as he sqwatted, back against the tree, sweating in the heat in the fullness of the day. Should he abandon post and follow Flick up the track to at least eyeball that Andaman fellow and his minders, or keep an eye on Baabi?

No. Had to stay on watch her. He felt so tired, worn down and almost hopeless, but still – job to do. He sank further into the undergrowth and watched carefully. There was no way this sheSnake was going to get near his daughter. One kid dead – he was not going to lose his second, and in his head he sent a rare prayer to the late Verity making good on that promise.

*

Over an hour later the convoy of official landVs and APCs swept down the hill and the small innocuous vehicle he was watching started up and cautiously nosed out. Kingdom let it turn right and down and, once out of sight, he slipped onto the vBike and followed, again the shadow. He knew where the whole 'kit and caboodle' were going. She'd be put under house detention. Into the upStreets of the North Ward where his daughter lived, a house which he'd checked discreetly in the past. Making sure she was alive and kicking.

Kit and caboodle: a Simon Bluestone phrase from way back in the Age of Steam. Bluestone liked his stupid archaisms.

Cars stopped outside the house, and milisi led her upstairs. Baabi tucked herself round the corner and he could just discern through oculars a tiny bee locking onto the house. He was kneeling against his bike under a poinciana, pretending to be fixing the chain. He knew where he'd be parked for a while now, because, while Baabi was exiting the scene, he knew she'd be back when the authorities cleared off.

He drove down to the store on the top terrace, bought some food and a bottle of rum, and returned to keep watch on his daughter.

*

Pushed by the monsoon, the clouds stretched a sticky, oily-Look ceiling over the Ville and the air was like steam. Two milisi were parked outside Flick's house, and her internal lighting was cutting though the louvres of the house wall in an old barcode pattern of bright and dark. Black and steamy, the sort of nite Kingdom knew all his life. Watching, preparing, for battle, for pillage and any other contingencies. Here the preparation was for the protection of his lastBorn.

He took a swig of sharp, sweet liqwor and thought about Flick as a kid, skinny and full of opinion. Her little frame, looking up with that qwizzical face, hanging with Verity's Dad — who'd been much younger'n him, at the boat ramp, fixing nets, or sails, or the hull itself. Fishing with her, discovering her likes and working out all her hates. Little curlyHaired buddy. He smiled and took another swig. He'd look after her, even if she hated him now.

Somewhere the air started moving weird, and he tensed. A qwiet tense. Didn't want to flinch outright. Something was wrong. He swivelled round, but there was nothing behind.

He stood slowly and wandered over the road and looked around once again, down the street to the corner. Only the milisi car parked at her house, with a shadow inside. Castle Hill rose above, a foreboding weight, with its granite cliff face.

Apart from that there was nothing.

Kingdom felt the rain splatter on the back of his neck, a hotSqwall from the sea, and slid against his vehicle once again with the activated rebut shield keeping him dry, although some drips got through, pounding hard into the forcefield. The monsoon, the 3 or 4 month permanency of the cloud overhead, was almost here, passing over Capricornia with its high mango bulb clouds and frightening stormcells rattling windows and drowning the unwary.

The relentless steamy heat carpeted walls and ceilings with mould & brought the edgy fear that lasted while the cloud was present.

He watched Flick's window, lit. He saw the milisi patrol pass and the guy on the top step wave to the vehicle. The patrol thought she was locked down and safe. Well, that wasn't true.

Anyone who'd been through the start of *the Blend* knew that Flick's little flat was the softest of targets. Soft to him, and nothing to Baabi. If she wanted, she could put a rocket – propelled incandescent through the front door to immolate the place. He'd seen her do that a few times in the past.

The hotSqwall passed and he got out of the bike and stood on the wet road, did a 360. He knew the bee on the eave wouldn't have the optics to reach way down the street. It was a 50 year old unit from the time he fought alongside Baabi, there to watch the steps and the front yard and not much more. Baabi and he, with others, had penetrated harder forward bases than this, right the way up to the mountains of New Guinea. She was a pro. She also killed with a savage intensity. Once he had to haul her off a dying man as she pounded him with an electric prod.

"Save yr strength," he'd ordered, "he's dead anyway."

"Not dead enough," she answered with a hiss, trying to strike him with the device, and that's when he first knew he'd turned her into a monster.

The light went out in the house and he looked at the timer. Past 1 am. Late late. 'Ville was mostly asleep. Rain was light on. He imagined Flick sleeping qwietly, hair splayed on the pillow like it fell when she was a little takker.

He hoped her dreams were sweet, but doubted it.

AFTER THE AGE OF PURITY & VIRTUE

CENTRL

CENTRL was not one person, but several. A unit of people, with a CJops, a Commander of Joint Operations, doing the talk. CJops were trained in clear decision making and logistical brains. Absorbing the recommendations (recs), and sorting the order of priorities (ops). Fingal Wen was the Commander, a 3 star, who had been at Centrl on duty during the endTime of Marko's kidnap and thermocell incident. And when Madrigal Phipps, Andaman Marko and the Slotters arrived, he was the CJops on duty that day also.

When told of their imminent hopper, Fingal Wen broke contact, handed over to his 1 star, and wrapped in a greatcoat, personally took the lift to the landing disc at the top of the Spokes to meet the party.

As soon as he stepped outside he realised the clime was unpleasant. A wind was lifting off the greenGrey ocean, and freezing mizzle stung his face. In the distance, he saw clouds scud towards the horizon where the hills of Hobarttown fell from the ends of the earth. Somewhere there, he and 'Arald owned a house, but they never saw it, as both were hermetically sealed for months in the "tin can" beneath his feet. Wen was unsentimental about the house, but 'Arald missed it.

The Spokes top deck stretched in front of him – 2 hectares of steel, mangaPlast, and Komms whiskers, both hex and cone.

Six or so hoppers were parked in one qwadrant, 2 being un-loaded with forklifts. Personnel were moving in & around the eqwipment.

The incoming hopper with Wen's people, was coalescing in the sky, a silver dot speeding towards the tower. Wen watched the hopper float down to land on a disc, correcting for the southern ocean gusts around the Spokes' microclimate, made as the surrounding waters were cooled by plant underneath his feet. A pause, then the hatch was pushed back and the passengers emptied out. Folly, Pearl, Marko, Dr Phipps, Chime and Dante in that order.

What a bunch, he thought.

Dr Phipps in particular – morfing so fast into a brilliant operator, but a problem child. He would be having words later, but now was the time to rejoice in her return. Whatever his current qwalms with Dr Phipps, he was pleased to see the group. His group.

His problem child looked qwizzically at the grizzled, bearded Wen with his blast glasses and woolly coat. He was slapping his sides to try and keep warm.

"Centrl – welcoming us in the sleet!" said Dr Phipps, "How are you?"

"Tops for an old fella," he said. "I was so sorry about Simon. I still can't believe it. We went back a long way."

Madrigal Phipps accepted the condolences. "You did. Much further than me. Brigadier Smith is still hunting the perpetrator, but the task is massive. The city's too big – 8 million people is needle and haystack stuff."

"Indeed," said Wen.

"To be honest, I'd prefer to be in the 'Ville," she added, "finding Bluestone's killers."

"Not your job. You've had your spree to the north. But you are n'fact a Courier, not the law. Need I remind you about your place in the scheme of things, Madrigal. Others to find the killer – yours to acqwit the strong fluid business of diplomacy."

Their heads were close together now, and they spoke soft.

"I know," said Dr Phipps, "but I want to do ... well, avenge Bluestone."

"Vengeance is weakness. You've been taught that," said Wen, ignoring her bitter tone. "Come. Let's go below. It's freezing on this flightDisc."

The party didn't talk in the cylindrical lift which descended, like a piston pulling 7 people silently down, half a kilometre below the waves. Madrigal pondered Wen's words. Folly and Pearl stood like statues. Marko was dumbstruck by the location and his claustrophobia started to itch. Chime held his usual craggy silence. Dante leant against the back of the lift and tapped his fingers. Fingal Wen was just pleased to be warm.

The lift hissed to a stop, and they disgorged in the main reception chamber with its whites, silvers and streaks of shiny timber panelling circled by openings into tubeWays. Deep down, chambers and engineers, analysts and tekkies keeping the AuZtralian world ticking along.

The Spokes was built on the edge of the southern continental shelf and extended out into the very deep ocean waters. While AuZgov used a small part of the facility to coordinate their social security operation, the main job of the Spokes was a factory filter – to keep the southern oceans liveable, the climate under control and the fish and krill alive.

The huge thrum of engines was not just pumping seawater coolant for the stacks, but also the engines and massively long delta points – the actual spokes – which radiated 100s of ks down, then to the east and west, correcting the ocean acidification, resuming carbon and acid. Other massive plants beneath them pulled the heat from the ocean waters, cooled the passing currents and corrected the ocean temperature, turning the excess heat in the ocean into electric power which was gridded to the mainland.

In those more difficult years, AuZgov had built the security base in the same location. Because of its climate corrective infrastructure, there was no chance that it would be attacked unless mutual destruction was assured.

The western hemisphere was also covered by a similar underwater factory run by the Brazilhoz (or the Brazilliance as the more cynical called that hegemony). The other biggies were in Hawaii, and the North Atlantic off Newfoundland, well outside the cloud, keeping the planet habitable.

Marko could feel the engines beneath his feet.

"This way," said Wen. Madrigal Phipps knew his voice very well and followed what was clearly an order, the others in tow.

"Canberra is very interested in the outcomes from all of this," said Wen, as they shifted into his office. Pearl and Folly were stood down and headed to look for kopi. Chime, being a senior officer, stayed.

Wen turned to Andaman.

"Mr Marko, I would like you to accompany our technicians to check their traces of your introodr. You will see the entrails of our methodologies, and I expect they won't surprise you, but to be frank – having protected you, helped you – you must help us. You must clear the air." He introduced Andaman to a pair of technicians who were waiting in the office on side stools. "Dr Lemno and Dr Vu." One was a tall guy with a shock of vertical black hair – he wore a scowl. The other was a small Asian woman, wearing a beige coat over a yellow frock, who looked a bit friendlier, if now qwizzical. Both looked tired, as if all the zizz had been extruded from them. Andaman could tell that they had the eyes of virtual engineers. He'd sported oysterColoured eyes many times in the past.

Andaman nodded. "I understand." He wanted his life back and would do anything to get it.

"Dr Phipps will check in with you later."

*

"This way, Mr Marko," said Dr Vu. They headed down the corridor. "We are amazed at your proficiencies in the virtual, but have some qwestions."

"That's fine," said Andaman, "but first can we look at your traces. I was 'mazed you picked out a lurker and I can find nothing. I have tried. How deep are we here?"

"Oh, around half a kilometre, Mr Marko," said Dr Vu. "The 'big deep' starts here, as we say, over the shelf." She pointed to the left. He could see the flicker of a smile on the face of Lemno. It faded almost as soon as it appeared. Didn't seem very funny to Marko.

Into a lab with screens, caps, the lot. There was noone else in the room. They sat on a range and Lemno played the scans and started taking Marko through the trace, the coding, the petabytes of material, on the blue, and he could still see nothing until a shadowy shape appeared in his transmissions of data, a hollowing out in some of his harpoons that were exiting and coming in.

"Ho ... yes. Lurkier and lurkier," said Andaman. He turned to Vu and Lemno. "I found your breach earlier, but you must have been tracing my work for a while."

"We are being all cards up on the table with you," said Dr Vu. It was becoming obvious that Dr Lemno was the datastream guy, and she was the more empathic one. "That's what we saw, that's what we followed."

"Oh," said Marko, "and you didn't interfere with any of my material?"

"No, no. We just watched."

"Like voyeurs?"

Dr Vu blushed. "Not like that."

"It's ok. All business with me," said Marko. He reexamined the traces, flicking them one after the other to enable him to check the warps in the code and the reshaping of the lurker's data, so they were almost invisibly similar to Marko's.

"This is good. That is so good," said Marko in admiration, flicking the wave images and then the numbers across the screen. "You must have slowed this down to microsec analysis."

Dr Vu looked pleased, and said "Yes," without embarrassment this time. "We were, of course, trying to analyse your scriptbuilds when we saw this shape."

"I'm sure you were," said Marko. "And do you understand my intellectual property?"

"Not qwite," she said, "because it's all compartmentalised."

Marko smiled.

"So, some compartments yes, some compartments no," she added.

"Sorry to make life difficult for you," said Marko pointedly.

"Difficult is a relative concept," said Lemno, speaking for the first time. "Difficulty understanding coding. Difficulty in the back of a sealed landV facing torture. Difficulty fearing death, or here, breathing fresh air in the Spokes, half a kilometre deep." He had soft voice, like soft young skin, or wallMusic. "As far as we're concerned, Andaman Marko, you being here makes it easy."

"Easy to pinch my strokes?"

"You are a citizen. You never harpooned AuZgov mainframe, so, we take it you are loyal ..."

"Mebbe loyal is a relative concept too," said Marko.

"No," said Lemno with a fixed smile. "Loyal is an absolute."

"Let's get to work," said Dr Vu, interrupting the escalating male tones with a bright smile, before any further philosophical badinage occurred.

"How do you do it? How do you tell which communication string is false and which is true?"

And there was the nub of it. How to know which data that hegemonies, syndicates and embassies streamed out from their meetings, their analyses, their decision making was, in fact, the real decision, in a tangle of similar false communications. It was too easy to break a code, so everything was layered. Couriers delivered the info on the genuine article face to face in person.

Marko's genius was in having harpoons and syntax sieves; going between electronic interfaces, and ratifying his "nugget", the true datastream as opposed to the "bad eggs", the falsified structures, transmitted to camouflage the real Komms. Long before the live Couriers revealed any truths, face on face.

Marko had to make a decision, so asked for a glass of water. A stall. He'd been thinking about it all the way from the Ville, and he still couldn't decide to "clear the air" and his prevarication was driving him nuts.

Better than water, an aide brought brewed kopi. He sat his captors and assistants down around a meeting table with red cushioned seats, and while wittering about the tropics, looked into their tired eyes. Was there goodness behind the tired? Empathy? Probably not. Hard nuts from the control centre. They were only being nice because they wanted something.

He remembered Dr Phipps and her lecture on iris and pupil movement, but couldn't for the life of him see any variation in size and shape as he talked. Both sets of eyes looked grimy with exhaustion. He saw brown limpidness in Dr Vu's irises, and a dirty green weariness in Lemno's. Madrigal, and Bluestone before her, must have practised the iris thing.

"Look. The truth is, I changed my strokes slightly, every time. At the beginning of each month I'd do the raw research, talk to people, work out what was burgeoning from the stream-Teevs and tickers. I'd translate programs for words my burrz could attach, y'know, jargon the burrz would stick to. Portuguese, Chinese too – it was about hitting or missing at the margins. And if truth be known, I only placed small bets, but a lot of small bets, so I just nibbled at dividends and things.

"Never wanted to wave my hands and arms in the virtual and say 'Here's me', if you know what I mean. That would be suicide. So, softly and qwietly. Play the margins. However, given the current circs, I was still too obvious. You guys found me. Other guys found me. But with AuZgov behind you, I can tell you what I was looking for, and you can take it from there."

"It's a start," said Dr Vu, her eyes clouding with what looked like concern at his bibbleBabble.

Marko felt pretty good. Safe and well slept. He'd then and there decided to stall again. Too proud of his strokes, the creations which brought him wealth, and in his gut, he felt they were none of AuZgov's bizz. He clasped his hands in front of him at the table and looked Vu and Lemnos direct in the eyes and began his story, hinting that it was more in his instinct and not the coding. He started to bend the truth, ever so slightly. Like one wire pulled from a much bigger piece of electronika.

*

At the same time, Dr Phipps and Fingal Wen were drinking small drams of Tasmanian whisketty, Wen congratulating her on the capture and transport of Andaman Marko. Wen had opened his buffer window on his patch of outer hull and flicked the lights, so they could see bubbles and fish and the massive steel feeder tubes of the Spokes fading into the black.

"Like we're the ones in an aqwarium and the fish are eyeing us from their living room," said Wen with a laugh as a school of tunny passed the porthole.

They reminisced about their mutual friend Bluestone for a while, and Phipps couldn't help feeling depressed about the death of her old boss, with whom she'd spent 2 years of almost every day. She'd banished her frustrations about him.

"Why kill him?" she asked. "I don't get that one."

Wen stood and looked into the black void beyond the glass.

"Either he had an enemy in the Ville. Or someone thought he knew something about them. He gave no indication he was on to a plot?"

"We were there to warn Marko and then come home. That's all."

"Someone tries to kill Marko and probably thinks they've done the job. And they then kill Bluestone, because they think Marko's given up his secrets – Marko's codes, mebbe? And you too. Marko informs and they want the message killed. There you go. All in the timing. Marko lives. They find out. They pursue him."

"Indeed. Marko lives."

Madrigal asked Wen when she could take leave to see her boy. A few days would be good and then she'd be back to work.

"Soon," he said. "You are Marko's mentor now – you have to see this through."

"Could take forever. Andaman Marko will obfuscate, you know that."

"Yes, yes. A given. These guys are lone wolves," said Wen. "We'll eventually understand his precious data methodologies, but he'll resist to the last. CyberSavants think they're smarter than everyone else. Maybe they have an edge when it comes to one small part of the machinery, but the rest of the machinery will eventually outThink them. One slip, and the machinery will chew them up. Andaman Marko's hand is already caught in a flywheel, though he does not yet know it."

"He's pretty scared."

"Yes. He doesn't understand what he's done, but understands there are conseqwences. That, as you know, is where fear often comes from."

"That and thermocells."

Wen smiled.

"Yes. Nice work with the thermocells, Dr Phipps. But not such a good move with Security Chief Jembrana. You know the protocols."

Madrigal was expecting this speech. Relations with senior figures without an AZSIS warrant was a breach, particularly having sexed a rep from ASEAN.

"You are a Courier. A senior person," said Wen. "We almost sent the cavalry in to haul you out of his bedroom."

"Glad you didn't," she said. "Counsellor Jembrana wanted me — made it very plain. I was intrigued with his obsession around the retrieval operation. And qwite frankly, you heard him ... he was in the intel stream for the whole 36 hours after we went north —"

"I think you were intrigued by more than that," Wen said with a scoff. She could see, through his layers of urbanity, Wen's long face rippled with disgust.

"True. He has a nice apartment and soft bed."

Wen snorted. "Don't goad me, Dr Phipps. It'll be etched on your record, this breach. You understand the principle that you are a senior official, and the event was out of wedlock."

Madrigal smiled thinly. Event! Wedlock! Old chestnuts from the fading Age of Purity being used against her by a grand old man. Her generation sexed when they wanted to, at least she did, and she was generally discreet.

He went on: "But you're not to be immediately disciplined — you are too old, smart and involved in this shemozzle for that." His tone was tart. Someone of her rank, sexing with a foreign bureaucrat, with all the risks. He certainly was not pleased.

She waited. She knew Wen was curious.

"So, did you find out about this obsession?" he finally said.

"Not really. He's a complicated character. He seems to distrust Premier Luff, but that always happens in a job sharing arrangement at that level."

"And you got that intel from him, by sleeping with him? Could you not have just had a chat at dinner?"

"No. We sexed because I was attracted to him," she said firmly. Wen winced. It was a genuine wince. His was a different generation that honoured marriage and reviled sexual experimentation. Bluestone had pretended to be the same. "That is the truth. There was some talk about my father's business – that intrigued him, but as you know, I am always uncomfortable discussing Phipps Industries with colleagues. That is my father's business."

"We know that's not true," said Wen darkly.

"Well, we didn't go there apart from superficialities."

Failing to be candid with your superior was unheard of. While she held her face in check, Madrigal felt physically wrenched at minimising the conversation about her family, and, of course, Jembrana's weird musings about future alliances. Though she'd never lie to Wen – lying being such a taboo – she downplayed the part of her pillowtalk with Jembrana that was meaningful. The fact was, Jembrana had mused about an alliance in a world after the Duumvirate, the shared administration of the continent's north. But they were just musings, she told herself. The exPrince could have just been talking about a romantic alliance.

"Anything else. Is the security chief in control of his patch?" Wen looked at Madrigal's serious face as she thought about it and picked her words.

"Apart from bombers and assassins, yes. He keeps the peace. Eighteen million people in his patch. It hums along – just."

"I think this information about his distrust of Luff is worrying. I'll consider ramifications. Jembrana, by all accounts, is an excellent appointment. Luff is, by all accounts, the perfect administrator."

Madrigal finished her glass and stood. "Frankly, I think it's simply the natural frisson that happens when you put 2 people in charge of one nation at the same time. There will always be chafing. I'm sorry, Centrl. I am going to The Hierarchy and sleep."

"So come for breakfast," said Wen. "Come for breakfast with myself and 'Arald and we'll talk more."

Wen watched his best operator (now Bluestone was gone) leave. She had been warned. He sniffed once and pondered the next move.

*

At The Hierarchy, the classy hotel within the Spokes where rooms were booked for Madrigal's team, the concierge gave her a wand and allocated a room. Her bag was already stowed in the apartment. As a Senior Courier, she received preemo accommodation. She sat in her apartment office and immediately scoped Todd and promised that she would see him very soon. He'd had a good day at school and was full of news about his friends, and was wanting to know when they'd be going north again. She told him, after storm season. Madrigal flicked off, feeling as empty as she always did seeing him on a screen without touching or hugging him. Her 2D son.

"Bath," she said. The bath started to fill as she added, "Medium hot with bubbles." She poured a restorative drink to cheer her up, locked the door, covered the one camera she could find with a pair of knickers, stripped, and lay in the huge tub full of warm water, thinking of Jembrana and his rather wicked ways. Half an hour later, she was falling asleep on a far less comfortable bed than the one she'd slept in 2 nites before.

*

Andaman's strokes were a syntaxSieve in the program called SQwizzy, which sat, at that moment, in one of the hardDrives he had retrieved from the safe in his house.

SQwizzy analysed the message strings which a hegemony or company, cartel or State, transmitted about a deal or a secret. The programs picked up the similar subject strings, and ran through the grammar and the nouns, and especially adjectives, in each message.

Andaman had explored the premise that when people lie, they tend to complicate word structures so the syntax gets more knotted. He found, on balance, that the simplest, most direct messages, were the true ones, and that out of, say, 5 or 6 messages concocted to fool lurkers and electronic surveillance, the truth was in the straightest string. The messages he caught were invented by specialists, clerks who came from creative faculties, who often couldn't help themselves from inventing detail. Even when the message was: *We will buy 300 tonnes of sphagnium, and the price is within the range of $New400 a tonne,* by even just the third wrong version all manner of detail was being added to "fool" the surveillance. The program assessed the developing versions and scrutinised them, working back to the original, which was more often than not the true reflection of any situation. And, of course, it was often in code as well.

The simplicity of Andaman's lucrative little theory belied the complexity of his program.

The initial harpoon had to find a datastream of messages, then pinpoint similar messages despite some being dressed up to be qwite different. The program had to retrieve these, and then move on to syntax digestion, done by SQwizzy.

The reveals of the coding would be analysed. Then followed the automated investment that the program put into the market to buy script – stock, or futures. The whole program had taken Andaman 5 years to design and test and he wasn't wanting to share with anyone, let alone AuZgov.

The illegal harpoons were a beautiful thing. Their booby traps were set off when pinged by security programs. On eradication, which security would flag as "threat neutralised" his program would harpoon a further, even more discreet, qwincunx into the "neutralised" message and the 5 nodes would piggyback to the security centre, and boy, they would burrow. A beautiful thing. Why share this with anyone?

Andaman lay awake in The Hierarchy, his own bed deep under the ocean in a room far less fancy than Madrigal's, and pondered the conundrums that faced him. The qwilt was warm and a console glowed dim green beside the bed.

For SQwizzy & Andaman, in the end it came down to numbers and his (their) commercial investments. Andaman, in better times, sat under a shadeClothed bayside table, looking at the yachts and the waves, making money and thinking of things he could buy.

He sighed in the dark. His was a supreme feat of interception & analysis.

He knew if the lurker had got past the barriers and into SQwizzy, past the firewalls, and the dummy software, someone else had his strokes by now, which to him wasn't that much of a personal disaster, but to a government that used the multiple deflection strategy was probably catastrophic. The program could pick the real from the unreal across a plethora of electronic messages before Couriers could even arrive to decode. Or messages could be sent in other ethery ways.

And that may be why they tried to kill him. He was able to reverse engineer and find out the culprit. But they wanted SQwizzy to themselves.

Andaman was thinking that the hegemonies would invent & shift to some other ruse to protect data. At the moment, the coded strings and decoding Couriers worked for them, but some bright spark would come up with something else. He knew they'd been investing in telepathy research for years, but he hadn't put a zack in that basket. He snorted. The telepathy conundrum had cost billions of $New and millions of research hours, but research had fallen well short. Brainwaves might exist, but they don't transmit between skulls, they had found.

No – everything was still stuck on the old virtual and everyone could see everything and still nothing was secret. Coding could always be broken, but lies were harder to pick.

AUNTIE

HER AUNTIE sat on the end of the bed, wrapped in an orange acrylic blanket. Her charcoalSkinned face glowed gently reflecting the clock light. Through the haze of sleep Madrigal could almost smell the woodsmoke and sweat. Auntie's face was puckered with age, but she had a childish smile, as if delighted to see her greatNiece.

"Hello, Maddy luv," said the auntie in English, in the contralto tone that Madrigal remembered. The auntie then reverted to language. Madrigal listened intently. She wondered how the auntie had found her, deep under the ocean, in a giant pressurised tin can.

"Look after little Toddy. He's a good one. He needs to go to country again ... you take him and the boys will look after him."

Madrigal knew in her heart it was time to go back, but she was stuck with the stupid Marko job.

"Toddy is an important boy. He needs to be an important man," said the auntie, one she knew well from long ago ... was it the turn of the century? Probably. Madrigal took such nocturnal visits and conversations extremely seriously. An elder who had died in 2105 or '06?

"Oh, and there's a k'daitcha man out looking for you and the tagalong. You gotta watch for your little tagalong friend. But most of all, look out for Toddy ... so I got to go, dear. You're looking well."

Madrigal slipped deep into sleep, then woke, brightly. On a knife edge. Like déjà vu.

The little tagalong friend certainly wasn't Todd. He was safe. She reached for the intercom and called the front desk, slid into skins and shot out of the bedroom and down the corridor.

*

They zipped Andaman's door open and entered, flicking the light. She could sense the introodr immediately. An old trace of cologne or shampoo, and breath. Not Andaman's. And a dark brush of shape against the lighter carpet grain. A weird shape.

Andaman's room was not as big as hers, but still plush and spacious – it was The Hierarchy, after all – and there was a lump in the far bed about ten metres away, where Andaman lay. Madrigal and the security chief gave him a shake and Andaman groaned, already half asleep. "Wha–"

Madrigal checked his eyes as he woke. "He's 'k," she said to the security guy. Andaman was fully awake now.

"What's happening?" he asked.

"Sh," said Madrigal, her hand gesturing for qwiet and stillness.

She 360'd the room, and sniffed.

Andaman thought: What's with the sniff? This woman's mad. The security chief, Colonel Starréd, raised a qwizzical eyebrow.

Madrigal's hand stretched to the security chief's belt and, to his surprise, she detached his zap, lifted it and pointed to the far corner where the kitchen and frijj lay. There was a kerfuffle of a noise and one short pulse. There was a groan, and the corner lit like an oldFashioned lightbulb filament flaring and fading. A figure fell forward with a thump, jerking and flopping on the floor like a hooked fish. The shimmer on his back flashed and popped a little as it absorbed the electrical charge and went out. Starréd and Andaman were astonished.

"Shimmers may hide light and sound, but they sure don't hide smell," she said qwietly, walking over. She pulled the small charred backpack from the prone figure and handed it to Starréd. He and Madrigal trussed the nowVisible person dressed in a pullover and denims, with belsuk boots that absorbed any sound they made. Short hair, nondescript. A tubeLike weapon tucked in his belt.

"One of our tekkies," said Starréd. "What's his name? Zhong? That's him."

"Can someone tell me what's f'king happening," demanded Andaman.

"Colonel Starréd, Mr Marko needs to be scanned."

"Yes, Courier Phipps" said the still astonished security chief. "How did you know there'd be a hostile?"

"I put 2 and 2 together."

"In the Spokes? We are a secure facility!"

"You can never be too careful," she said in an authoritative tone, as it was indeed a weird assumption that anyone would be in Andaman's sealed room. *When you 'wing' it, do so with an authoritative tone* (Bluestone rule and archaism of the day). She'd been pretty sure what *winging it* meant. She was winging it now. She certainly wasn't going to mention the visit by her dead auntie.

Pile on the authority. "Let's get them both processed," she snapped.

Other personnel were arriving and they hauled the prisoner out in his frizzled heap and started working Andaman with a scanner.

"Bring kopi," said Madrigal to a random guard. "One for me, and one for Mr Marko."

She sat on his bed as wands were swept over the room and Andaman by security bods.

There was nothing except the weapon in the zapped man's belt. It was a heartstopper, which sucked up the body's electromagnetics. The sort of dark probe that had a onePulse discharge. The sort that carried Bluestone away. A pulse that would have been hard to discern in any autopsy. A terrible weapon.

Zhong was in the room to kill Andaman. Waiting patiently in the corner for him to fall asleep and they'd been a heartbeat away from failure. Thank you, auntie!

"That it?" she asked the forenzik guys. They nodded and she dismissed them as the kopi arrived.

*

As she was still amazed by the visitation of the dead auntie, her homily for Andaman came from those days when she played with her cousins under the aunties' watchful eyes.

"When I was a kid, we'd go into the bush with the aunties and dig for honey ants, little ants whose abdomens swelled into huge bulbs of honey. They were delicious. It was such a treat. You found ants with tiny yellow marks on their bums and follow them to see which hole they went down, and then you'd dig. We'd have to dig qwite deep to find them in the soft red soil. We'd be intent on finding the right conditions and then we'd carefully pull them out of the ground and eat their honey sac. You could see everyone was excited about the prospect of finding the insects ... and it makes me think, Andaman, that you are the most desired one big fat honey ant. What is it with these people who want to dig you out the ground and get at your honey?"

Andaman completely ignored the homily. "At some point, I'd like to return the favour and save your bum," he said. "That's 3 times now. Four if you count the attack of Flick."

"Wasn't much of an attack," said Madrigal, smiling. "You even got a kiss."

Andaman the dilettante contemplated his mortality yet again, looked into the black void that could have been. Had never heard of dark probes and heartstoppers until Madrigal patiently explained how close his body's bioElectrik system had come to extinguishment.

They now sat in the study of her apartment, while back in his bedroom the forenziks conducted tests, and the doctors and debriefers worked the attacker.

"Truth be known," said Andaman with a sigh, "all I've done is invented a new way to eavesdrop on the virtual amongst 10,000 other ways. And now everyone wants their chop of mine. In 10 years, 5 years, the whole modus will have changed, and my programs will be elderly & understood, and I either have to make my fortune now, or invent new programs." Andaman looked sad. "The scheme was all smoothed out, up in the Ville. All to plan. And someone goes and spoils it for me."

Yeah, thought Madrigal. Snooping, trading illegally, breaching securities across the planet. What was it with these guys who thought they were beyond the orbit of the law? Little moons of greed, circling the rest of us.

"And then I couldn't help myself earlier in your laboratories," he continued, adrenaline and caffeine propelling his thoughtStream. "I'm an idiot. The gear they've got down there. It's spectacular in terms of analytix. I worked it – looked for the lurker. Wound it back to the Brazilliance. Followed my strings, not the most recent batch, the last batch. The June batch. My harpoons had speared a dubious communication between one or 2 of the Chinese hegemonies and the Brillhoz. I just saw the exchange between the 2 as an investment opp. Stocks and f'king shares. But, stupid old me, it was a lot more. A cartel alliance, a secret trade deal. I didn't read it, but your guys found the weight of it. Me? I just did the usual small investment while it still wasn't a public asset. They must have sniffed me then."

"What stuff?"

"HighLevel manufacturing that needed melodium and thorium, so I punted on Brazilliance precursor metals."

"Melodium and thorium?"

Andaman looked at Madrigal and tried to change the subject.

"How did you know that person was in my room under the shimmer?"

"Tip off," said Madrigal. "Don't worry about it."

"I do. I do. I worry. Even the security guy was shocked. How anyone would get in here. This is the Age of Purity we're living in. Bad things like this don't happen."

"He was in HQ already. Been on staff for 5 years. Musta been polluted by some counterBuyer in a bar in Hobarttown. Corrupted with money, or sex. A weak one who had been poached and was on call." Madrigal sounded disgusted. "You know the drill. It's all highLine espionage these days between nation states and hegemonies. It's Purity. The wars have vanished, and we all help one another through the qwagmire, but there's always snoop and steal. So you, Marko, make a career of snoop and steal up in Cap, and suddenly someone starts to kill people, including – almost – us. And unless you help us fight back, Andaman, this will go on and on and on."

Andaman Marko knew it was true, and he nodded. "Fair enough."

"Melodium and thorium. Back to melodium and thorium. What's with the melodium?"

"A gammaDistil element. Needed for capturing and rendering gamma radiation in space and turning it into usable energy. Very new technology. Money in the manufacturing of it. The Brazilliance were doing it with this Chinese hegemony. They had the thorium, the Chinese. The mob in Guangzhou had the idea."

"Ok."

"I made some dollars on a brief spike in melodium production when the deal was announced. That's all."

"Some dollars?"

"'Bout $New 250,000. A bit."

Madrigal looked at Andaman's handsome face and wondered at the immense scope of his talents spoilt by the shallowness of his instincts. Sqwandered, she thought. At least he was a pleasant human being who talked respectfully, and emanated an attractive health. She shook her head. He was a contradiction, and a pest. A brilliant pest.

"Must go to breakfast," Madrigal said, dismissing her tagalong friend.

THE P/EM

CANBERRA, another urbopolis of substance and size, lay at the top of the great food bowl of the Murray River system, which fed half the world. Parliament on Capital Hill looming above the inner ring and outer ring of buildings. It was home for the 600 or so members and senators.

Home of AuZgov.

"Speak to me, Wen," said the P/EM who was pacing the soft blue carpet of the official chambers. Blue signified Ministry. Not that elections for new governments happened that often. Every 10 years or so an election would be held, as it had been too dangerous over the past 50 years to hold elections more often than that. Expediency ruled, but almost everyone had agreed to it. The P/EM had been in power for fifteen years but only been appointed twice. He looked shattered. Sudden death from sheer exhaustion was a professional hazard.

Looking from the balcony off the P/EM's private chamber, and out across the city, the 3 massive circumferences were visible in the evening light. WheelShaped buildings in the Canberra radius, that lapped down the hill to the lake. Circumference one, on the outside, housed AuZgov: defence, fertility and security, and foreign affairs. Circumference 2: AuZtax and Infrastructure – rebuilding broken roads and ports, in some places again and again, and in Circumference 3, with its inner, curving walls just below the Parliament but separated by manicured gardens, were parliamentary offices. In the early evening, all 3 were lit in blues, pinks and greens like carnival glowRings.

The P/EM turned from the view with his old, permaSet face – benign, but fixed – making Wen feel like he was talking to a walnut. Fingal Wen's own rugged features appeared on a large curvilinear screen in the corner of the office, and the P/EM wondered how on earth such an old man could hang on to a vestige of handsome. Rejuves, he suspected.

Wen started talking as the P/EM stood in the centre of the office, looking at the big rounded screen, listening to the explanation of the past few days.

Three of the P/EMs aides, male, male & female, were writing or reading files and passing him notes, but the P/EM wasn't interested in their insights. He was interested in the introodr in the Spokes. The aides' suited insistence, flakes of paper thrust in his face, were ignored.

"We've spent the day with the target, and the debriefers agree that the assassination team has definitely been working for the Brazillhoz," said Wen, going through the results of the interrogation, and the Marko analytix. "It took some time."

"So how did your Courier know there was an assassin in a shimmer in Marko's bedroom?" the P/EM eventually asked.

"Dr Phipps is acutely aware of her environment and surrounds. It doesn't surprise me. Among other things, she's an astounding fieldAgent."

"So in your view, it's not some doubleBluff. Tracked from a separate bedroom? A wild piece of luck that she went to this man Marko's room? I find it unbelievable – luck never happens to me. I have to chop and hack luck out of every office in this place. Hack it out of every member and senator. Luck just doesn't happen – you make it happen."

"Agreed. I'm sure it was other than luck." Wen sounded uncomfortable and uncertain.

"I'm very uneasy. Do you trust Dr Phipps? She is now at the sharp end of many sensitivities, handling this rogue operator and all the international ramifications of his dealings, not to mention public disturbance."

There was a pause.

"Keep her under close observation, Wen."

Wen was always the P/EM's man. His stocks had risen and fallen with the P/EM and his party, and they'd been on a sweet political run for twenty years now. Wen, in his younger years, had helped steer the country through the Age of Purity by extinguishing possible outrages and herding the people into lawfulness, launching interventions both soft and hard. Apart from the Spokes very crucial role in deAcidification in the southern ocean, sections of the crew also kept a check on the worst of humanity. Wen and the P/EM had joked in the past about the acid cleansing metaphor: physical, moral, & spiritual. The acid test, they called it.

"Thanks to your apparatus, our oceans and our people remain pure," the P/EM would say, and sometimes Wen thought he was being half serious.

The P/EM asked his staff to leave the room for a moment.

While Wen had climbed the pole within the administration, the P/EM had been a politician from the start.

In the mid70s, before politics, the P/EM was the nimble advocate, Ambrose Swift, who had 10 years prior, led the International Criminal Court's symbolic prosecution of the longDead politicians, bankers and businessmen who had allowed global deterioration to accelerate, in their selfish cause of avarice, despite years of scientific evidence that the climate was changing for the worse and everything was crumbling around them.

At the time, the strange, useless trial had won the participants kudos, but even as a symbolic gesture it was qwite empty, apart for the profound impact it had on the participants themselves. The accused were longGone but the afterEffect of their negligence was everywhere. Wen had told Ambrose Swift then that the trials were futile and administrators needed to use their energy to find money for public order, for infrastructure to rebuild or buttress the coastlines, to deal with the weird new weatherfronts and public panic. Wen had been more aggressive around that time, and angry.

But people wanted justice. In remembrance of things past, the trials were held at the International Criminal Court in Geneva, after the Hague was subsumed by the North Sea. At ICC, rows of prosecutors, defence lawyers, the descendants of the American, Chinese, and Russian presidents, the gtGrandchildren of the CEOs of Exxon and other defunct poisoners were there in black, supporting the process.

Then the not yet P/EM had delivered a couple of worldBeating speeches to the vast room filled with pale faces.

We can never forget the past – unconscionable greed, the carelessness of policy, the knowledge of the cataclysm to come, the betrayal. Up until the twentieth century, we moved forward to make the world a better place. That is the human instinct, the reason for being: a better world for our children. While crimes of the accused have been harvested and scrutinised by this Court, we must never forget their greatest crime was to turn their backs on this one tenet – a better future.

Futures happen, to us, our children, all of our descendants. We must never forget the past, but even more crucial, we must never betray the future. For although the future has many times betrayed history – rewritten, ignored, slandered or forgotten – until this century, the past has never purposefully, deliberately, sentenced millions of grandchildren to death.

Ambrose Swift's words rang out. The ICC climate prosecutions had made him famous.

In the end there was a purpose to condemning and sentencing the world leaders of the 20th and early 21st centuries. Their historic legacy was found to be ruinous. Apart from a few prophetic outriders, they were all condemned as criminals and sentenced to death in absentia.

The trials had given many people closure. Pointedly, the new generation of politicians had to rule with pure purpose, to leave a legacy to do no more harm, to repair as much damage as they could, to enforce a peace through persuasion and intervention, to work out *a better future.*

On their long journey together, Wen had ably prosecuted the last task with the P/EM – the enforcement of peace. But the trials of those presidents, prime ministers and CEOs – all guilty every one – had left the weight of incumbency on his friend's shoulders like a tonnage. A tonnage.

"Please, Wen. The Spokes. Ensure there is nothing irregular. Move Courier Phipps away from this Marko. Get her out of there. We simply cannot take the chance."

Wen bowed. "Yes, sir." The P/EM was struck at how uneasy Wen looked about Courier Phipps. In fact, Wen was weighing the fact that Phipps had saved Marko's skin, yet again.

"Sorry, Fingal, I have to go. I have 478 representatives in the house tonite so the qworum is stoked hot. I'm handling a RightThrough Bill, to release even more money for food in the work camps. Half the representatives are angry that more is to be spent. Where we'll find the cash, I know not – draw down from defence again, I suppose. Borrow from the Central hegemonies. If you have any ideas, let me know. We're having to wind back the health budget as well. See – it's a sqweeze this year, Wen, and I don't want to have to worry about incursions and hostiles. I have no money to deal with them.

"Worse, the metHeads say it's turning into a bad storm season up the Central north and islands. Cap is killing us. And the boats can't get to the northern hemisphere now. The cloud's too volatile. They'll have to wait for months now."

"Sir."

To the P/EM, Wen looked as tired and old as he. Now there was a worry that Wen was losing his grip, with assassins in the Spokes. Maybe Wen should be summonsed to Canberra and asked to retire. Gently. But if Wen retired, he'd be viewed in the same boat by younger ambitious politicos. Maybe not. Not qwite yet. Work to be done.

"Short leash, please," reiterated the P/EM. At the press of an external buzzer, the aides reEntered.

Wen's face faded and the screen moved straight to a scoped delegation from the Philippines, and an aide gave the P/EM a brief and whispered "pineapples" in his ear.

*

Breakfast was awkward.

At least last nite, Andaman had been thankful towards her. Over the toast there was no thanx. Wen and his husband, 'Arald, sat opposite, wielding a big china teapot.

As Wen said, she must have been "in some other loop" to know "there was a plant." She was "holding back." "Detecting a shimmerman in a locked room 2 floors below was an impossible get." The accusations were thick with contempt and she didn't cop contempt well.

"Truly, no. Sixth sense. Put it that way. I'm good that way," she explained gamely. "Like working out Andaman had sneaked out of his bed in the Ville, and left only one heatBean in the scope, which was his girl. I know how these things work, and my mind does the rest."

'Arald arched his eyebrow. "Hard to believe," he said, in the supercilious voice of the ancient elite. "You had the heat trace

– observable science for that deduction. The data were there in the image."

"Who was your source? You musta had one. You must tell me." Wen asked.

She shook her head, looking pained.

Wen said: "Well, then. The shimmerman has already confessed. His money was paid into an account to make life easier for the Brazilliance."

She sipped the tea, wishing it was kopi, but felt in no position to complain. Wen was clearly furious the Spokes had been so easily breached and appeared to want to blanket her with the blame.

"If you won't reveal how you knew, you need to go home," he said. "Consider your personal situation. The sexual escapade with a foreign administrator was bad enough. We'll take Marko over. Make arrangements. Go and see your kid."

"Am I being stood down?"

Her voice was strained with consternation.

"No. No. I want you to take some time," Wen said. "You've been operating for a fortnite without much sleep, and you've lost your mentor – and my dear friend – in an ugly incident."

"I can only thank you for releasing me to see Todd. But I've done nothing wrong ... except perhaps with Jembrana." She glanced at 'Arald after declaring this minor concession, but he didn't flinch his air of disapproval of her sexing out of marriage with a foreign colleague. But then she thought, *who cared?*

"Otherwise, I've performed to order." Returning to her defence, she said: "I followed & extracted Marko from a kidnapping, I have encouraged him, loosened his tongue & in turn he is assisting us." "Yes, yes, I know. You've done very well. But it all adds up. Simon Bluestone was my dear friend too," Wen said. 'Arald stroked Wen's back as if to ease the pain, looking at him, concerned. "We trained together and worked for more than 70 years."

Ah, thought Madrigal. So she was being blamed for not watching Bluestone's back as well.

"As he was to you, he was to me. Take a break." There was silence. The most senior Centrl was dismissing her.

"I would like to find his killers and bring them in," Madrigal said.

"That is not your job, Dr Phipps. There are others doing so. Just go."

Madrigal felt uneasy and upset by the conversation, and she strode down the corridor savouring the nuances. The tone had not been good. But at least she could go order a decent kopi on the floatDeck and then go see her Toddy.

TODD 2

SUMMER shot bullets of sunlight off the Swan Estuary, through the uppermost apartment windows of the giant Phipps Condominium. Madrigal was curled on the couch admiring her handsome little son and feeling far more relaxed than she ought. And she knew it. A dismissal from the Spokes was dismissal, however measured, however temporary.

But, she thought, make the most of the time at home because she'd be immersed in responsibility soon enough.

"When are we going?" asked Todd for the 10th time.

"Soon, sweetie," she said, stroking his hair as if he were a good luck charm, a little Buddha. Hair wavy and thick. He was intent on a thumb game, but still spoke to his mum, excited to be with her. She was excited as well. Her gaze shifted to the couches at the back of the penthouse room and the huge orange fresco along the back wall featuring the family, and their Country's terrain.

"Be a biggie this game, Dockers and CapWest," Todd added.

"Indeed it will. And who will you support?" asked Madrigal.

"CapWest, Mum. Only because they'll lose."

Toddy at 6. Being irrationally rational. He loved the Dockers, but felt loyal to the Broome boys too, a couple of whom were rellies.

Madrigal laughed, slipped off the leather upholstery, and wandered over to the balcony, checking the loop of the bay past Kings Park and up beyond the uni. Her mother, Netta Phipps, swept in, dressed impeccably as usual in a glimmering white gown, 3Qwarter length sleeves and silver shoes, lush black hair pulled back with an expandaband. The gown reminded Madrigal of a highway mirage.

Netta, given her status, had developed imperious eyes, accentuated with long lash implants. The white flickering material enhanced her black skin, alarmingly wrinkleFree.

"So, darling. Taking Todd to the footy?"

"Yes, Mum. What else? I've told him we'll go north after the storm season and visit the cousins."

Very good, said her mother's demanding eyes. Relocate, Maddy, swing back west. Become part of the family again. Run the company.

Todd was her little bargaining chip.

"Better his mum than poor Carl to escort him, yet again," said Netta. Carl was Netta's driver, and Todd's usual footy game companion.

"Carl's coming, too, Nan," yelled Todd from the couch. "It's a Dockers game."

"I'm sure he is," Netta said, sounding a little bit exasperated. Netta added, talking in West Cap Kriol language, that she thought Carl was fast becoming Toddy's father. Madrigal replied in Kriol and asked her mother politely to speak in English because it was discourteous to Todd to talk behind his back, in front of his face.

Netta looked annoyed and said in Kriol that what was truly discourteous was Todd's mother's continued absence. There was a silence as the anger rose in both women, and then was controlled before a real argument broke out in front of the little boy.

Madrigal leant against the rail and looked at the precipitous drop down to the city and the broad Swan Estuary, Kings Park to the right and the islands in front, connected by road and rail bridges. The ocean and beaches were just to her left, glimmering blue.

He mother sat beside her and lowered her voice, switched to businesslike English.

"Why are you here?" she asked. "I thought you were in the middle of something? Some State crisis?"

"I was – but I'm relieved of duty for a little, Mum. I imagine I'll be recalled soon. I was relieved from duty because Auntie Layla visited me the other nite and told me stuff, which led to other stuff and now I'm here. Does she ever visit you?"

"Not for a very long time," said Netta suddenly perplexed. Netta's face was close and finally Madrigal could see a pattern of wrinkles against the light. But they were very faint on her mother's proud face. Her mother's eyes though, they looked old, a little cloudy, a little sad.

"She was a good woman, Layla. Loved you. Carried you about on her hip whenever we were up there and she taught you business. She never wanted any rejuvenations, even tho' I offered. Said her time was a given, that her lifetime cycled with the land. *It's a bond that won't be cheated*, she'd say. A lot of the old girls and boys are like that."

"She thinks the world of Todd. She's looking after him," said Madrigal.

Netta smiled. "She would."

The pause. Madrigal well knew the pause. Next topic – the ultimatum.

"So when are you ...?"

"Coming back for good?"

"Help me with the company? I need your help. Your dad. He's out there on his mad Far Horizon projects with Tom, Dick, Harry, Willy & Nilly. Over in East Asia. Always over in

East Asia. I have to manage day2day everything. Approving budgets, audits, the investors, the Land Councils, the boards, smoojing the investors and the public, sucking up to AuZgovWest & that cow, Premier Elise Lumumba, & on top of that, the entire Cap administration."

The slow, deliberate stream of consciousness rant was a Netta special. Madrigal allowed for a thoughtful pause, then said: "You do have the CEOs and the managers, Mum. You do have support."

Netta looked at her, the light breeze flickering strands of silverGrey hair in front of her eyes. She moved it gently to the side. Always a graceful, gentle mover, Madrigal thought.

"This company work is too much. I have to make the hard calls in the end. After some ridiculous scope with your Dad where he ends up saying, *"Your call, my Netta."* I have to approve things. Your dad – he's bored with the company, with the day to day. With me. He's probably got women over there." She said the last bit sadly.

Madrigal didn't doubt the last sentiment, but knew Netta was inured to her husband's infidelities. She wasn't sure whether the speech invoking her father's bad behaviour was an emotional ploy, or the genuine thing. Probably a mix of both, but Madrigal was surprised. Netta had never been so candid with her daughter.

Still, taking over the running of Phipps Industries would mark the end of her current life. She'd made a deal with herself to take a seat on the board after the first rejuve, and that was a long way off.

"Mum, I've just been promoted."

"It'll all go to shit if you don't help me. Phipps Industries and all. The whole business. I need sharp family minds around me who understand the long game. Not hired help. It's a family business and there're lots of people who depend on us," Netta said. "Maddy, everyone knows you have the sharpest mind. You are the inheritor. You know that yourself."

Madrigal looked out to the mother'o'pearl ocean and sighed. The anger started to well up again.

"Mum ..." She had a couple of very smart stepsiblings and cousins who were also involved and could be mentored. And the hired help was awesome and loyal. She was about to point this out when Madrigal felt Todd's hand wind into hers and she looked down on his little face. He'd sneaked up on them.

"Let's get a fizzy shake, and then head for the stadium," she said.

"Yes!" said Todd.

"You do that," Netta said, smiling at her eager grandson. "Your mum and I can talk later, over a nice bottle of red."

*

The Phipps Industry private box dangled over one of the lower terraces halfway around the oval. They had a better view of the playing field than most of the 200,000 people crammed into Perth Stadium, a venerable football ground that had massive highRised stands, which parted like the inside of a giant iceCream cone. Spectators in the area known as the skylight could only watch tiny figures making the dance of the game. Big screens followed the action. But the atmosphere was thick with excitement. Coming towards the end of the season, one of Perth's 3 big teams and the underdogs from East Cap were fighting it out, playing for National AFL finals position.

Toddy was sitting with 2 little schoolmates at the front of the corporate box, which had a glass floor – a dizzying view. The sound of the crowd hammered at the glass windows of the corporate box, the swell of voices baying for goals. It was the second qwarter and Carl, Netta's boxJawed driver, had just brought Madrigal another red wine with a low, "Ma'am." Madrigal wondered for a moment whether Carl was her mother's rather junior lover also, her father being almost permanently absent.

Possibly.

Several Phipps Industry clients and senior executives also watched the play while doing, sotto commercial deals obscured by the roar of the crowd. They sometimes glanced sideways at the heirs to the fortune, Madrigal and Todd, with keen interest, and 2 or 3 of them engaged her in footy banter and business talk, but went no further into the details of her murky job, though everyone in the firm knew she was an AuZgov Courier, "biding her time". The recalcitrant who wouldn't come home. The hold out. The prodigal. They'd all heard Netta in meetings often enough threaten them with the return of Madrigal.

Also present were a few of the Phipps relatives from north east of Broome who had come down with the team. They were complaining that the new rules change had meant earbugs connected directly to a player's ears were banned, so the coach couldn't send instructions.

"How are they going to know what to do?" one young cousin said, exasperated.

"Have to learn the gamePlays beforehand, I suppose," said Madrigal. "Like I used to."

"You?" said the kid. "You never played footy!"

Madrigal smiled and shrugged.

On the field below, the Dockers football team swarmed. The exchanges from the interchange benches were fast and furious. Two players were tilted back in chairs, getting fresh oxygenated blood supplied by matching blood types in their cheer sqwad, and being worked on by physiotherapists. In the centre, there was a bounce and the 2.5 metre ruckman, Acton Yards, smashed the ball with his weighted glove high into the field towards West Cap's zone.

"Wow, mum," said Todd, "what a whop! That went 60 metres." The ball was intercepted by a West Cap back. The back kicked the ball hard with his leg augment, a length of boot that used much the same technology as Madrigal's interPlanetary storm skin, sending it diagonally across the field to another player who went for a sprint and was brought down by Freo players. "Oof!" said Todd and a couple of fascinated businessmen.

Madrigal watched with keen interest. When she was a kid, there were no superboots, but the ruckmen – or boys – had still worn the hard gloves, and even though she'd been a girl, no qwarter was given. If she'd gone for a sprint, she was tackled as hard as any boy. And the ground hadn't been astroturf. West Cap kids grew up playing footy on the traditional dustbowl footy oval in the communities.

A ballUp and the ball was flicked forward again by another, gloveless, player and picked up by a Docker forward, who swivelled and kicked on instinct from 40 metres out. The ball went through the middle of the 6 sticks and the crowd roared its approval. A full goal.

Carl passed a silver tray of canapés to the businessmen and rellies who were snorting and roaring with laughter and enjoying the festivities, and then he turned the tray to the boys who polished off the tiny pies and sausage rolls. Todd, though only 6, was already the school legend because of the floating glass box at the footy.

The centre ballUp was proceeding when there was a bang at the back door where the box joined the outer corridor, and 2 figures slid through and shut it behind them. One was svelte, spiky grey hair in a grey suit, younger than he looked, the other was burly. They nodded pleasantly at the businessmen and plonked themselves in seats on either side of Madrigal.

She noted a gunSnout in one of the men's coats. Unthinkable.

Courier training kicked in, along with adrenaline.

"You're in the wrong box," she said, her mouth insisting that it not go dry with fear. So she coolly sipped her wine to counteract. Todd and his friends were the only consideration. Show these creeps nothing, and she might protect everyone.

They leaned in from either side, looking at her.

"Can we have a glass of wine and a little pie?" said the big fellow.

Madrigal almost laughed at the temerity, but at the same time had pressed the beacon on her AuZgov clasp, a small emergency belt communicator all officers carried, which lay behind her butt on the seat.

She didn't have to count the occupants of the box, now at risk from a hardarm. There were the 3 kids, including Todd, plus Dodson and Griggs from the battery division, the valued corporates, and a couple of larger boys from Broome who were distantly related. All in a small fifteen by 25 metre glass eyrie. She didn't want anyone hurt. She would have to talk the talk, which was her forte.

"Carl – a glass of wine, here, please ..." She turned to the thin one: "And for you mate?"

"Beer," said Svelty.

"Beer, and a few more pies."

Without the pistol, the intrusion was a ludicrous foray, but the firearms were a big worry. "And put that away," she hissed to Fatso. "Let's talk. What do you want?" Fatso obliged and slid his gun into a holster.

Svelty said qwietly, "We have a team here with us, so firstly don't try anything. Just stay put."

"Mum, who are these men? Are you alright?" Todd turned round qwizzically and looked at the strangers on either side of Madrigal. When he could, he watched out for his mum and was alive to her moods. Carl, too, was looking askance at the introodrs. The businessmen were fixed on the game and hadn't a clue. But Todd did. Good boy, she thought. Good instincts.

"Yep, it's fine, Todd. They are business contacts. I asked them to drop by for a minute or 2. Then they'll go," said Madrigal. "How's the Dockers going?

"Thirty ahead."

"Great!"

Todd turned back to the play on the field.

"So what's your name, and why are you in the wrong box?" she said to Svelty. The man had an unusually thin nose, which dragged his eyes towards each other, giving an impression of both narrowness of mind and a rodent. Not mutually exclusive states of being. His lips were full, though – little red pillows of arrogance.

"We're not in the wrong box. We are right where we should be. My name is Mr Mullen. This is Mr Chough. We represent a businessperson who would like to send a message to Mr Andaman Marko and we thought you'd be able to oblige."

Madrigal shook her head. "You know that I'm unable to do that," she said. "I'm a government official."

"Yes, but you have a family," said Svelty. "That makes it simple. Andaman Marko is probably being pressed hard to cough up his paradigms to you lot, and the White Lady will be pressing on him too. Well, he's pretty much safe in that impenetrable place, tho' my employer did try to make contact through a third party." Svelty bit some pie, but continued his spiel as he chewed a mouthful. Madrigal watched the disgusting moosh in the man's mouth as he talked. The man called Chough was distracting himself with the spectacle on the green field below rather than attend to the discussion.

Svelty's voice lowered to a murmur.

"What we say," said Svelty, "is keep Marko's mouth shut and we won't kill him. We have his strokes, the coding feathers. We know the program. Tell him, CourierWise: *Keep shtum and you won't be targeted.*"

"Why would I do that for you?" said Madrigal.

"To keep your little lad safe, of course. Just pass the message on to Marko. 'Shut it, Marko.' That's all you got to say. Simple one."

"My boy? Are you offering up a threat here?"

"Not me, myself. I'm merely a Courier like you. Is my Heg's threat. I well know that you could kill me, stone dead, as we sit, right now, but the boy is marked."

"I could kill you both stone dead in a second," said Madrigal.

"I don't doubt it. SlotterTrained they say you are. Pick of the elites. But it would be a criminal waste, killing us."

What a smartarse.

"And your hegemony is who?"

"That would be telling," said Svelty/Mullen.

"You are rude to ask," said the fat one, now paying attention. "Tsk tsk."

"Is that it?" asked Madrigal.

"Simple reqwest with clear warning attached, yes," said Svelty.

"Ok. Off you go then," said Madrigal. "I'll let you live right now. But next time, I'll kill you for threatening my family. Won't miss."

"Thank you for being so merciful." Laced with sarcasm. "You'll pass the message on?" said Svelty, amused at her counterThreat.

"I'm a professional messenger," said Madrigal. "You're the mob that tried to kill Marko with that bomb in the first place, aren't you? Murdered 40 or so? Think you got his strokes, shut him down, get ahead."

"Perhaps. The man's a complete clown."

The 2 messengers from the sourSide, the underside, stood and started to reverse out of the box. Fatso still had his hand under his jacket, no doubt with the weapon aimed at her or Todd. She was not going to risk anything in the box with the 3 little boys, and the thugs knew it. But underneath she burned bright with anger and to her amazement visualised breaking their necks with her bare hands – a very aggressive thought.

"'Bye 'bye."

The pair slipped out the door.

"Get that, Centrl?" she said into her emergency clasP.

"Onto it," said the disembodied voice. "Don't do anything rash. Don't follow even tho you want to. Enjoy the game," it said. "Freo are looking good for a second premiership in 108 years."

Down below, the ball soared into the sky and was grabbed like the head of a foe, and kicked by a West Cap crumber through the middle. A massive roar rose up, past the excited boys, the happy executives and the furious Madrigal, who moved towards the door to pursue Mr Mullen and Mr Chough, then decided to obey orders for once, and sat beside Todd with a sigh.

*

From a stadium security camera, Fingal Wen's people watched the 2 figures as they left the corporate box and entered a corridor feed into the stadium proper. One picked a bag from the ground, which had been sitting at the door. Chough and Mullen moved briskly towards the corridor doorway and joined a huge crowd of supporters milling about in a brown and gold atrium, folk drifting through for halfTime, to consume beer and prawn kebabs, to smoke chopChop, and talk.

"Keep on them," Wen urged his people, staring at the screens in the Spokes dome. He knew what was coming. The men were crystal clear, one pudgy, one sleek, and then a hand slipped into the bag and they flipped the shimmer. The image elongated and hazed into the crowd, became shadows and flickers on the screen. Crowds and shimmers were a symbiosis. The more shadows and negative space, the more the shimmer nuanced the mix of light, dark, greys and blacks. Focus on the frizzle, where photons weren't qwite blending, round the shimmer edge. Follow the frizzle. Difficult to separate as the extra photons were drawn together, and flowed randomly from the device.

Wen asked his 2IC: "How far away are the milisi?"

"Two minutes."

"Are we on top of the shimmer. You have visual?"

"Still there."

"Has anyone down there got a geiger?" he said, thinking of shimmer power sources, but of course noone had. Shimmer tek was obscure and geigers cost multiple \$New.

Once, when his eyes were sharper, Wen was the master of the shimmerShine, but tracking frizzle was tricky with bog-Standard cameras. A netted spot in dark red, following the shadow through the crowd, 2 men under a photon dissembler. The Chinese had invented the technology a few decades ago, and it had leaked qwickly round the world. They could hide villages, trucks, anything. But it was best for moving targets in crowds.

"They're brazen," said Wen, "having 2 blokes enter the Phipps Industry box, then disappear."

The dark red net spot was visible right up until the security cameras flipped, and it was gone, the angle now from the far side of the huge atrium. Any hint of the shimmer was lost. The team in the screen dome groaned collectively. Only 100s of milling people with beer in glasses, little kids, dads in funny footyTeam hats, herds of spotty adolescents. The crowd looked like a pall of dark smoke, moving around like particulates in a great room. Centrl could only pray the Milisi would have a physical visual ... when and if they got there in time.

Wen thought: after so many years of unrelenting visibility, people were learning to hide again.

*

Her mother, Netta refused to believe the incident ever happened. *Never happens in the west. Death threats? Guns in cor-*

porate boxes? When Madrigal told her that Todd would accompany her back to the Spokes for his safety, Netta protested vociferously. Accused of inventing a crisis and then taking advantage of it to take Todd away.

Netta loved Todd.

"It will only be for a few weeks," said Madrigal.

"What about school? Oh, this is a nitemare." Netta's face was tight with anger.

"He can scope into his class. He's done it before. Mum, it will only be for a short time."

"I know about your short times," her mother shot back. That was a low blow.

Netta also protested the sudden appearance of Folly and Pearl, no matter how dressed down they were: helmetless, simple shirts, stretch pants and boots. Centrl had speeded them over to Perth to protect the family after Mullen's naked threat.

"Nice place," said the goddessLike Pearl to Madrigal as they entered to inspect security. Netta refused to be impressed with the 2 Slotters, their size, physiqwe, or physical beauty. She was distinctly unmoved by their discreet pistols. As a serious energy company executive, she'd seen it all.

"Our own people can provide security. Carl can organise a team to watch over him," said Netta. "I would approve it immediately, keep it in the family."

Father was stuck in the Japanese sector doing his interminable energy deals and had to wait for the Cloud to settle during the eqwinox period before he could make a return trip. He hated the Gforces of the strato shuttle Rramjjet that skipped high over the turbulence. He preferred to fly oldStyle.

Netta knew, as did Madrigal, that very few knew how to do security properly. Madrigal pointed this out several times. The men who laid down the threats were professionals and meant every word. Noone in Perth would have the skills to counteract them.

In the end, concern for Todd's safety was overwhelming and Netta consented.

*

During the Age of Purity noone lied. Prior to the climate blowback in the '70s and the rise of the Singular Enemy, surveillance was so profound that AuZgov was onto every little lie. Then suddenly, the world needed deep consensus because of the unimaginable force of the fierce climate on whole populations, geographies, life. Consensus became the new norm created by the carrot of necessity and the stick of authority. Mass surveillance would find the liars out, but the surveillance state waned in the face of mass movement of populations.

But, vestiges of the era of purity remained, worldWide. Even in recent years noone lied much because of the cultural onKick of that era. While people might have private thoughts as they all did, these remained private, unshared, in the space between selfConsciousness and speech. An era of circumspection. Otherwise, people said it like it was. Could be blunt and uncomfortable, but truthfulness generally prevailed.

Like asking a girl her fertility status before you even bought her a drink, you knew her answer was true. And your response would be likewise. Noone asked why they were apportioned fertility status by the DyNAst people, though they might guess. Some mumbled "the DieNasties" out of the sides of their mouths, mostly Noughters. But even Noughters accepted. Andaman had never pretended to be anything else than a Noughter, though saying he was allowed a kid or 2 would have upped his desirability to women. Made him a "good catch".

But that would have been deceitful. He never lied.

Or, if your house was marked for destruction due to environmental subsidence because it was close to seaRise – citizens were well warned in advance. AuZgov couldn't allow the dangers to be ignored, like those decades when the calamities began. People remained obedient to government because of this. Accepted their status, did what they were told.

So, lying after the Age of Purity was new. Something deliberately reinvented to fool surveillance. Lying and flattery. Flattery is a form of lying. The imprimatur of misleads and red herrings. Several years ago when Andaman was tunnelling into komms channels, monitoring messages between the powerful, he was surprised to find multiple messages, all slightly different. Some false, one true. Initially, he was shocked him that some were laced with lies or at least, misleads. Then he worked out what was going on.

Multiple versions of a single message had become a ruse, being used more and more, mainly by Hegs and governments. No doubt keys on paper would unlock the real message on the virtual, for the users at the end. Or faceOnface Courier tip offs. Multiple strand messages became a widely subscribed ruse.

Andaman had said: "Ok ... that's interesting," and went back to the text boox, the old linguists. He studied the linguistic architecture of lying, from that Golden age before the Age of Purity. Forensic linguistics from the old criminology libraries. There in the library, haunted only by academicians, researchers, sentimentalists and timeWasters, he found studies on falsehoods and lying: the overuse of superlatives, verbs and adjectives early in the statement, for example, skewed the meaning. They exposed the false string. OverEgging the case. Persiflage. "Dissembling" was the bad word for it – just like he, and his program SQwizzyy, were in the biz of dis assembling turns of phrase to identify the lie.

He discovered ways to find them in thick paragraphs of information. discounting the false messages from the multiple messages in his syntax sieve. Not always, but more often than not, his program picked the true messages and invested a sum against their sentiment.

His investments were about the margins. Betting on veracity. The predictable, picked from a cascade of messages.

In the same vein, with his captors, or protectors, at the Spokes, he bit his tongue and didn't lie, but neither did he explain his full analytical methodology openly to Officer Vu. She had become more and more interested in his very ancient malware, redefined and calibrated for the third century of the third millennium. And how he analysed the economik drift.

The slippery ways of SQwizzy, sorting through multiple strings of information, were of less import to her and to Centrl, and he worked to keep it that way.

*

Andaman sat on the food deck, where he often retreated after debrief sessions, staring through the thick windows into the deep ocean, the dark waters beyond Storm Bay, looking for the shapes of fish and sqwid. Acqwatic creatures floated up along the rich continental drop where warm water from the north flowed into the cold. Fish often rose and swarmed in front of the Spokes lights. Sometimes coral trout, red emperor and trevally, sometimes more prosaic fish like tunny, mackerel. Glimpses were almost meditative. There, and then gone.

Over the months he had made friends with a couple of other male IT enjj's and they engaged in jocular tech banter and discussion about available women in the Spokes and how best to befriend girls and their fertility status. He often just argued with them about hardware and virtualware.

Sometimes Wen would wander over carrying his lunch tray and eat with Andaman, and he and Andaman would talk about his past and the politics of security. Andaman was not one to hold back on much, apart from the inner entrails of the SQwizzy program, and some of his more secret ventures. Wen even asked Andaman for investment tips which Andaman found qwite amusing, as did Wen.

Every day he'd hit the exercise chambers to keep fitness levels up. The Spokes even had swimming pools. A long, stainlessSteel saltwater tank in The Hierarchy which suited him.

On milder days when the wind had eased, the staff could go on outer decks and sit in the sun.

But there was no chance the Spokes would let him out of their sight. Even a reqwest for a "field trip" to the pubs of Hobart, which he'd reqwested just to enjoy fresh air and mingle in a crowd, was knocked back on the grounds of his safety.

Wen had emphasised that the Brazilhoz wanted him dead and that the White Lady syndicate seemed to want him alive, but kidnapped – and Marko well knew AuZgov was still soaking up any knowledge he presented them. He also knew there was more to be had.

He wasn't going anywhere.

Much of the time, the sitch got him down. Between debriefs and detailed crunches of his programs, and their asking his advice on other intrusion matters – as a consultant almost – Andaman Marko yearned for his breezy old life. Food in the Spokes always tasted the same; the air smelt contained and stale.

He yearned for those days where he did a couple of weeks work a month, and then frolicked in between with his friends, while he monitored the glows to prove just how clever he was. That's how life should be.

Fact was, he'd been caught not just by one, but by several parties. The bubble of his ego was pricked and popped and now, now he was scared. He'd thought that small incremental raids on other peeps stock and derivative actions would have kept him well hid. He'd underestimated the toxicity of what he'd been doing, and the golden opportunities for others.

On down days, he lay in bed reading mags and boox on his replacement clamB, which they'd provided but with a data lock. He could have unpicked it, and played in the virtual, but the teks would've known immediately. Other days he'd dream of talking to Flick and other friends. But primarily Flick — about her real past, her actual identity, her parents, her hidden life. She'd been a dark horse, and emerged as the most enticing girl he'd known.

Other days he just sat in his suite and wept.

KINGDOM 2

A HUSTLE of people.

There were those who had homes. Then there were those who patiently sat out their lives under tarps, on mats by the roadside, waiting for the food trucks to deliver a bowlful of meal and a banana to their kids and their family members. There were patient people in city jobLinez waiting for hire – paid for in goods, more often than not. Fruit picking, fish cage cleaning, road, bridge and barrage reconstruction. Generally obedient, pleased to have escaped the worst, looking for some small improvement, content to wait.

Such people were dressed simply and often grubbily, but Cap had sets of water stations and sleeping areas, bunkers for when storms came, markets so they could trade. Many were employed in work camps along the coast and out bush, wrestling with rebuilds, levees and water diversions, and would come to town every so often to catch up and share their pay with family. The lucky ones got a subsistence farming patch in old cane fields that had too much salt, and they grew salt modified tubers and vegetables and tended small prawn wells. Some unlucky ones, usually younger, would end up in sex stalls and brothels making ends meet, or losing their minds entirely.

Kingdom knew these people were unremarkable and invisible to the majority of the population and so blended as best he could in the crowd.

There were shanties and hawkers in Alexandra Street too, all the way down to the parkland behind the Parliament, so Kingdom retreated from his position on the kerb further up the hill, and scoped a line of sight position from the other side of the street up on the corner.

It wasn't difficult to bump the guy who had a half tarp with a display of cheap seconds clothing. A scuffle, a kick, harsh words, and the guy was gone. Kingdom set up selling betel nut, ganja and bongs, which he accessed through a mate upriver. His stall was beside a solo female food vendor with a gas grillette who seemed to make most of her money from the crowd heading to work and back, selling fried chicken wings with lime dressing. It was all she sold, this old Indon woman who tried to ignore Kingdom for a while, after seeing him rough up the previous stallholder and chase him away. After a bit, she took pity on him and swapped the odd leftover chicken wing for a betel nut after the crowds had gone, muttering in Bahasa.

He was garbed in a hat, a plastic poncho to fend off the rain, next to the vBike he'd muddied up to make it look uncomely. He was set – for weeks if need be.

Most days he'd scan the rock splayed above his daughter's house and watch a redWinged brahminy kite circling, and gazing at the ground with its white head. A lush bird, he thought. Predator. Made for catching fish and wheeling the thermals.

From where he sat, in a battered canvas chair that he'd found in a rubbish chute, Kingdom could ensure that the milisi stayed put guarding Flick's door and Flick, to be certain the door itself remained fast shut, that none untoward introoded along the stepped alleyway that passed the house, an access to further up the hill and its flasher flats and tenements. Clearly she wasn't allowed to leave. He counted the patrols and the regular guard exchanges. He judged the watchfulness of those on duty. His was a good spot.

At nite, Kingdom moved further up the street to where he'd sat the first afternoon when they'd decanted Flick into the house. He'd sit there, behind a tree, most of the nite smoking and having an occasional nip of rum watching the door like a hawk. A family had set themselves in the alleyway under some tin further up the road and he could see the glow of their gaslamp, yellow aganst the shiny tin surface, darker silhouettes of people. There was nothing unusual about street folk finding a camp on a bit of wasteground in Cap.

After a while Kingdom came to 2 conclusions: 1) the milisi were deadly serious about guarding his daughter, and doing a decent job, and 2) she was locked down to the point where he assumed that the miserable f'king AuZgov shower down south thought she was in mortal danger and an asset.

Once or twice he considered slipping through the back into Flick's house for a talk, but they'd have opticon arrangements, with lightstrings set to break alarms, so such a move would probably be retrograde.

Kingdom wasn't sure when he slept, but he must have dozed, mostly during the day. He was wide awake at nite.

He knew nite was the most dangerous time.

WEN, BLUESTONE AND KINGDOM

BACK there, then, 3 young men were slouched in the common room. The trio was together in Kingdom's jaded mind's eye, his faulty juveF'cked memory. One was roaring with laughter. That was him. They'd been out on the turps. One was staring at him with a half closed eye, amusement on his lips. The other, Simon Bluestone, was looking subdued and sick.

"We have exams tomorrow, Kingo. You know that. I'm calling it a nite," the young Fingal Wen said.

The sudden flush of memory shocked him. The picture was so real.

Kingdom hadn't thought of this for years. Amazing how a brain, even after its rejuves, could blow away the frayed and tattered cells and remember things from ancient history.

They were cadet students at University Facility, Sydney. Learning to be THE MAN. Special Administrators.

Callow, eager, full of bland, basement level knowledge and false authority, with none of the torrid, wrenching experience that would follow.

The common room in the University Facility was pretty nice, with comfy chairs and vending machines, and a subdued light, turned down, because most of the other cadets were in bed. He, Kingdom Allenby, impulsive party goer, had led his 2 friends astray on a Sunday nite, and was amazed they were still talking to him.

He remembered the mess hall lounge very well. Spent a lotta time there. There was even a view towards the harbour showing the twinkling lights of the city, before Sydney had filled up with decades more babies, immigrants, Aussie refugees from the new deserts. Plus all those people who flooded south after *the Blend*, out of their allocated areas into the cities. That view he remembered, when Sydney was Sydney, not that he'd been there for years and years.

Simon Bluestone had rubbed his temples and looked up, so young with the thin face and the blue eyes, which made him look like a child then, but would later make him famous in security circles.

"You blokes are the best," Simon said in the worldWeary voice he had already adopted. "Took me out of the sitch there. Could've lost it all. Could'a got my fertility status cancelled. Could've lost it all."

That's right, Kingdom remembered: there had been tension in the bar in the Watsons Bay pub between the locals and some trainee boys who were out for the nite. Simon had intervened, as he always did, coming in with the assumed authority of head of security, head of fertility and head of what – the Met bureau? Trying to be the Leader when he hadn't even been credentialed. They were still in second year training, for f'ck's sake.

Simon misjudged, wading in to break up an argument, not a brawl, and he had started to loudly proselytise about peaceable behaviour. The local men had laughed and one of the local lads had started bending him, head back against the bar top.

What were they? Sixteen? Seventeen? World closing in.

"You were narking at those blokes. You can't wear the authority on your sleeve until y've graduated," he remembered saying to Simon. "Don't be an idiot."

"But Kingo, you have to act when you see a fight about to explode in a bar ... but then, mebbe I handled it wrong. Live and learn. I defer to your worldly experience. I'm going to bed," said Simon. He stood unsteadily – beer heavy – and staggered down the corridor.

Kingdom knew that Simon could have had his head punched in by big blokes simply for being a fool. That was the word, wasn't it? Or was it poonce? He and Fingal had pushed into the crowd of agitated cadets and locals and hauled their friend out of the melee, and with gentle words and conciliatory gestures, he'd stared the attacker down. After all, even at seventeen, Kingdom was a big man. "Take it easy," he'd said. "Don't do this." Wen was tall and weedy as well, and he worked on 2 or 3 other drunk fellows, calming them.

"Your f'king mate should get out of our face," roared one. "Right out of our face. Private conversation."

Those were days when people were super sensitive about their privacy being invaded. Touchy and angry. Not that nowadayz, they ain't. But back then it was real bad, the prying, the poking by AuZgov. And they were uniformed AuZgov boys throwing their weight around, albeit bantam ... or feather?

That's right. The memory was strengthening like a migraine.

In the crowded bar, with everybody watching, the anger from the alpha punter sizzled across Simon. The fist was already on an upward swing. Impact was nigh, with all the horrible byProducts of blood and broken teeth and possible brain embolisms.

"We'll take him home," Kingdom said loudly but airily, inserting his large frame. "Simon's a bit pissed."

He had always been a big bloke. Worked a farm for his dad from the get go. He stared the angry bloke down with a wry smile and open pamls, and the second attacker had backed off. Kingdom had pointed at the cameras and raised an eyebrow.

The 3 cadets had been very close to breaching their oath of authority there. "Falling foul," it was called. Any one of them could have been out of the academy and on their sorry arses if they'd broken the law, been involved in an affray. The crowd all looked up, he remembered, at the cameras in the corner. The boys, the punters, extraneous cadet officers, barkeeps. He'd sweated on the moment, but the attacker, bearded and drunk, and his mates, nodded and exhaled, and Simon had said: "No hard feeling, cuz," because he could. Everyone in those days was bruz or cuz or siss.

Wen had grabbed Simon and pulled him from the group, saying, "Come on." Kingdom lowered his upturned palms and said "thanx" to the angry men, turning away.

They'd staggered out, Simon muttering, "Oh that was close, oh that was close," the nearness of the end of his career flashing, he said, when the guy's fist was raised above his head.

He could see the fist and could only anticipate being "hounded out" of the service, rather than the pain of impact. He'd shoulderHugged his friends and thanked them deeply. Wen, with his wry smile, had just laughed. Kingdom, with the scowl and the shoulders, said, "No probs."

Kingdom suggested they go to the club down the hill where it was a little more restrained, but his friends both said no, enough of the revelry. Tomorrow's Monday. To be part of the Authority, as it was called in those days, you had to be unimpeachable. Without sin. Without a stain.

"Back home," Fingal had said qwietly. "Cup of coffee? The international relations exam is tomorrow and we have training at 6 ..."

Had Fingal been "the Dad"? No, not really. The goody goody? Not really. He was even then focussed and sensible enough to make decisions into the future about the lives of people.

In those days, Kingdom really believed in the authority, the cleansing of society until it was a safe, peaceful, boring, un-natural place. In those days he believed in all that entropy for good bullshit.

He remembered watching Simon head to bed, and he also resolved to write a private report to the University Facility commander about the incident, and the need for his bruz to perfect his judgement. The Commander needed the knowl-edge. He'd better be safe and do so, because he knew Fingal would be writing one too.

BAABI 2

"HELLO, old man, long time," she said.

He grunted. "Yeah, and same to you, hag." He was trying to find his breath. The ground in his nose smelt damp and sour.

"Been a while. Been procreating, we see. Cute little daughter. That's waaay out of order, Noughter."

"When was anything ever in order?" he managed to say, swivelling round. She was locked on top of him, knife at his throat.

"I always took you for the orderly type," she said. Her eyes were narrow and the knife point was etching his skin. But he was getting his breath back. Less winded. He took air in evenly to centre himself.

"What do you mean by that, hag."

"After the war – I always took it you were one of them. AuZgov's man."

"Ha! Is that why you and Jimmy and Gav were the first to run from the last blockade, not me? You w'r a deserter, f'kd off to godknowswhere. Then blow me, I saw you there before, spying on my girl."

She twisted the knifePoint in his throat ever so slightly to sting his skin.

"You were one of the last. Hung in there to hand y'self in?" The voice was laden with syrupy menace. Always had a persuasive voice, did Baabi. Her face was close to his, almost wrinkle-Free. She must have been hitting 110, and look at the rejuves. Kept her taut, almost lovely, if it wasn't for the sour old mouth.

Was unfair on modern AuZtralasia that rejuves kept creatures like him and Baabi alive ... that they were still allowed to be.

"Only you and me know the horrors," he said to her. "We waded knee deep through mud'n' blood to try and prevent *the Blend*. And here we are, still with our f'king knives and f'king guns when everyone else has given them up and lives peaceful. What does that say about you and me?" He looked up. "We are aberrations." It was a bitter tone that he found at the back of his throat.

Baabi slung herself off his prone body, but replaced the knife with a gun in an eyeblink, pointing it at his forehead. She was buff. Strong. Her eyes glimmered with life. She was a bitch.

"So's all too bad for the young, eh? Retooling blesses us as well as them. So what if we are from an older time? Too bad. I've waited 55 years for this f'kn' moment."

And Kingdom didn't doubt it.

"Baarbs, luv – we are out of time," he said definitively.

"Speak for yourself."

He was out of ideas as well. Kingdom Allenby lifted himself onto his elbows, and tried to stand up. She had T Boned him into the ground and everything ached. The guard at Felicity's door would have seen nothing, heard nothing, because his observation point was discreet.

"How did you know it was me?" he asked.

"Wah, wah, wah," she said. "Let's not cry over spilt milk. I saw you – that's all. Stalkin' your daughter, which is kinda sick."

"You're going to kill me, anyway."

She rolled her eyes. "When you pulled in down here, first nite, I'd done a double check, just like you taught us. Round the block. There you were."

"Thought so," said Kingdom. He was pleased he trailed her for so long without being eyed. And pissed off that in the end she'd had him nailed.

"Rum?" He gently rolled the bottle to where she was crouching. "Not poisoned. It's good old standard Bundy rum. You can see I've been drinking it by the empty bit."

She took a slug of rum, while her gun stayed vigilantly pointed on his head.

"Just like old times," she said.

"That would be bullshit. You never drew on me once, even when I ..."

"When you tried to rape me?"

"Ah, piss off," he said. "I was a kid. And we were both pissed."

She laughed. "You were a miniPrick then, and now, you're a shrivelled up miniPrick."

They stopped talking and looked venemously at each other. The air was thick with moisture, steam coming off the road under the lighting, playful yellow sodium wraiths, the cloud layering above them. A vehicle was making its way through the lower streets, he could see the lights. Hopefully, it was the patrol. His kid was alright. Flick had whacked him across the head a fortnite ago, and that had hurt. She had pluck and the smartz, was off the zizz and the piss, as far as he could see. The lights crept closer.

"I'm done now, Baabi. Don't know where you've been and how you've got here ..."

"China," she said. "For over 55 years. A lifetime, in old money."

"Can you roll me the rum," he asked. Without the gun barrel deviating from his forehead she pushed it across the kerb to where he was propped. "He opened the screwTop and took a slug.

"Was pretty sure you'd given The Man my biometrix on a plate. Am I wrong?" she asked.

He didn't answer. The lights were now rounding the main hill and heading up the nearby side street.

"So I'm stitched up in the AuZgov intel. Fuck you Kingdom."

"You've changed your face. For the better, I may add. Apart from the sour old lines at the side. You'll never hide those, Baabi."

"Fuck you," she hissed again.

He flipped the rum bottle high, at her face, and rolled. There was a gunshot. He skittered over the vBike and flicked on the rebut before the second bullet caught him in the neck and the third in the shoulder. But the bullets had pierced the protective photonic rain shield and the umbrella started to smoke and glow. Shields try hard to keep objects out and react intensely when hard things penetrate – like gun slugs. The patrol car lights stopped at the crest and milisi got out to investigate the big red mushroom floating in front of them, and the gunshots.

By that time, Kingdom was almost unconscious, and dying.

"Aw, fuck it," he was thinking, as he heard further shots, but the hardArms weren't aimed at him. She'd done the job and got him first. His eyes stayed open, until nothing remained visible. Then they closed.

WEN

AN EXTRA Tropical ''phoon had blistered in the currents of the south east Pacific over the past few days, ahead of the southward cloud, and the metHeads in the Spokes knew that when the storm reached superIntensity, then several days of bunkering down would be reqwired, as supercharged currents and wind would drive smashing oceans south, butting heads with the cold Antarctic swell. The 'phoon was deepening hourly.

Always a problem in the hot/cold confluence between the Antarctic waters beneath New Zealand waters, and the great wells of hot moist air powering down from the Indian and Pacific oceans into the soupy waters south. The superstructure of the Spokes was designed to withstand those storms, but for the duration the only safe access between Derwent and Spokes was by sub. No boat or hopper could survive a minute in the open.

SuperIntensity warnings – once the pressure had slid more than 50 points and the isometrics red lined – were issued for the southEast coast, Bass Strait and Tasmania. While mainlanders had adapted and built shelters in their houses, and casualties were rare, the worst thing about the storms now was the amount of salt from the water that ended up inland through water tubes and other unknown weather elements.

Those salinity dumps were very bad for horticulture and needed a lot of flushing.

Being on the Spokes was a different kettle of fish, so to speak.

Commanders such as Wen pressed the staff into red mode and everything was battened. Top side hoppers were evacuated and hangared in the hillCaves above Hobarttown, food security was checked and supplemented. The engineers doubled efforts over the antiAcidity flumeTubes to ensure they were lowered into the qwieter deep over the edge of the shelf, away from the turmoil.

Wen had watched the last hopper leave from the top deck and looked at the roiling swell which would reach 50 to 80 metres, and shook his head at the thought. The wind was really feisty now, and the top deck enjj's and gaffermen in gravSkins moved slowly about, like beetles, painstaking in their storm-Prep.

As the world constructed more technology to ensure human safety, the worse the weather got. The exponentiality of the weather frustrated Wen, and the leadership of his generation.

"We live on a dynamic planet, and still don't know how dynamic it might get," 'Arald told Wen that morning as they lay in bed drinking tea, and checking data glows.

"At least we won't be around to find out, my dear," Wen had replied, looking rueful. "Maybe the long awaited tipBack will come ... and the weather will brighten."

"And mebbe not," said 'Arald.

The rueful mood then followed him like a wet dog all morning.

*

Wen kept thinking about a conversation he'd had with Marko the day before on the facility deck. They'd faced eachOther with their trays of bread, fish and vegetables, while he tried to gauge Marko's state. With Courier Phipps away, he'd kept a closer eye on her exasperating bunny.

Marko had asked, "Is it true the whole economy went stagnant and flat when you and the other Administrators purified Australasia?"

"Where'd you hear that?" asked Wen with an amused smile.

"Flick. My friend."

"That sounds like an intergenerational paranoia passed on by Flick's father, Kingdom Allenby. I'll tell you something, Andy – my colleagues in the prior generations before I came on the scene, designed and prosecuted the most stable, peaceful society, worldwide. And it was democratic. People accepted our strictures. Global violence plummeted. The plan worked this way: we helped people who were struggling. We either arrested the more destructive psychopaths & sociopaths or at least diagnosed them, and kept many out of leadership roles. We put a lid on the fire of crime and violence, and snuffed it. Granted, people lived duller lives, but as for the economy stagnating ..." Wen shook his head and wiped his lip with a napkin. "Here in Australasia we had to contain one small war, but that was during *the Blend*."

Marko forged on. "So, allowing me to operate in the way I did ... to create 'ripples' and galvanise the economy ... I wasn't beating back entropy by taking risks. Feeding into the economy to make it dynamic?" Marko obviously enjoyed imagining he was doing his bit, however illegal.

"Sorry, Mr Marko. That's Kingdom Allenby talking. He is a very bitter man. Surely you realise the government allowed you to operate so they could tax you, huge sums, which you faithfully paid. Nowadayz, we need all the money we can get to rebuild infrastructure, to feed the work camps. We don't even have a defence force with fighter bombs, tanks and rockets any more. No country does, because the money is needed elsewhere. That was the one great bagatelle from creating world peace just before everything went to shit."

"What would have happened if there hadn't been international tranqwillity when the climate changed?" Marko asked. But they both knew the answer. Fingal Wen shook his wrinkled head and Marko stopped chewing his bacon for a second.

"We'd all be gone," Wen said. "From space, the world would have looked like the head of a burnt matchstick." Wen looked closely at Marko ... he was nodding, so seemed to understand what a matchstick was. "Now, at least we are hanging on by our fingernails, and life goes on."

"Well, people still obey things, like the fecundity rules, and the pax protocols, and the 10 ways of good neighbourliness."

"In the main they do, and isn't that good," Wen said. "You need those structures and discipline to work your way through the chaos that we have inherited."

He realised he was indulging the lowlife hacker when he was needed in the secure area. For some reason he continued to indulge the confused young man. Maybe on principle to counteract Kingdom's lunatik bullshit.

"So, the Nest. What was that place? It was the weirdest place I've ever encountered." Marko was taking advantage of Wen's candour.

"A place of refuge for those who didn't fit with our structures."

"They all looked like pirates. I couldn't believe my eyes."

Wen raised an amused eyebrow. "I must admit I never had the pleasure of visiting the town," he said.

As Wen reflected on the conversation, he thought, Marko is still a liveArc unit. Asking qwestions. Full of curiosity. Showing no signs yet of deference to his elders, or folding into plain civil obedience.

*

A couple of hours later, still feeling dour, Wen elevated topside once more to check progress. Gaffermen had pulled the more vulnerable parts of the infrastructure down and stored the machinery below water – whiskers, radar, pv nanoPanels that sucked energy from the atmosphere and upperShield management units. All were stripped and stowed.

Hooves to stabilise the hoppers were unbolted, removed. Wen kept a close eye on activity, but the crew knew the drill and he had nothing to add. There were one or 2 such events a year, and worldMet, as well as the Spoke's own metHeads, predicted a further escalation to the point where 'phoons would be a constant in the summer months. Great wads of cold air sucked out of the Antarctic circle, slicing against warm fronts and being corralled into gigantic sea blizzards with tubes and massive 500 kilometre gusts.

Above deck, the weather was getting willing. A sudden icy blast caught the exposed enjj's who were battening down. All personnel hung onto the nearest pipe, or rail. Wen held a large bollard, and leant into the force of the wind and felt wads of sleet slap his face.

The sky was now almost white, the ocean slateGrey and whipped into huge waves. A gafferman high on one of the steel antenna platforms lost his grip and swung wildly on his harness, crashing back into the metal. A spanner fell from his hand and blew like a twig over the side. The man hung backwards, stunned unconscious and his mates headed to help winch him from the rig.

"Bring him down," said Wen into his scope. "Get him to medix now." The force of the 'phoon was now too strong for him. He wasn't wearing a skin with a boson enhancer, so he retreated into the lift vestibule and left it to the men who wore skins and were much younger and stronger. The huge water tornadoes were not far off.

As the lift descended he wiped his face and hands dry with a kerchief and barked a couple of orders into his scope, answers soon arriving: yes, the booms and deAcidification tubes were lowered into the deep level. Yes, the hoppers had made it to Hobarttown without incident.

Yes, audit was done, and yes, there was at least 30 days supply of food and water before a submarine would have to replenish, but the storm wouldn't last so long. Wen hated being so physically isolated, but that was the price of nominal security.

As he strode along the executive deck to the bridge, he almost collided with little Todd, who over the past week had claimed the run of the place and escaping Angie the young cyberEnjj who'd been dragooned into nanny duties.

"What's happening, Fingal Wen?" said Todd.

"Big storm. Go and see 'Arald. He'll tell you." An attempt to get rid of the eager boy. Didn't work.

"Is it dangerous?"

"Not down here, little Todd."

"If it's dangerous, Mum should be here," Todd said bluntly. Todd looked very concerned.

"Where's Angie?" asked Wen to the small boy.

"I think she's looking for me."

Wen felt the dour mood lift slightly as he looked into the little escapee's face.

"Your mum will be here very soon. Next few days. I'm very busy now because I'm boss here, so you should either go and visit 'Arald or find Angie. She'll be worried. Off you go."

Todd nodded and pottered off. The boy made him feel very, very old but Todd was so obedient. Good to see, thought Wen, as he buzzed Angie.

The bridge was not the ops room, but the infrastructure control centre. The bridge also facilitated air and sea control around the Spokes. Its Naval commander was a fellow named Hoggett, who was keeping tabs on the stress sensors.

"Hoggett," said Wen.

"All looking fine, Commander Wen. It's a category 8 'phoon, gusts up to 450/480 kilometres and we've dealt with those before."

"Good to know. I've just heard the hoppers made it in, too, so they'll be hangared safely. We just need to bunker down, I'm afraid."

"You and 'Arald are very welcome at the mess tonite if you feel like company," said Hoggett.

"I'll check with 'Arald," said Wen, looking for a way out. The military stiffness of the milisi officers Mess and their ancient rituals irritated him. He'd use 'Arald as an excuse. Not that it worked. 'Arald liked the finicky ways and solicitous serving staff of the mess and after a short intense discussion, they ended up going.

"It's a serious storm, Fingal," 'Arald had argued. "You need to show the flag with our military colleagues. Our collaboration. Our unity."

"You just like their liqweurs," grumbled Wen, but 'Arald was the one person he couldn't say no to.

As the mess party sat around the ovoid dinner table, and smoothly attentive subalterns brought great plates of food and wine, the structure above them occasionally clanged deep as a larger than usual wave landed directly on the platforms above. Out beyond the windows it was as greenDark and calm looking as usual, though any zoan had withdrawn deeper. Both Hoggett and Wen chatted with half an eye on their clamBs, which were set to the storm freqwencies and structure pressure nodes sending signals.

"We seem to be weathering this one," said Hoggett.

"It'll take 3 days at least to clear," said 'Arald. "I looked at the heat ring signals from the far south HighEyes and it's qwite a blister. Stretches up to Norfolk Island."

The head of SpokesMet nodded in agreement. "At least 3 or 4 days of full strength, and no inFlight for a week," she said.

"That would be my analysis too, Jenny," said 'Arald.

"So we are pretty much encased here for a while, like oysters in a shell," said Wen. "Twiddling thumbs. We did a pileFoundation assess, I presume?"

"Yes, commander," said Hoggett, wearily. "All checked." Dessert, in chrome concertinas, was served: fresh berries and gelato with homeMade chocolate.

"I don't know how they do it in your mess kitchens," said 'Arald in wonderment.

Wen was studiously bored, but even the appearance of dessert impressed him, and he chuckled inside at 'Arald's delight. He looked around at the faces, serious faces who were scooping custard into their mouths, and listened to the shudders across the infrastructure.

'Arald, who'd been a very senior met technician and had developed and run vast weather modelling programs all his life, and who was scooping custard with the best of them, would tell you that, in the end, it was impossible to predict what was going to happen in the outYears. The volatility made everything even worsely unpredictable.

Hoggett continued: "That Marko bloke was talking to one of my lieutenants, by the way, about the primary shutdown and the various stagings. He's a strange one."

"What, the lieutenant?" asked Wen.

"No, Marko. Got Lieutenant Chivvers to go through the whole drill, beginning to end. In detail, no less. Chivvers didn't see any harm as everyone is in it for the duration, but as Marko is a target, I thought I'd let you know."

"Did this informal briefing by any chance include the lowdown on the landBasing of hoppers?" asked Wen.

"Well, that's a key stage of the preparations," said Hoggett. "Beats me though. Why do you think he was so interested?"

But Wen had already thrown his napkin on the table and was heading out the door.

Wen was almost running and at the same time thinking: "I am losing it. I am getting too old. 'Arald was right." There was even a rising panic in his chest which was an almost alien feeling for Fingal Wen. Never had a single human being caused him such anxiety. Not in recent years, anyway. He'd buzzed security to meet at Marko's room in The Hierarchy hotel. They banged the door. No answer. Wanded open. No Marko. Wen swept in and checked clothes and effects. They appeared reduced in number, and his toothjell was missing.

"Call the hopper base at Hobarttown and get them to check the hoppers, and any vidz of people leaving the air base. See if Marko got there. Red code."

"Sir," said Security Chief Starred, face dropping in shock, "but the storm?"

"Just do it," said Wen, slapping his hand on the wall. "This is a disaster."

LUFF

JEMBRANA strode round the outside terrace on the 8th floor of Capricornia's mighty Parliament, with the motion sensitive mist blowers sending puffs of cool moisture across him as he and his party passed. The mist sheened their sunshades for a second then evaporated in the heat. The terrace was an echo of the verandah culture of 300 years prior, an architect's whimsy. Despite the cooling mist, it was still troublingly hot in the height of the day and the sun glared like a furnace.

The security chief was followed by Yovo, who carried some papers. Jembrana himself had his leather wallet firmly underneath an armpit.

"Don't you think Dr Phipps is hugely talented?" he said to his young aide.

Yovo knew that Jembrana was a huge fan of Dr Phipps and qwickly assented. He himself found Phipps to be somewhat evasive and distant, even in Jembrana's orbit. But she was a diplomat and, metaphorically, went through life biting her tongue, like him. The "incident" where Phipps and Jembrana may have *consummated* in his boss's private qwarters (the talk of the town) was not lost on the aide either. Yovo, tho', like his boss Jembrana, was thoughtful, humane and smart and, qwite often, fun. But he was discreet, like now. Sometimes the wrong answer could cause an angerFlash.

"Are you contemplating an alliance with Dr Phipps?" he asked.

Alliance meant many things, of course. Open word.

Jembrana stopped in his tracks and looked out to the ocean.

"She is from Cap. She is the heir to a vast fortune, controlled by her people. And yet she plays in this great big political pigsty with the rest of us. I find that interesting. She could be important to us."

The aide wondered whether Jembrana meant the royal "us" (he was a Prince, after all) or the collective denizens of the huge sprawling overpopulated state they administered from this very building.

"You'd also have observed, Yovo, that she's very, very attractive."

Yovo was surprised. Jembrana often asked him for opinions on everything from the food they ate to complex policy. But the attractiveness of a woman was a new one. Looking for a masculine insight from his aide.

Yovo didn't hold back on Jembrana's observation though.

"She's beautiful," agreed Yovo. "And always immaculately dressed."

Jembrana nodded and headed into the shadier halls and through a door. The slight film of mist on his skin cooled rapidly in the airCon, a pleasant sensation.

"I'm warned by his staff that the Premier Luff is low," said the aide as they made their way to Jembrana's administrative chambers.

"Low? How."

"His people said the admin tours of the far north were a real eye opener. Deteriorating sitch. Terrible scenes. He's depressed about it, shocked even."

"Ah, we've coped with this sort of stuff before," said Jembrana airily. "He'll be fine!" They bowled through the high open arch through Luff's reception area, and passed the executive assistants with a nod.

"Call the Premier and tell him I'm back. His turn to come to me," he said on the way through.

*

Luff sat in Jembrana's office on white leather, the couch adjacent to the security chief's large desk. Jembrana leaned back in his airChair sideways, looking out the window, and not at Luff.

The steel tint on the window kept the fierce glare from warming the air in the room. The everpresent glare, which to Luff was sometimes like a knife in the back of the eyeball. At that point, the tint was the only thing that pleased him.

The men were enveloped by a long pause during a catchUp conversation. Luff had been away, avoiding the Ville for a month and a half.

By consent, they'd removed their aides from the room so a more candid and friendlier atmosphere prevailed. With less formality and likelihood of leaks.

Jembrana kept his eqwanimity, eyes slightly closed. The Premier of the vast territory they jointly administered watched him, his eyes dark ringed, his head shaved. Luff was thinner, more gaunt, and he felt his energy levels starting to drop. He was wrung out.

"Sometimes I think our State ... our administrated area ... was deemed a separate entity because the rest of the world didn't want to deal with the chaos. Put some new suckers in charge. Make them responsible for the disaster," Luff said.

Luff was being remarkably candid and sharp, although like all high ranking administrators, he spoke in subdued tones, as if sharing a secret. "As you know," he continued, "I've checked out the top end. From Tennant Creek through to Kununurra and up to Wyndham. A look at hardening the infrastructure, but in reality, we're just going to have to pull people south. Like we did in the Cape York region 30 odd years ago. It's becoming uninhabitable above the 16th parallel in the west High Capricorn as well."

Luff told of the cloud, the almost unstoppable rain; the impassable roads. The erosion as the ocean ate its way up estuaries and mangrove flats into the hinterland, flushing great brown clouds of sediment into the ocean. Sometimes they couldn't even get the Premier's hopper into towns because of the weather, and had to change the itinerary numerously. Many of the people of *the Blend*, refugees from the elements, had come across from further north to grow food as subsistence farmers, as they had done in Indonesia and the Philippines. That was the compact – likeforlike. But after 30 or 40 years, things were worse. They were moving involuntarily, in dribs and drabs, but the volume of refugees from the far north to Central Cap was growing and creating tensions in towns further south.

*

Rows of cycads with stripped leaves and black stumps dotted the rubble that had, a few days before, been a massive West Cap work camp. Luff had been there a few months earlier troubleshooting and jawing with enjj's, logisticians and accountants over the micro details of storm walls, food routes and whether (big qwestion) the port facilities, docks and swing cranes was kat6 safe for bigger cargo haulers. He'd explored all the hooks and catches with the riskWranglers and the Wyndham portmaster's people.

At that time, 100s of people, mostly Indon, but qwite a few Indijj and Euro workers as well, were pitching and meshing storm walls along some of the inner estuaries. Hundreds more were retrofitting the railheads and dams, from the last season, around the district. That's what the work camps did: maintenance and repair while the *Singular Enemy* fought back and tried to strip the work of humankind off the earth's crust. They had lived in the now rubbleStrewn plain – not well, but not uncomfortably, with their wives and kids. Now they were pulverised and on the move.

The Wyndham work camp meant a lot. Was a great experiment that he'd overseen. The population had adapted and worked there well. Further south, the Ord area was holding up to the seasonal downpours and producing. Luff hadn't wanted that lost. Oh no. Meant valuable $New exporting south and to the northern hemisphere. The Ord was his baby. Now in Wyndham the cycads were stripped mostly of their leaves. They held their ranks, but looked like crushed fingerbones. Like they were giving him a salute of failure. A guard of dishonour.

The scene boded very ill for future human habitation.

*

Jembrana had heard and seen it all before, but his coAdministrator was pretty boggled with his visit, this time.

"How long before we need to act?" Jembrana asked.

"Now. We have to act now. It is … uninhabitable. But somehow there're over a million people in that qwadrant who still give it a go. Some of them don't even want to leave, specially the Indigenous which is understandable."

"What do you want me to do?" asked Jembrana.

"I'll talk to Canberra, when it calms off in April. We need to move them all west of the Tanami Crescent. Or the Arables along the mid west coast. Fit them in. They can give it a go there."

"All pretty far south for Cap."

"Long way. I'll have to marshal our milisi and get help from the south. When the roads dry."

Luff was always uncomfortable in Jembrana's sparse office, but the smell of kopi steaming was reassuring.

"Will the settlers object?"

"Most of them are begging for reassignment. Some of them are already moving south without the permissions and claiming smallPatch acreages in the southern Tanami which is causing some consternation among the current residents." There was another long pause.

"We knew all this already, Paul. You seem disturbed. What happened up there?"

Luff groaned. "The day before I got there, a group of thermocells had gone through my big work camp at Wyndham. I arrived to find that crews were on a rescue job. A container had been picked up and flipped –"

"What? The cell flipped a shipping container?"

"Hadn't been bolted to a slab. It was a public storm bunker. There were 5 in a row. Three red. One yellow. One Blue. Four of them had been bolted on twenty by twenty slabs. The blue one was an afterthought. Because of growth in that qwadrant of the camp, they had needed more shelters. Kids. Somehow a couple of families had multiple permissions. They'd had kids over the last few years and needed a further bunker.

"So our men hitch up a crane and pull it out of the mud where it had flipped. They lifted it up about 8 metres so we could set it right, and the door just swung open with the weight of what was inside. I was there. So people, kids ... and their mums and dads ... just started pouring out of the end of the container like slop. Like slop from a big blue jug, into the mud. There must have been up to 50 of them crammed into the space. All dead. Suffocated when the container was up-ended and the door was flattened against the ground.'

"What," said Jembrana in horror. "It hadn't been ventilated?"

"Not properly. Just another infrastructure job waiting to be done. Bolting and ventilation drilling. A pile of corpses. Crushed together and suffocated, Jembrana. Piled on top of each other. Mostly littl'uns." Luff's hand was shaking as he lifted his cup. He took a sip of the strong kopi and closed his eyes.

"These things happen," said Jembrana flatly. "Millions died in the step change."

"Well, they shouldn't," said Luff. "I can't abide it. Some of us are not so lucky as to have children. Some of us have to absorb the criminal waste of our mistakes. The contractor who had the task to bolt the container has been arrested, of course."

"So they just entered an unsecured, unfixed storm bunker?"

"Should have been padlocked to prevent entry. But the community told me the others were just as crowded. They had nowhere else to go. And the houses, the shanties, the whole area was torn apart by the tubes, of course, and some of the reconstruction along the wharves, which the work camps were established for. Torn apart. But it's the pile of dead kids that I can't get out of my mind."

"Of course," murmured Jembrana. "I'm sorry."

He paused. "When I was a kid, the politicos in this country talked of achieving a perfect society. Was everyone's dream," said Luff.

"In my country, my father said that too," said Jembrana. "He was a leader. It was the aspiration, and he fought for harmony and virtue." He thought of the picture of Rama, above this father's desk, greeting the monkey god.

"But the past has a habit of sneaking up from behind and robbing us some more." Luff's voice cracked with despair. "Those dreams are bullshit." A tear started to well in his face, which he then covered with a hand.

Jembrana looked very concerned. He leaned forward. "Can I get you something? A brandy? A flute of zizz?"

"Don't touch any zizz," said Luff in a flat tone. "Purity is important – of mind and body."

"Then is there anything else I can do? Our tenure has 6 years to run. You are one toughNut colleague, although I hate to admit it. Maybe you could take some leave? We can get Chance Cargill to deputise."

Luff took a sip of kopi to steady himself and clicked his cup back down on the saucer. It was a sharp noise given their qwiet conversation.

He ignored Jembrana's genuine concern and continued: "Chance? She's too young. No, I'll start looking at the logistics of an evacuation from the very top. The Wyndham sector. Pull the town and 2 big camps south. I will scope Canberra and set up a meeting. You'll support the evacuation, won't you?"

Jembana looked at Luff. He was emotional and shaken and Jembrana wondered about his colleague's decision to persevere. Their next election was far away. The wily security chief sighed. He was the one who could authorise milisi and trucks. The Wyndham area had more than a million inhabitants.

"This is a massive population shift you are contemplating. Much bigger than the Cape York exercise."

"It is indeed. I was one of the junior subaltern administrators that organised that shift, back in the decades."

"Right, get your people to send me a report of the tragic incident, please. And the Portmaster of Wyndham can send me metEvent records for the region, too. I'd have to see the evidence on paper, as will Canberra and Jakarta. If it is as you say, with escalations outside the parameters of our current regional climate models, I'll back you, yes."

Escalations would have to be proved. Jembrana knew this would not be difficult.

Jembrana's caveat was now fixed to the evidence, and Luff knew it, but he still nodded and said thank you. Luff himself knew too that he was in no fit state for a fullFrontal argument with Jembrana about a worsening stepChange in the weather. That could wait while he got his untoward depression under control and the evidence was presented.

But Luff had been around and he knew what he'd seen.

"What now?" asked Luff, who was usually the one issuing directives.

"I'm meeting Courier Madrigal Phipps. She's back in the Ville after the death of that Kingdom Allenby fellow. Centrl wants it checked out. We've made no headway with any of the other mayhem that happened last October, so Dr Phipps is back."

"You'll be pleased!" Luff said drily, looking darts at his colleague. The single assignation between Jembrana and Dr Phipps had been the talk of certain, rarified parts of the town and word of the "sleepover" had reached Luff when he was in Tennant Creek and he answered a breathless call from an assistant who was trying to win favours.

When he'd heard the gossip and scoped off in the poky hotel room, the news had caused a worm of anger in his guts. Not so much jealousy but a sharp sense of propriety being broken. Jembrana had sexed with a senior AuZgov official, breaking certain, unwritten rules.

But that anger had evaporated. Now, shattered by events in Wyndham and what he had witnessed, Luff had summoned much effort to get a needling tone into his voice.

Jembrana didn't flinch at the "You'll be pleased."

"It will be nice to see Dr Phipps. She is an interesting woman." Deadpan return.

"She is the daughter of Derek Phipps, of Phipps Industries, in my experience a man not to be trifled with."

Jembrana knew the old term "trifled" He shrugged. Luff's comment was surprisingly guarded and even advisory, given his clear disapproval of the relationship. Derek Phipps basically "owned" West Cap through his web of companies, and could be extremely vindictive.

"Hopefully Courier Phipps will shed some light on the murders and the subseqwent attack on my men," said Jembarana, changing the subject.

"I hope so, too," said Luff, sounding punctured again, coping with another wave of sadness. "The bombing of that bar was incomprehensible."

There was a knock and a bearded assistant stuck his head round the whitewashed door.

"Your 11 o'clock appointment, chief."

Luff stood up.

"I'll get you that information first thing tomorrow. The crew is onto the logistics projections already."

"Fine," said Jembrana and offered a folder. "Here's the paper file on the investigations into the bombing as well as the 2 discreet murders, the latest being Kingdom Allenby." He handed over a wad. "I've kept the details on the discreet channel for security. No sharing. Paper communication only."

Luff nodded, but didn't seem interested. He was more concerned about the deterioration in the northern areas, than with the police investigations.

"Thanx. I'll look at them tonite," he said in a flat voice, taking the files.

*

Jembrana watched Luff leave, perplexed. The man had seen 100s of terrible things in the past. They were youngsters together in *the Blend* – which, as far as Jembrana was concerned, went well. Millions had lived and escaped the devastation. What was with Luff's trauma? It was as if the Premier had lost all spirit and energy for a task that he relished.

In fact, Jembrana had been delighted at Luff's late jab – *You'll be pleased* – because it showed the old Luff was still there – sharp and snide, with his judgemental backhanders. The comment had taken a fair bit of effort though. And the seemingly friendly warning about Derek Phipps. Something was odd. Mebbe he needed a tonic. He knew Luff had had 2 rejuves. Was that it? Running out of fuel third time round, even with the pills.

Jembrana composed himself. Centrl has already exchanged snippy words with him about his relationship with Dr Phipps and he'd mostly agreed what they'd done was inappropriate, even though it wasn't really Centrl's place to scold him.

Inappropriate it had been. Yes. But he disagreed on one thing. If an interesting woman comes along, then you have to come together, see where it takes you. That was one of his rules and it had cost him a marriage or 2. Perhaps he'd gone too far with the Courier? He didn't think so. And she was indeed her own woman and would have her Dad sorted. Old Derek Phipps didn't worry him either.

A valet removed the dirty cups, straightened the cushions on the couch and then nodded on his way out. Jembrana went to the door and personally ushered Dr Phipps in.

As usual she was beautifully dressed, not in any uniform, but this time in a very light gold business jacket and skirt. The door shut and she pecked him on the cheek. They sat down on the comfortable lounges. No official crossDesk positioning business for those 2.

"Jembrana."

"Dr Phipps."

"We could keep the door closed to keep Centrl guessing," she said. "I was sin binned for a fortnite because of our evening together."

"Sin binned?"

"It's an old Australian football term where you are sent to the sidelines for a while as punishment. I was sent to my family in Perth for a break."

"Oh, I didn't know. Thought you were still tracking through the binaries for Marko."

Madrigal smiled. The rare smile of affection.

"At this juncture," said Jembrana, "I think a couple of aides should be present and take notes."

Madrigal nodded with another fixed smile, mildly disappointed that Jembrana wouldn't bait Centrl by closing the door, but he was one prong of the Duumvirate and owned a public reputation. She inhabited the sidelines.

"You could at least get them to bring kopi at regular intervals," she conceded. "Let me fill you in."

She briefed him on the Spokes, the attack on Marko by the shimmerman and her winning sense of smell (which amused him), the issues between the White Lady and the Brillhoz; who was who in the plot. She told him of the heavies in Perth who threatened her at the football game and who subseqwently disappeared without a trace, which horrified Jembrana.

"They outwitted Centrl? That's astonishing!"

"Didn't make me happy after their filthy threats."

Jembrana then briefed Madrigal on the Kingdom killing. The crazy shooter – Milisimen tagged on their cameras as a woman with blonde hair – had fired a bullet through the energy shield on the bike, which was turned on for the rain sqwalls; the vibrations and flash the bullets had attracted the patrol's attention. Then he went into the gruesome details of the gunfight, the milisi had engaged in, and wasn't the fact they were armed a miracle? And Kingdom's corpse.

"Have you tagged the killer apart from gender? You did get some biometrix from the Milisi landV sensors?"

"Not anything hard. Killer moved qwick."

She shrugged. "Where's young Flick?" she then asked.

"I moved her to the barracks, I'm afraid. For her own protection. We assume this assassin was on the way to kill her, and instead killed her father."

"I'd like to see Flick," Madrigal said, and Jembrana acceded immediately.

Madrigal took a sip of the kopi and glanced at a young male aide who had stopped taking notes and was listening like an alert dog. She said: "It's like there are several teams, including yours and mine, thrashing around, trying to find the key to it all," Madrigal said. "Like a murky tank filled with slippery fishy shapes. My view is that somewhere the 2 teams were both in on the plot, but at other times, they worked to a separate plan. The Brillhoz think they have the key to the coding and just want Andaman dead, along with anyone else who had any idea of his program – which I surmise, noone does. Then they have a powerful tool; to spy on their rivals.

"If they can't kill him, they want him to shutUp, hence the death threats. The White Lady from the Chinese Hegs has some of his program and they want the rest, which is probably smart. That's why the kidnapping on the Cape.

"So – we have Marko and yet he's not coming completely clean on how he punctures secret communications to make money. He's a real sneak. The 2 hegs are not natural allies, and mistakes have been made. Their submarine and raiding party was a massive overReach," she sipped the excellent smoky kopi again. "And it's at a point where somehow young Flick, myself, my son Todd even, are all in danger because these people have no idea of exactly what they want. And I'd further bet King-dom Allenby was in full watchfulness over his daughter and someone decided to remove him before killing Flick. He was marked, because he was guarding the girl. Perhaps he posed a danger to the killer ... a woman, you say."

"A woman."

There was a pause and Madrigal spoke awkwardly, as if ask-ing for a strange favour. "My lead Slotter, Chime, is insisting we examine Kingdom's body, on orders from Centrl. Something I find rather odd and unsettling, but there you are – under these extreme circumstances, can we view it?"

"Of course. The whole family are out at the barracks. Flick, plus her dead father in the cold storage. And her dead brother too, tho we're done with him. As you know, you ambushed him and his crew north of Cape Flattery."

"Does Flick know the brother is there?"

"Oh no, no, no. We want her compliant,"

"Fair enough," said Madrigal.

There was a pause. They flashed conspiratorial smiles at one another.

"So you have your whole Slotter team with you?" Jembrana asked.

"I'm sorry, but I've imported 2 of them into East Cap again. Chime and Folly at least. The others are with Marko. Once this is over and safety prevails, I'll be free to move to my own beat."

Jembrana laughed.

He turned to the hovering Yovo and asked that a visit to the barracks be arranged immediately and a VIP cruiserV provided. The aide closed his notebook and strolled out of the room. Jembrana, with his calm, slightly hooded lids, watched Yovo go, then turned to Madrigal again. He observed her honeyBrown face, dark brown eyes, amused lips.

"I'd invite you out to dinner, for a prawn something, but ..."

"In a couple of months, when this is all over, I'll pay a proper visit. I'd like that."

BAABI 3

THE GAUNT old woman spat a gobful of chopChop juice over the canal bridge where it splashed in the murky water. She realised she'd been chewing too hard, too fast, in anger. The milisi mopUp over the past week had enraged her, though she'd easily evaded their sweep. There were bucketfuls of old women in this town. She'd become one of the invisible ones.

Baabi, although she preferred Three, had ditched vehicles (sold real cheap to a stallholder), and her weapon (in the canal), and had augmented her face, coloured her hair to grey and curls. She was still seething. Aiee! She'd been tricked by the old fool Kingdom, the traitor, the cankerous bastard. Eyes on him and ears on his patter, thinking she'd had the upper.

As they'd talked, memories of the insurgency, the adrenaline of that time, had flowed through her veins like poisonous tingling hooks. During the war, in the various camps and hideouts, their nervous systems had been on overdrive and his grog had been powerful – he'd seduced her. She'd seduced him. When they'd got drunk and dirty he'd beaten her on occasion. But she hadn't minded. She'd fought back – bashed the shit out of him once until he passed out, begging her to stop.

Very qwickly, she'd risen in Kingdom Allenby's pantheon of fighters and he'd appointed her a commander, leading a platoon, which was enthralling. He'd taught her to fight, to kill effectively. Really kill. He'd trained her, used her and then betrayed her. And here he was, 50 years post *the Blend*, post every hideous recalibration of the world.

He'd been the reason she'd come back, from H'Kong. Didn't care much about the job, but the assignment gave her a chance. A chance to find and kill Kingdom Allenby.

Lying there, a human wreck half conscious on the grass verge, under the poinciana tree, in her gunSights, and in her revenge charged delight, she'd forgotten the ambient awareness training that he'd banged into her brain all those years ago.

Listen up teamsters ... Most important warning you'll ever get is from your neck hair... Watch for reflections... Listen behind ... new noises ... airflow ...changes in the light ... new light sources ... are a DEAD give away ... command your surrounds, don't let them command you.

For god's sake, she thought, headlights of patrol cars had been licking the house windows all the way through their ugly convo, their verbal duel of abuse, recrimination and reminiscence, and she hadn't noticed.

Though she'd watched it pass, and clocked it, nite after nite, from her vantage point above the house she hadn't heard the approaching patrol vehicle. Forgot clear about it. He'd muddled her slightly with his rolling rum bottle and the rum. Old times' sake. She'd lost discipline. He'd messed with her head. Or rather, she had messed with her own head. The rum bottle trick. One last drink for old times' sake? Fuck's sake! He'd forced her to concentrate on her aim, a ploy to draw the backup close and sacrifice himself for his daughter, noble in death .... for once. F'king bastard.

He had fought hard in the final skirmishes of their pointless civil war, but he'd brought all the warring groups together, in one place, to face the ultimate enemy of AuZgov. A full frontal attack. They'd been so successful harrying government troops, and towns, sinking barges which were bringing people across the Timor Sea. And he'd cajoled the rebel military groups into one place, waited for a weather window to allow full visibility. Purposeful, duplicitous. He knew they would never beat the AuZgov forces, but led them to trust him & believe they could. They were all led down the garden path into open fire where 100s of her comrades died at the Battle of Normanton. After that she'd deserted and a few weeks later twigged to Kingdom Allenby's deceit. But by that time she was in the Philippines.

She was walking through a laneway and over a couple of canal bridges in the flats, dressed like a hawker, to the safe-house. There she'd check for any new orders. Currently in town, were targets still. Kingdom's daughter, and wasn't she marked! Finish off that despicable lineage. The Indijj woman, she'd seen her. Three was being paid to deal with them all, and she would. And yet, she was now being sought. Slight woman, old, dangerous. Killer.

At the safehouse, with its hardplast walls, louvres and steel roof, she let herself in with a wand and went straight to the frijj, an old one that hummed. In the crisper tray were a new firearm, rounds, explosive knuckles and detonators, and a wad of $Old to keep her going. She found a token behind the poster of a dog and stuck it in her Frisky, a small Scope'n'lock device, and grunted.

It read: *Original target only, on his return. Crisper tray.*

She'd already done the crisper tray. Scooped its contents. Wait for Marko now, and his inevitable return to his assigned town. She was a soldier, so she'd do as asked. They'd send the cash through eventually. But if that AuZgov bitch tried to find her, bitch would pay her own very private price.

Just like her exLover, mentor, and finally betrayer, Kingdom Allenby.

KINGDOM, POSTMORTEM

AT BARRACKS, Madrigal and Chime were taken into the cold-Store to look at the corpse of Kingdom Allenby. Chime held the door open as she entered.

Chime's take was always a useful sounding board, with his situational insights. He was good backup. And his unconscious oldWorld gallantry amused her.

"Two clean shots," said Chime staring qwizzically at the naked corpse. "But looking good for a 93 year old."

A tech who'd scanned and dated the victim said he'd had one illegal rejuve. One too many. Four in total.

"Must have been hurting, really," said Chime. "Four's a lot. Joints start getting inflamed. You lose body mass as stuff starts to eat away from the inside. Looks like he's been weather-beaten from the age of 10. Look at the scars."

Madrigal noted: "Skin and scans show a man who had sustained a lot of injuries. Broken bones, bullet wounds ... very rare on anyone nowadayz. Old burns. Raddled. It's the only word I can think of."

Fingal Wen's sonorous voice chipped through their earbugs. "The man was a warrior. Worked with us throughout the insurgency during *the Blend*, 60 year ago. Underground. Trained a lot of bad people, I daresay, but in return, he almost single-handedly wrecked their rebellion. Made it implode. We have him to thank that a wildfire civil war was ended before it really took off."

"During the Age of Purity?" asked Madrigal in disbelief.

"It was a nasty little war. Passions were very high up north, and they were getting archWeapons through from Asia. HardArms, explosives. Northerners were cashed up in those days, from minerals. Kingdom Allenby was very badly injured in the last stand near Normanton. Burn wounds. Lost half his liver to a bullet. Our people patched him as best they could, with synthetic skin and rejuve stem cells in a field hospital. But before he was lifted out, he disappeared one nite from the hospital," said Wen. "No time to track him. There was too much mayhem, fires to put out. We were pretty sure he'd headed up to Cape York rather than the northern hemisphere. He floated into view every so often doing his own thing. Smuggling, gun-Running, growing cashDrugs, being a boat raider in the waters under the cloud. Told me once, very rudely, that he'd paid his dues and to forget him."

"You knew him?" Madrigal said astonished.

"We went through training together," said earbug Wen. "We were once friends."

Both Chime and Madrigal looked at one another with im-pressed eyes. They were in the presence, though deceased, of one of the unknown legends of the security service, surely.

"In the end, tho', I ... myself and others, turned Kingdom Al-lenby, my friend, into a throwback." Such a bitter tone.

Madrigal looked at Chime's face, but he didn't flinch. Pro-fessional, impassive.

"So what can you tell me?" asked Wen.

"Centrl, we know that he was shot by a single person with an oldStyle weapon. The milisi patrol who intervened were armed. Because of the high state of security around Kingdom

Allenby's daughter, everyone had a hardArm. They were qwick to return fire. One was seriously injured in crossfire, but the assailant ran before milisi could get a bead on her either with HighEyes or an angel. The unhurt milisi tended to his comrade without pursuit. She escaped into the crowd down the hill and from there we know not."

"Her?"

"Yeah. Milisi definitely report a female."

Wen groaned. This was too weird. Weren't the last remaining tough nuts, Kingdom among them, all men? But there was the seed of a memory there.

"Can you repeat that?

"Female," said Madrigal. "Definitely." She evoked a shrugging motion to Chime who nodded back.

"I think this is all a legacy matter. From a very long time ago," said Wen distantly. "I'll send you some images if I can find them in the archives," and he signed out.

Madrigal walked up to the body, looking at the matted hair and beard, the bushy eyebrows, still reddishBrown. A nasty neck wound that was cleaned. Here was a comrade of Wen's and probably Bluestone's. They came through training with the enforcers at the end of the Age of Purity & Virtue, invisible men and women who were the guardians of the increasingly vulnerable nationContinent. The people who saw to the transitions, and ameliorated the disasters, such as the time of *the Blend*, when the worst climatic stepChange (so far) had happened.

They took the worst off the streets and remediated the confused. Worked with other governments to curtail national aggression, while the politicians worked on the "ties that bind" between nations, states, tribes. The war, they declared, was against the *Singular Enemy* – the climate – and couldn't be won if humans fought each other.

She respected the older guardians in theory because they'd kept the peace when everything could have unravelled to the point of species extinction, but she now found that entire generation to be patronising, full of themselves, and unaware that more change had since occurred.

"How old are you, Chime?" she asked.

He laughed. "Late fifties, ma'am. Never had a juve."

"Well then, I'm just a baby compared to you and the late Kingdom Allenby," she said, sliding the corpse back into the cryogene.

"And he's still probably old enough to be my grandfather, ma'am."

*

Back in his qwarters, Fingal Wen stared into the ink of the oceanFall from a battened window. There were no creatures visible. He stared at where the black went endlessly onwards through currents and eddies to the chill of Antarctica.

Wen remembered the hasty signals coming in from the heart of the civil war. He shuddered at the memory of the packed evacuation barges crossing the Arafura Sea and Torres Straits that were torpedoed by small, unmanned fishing tinnies.

The tinnies had been malevolently loaded with old mortar rounds and aimed at the barges by the anti*Blend* rebels. The coastguard picked up the dead and wounded refugees, who the Authority had invited to come. And the naval personnel, both AuZgov and Indon who were crewing the barges, well, many of them died also.

He remembered the secret signals from Kingdom, as their doubleAgent played the various factions. Dissembling, lying, cutting against the grain of truthfulness.

Kingdom's work, and the support of Centrl security, had made everyone involved in the op qweasy with guilt, but there was no other choice. The conflict was generally kept hidden from the general population. AuZgov and ASEAN found the wherewithal (somehow) to protect most of the refugees who escaped the closeDown along key eqwatorial areas, and snuff out the dissent.

Oh, thought Wen, if they had only anticipated. Never had AuZgov anticipated such anger from people. Wen and his fellow Administrators were caught by surprise at the local reaction to *the Blend*.

After decades of calm, through the slow weeding of those with psycho/sociopathogies from senior positions and qwelling rebellious instincts within the people, the proposition of civil war had been some hallucination from previous centuries that suddenly manifested in the image of furious red-Blotched, leathery men in homemade fatigues, bearded, bloodied and unbowed.

Kingdom was a young livewire then, enthralled with the challenge. Wen remembered his energy as they planned and briefed and prepared. The big man, undercover, ready to rip the heart of the rebellion apart. Centrl concluded the scheme would take "some weeks", but things dragged on, as only the impure chaos of war can. War had become a forgotten state of being and they were caught offguard.

People died, bodies piled up. Northern Towns were burnt to the gound – Cloncurry, The Isa, Weipa, Mareeba, and milisi posts were smashed. Kingdom was embedded to unite a bunch of unfocussed guerrilla bands, train them and then lead that army to its doom. The most costEfficient way of dealing with what was truly a savage conflict. Snuff it qwick as poss.

Fingal Wen knew his old friend Kingdom had suffered horribly: physically, mentally. Prior to volunteering for the job, he'd been a slightly wayward member of the administration, but effective, and a believer in peace. Afterwards? Afterwards, he was a man torn asunder.

In the end, the Civil War was Kingdom's suicide mission – a long lingering, walloping, drunken, violent life of a suicide, which took his old friend the rest of his century to complete.

*

Madrigal met Flick in her barracks suite, where she lived for safety. A very pleasant set of rooms, plumb in the middle of the campus, with a big bed and kitchenette, and a ground floor apartment, out of sightline from the roads or hills. A safehouse surrounded by milisi.

Flick was genuinely delighted to see Madrigal who couldn't help but smile.

"You've come back!"

"Not for long."

She looked at the young woman and her disingenuous face, and suddenly felt old. Flick had slept, looked fresh. Obviously hadn't been crying or mourning after the death of her dad. Eyes were bright and clear, free of grief and zizz.

"Come and walk with me in the garden," said Madrigal.

In the well of the barracks was an excellent central park shaded with eucalypts and palms. Further behind the park was a cluster of cafes and shops for the milisi residents and contract workers, and while the morning moist was starting to hit the forties, there were fans and sprays keeping the microclimate cooler.

"I am sorry about your father."

"So am I," said Flick simply. "But he was difficult. A very hard man. You have to understand that. When I was old enough I left. I avoided him."

"You know what he did in the past? His history during *the Blend*? He paid the price."

They made their way down one of the paths. Though it was sweltering, Flick kept her arms crossed.

"Don't want to. Whatever he done screwed him up. He used to beat my mum. He was never there. He drove away my brother, S'mon, who I lost – and now it seems S'mon is dead as well. Killed in an accident I've been told." She shrugged. "S'mon worshipped Dad when he was a boy, and got treated like the whelp of the litter. Least Dad never beat me, unless he was drunk and out of it, and I was pretty scooty – got out of his way."

A flock of lorikeets landed in one of the high eucalypts and started noisily feeding on the flowers. Bits of dead leaf came floating to the lawns.

Madrigal looked sideways at the girl who was looking at the ground as they walked. She didn't appear troubled. But very solemn. She couldn't tell if Flick was bottling things. She had such a sweet face.

"It's been a rough few weeks. We moved you here for your own safety. You're not a prisoner. You are a guest. Can't risk losing you too."

"I know," Flick said.

"In recent times, did your dad ever mention a woman called Baabi? From his past?"

Wen had found the file in the archives. He remembered something from Kingdom's ratty debrief in the field hospital after the Normanton event. She was in there. Kingdom had then itemised her savagery and the authorities looked for her, but she'd gone. Wasn't among the dead. Wen read the reports and relayed it down a scope that morning, the type of mercenary Baabi was, Kingdom's worst creation. Madrigal thought she'd try asking Flick about her.

"No. If this person was from before he met mum, then he never talked about it."

"Baabi is really dangerous," Madrigal volunteered.

They found a table at one of the courtyard cafes which was inhabited by a few morning kopi lovers. A steward took their order and delivered a flute of zizz from a tray to a couple of soldiers sitting next to them. They sniffed noisily.

Madrigal asked whether Flick was ok at the barracks, whether she had people to talk to, and assured her that no recriminations would happen due to her zeroNatal status. She said Flick's DNA identity was now with DyNAst, but authorities always understood that in the rare event of a child born to Noughters, it was because of the sins of the father and mother, not the kid. There would be no blowback. Flick just shrugged and nodded at the reassurance.

"That's just the law. It's fair," added Madrigal.

"He called me his little abomination."

"Who?"

"Dad."

"That's horrible," said Madrigal.

"It was his joke," said Flick. She even smiled slightly. Madrigal could tell now. She was mourning in her own way.

"Will Andy be coming home?" Flick asked.

Maybe Andaman Marko was her family now?

"I can't guarantee anything, Flick, until Baabi is captured. She obviously has orders to kill Andaman and you, and possibly me. Your dad was keeping an eye out. That's why he was killed."

Flick nodded. She knew. Dad was looking after her at the end.

"When this Baabi is caught, make sure she suffers," said Flick, looking down at the table.

*

Ronny, the very decent bruzz from the Ville who'd welcomed her all those months ago even buying Madrigal a drink at that bar, again welcomed her with a joyful hug and led her to a group of people in the large suburban backyard. The yard sported 2 ancient mango trees and a small steelFramed house. The traditional Wednesday barbecue Ronny had extolled during their brief chat, before the unpleasantness began, was host to mostly Indijj, plus a few Euro and Asian rellies. A big family. Groups of folk were sitting in chair circles gossiping, or clumped beside the barbecue, or watching kids. They were laughing, and kids ran round the yard playing tig and kicking a footy.

"Nice to see you again, sister," he said and she nodded.

"Maddy," said Madrigal. "Call me Maddy. Dad's family's from Kimberly country. Mum was from further east till they moved to Perth. It's nice to meet you all. Been out of town, but now I'm back and thought I'd say hi. Thanx for inviting me along."

"Would you like a steak sandwich?"

Madrigal was impressed. Steak! She nodded and a young man bustled off to organise one.

"In fact, I have to be upfront and truthful with you, Ronny. I need some help. I work as a lawyer for the AuZtralian government. I wouldn't ask you if it wasn't critical, and I'm not asking you to do much. We can talk about it later. Can I meet your family?"

Ronny nodded. "Not a prob," he said. He called a couple of other brothers and sisters over and they were introduced and the women welcomed Madrigal. They talked for a while about the family connections in the Ville and beyond, and what was important and what was annoying, and the kids ran around, and they ate steak and sausage sangers and a few of the adults drank beer and others didn't.

To Madrigal, they looked prosperous and healthy and she wondered how people of her ancient culture ever managed to reach a place like this happy backyard, chatting and in one piece. She knew it wasn't because of the cards they'd been dealt for 300 long, horrible years. Cards dealt by both the cruel & the foolishly wellMeaning. She smiled at the conversation and chipped in about raising boys, and what it was like in the west and how the weather up north was making it difficult for youngsters from Cap to go to ceremony every year.

"The whole thing's buggered up," said one young woman.

"Ah, well, at least we know what we're in for these days. Not like before," said Ronny. "And we pulled it together, didn't we?"

"That we did," said Madrigal.

So she turned to business, and explained about a lone woman who was somewhere in the Ville, lying low, dangerous to everyone. Probably responsible for the fatal explosion in the Northern Lights, killing people.

"That was the nite I met you," said Ronny. "I saw the fire trucks and everything, but they kept us away down the block. It was a disaster! All those bodybags!"

The circle of people were silently listening to this terrible story.

"Wasn't long after we chatted that it happened," Madrigal answered. But she left out details of the meeting in the sexSalon, the man with the fishlike eyes, the explosion, and the horrible tang of burnt plastic in her mouth that had lasted for days.

At the barbecue, she was just being a concerned official combining a bit of business with some welcome interaction on a social level. Which was all true.

"We have to track this dangerous person down and we still think she's around. This woman will probably be living alone in what was a rental house, in an ordinary bit of the town. She'll be alone, but won't be sleeping rough. She'll be staying somewhere clean. So what does she look like? She's a whitefella, thin, a bit old, could be blonde, could be grey, could have gone black on top, but that would look weird for her ... she's had too many rejuves so she'll certainly be stiff."

"Ah, those rejuve things. Can't people just let life be life, and life last as long as it does?" said Shirley, one of Ronny's relatives. Madrigal smiled – she knew older Indijj people found rejuves contrary to their custom.

"Have you had one," Ronny asked Madrigal.

"No, Ronny." She laughed out loud. "I'm far too young. I'm like you – a spring chicken."

Ronny smiled.

There was a pause, and she stared at the sky, with the clouds lit sodium yellow from the bulging up glow of the Ville.

"So you guys, as the most local of the locals, just have a think ... if anyone has seen or knows about this person, scope me. Just scope me. Let me know. Here's my chip." She handed them to everyone listening. "I'm at my wits' end. Don't go near her or try and talk to her 'cos she's dangerous. Just let me know. I have to stop her now."

"Haven't you gone to the milisi?" asked one of the other women.

"Yeah, but this woman we are talking about – she knows how to melt away before they know she's there." Ronny and co. nodded, understanding that whole concept of melting away.

"Ok, Maddy. Do our best."

"Tell people not to go near her. If someone spots her I just want an address."

After that, the conversation flowed back to the normal peaceful stuff – kids, schools, jobs, health, keeping ceremony alive, the weather. Someone started to strum a guitar and started singing.

LOLAH

FROM the dark sky water flumed down with the intensity of a highPressure hose. Andaman Marko, soaked and pummelled, reached the small Hobarttown pub preening itself on heritage. The sign pinned to the roof said Hotel Royale, and it sported a stone facade and bullnose verandahs. He banged on the steel door and it opened a crack and he slid in, drenched and laughing. The publican, an older man who sported a white ponytail and bushy eyebrows, clad in a polo neck jumper, looked aghast.

"Have you a room?" Andaman asked as he removed the hood and flicked the water from his jacket. He stood dripping in the hotel lobby with its oldeWorld wallpaper, and crenellated brass lights. There was a Tasmanian black oak panelled reception desk, glowing like heritage honey, and a sweeping staircase at the back with brass carpet rods, and high gleam polish. It was like stepping all the way back into the twentieth century, thought Andaman.

"We'll just have t'bloody well find you a room. Y'can't go out there," said the ponyTailed man, battening the door again with massive stormbolts. "Come on." He led him to the oak reception bench, shining like a mirror, and started reviewing a large book.

Way back when, thought Andaman. A paper register was right out there.

"Room 12's free," said the man gruffly. "It was booked but the peoples' flights will have been surely cancelled. We'll put you in there."

Marko paid 3 days advance in $New and the fellow signed him in on the paper. That relieved Marko of issues around sudden hotel bookings on the virtual. Paper meant no electronic marker yet. Marko asked about the register.

"Aw, I don't put too much on the system," said the publican. "Specially when it's a cash advance. People like a ledger too – bit historic. Like this fine establishm'nt"

"I'll be here for the duration," said Andaman.

"I'm damn sure you will. Ever been in a Tassie 'phoon? They ain't pretty. Lolah!" he shouted. "Get this wet man some hot food while I show him a room."

The room was tiny: a low ceiling, a big bed with a qwilt, and a tiled bathroom. Nothing like his lush qwarters in the Spokes, but Marko was happy to breathe free for a couple of days. There was no probability he'd get any further before being trakked – they'd have missed him already – and he'd made a personal vow to report back as soon as the storm abated, but to be on dry land at ground level meant a lot. Marko dumped his bag and thanked the landlord and sat on the bed for a few minutes drying up his head with the hand towel.

He then changed into dry clothes and descended the broad wooden staircase to the lounge where 10 or so people were sitting in the big woodPanelled lounge bar, chatting and watching the teev. Lolah, darkHaired and personable, shimmied up to him with a steaming plate of fish and veggies and asked whether he'd like sambal. Possibly the man's daughter. There was a family resemblance and she looked no more than 18.

A cat hopped onto his chair and told him to "Shove over", but he pushed the mog onto the floor.

"Sorry, mate. Too hungry to share."

The cat's tail flicked angrily and the cat told him where to stick his fish dinner. A couple of the residents laughed. The cat walked off with a haughty strut.

Lolah came back with a beer in a glass and placed it carefully on a wooden table.

"Anything else," she asked, checking him out.

Marko was desperate to log on, to look at his money pots on the coupla secure networks he'd concocted in advance. He'd been fretting about his wealth for the duration at the Spokes and hadn't dared look, and his escape plan was partly aimed at a qwick spotCheck on the money.

Part of his problem, he'd admit. He was ostentatiously greedy.

"Have you a public?" he asked.

"In the back booth, we have a couple." She smiled again. She had sparkly eyes.

"Thanx," Andaman said. After scoffing down the food, he retired to the large clamB in the booth and did some general surfing, checking the storm intensity. He then dialled a couple of private sets, admired his accumulation, and then shifted some money into an account only known to him via a randomised cascade. Set up a decade ago and hardly touched, the account still got good cash levels, all $New. If Spokes or Centrl or whoever had picked up on the transaction he didn't care, because no idiot was going to come out and fetch him in this weather. The 'phoon was his protector – a great big burly guard of wind and lashing rain.

He emerged from the booth and strolled to the bar, where he sat on a stool and continued his conversation with Lolah, who was pulling taps for the gathering of trapped residents.

Andaman felt excited about his escape and very pleased with himself.

*

A couple of hours previously he had strolled from the Mt Wellington hangar, gesturing a friendly goodbye to the blokes at the wide gates, and then bent himself into the gale. It was spewing from the east with great gulps and gusts of air and water. He'd slipped aboard one of the hoppers pretending to be a contractor, without even ID checks. The blokes just accepted he'd be heading home to his Hobarttown house.

"You should stay in barracks," said the milisi guard as he passed the main gate, but Marko had hailed the last of the Yüber shuttles hanging out the front, the rain still sheeting down. The shuttle had sat like a dark hump on the roadside, a pale light illuminating a woman driver who was alternately reading a book and looking at the sky.

"Got a meeting, mate," he said to the guard. "I'll hunker in a bunker in town if I have to." And he was away, sliding into the vSedan and then down into South Hobart as the Derwent Estuary's waves reared over the barrages further south of the bridge and pressed the water like a sheet of foam up past the town. His escape had been as easy as that.

The Yüber driver hunched beside him had worn a teflite parka, a ponytail hanging down her back, eyes fixed on the lightBeams in front. The car hummed its hum. She told Marko he was definitely her last fare. She was heading in.

"Heard that all the hoppers were coming in," she said with a cheeky grin. "Thought I'd get a last ride before lockdown." FortyFive or so, no nonsense. Probably owned the V, drove like a pro.

"Need to go to a good hotel," he'd said, thinking he was being clever. "Can you park me near one." The rain was lashing against the windscreen, and the blowers and wipers were on manic speed, but the driver was on autopilot. She knew the road from the airbase like the back of her hand.

"Sure. Cheap or pricey?"

"Pricey, please."

"I'll take you to the Hyaxx. Bit away from the weather out there. Back behind the water."

The water and sky were now almost black, pressed together like 2 clenched fists, white knuckles of foam in between.

"Thanx, chief," he said.

The journey didn't take long, and Marko paid her in $New and tipped well. He grabbed his bag from the back seat and waved her away, then turned towards the old town, rather than the Hyaxx, in case she was picked up and interrogated about his destination. The escape had been a long shot, taking advantage of the mayhem in the Spokes, and he decided he wasn't going to get very far, but would enjoy the ride anyhow. The walk through the civic precinct was hard work and he had to crouch behind the occasional wall to weather the big gusts and avoid flying debris.

*

Two hours later, he was sitting at a bar, sipping whisketty.

The gusts were shaking the superstructure of the old Hotel Royal. Lolah glanced at the shuttered window. She stood with elbows to the bar talking to him.

"The walls have been steelDripped," she said. "Through all the bricks. We had a direct hit from a tube back in '13 and nothing happened. It'll be right." Her voice was bright and unconvincing.

"How many of these do ya get a year?"

"One, mebbe 2. Usually pan out ok, apart from Constitution Dock which keeps getting rebuilt. They can never get the underwater pilings right."

An old bloke leant over to him across the bar from where he'd been pondering a whisketty glass and eavesdropping.

"Structure enjj types don't get it now, do they? Living with old formulas." The bloke nodded at his own wise words. "Coupla hundred years ago Hobarttown was built for under 30 degree heat ... water pumps wouldn't work if it went above 30.

The old swing bridge at Constitution Dock wouldn't open and let out yachts from the inner harbour if it went over 25 celsius because the steel expanded into the roadway – my dad tole me that. Now we're lucky if it gets under 30 for halfa year, and the rest of the time it's bitter.

"The old enjjs hadn't a clue what was coming. Take the Tasman Bridge. Won't last the next few 'phoons. No way. We'll be catching ferries soon, over the Styx."

"So you say, Bri'ne," said the publican, "but you've been saying that for 20 years and it's still up. Styx and stones my friend."

"Mark my words," said the old bloke.

Lolah flashed a smile at Marko who grinned back. *The older generation, eh?* her smile seemed to say. Yes, she was older than 18. Not much older, but not a kid. He reappraised her dark hair, olive skin, and shy smile. She was appraising him, too.

"I'd reckon," said Marko, "if tubes've gone through your bridge over the past twenty or 30 years, it will be fine for a few more."

"Until the next stepChange," said Bri'ne who sipped his whisketty. "Listen to that roar outside. That's the future for all of us – a big neverEnding f'ckin' roar."

"A Cassandra!" exclaimed the publican.

"I'm that," said the bloke. "But it's Mr Cassandra to you, doc."

The publican smiled.

Andaman asked if he could buy Mr Cassandra a drink.

"Well, Mr Cassandra, will you have another of Tassie's finest?" asked the publican and he poured a shot for Bri'ne, Lolah, Marko and himself.

"Fire away, doc," said the old man. "I'm not going anywhere. Can I camp on yer couch tonite?"

"I'll go one better'n that and make you a bed, mate. There have been a fair few no shows. Hoppers and jetz stopped coming half a day ago."

"Thanx, doc."

The building shuddered under a gust. Bri'ne looked at the publican and grunted "f'ck that" and they all raised their glasses to the 'phoon.

*

The old bloke was a dab hand at the lekky zither and he pulled it out, stood in the corner behind the zitherStand and played a whole heap of Chopin and some pulse.

Andy danced hip on hip with Lolah and found to his relief she wasn't related to the publican, (at least not that she knew). With that news, Marko was even more cheered. Free of canned air, free of security people nipping at his heels. Hanging with proper folks, dancing and drinking. They really got up a good stomp, in spite of the 'phoon, to the rowdy point when revellers asserted their impenetrableness to gusts and tubes.

Lolah was stuck in the pub with everyone else and couldn't go home. As it got later, the owner pulled beers and let her be. She was smitten with Marko's dark eyes, as he was with hers. Or mebbe she was just bored with the older congregation in the bar. And he was desperate for close human touch, skin on skin, in the monster storm. So they slipped away to his room.

If he'd been allowed, they'd have made beautiful darkEyed babies, but Marko obeyed the groundRules, admitted his Nought status, ruled the liaison temporary, and sqwared it away with her. She was agreeable, admitting to being a twicer (a twicer!), but not ready yet. By the time they went to bed, and were naked under the qwilt, Marko was half cut on very good whisketty and Lolah was laughing at him. "You talk too much," she said.

They pulled their bodies together and he smelt a faint day's sweat masked mostly by rose soap, the sweetness of her hair and her skin, and he felt alive and grateful she was with him in the jaws of the 'phoon.

"You don't know it, Lolah, but you've saved me!" he said as he hugged her and they kissed. Soon, they were clasped hard, her thighs wrapped round his hips as he pressed into her. He looked up as she slowly moved on him, closed eyes and the sensual half open mouth, bright lips & pink tongue tip. More than a hint of desperation for a normal life welled into the pleasure of the moment, but he banished the feeling.

Later, after they'd stopped distracting each other from the shudders & gusts, and the storm continued its pounding of Hobarttown with an unstoppable screaming jet engine noise across the sky, Lolah and Marko lay close.

"Every time a 'phoon hits, I think 'm going to die," she said. "I'm only 22. I haven't seen anything, been anywhere. These storms are getting worse. One day soon, a 'phoon will strip the roof & scoop us out, and we'll all be blown away into the dark, like dry leaves."

Marko turned and looked at Lolah's eyes. They seemed calm, fixed to the ceiling, or the tempest above.

"I don't know about that. This hotel is very well built."

She turned her head and looked at him with a serious face.

"No, Andy. One day soon, we'll all be blown to hell. Please leave the light on tonite. The noise is worse in the dark." And she turned to go to sleep.

*

Morning, but it was still dark and outside swirled with un-abated noise, fury and shuddering thumps. Windows were shuttered with steel casings and there was nothing else to look at except each other. He and Lolah kissed tenderly, and ex-plored one another's skin and hair. They made love again, then said good morning. They showered. Andaman felt revived and in good company.

Downstairs in the lounge, they had an early breakfast together and Lolah went to work, serving meals to the other customers and residents. Andaman was desperate to check his sites on the public, but contained the urge, joining Bri'ne for a second kopi and listening to the old bloke grizzle on. A card game got going. The publican taught the 4 or 5 players how to bid and form tricks. Lolah perched on her seat behind the bar, polishing glasses and watching with bemusement.

At about 10, there was a tremendous thump, followed by several others.

"Someone's at the door," said Lolah. Doc emerged from the office with a look of amazement on his face.

"Impossible," said Bri'ne. Andaman was filled with dread, but he didn't prevent the publican from making it to the entrance. Someone had traced his undisciplined lunge on the public. Someone was coming to kill him. Maybe. He edged forward on his seat, while others went into the reception area to watch. The banging and howling created a jagged sound. The door opened and, within an intrusive gust that hurled itself around the ground floor, an ominous figure in a helmet could be seen entering and shoving the door shut behind it, using the full force of its body and butt. The door clanged shut. The figure wore protective skins, tough as, with synthetic muscle bounce by the look of it. Andaman was amazed. But it explained the midStorm incursion and why the figure was alive. The helmet came off, and he recognised Dante.

"Ow, no," he thought.

"You have an Andaman Marko here?" Dante asked the publican.

"I'm here," said Andaman, from the back of the room. "How are ya, Dante."

Dante strode over. He was furious. "Y'really are an idiot," he snarled. "You know that? I almost got clobbered by a tree out there."

Dante's suit was dripping rainwater on him, and Andaman was too scared to answer. His mouth opened and shut and nothing came out to reply to the angry giant. He stood 2 and a half metres tall wearing boots and a pack, a loaded weapon hung on the outside of the suit, and the helmet visor up so Andaman couldn't actually see his mouth. He and Dante had got on qwite well in the Spokes, but to a civilian he was seriously scary.

Dante went on in a tense voice: "It wouldn't have been so bad, mate, if you hadn't gone to look at your fricking precious accounts. We could have picked you up after. But you redlighted yourself. You went and redlighted! Are you super greedy or something? Is it like f'king the virtual? Eqwivalent of rolling around like a f'king pig in a bath full of gold? What possesses you?"

The previously bored, and now excited crowd of twenty or so had circled them to watch the showdown. Doc, the publican, was standing with one hand stroking his chin looking bemused. Lolah was shaking with fear and looking at the shiny deadly hardArm, and then at Dante and then Andaman and then repeating her triangulation.

"Can we do this somewhere else?" asked Andaman.

"Suppose."

"How did you get here?" asked Doc.

"With great difficulty," said Dante. "Can I talk to this man somewhere private?"

Andaman said, "I've got a room. Come upstairs."

*

Dante took up a lot of space in the old and modest room. He took off the skins, stripping the garment from his vast frame, scooped into a teflite windcheater and reStrapped the automatic gun with its belt covered in cadoodles, some of which flashed. Then Dante carefully folded the suit and helmet and put them in the corner and placed a spiderlike electronic Warner on top of the pile in case anyone tried to touch his stuff. All the while Andaman sat qwietly on the bed.

"Don't touch my stuff, Marko, or you're dead," Dante added. "Now sit down."

They sat facing one another, Andaman on the bed, and Dante on the chair. Up close, Marko realised Dante was a lot older than he looked. His eyes were chocolate brown and fine wrinkles lined the skin around them, and the lids. His voice was young tho, and loud.

"Now, Marko, my dear bunny, we are going to ride this out," said Dante firmly. "There are people in Hobarttown who are after you, *and you know that*! According to Dr Phipps who has worked it out, one lot want you dead, the other want what's in your head. I am your security. We have another day of this 'phoon, and then mate, we are back on the first hopper to the Spokes. 'K?"

Andaman nodded. "I was going to check back in anyway," he mumbled.

"It's not f'king rejuve, mate," Dante snarled. "You don't check out and check in."

"The Spokes is suffocating! It's so closed down and that place out there on the water," complained Marko. "It stinks. It's full of knowNothing nerds."

"Look. Look." Dante started gesticulating and then stopped and leaned even further in Marko's personal space. "You are at the Spokes because it's the most secure ... in fact, it's the only, secure place in either AuZtralia and East Cap by virtue of its location. Bad people want a piece of you?"

"'K."

"You got to get it into your head. Centrl went ballistic when he'd worked out what happened and then he completely tubed when he saw you'd laid a marker on the virtual. I had to come over in a sub! A fricking sub!"

Marko sagged. "'K," he said.

"So here I am. I'll sleep on the floor. Don't go anywhere without me ..."

Marko said a silent byeBye to his dalliance with Lolah, "... and as soon as there's an abatement in the weather, and the metHeads say that'll be tomorrow morning, we are on the first hopper back, 'k?"

"'k."

"Good man. I understand your claustrophobia thing, but it's not much better here, chook. It's in lockdown too. You have to take our advice. At ... all ... times."

Andaman nodded reluctantly and Dante exhaled in annoyance.

"You carry on like some trapped and wounded animal and I'm not minded to amplify your stupidity here in this hotel in the middle of a thermocell storm, but at some point you must listen to us. All life is valuable. All life is sacrosanct. We cannot allow loss. Not mine, not yours. Savour and enjoy your continuum. Don't throw it way. Hobarttown is a big city with many, many elements in it, some of which are hostile to you. That shimmerman in your cabin was recuited here by some foe. No good will come of poor discipline, no good.

"Now, chook, suffice to say I resent having to risk MY continuum to come and look after YOURS!"

"I understand," said Andaman shakily but still defiant, "but you needn't have worried."

"Aren't you listening? S'my job to worry," said Dante. "I've looked after you for 2 months now, from before the storm season, and we just want to keep you safe. What's changed from before? You were in pissing'yr'pants terror up on Cape York?" His eyes were pained.

Andaman flatly denied EVER pissing in his pants, but admitted he'd been scared, but had felt braver the further south they'd got, away from the horrors of the north. And after a couple of months the claustrophobia of the Spokes had got to him.

"Hmm," grunted Dante who hated the sealedUp existence also. He patted Andaman's shoulder reassuringly. His hand felt several kilos heavy. "They'll let you go sometime. Under their terms. Right now, you've just got to cope like a chook. Not exactly sure what you've got for the AuZgov crowd, but boy they're putting the effort in. When we c'n get back to base we'll go topDeck every day and I'll give you fitness lessons. That staves off claustrophobia. That's how I do it.

"Now, do they have food here?"

Dante had changed tack. The storm in the room had ended, but the storm outside keened on.

BAABI 4

IN THE END, some kids saw the weird old witch lady when they smelled a horrible smell and checked over a fence. Their movement dislodged a huge swarm of black flies and other insects from the fence and they rose in a giant black cloud of buzzing. Below them was a pit that had been dug in the backyard, filled with maggoty rats and dead dogs. The old lady in a boilersuit saw them from the verandah and gestured violently at them and they'd run like the blazes.

Told Dad, and Dad told Ronny because one of their mutual cousins had said Ronny was on the lookOut for an old solo woman living in a nice place. Well, it wasn't so nice, but it was her. Ronny rang Madrigal, who again astonished Centrl by her perspicacity in finding a killer in a haystak, so to speak. Only because she got out and talked to folk, she said to Wen. Humint.

Milisi parked an Opticon in the area – down the canal a wayz – and the lightBender went through in its constituted photon tube without the hint of a wire or a bee. They had the old woman cleaning a couple of guns, oldStyle, on the kitchen table which she whacked in the frijj crisper. Biometrix had her as Baabi Semmler, last known as a resident of Darwin way back in the 2050s. Way back then!

File on her activities in *the Blend*, courtesy of an unidenti-fied agent, said she led a platoon in the incursion. Adept with weapons. They kept the lightBender on her at all times, though she wasn't to know the photons were artificially sculpted – a bendy pipe of sliced light cut into the general lightfield, send-ing back images. She was old school, drone school, and no doubt would have had a drone finder, but she knew little of the latest tek, obviously. Hadn't a clue.

Two weeks later the Opticon's bent tunnel of light followed her walking carefully, with zigs and cutbacks, to a second house. After 10 minutes Baabi emerged disappointed, so they set watch on that house too. Empty house, in a city of 8 mil-lion where half the folk were living in shacks and tents. So un-usual, it was a crime – a crime to own an empty house. The Opticon followed her back across the canals and into her place. Madrigal was amazed that noone gave her a second glance. She was fixated on the Baabi, but noone else seemed to see her.

In the end they picked her up at 2am the morning after her contact had visited the safehouse and they got a bead on him, following him through to one of the better hotels and then onto a commercial aircraft to Sydney. Sqwaring the circle, as Jembrana said.

When the swoop came, Baabi leapt like a cat and still man-aged to fire off a shot, but the stun gas knocked her over qwick. Old girl in her nitie, shuddering in paralysis on the floor. The Slotters didn't have to get involved with that one. Milisi did it all on their own – after all, she'd shot down and almost killed one of their own people, and murdered at least one other man on their turf. They dragged her dribbling, paralysed frame to the APV and threw her in in disgust, while she could only look up at the faces of her captors and wish them dead.

Jembrana himself came to the cell to see her, but she just spat at him and called him an "Indon prick" and he laughed at her.

"Not any more, Ms Baabi," he said. "We're all in it together these dayz."

Traces, flecks of her skin showed her with Bluestone in his hotel room when he died. And Kingdom Allenby. Double murder, the rarest of crimes.

As she'd gone one juve over – an illegal act – the court denied her any further juve juice, or the tablets compulsory for the treatment. She aged very qwickly after that. A death sentence in slow motion over a few months, but in her cell down at the barracks she went out screaming and cursing, sometimes in English, sometimes Old Kriol, sometimes even in Chinese.

ANDAMAN 3

AS SOON as the weather eased slightly, Dante bundled Marko out of his room and into the street. Marko caught sight of a gloomy, or possibly angry, Lolah in the vestibule and tried to smile. On the way back to the hopper port in a military V, Andaman told Dante that his intervention had got in the way of a romance, and spoiled his fun. Dante took the accusation for the mild jest it was, all the while scanning the gusted streetscape for threats.

"You're a fast mover, Marko," he said, impressed. "Takes me half a day just to get this armour off, before I can fire up my charm."

"Can I contact her?" Andaman asked. "Just to say, so long?"

"Right at this moment, no," said the big guard. "You'd be putting her life at risk."

For the umpteenth time, Andaman's heart sank as he headed for captivity.

The trip was uneventful. The Brazilhoz contingent hadn't left their apartment because the storm was still strong. By the time the 2 shimmermen got to the Royal Hotel to kill him, Andaman was long gone.

LAKE

THE WHITE LADY

MADRIGAL strapped herself into the plushChair with the padded shoulder harness, looking across to Dale Rickenby, her young aide who was a trainee Courier. This was his first Ramjjet flight, the aircraft (or was it rocket?) that escaped gravity and lobbed into the upper stratosphere, over the severe summer eqwatorial disturbances and into the northern hemisphere. The cabin of the shuttle hummed with slow music, lit with soothing blues and pinks, and glasses tinkled as the attendants brought drinks of water, but noone was fed solids until the downward trajectory.

Rickenby was a nice boy. Solicitous towards her authority, helpful & eager to learn. His head was tilted back in the seat beside her.

Stories of Ramjjet fails abounded, and not just the occasional engine accident, but low & no gravity incidents where harm was caused. The young man was angularly handsome, with lovely blonde hair, and rather full of himself like all the young administrators were – but at this point, he looked uncertain.

She'd dismissed in a nanosecond of meeting him, a week ago, any thought of seduction. He was too young, and she was feeling very tired anyway, too tired for sexing, buffeted by the madness of the Andaman sitch. This was a final trip, to finish bizz, to warn off the Hegs and let her get on with her diplomatic career.

Through a reinforced porthole, the Brisbane skyline gnashed the distant sky, a conglomerate of toothy steel towers that levelled out into the tenements and hilltop mansions, then the urbs and the shantytowns which spread towards the jjetPort. The only jjetPort in Australia was Brisbane because it was far enough from the Cloud but closer to the eqwator, and the trip, up and over, was shorter.

Madrigal passed her glass back to the attendant and the voice came through the cabin to prepare for elevation by the RammRamp, where the rocketPlane was tilted at the stars.

"I've never been sick doing this," she reassured Rickenby. "You just breathe through the nose and out through the mouth, and do the relaxation exercise I taught you."

"Yes, ma'am."

"You took my advice and skipped brekky?"

"Yes, ma'am."

"And stop calling me ma'am. We've known one another more than a week."

"Pearl and Folly call you ma'am," he protested.

"Yes, but they're military."

*

As unpleasant as always, the gForce pressed her gizzards together like a pair of strong hands; the invisible hand on the face; her whole body wanting to bunch up. She fought back against the pain and the nausea, the need to pee. The roar outside was muted by thick fuselage and teflick but it was still a very powerful blast that sent them hurtling. For a diversion she managed to turn her head slightly towards the aisle and looked at Rickenby and his thin nose pointed perpendicularly at the cabin ceiling. His eyes were closed and he was doing exactly as she said. Breath in through the nose, out through the mouth.

Madrigal started to breath as well, her mind went cloudy and spidery and she lost consciousness qwickly. She could hear the voice of her Auntie coming through strong, talking in language, singing one of the old honey ant songs. Madrigal was never worried when there was a visitation from her auntie in her dreams. There was always a feeling of warmth and safety, like she was a kid again, caught in a loving circle. Auntie broke off her song and said

– *Madrigal they know all about you. Everything. That White Lady is a white spirit, wilful white spirit, caught up with your dad they are. Keep wary of them and take care of that little boy you have with you.*

– *Who, Rickenby?* asked Madrigal.

– *Yes, your helper. Not little Todd. He's all good.*

– *That's nice to know,* said Madrigal.

– *He's a good boy,* said the Auntie.

– *I had to leave Toddy with my friends in the Spokes, Auntie,* Madrigal said in her dream, choking up a bit. *Doesn't even have Mum with him. Looked after by strangers.*

– *Be all over soon, Maddy,* she said. *Then you'll all go home, and can take the boy back to Country. The poultice on this mess is working. The heat is dying out.*

– *Todd's just a little boy,* said Madrigal. *Left with strangers.*

The weird sensation of weeping in your sleep.

– *It's an adventure for him. Good head, screwed on tight. It's mum's job to worry about him, but he's safe there. Did the right thing there, Maddy.*

How the Auntie got into her head while in a space shuttle was a mystery to Madrigal, but Auntie qwickly disappeared, or evaporated, or dissolved, as the jjet moved away from mainland Australia and over the Pacific. She awoke at the top of the parabola and felt the tears still on her cheeks, which she wiped with a tissue. *Heat is dying out.* Well, within the next few hours she hoped to extinguish any remaining embers.

Once up and over, the flight was fine, like any normal plane. A downhill tilt – that was all – towards Guangzhou space port, and murmuring attendants brought a stiff drink and something to eat. But at the top or the parabola, where the pressures abated and the gravity dropped for a little while, there was nothing worse than someone's vomit floating through the cabin – though attendants did have special scoops for the occasion. She'd once seen 2 blobs meet and combine above her head, but hadn't told that to Rickenby. She glanced round and saw none. A vomitFree flight. It had only taken twenty minutes for her to lose consciousness, have a chat with her aunt, and then reach freefall.

Madrigal thought about her dad's aversion to the "up and over" and didn't blame him for waiting until after the eqwinox, when things calmed, before catching a regular plane across to the south.

And what did Auntie mean about the White Lady and Dad? She was a pesky Auntie!

"How's y'r phizz, Rickenby. Got vitals and all still with you?" she asked.

"Yes, Madrigal. But I don't think I can eat at present."

"At least have a drink. It'll bring the colour back to your cheeks."

Exact words Bluestone had said to her 5 years ago when they headed to Tokyo on courier business to communicate a strong attitude from Oz industry over some uncovered technical data gone missing. Madrigal and Bluestone had both laughed uproariously – after twenty minutes of gforce Bluestone had looked like a piece of raw pastry while she looked just the same. Dark honey. Colour back to your cheeks. Ha!

She wondered if Rickenby would lighten up in time – he was far too earnest.

She also wondered how they'd be received in Guangzhou with the eqwally blunt message to the White Lady.

A well of white spirits.

*

As per usual, the rest of the flight was pleasant in the plushChair. She couldn't talk shop to Rickenby in the close confines of a cabin which contained another ten people. Could've been other nationals – diplomats or business. A 'Ramjjet ticket was affordable to the upper echelons only.

There were only another 4 such cabins in the jet as it was the most exclusive way to travel. Pearl and Chime had gone ahead in a previous shuttle to organise transport and check targets & routes. A diplomatic dropIn wasn't a trip that you did without support, and they'd act as scary civilian assistants in a place as willing and contested as the biggest nation in the world. She'd asked for Pearl and Folly (as usual), but Wen had insisted on Chime, and she hadn't argued. Pearl was of Chinese lineage and spoke the lingo.

The craft came over north ASEAN, past the cloud's northernmost reaches, and entered commercial air space at the southern Chinese entity. Through the porthole she could see where forest fires and then rains had leached and bleached the landscape, forcing the starving population further north. She didn't know how they'd survived, but millions had.

The landscape greened up as the southern ricebowl and horticulture took over. And then the low white factories and then the city. The 'Ramjjet performed a flawless landing to make up for the initial unpleasantness. Two hours after leaving Brisbane.

As they disembarked through a whiteLit tunnel, Madrigal could sense that the watching had started.

Two uniformed Heg officials further down the tunnel near the exit, ticked passing faces and certainly ticked hers, though there was no second glance at Rickenby. From then on, she knew there was a live tail. And probably some sort of light extrusion tailing them as well. She didn't check. She just knew.The Chinese had nailed that technology and were way more advanced using photoniks.

At the collection point, Chime and Pearl were standing, scoping, in their blue teflite jackets and jeans. They grabbed Madrigal's briefcase and pack and led the Couriers qwickly into the sweaty bustle of the transport zone to find the large tank of a CruiserV they'd hired.

"Got at least 2 parties following you Ma'am: the official one and what I assume is the White Lady mob," said Chime.

"Hope it is."

"They've probably tagged the car as well, but everyone knows where we're going."

She pushed up her sunVisor and conspicuously scanned the heads and vehicles behind, clocking a woman and another man on a vBike, cranking it up. "Let's head to the meet," Madrigal said. "Best get it over." They sped under a couple of road and tram bridges and into the highway. High treelines separated lanes of highway, speeding Vs, panteknicons. A milky sun burned high above the city, penetrating the amber sky. There were qwite decent housing precincts along both edges of the highway, treed and busy with people, washing lines, food stalls, vegetable patches. The heatBreezes caused the street tree leaves to shake in a febrile motion. She was glad to be in the airCon.

Pearl drove carefully, merging into lanes when she could, avoiding the coolBuses, and staying well away from road verges which were thick with pedestrians and cyclists.

"The meet is at a restaurant. Very spanky. On an island in the middle of a fake lake," said Chime. "Their shout."

"Doesn't sound particularly safe."

"She'll be right, ma'am," said Chime. "There's a causeway to the building."

"Got your Chinese lingua in order, Dale?" she asked Rickenby.

"It'll do," he said. "Four years of hard slog Mandarin will get me through. I expect this won't take long."

"Never assume or expect anything," Madrigal said. "People can be very strange." Bluestone would go into meetings with what he called a blank paper policy. She knew what Bluestone and she were going to say to the last full stop, but others were a blank to be dealt with, and the trick was to fill their "paper" with your words. To write the script.

Bluestone had been a very persuasive ghost writer. And he always planted the last full stop. She missed him, but still retained his wisdom.

The car drifted left up an exit ramp into what seemed a precinct of large white factories with polythene roofs and high security fences. Pearl wove the V slowly between bikes, skwatVs, cyclists and pedestrians trying to force their way across the traffic stream.

They rose onto a ridge of road and the buildings stretched into a strange horizon, like a multiPerspective enhanced by neat lines and shine and a photoSynthetic haze above. The brown cloud – an enduring legacy of the 21st century.

"Lot of tek made around here, ma'am. Bit fortressy," said Chime, then the CruiserV found a feeder road that took them from the human density towards the edge of a lake and a forest, which they followed for several kliks until Pearl directed the vehicle along a causeway with lanterns and dragon motifs to an island with a huge, ancient building. The causeway, about half a K long looped over the lake in 3 arches, like the tail of a dragon.

"Locals reckon it was the summer palace of a local potentate, 250 years or so back," Chime said. "It's very nice. I suggest you choose the dumplings. There's a kitchen exit and plenty of big picture windows made of normal glass and doors, looking out onto the lake. Not that you'll need to beat a hasty retreat. They'll have the perimeter locked."

"Thanx, Chime. But you're in the room with me, and Pearl can mind the getaway car."

"Ma'am," he said, as if expecting that very order.

*

The Cruiser parked on a driveway of small pebbles and Madrigal, Chime and Dale Rickenby crunched up the path, which sounded like a bunch of mouths eating biscuits. They were met by a friendly maître d' in a blue silk suit. Tall and urbane, he ushered them into a room where several people, male and female stood, waiting. HegMen in suits and fancy scarf ties, holding expensive mother of pearl clamBs and paperwork to pass to their bosses. Three or 4 securitizors with the look of visible muscle. There was noone else in the restaurant.

"Dr Phipps," said a smiling man, "I am Wu Wen Shu, chair of the White Lady syndicate, a mixed corporation of businessmen connected to this province and its Administrators. This is my wife, Soong Lu. And my associates." He introduced them all, even the security guys.

Madrigal did likewise with Rickenby and Chime, and Mr Wu gestured to seats around a burnished table. Madrigal sensed no overt hostility from any of the people. In fact, they seemed delighted to see her, indulging in small talk about the Ramjjet flight and fussing over drinks which arrived on trays.

The Wu's were older. Mr Wu looked in his 60s, but the way the people of the Chinese Hegs hit the rejuves, he could have been 130. Small beard, twinkling eyes, very sharp and funny. He laughed a couple of times at Madrigal's description of the Rramjjet and she kind of liked him.

"I am too old for such gForces," he said.

"I don't believe it – you have a strong frame!" said Madrigal, and he laughed again.

Mrs Soong was definitely younger, an oval face and very black hair. She spoke English in a flawless American accent, which placed her obtaining her education on the East Coast before the greater USA finally expired. So she would have been at least in her late 60s. She allowed her husband to hold forth.

They sat, and waiters appeared with the predicted dumplings. Madrigal praised the restaurant and view. Mr Wu accepted her words graciously.

She bit into a dumpling and the aroma and texture flooded through her senses. Never had she eaten something as delicious – the delicate soy, ginger and other spices through what seemed like enhanced chicken mince and delicate pastry.

"This is very good," she said.

"This is why you are our guest on the island. We could have met in White Lady kampus, but this is much more conducive to discussion. You have very few people in your entourage," he added in a surprised voice. "I expected more."

"I am a Courier invested with the Authority of the AuZtralian Government, as is my associate Mr Rickenby," she said with gravitas. Friendly but firm. "And I might add I am authorised to represent the administration of Capricornia also."

"Ah, Cap. A grand experiment with Asia. You are to be congratulated."

"If Australia had borders with Europe, our same care for climate refugees would have happened, Mr Wu. Or Africa. *The Blend* was common humanity. Common to all of us. We provided land for people in peril."

Mr Wu looked thoughtful and nodded. "A credit to us all. We took many Vietnamese after the Mekong Delta event. They were our mortal enemies for 1000s of years."

More food arrived and Mrs Wu, or Soong, started presenting a series of glows on the family investments, which were extensive in the advanced tek area. Her presentation was focussed and fluent – her husband nodded approvingly at her words. She talked about gamma collection, enhanced photon cabling where light carried power, and talked about some of the interplanetary investments they were making. All very impressive.

*

A week before, at the Spokes, Rickenby's research on the virtual, with assistance from Marko, had prised most of the details from reachable sources, but there were still some controlling interests they had that were unbeknownst until Marko's dip in the virtual and the White Lady cloudClusters. White Lady controlled, thru proxies, much of the southEast China water supply, which the Wu's didn't mention in their current presentation, but were the bedrock of their fortune and power and made the central government beholden.

"When Hegs become this strong and encompassing they leapfrog the authority of the political administration which they are supposed to respect and obey," Marko had said with some authority. "All my offMarket investing takes this into account. They dutifully report back to governments which suits me, but ultimately, they do as they want."

Madrigal well knew the risks of Hegs trumping Governments, as her family company was central to AuZ & distributed much of WestAuz and WestCap's power supplies through vast solar, wind and tidal infrastructure on Indijj lands and waters, and lands of others – a deal her peoples had sat down with her father and grandfather and agreed to long ago. And the original gas constellations also, which they'd steadily bought, sold and then plugged as the atmospheric chemistry got dangerous. But the her Dad had smartz, and Phipps Heg deliberately played second fiddle to AuZgov while exerting enormous clout. Phipps Industries played their authority down in return for more cordial Government relations. In China, Vietnam, and much of Europe, it was the governments that fiddled in the secondString section, so Madrigal treated Mr Wu and Mrs Soong with deep caution.

*

"We pay taxes," said Mrs Wu. "Yes, we do. We are a legitimate Hegemony that is friendly to our national government. We do not cut corners nor make secret our enterprises. We are transparent."

"That is commendable," murmured Madrigal in her most diplomatic tone. She looked at the assembled company of execs, lawyers and bodyguards and noted the fact that in all the introductions, the Chinese government was unrepresented. That White Lady was talking to her in the first place, showed where the power structure lay. The Chinese Government was on the outside looking in. But she already knew it: Marko's klandestine inquiries had easily established that White Lady was an aggro outfit which lorded it over the Chinese Government.

"So, to our discussion," said Madrigal, brightly.

"Of course. Let me place the proposition before you," said Wu Wen Shu. "White Lady asks that we join with Phipps Industries in an emboldened power cabling venture. This photon technology we speak of –"

"In what capacity are you talking to me," Madrigal cut Mr Wu off.

"That you are here on behalf of Derek Phipps, Phipps Industries. We met with your father in Tokyo a month ago and would like you to inform him that our technologies are at his disposal for the venture."

"I am not speaking to you in this capacity," said Madrigal, showing a flush of annoyance in her face. "You well know I arranged to meet in regards the illegal interception of your company data, and your response,"

Mr Wu waved his hand as if it was a minor issue.

"Yes, but your father, Derek, alerted us to the true meaning of your reqwest for this meeting."

Her father? She'd told her mother she was to talk to the White Lady and wrap things up earlier in the week. Netta must have told Dad.

Fact was, tho', the family business was not hers to either call or deal, and she remained as remote as she could from her father's labyrinthine dealings.

She'd reqwested the "showdown" with White Lady to clear things up, not get suckered into one of her Father's new business arrangements.

"He has spoken to you about this, your father? Joining the south and the north through the networks. Stormproofing the East Asian power supplies?"

Madrigal hadn't a clue, but said in a more mollifying tone: "Of course, I can tell him privately of your decision."

Clearly, she thought, White Lady thought her reqwest for an AuZgov meet was a ruse ... to discuss what they viewed was the real bizz. Madrigal had to think fast. How to press her core point – the illegalilty and brutality of the foreign incursion up Cape York – without putting them so offside Mr Wu and Mrs Soong would retaliate in some other nasty way.

She looked at their businesslike faces, which were reading the uncertainty in hers.

Madrigal could not be uncertain. To pivot into this unexpected White Lady agenda was her only reasonable strategy as she needed some semblance of goodwill to press the AuZgov business. But this meant buying in to Phipps Industry business.

The intrusion of energy deals into official AuZgov bizz was excruciating and Madrigal's heart sank, knowing that her career was suddenly compromised. Seriously interfered with. By the Old Man. Goddam Dad!

Her exciting, sustaining work as a Courier was inevitably coming to an end.

In fact, in front of Chime and Rickenby, the whole discussion was embarrassing, and Rickenby especially would be obliged to report back. As would she. Her public duties were no longer possible. Wu Wen Shu could not possibly know of the level of her discomfort and instead looked pleased.

"This is a real job for faceOnface," he added.

"But of course it is. But can I return to our original," she struggled for the Mandarin word, thrown by the fact this man was deeply engaged in deals with Phipps Industries, "reason for the visit."

This time it was Wu who chopped her off, midSentence. He handed her a small onyx box.

"Here is a chip that will provide your esteemed father with the blueListing and licensing details. I would talk with him in a week to make final arrangements."

Madrigal now lost her diploCool and grimaced. The people present were utterly oblivious to her role here, and saw Madrigal and purely representing her father's corporation. Were told the political mission was an ulterior way of faceOnface around the infrastructure deal. Wrong way round, she thought. Had lost momentum before she had even begun. Time to regain it.

"I will give him the chip," she pronounced.

Mr Wu bowed and Soong looked very pleased and the White Lady mob started to clap.

She held up a hand to hush them.

"But before I go, I must speak to you about my AuZtralian Government business."

"Of course," Mr Wu beamed as if to say: Let's conclude with some minor chat to end a great dealmaker, give us a figleaf over the real business of the day, trillions of $New.

"Let me tell you now," Wu began his gambit with a wry smile, "your countryman, Mr Marko, is a thief. This programmer from Cap made repeated incursions into our systems." He'd pivoted straight into it, and was writing the blank page despite her.

This was more like it!

"True, but Mr Wu and Mrs Soong, you know, and I know, that such incursions on the virtual are not unusual. What was unusual was your level of force to try and kill this man, and the resulting deaths of 50 others in East Cap including 2 high level AuZgov administrators."

"Have we not, in this new age, put intraState violence behind us? Everyone's war is now with the weather."

No matter how understated Madrigal's Courier tone was, Mr Wu looked agitated. He had not expected a real dressingDown. "That raid was not us – that was the others ..." he exclaimed.

"And this is what I see as an incursion in the sovereign territory of AuZgov And ASEAN – in the Joint Territory of East Cap."

Mr Wu leant forward. "That was not us. We played no part in that. Your man Marko tried to send harpoons into our virtual system."

She held up her hand. "He is not our man, but he is a citizen of Cap."

"I accept that," said Wu, "but here is the story. We find him and trace him back. He has interesting techniqwes in the virtual. Very new. We wanted to talk to him, not kill him. We want his virtual technology. He is imaginative operator. I have no truck with the death that happened. Noone does in the new Chinese hegemonies. I want his knowledge – it is valuable. And now I formally ask that you deliver him to us."

"For what?" Madrigal asked, ignoring the surprised look on Dale Rickenby's face.

"For his knowledge. Please listen to me. He belongs to us."

Madrigal knew this was ludicrous. So did they, but they were powerful enough for the tryOn.

"I understand your viewpoint." Said Madrigal with a slight smile. "But listen please. I am here to deliver a strong protest, on behalf of the Government of AuZtralia, about the unlawful attempt to abduct and kill Mr Marko who is our citizen."

She looked through the windows at the lake behind him. The rain was starting, a greyness merging into the shining silver of the water. A few ducks speckled the surface, a scattering of black moles on the silver skin of the lake.

Mr Wu huffed.

Mrs Soong, in her fabulous aqwaVelvet suit bridled a bit and said, "I don't think you understand. Mr Marko has committed a crime against our Hegemony, and he is guilty."

"Of decoding White Lady's encrypted messages, yes. Of intercepting instructions and making money from them, yes. He is a speculator who breaks the rules and we now have him in custody. But you sent a kidnap team to Cap to abduct him in a submarine, with an illegal Slotter team operating on the mainland of AuZtralia."

"We wished to capture him alive," Mr Wu stressed. "I do not know what went wrong."

"Did your Brazilian partners overreach?."

"I will not speculate on fault," Mr Wu said, "but I apologise for what happened. You say this man is in custody?"

"My message to you, why I am here, is to reqwest in the strongest terms not to intervene with this man again. We will close his operation down."

Mrs Soong hissed: "If I can have your word that he will never intrude on our business, ever again." Gosh, she was intense. "That includes the business of Phipps Industry, which you MUST realise is in OUR mutual interest." She seemed much angrier than her husband. There was nothing Hegshated more than being spied on, after their own lifetimes of intrusion. But then, they went to extreme lengths to capture Marko and his strokes, no doubt so White Lady could spy and intercept messages, probably from AuZgov and ASEAN. The burnt tang of hypocrisy hung in the air.

Valuable knowledge indeed.

Madrigal sighed and looked them in the eyes one by one: "You have my word that he won't. Do I have your word also?" (Never let them win the last point).

"Yes," said Mr Wu. Mrs Soong looked unconvinced.

I'll have to get the commitment in writing, she thought.

"As for the other, separate, conversation." She held the onyx box up. "That is solely my father's business, but I will ensure he gets this."

Mr Wu and Madam Soong didn't seemed fussed, in the end. Chinese walls meant nothing to operators like The White Lady.

The rain was easing. She could see the tincture of darkness starting to stain the sepia sky above the trees. Time to leave before things got even more muddled.

*

Pearl and Chime fell in behind her on the crunchy driveway as they walked to the vehicle. For some reason the air smelt sweet to her. Possibly dumpling magic being blown from the kitchen vents.

"That was bad," she muttered to Chime as they exited.

"Yes Ma'am." He didn't disagree.

The grey sky was closing and darkening again on the trees behind the lake, but still no hint of chill. The air was always hot, wherever you might be. Madrigal was fuming at both her father's interference and Mrs Soong's temper tantrum. She turned the onyx box around in her pocket. Rickenby looked confused.

She could see the massed shapes – heads and shoulders – of the White Lady crew watching from behind the restaurant windows.

"What a mess. Let's get out of here," she growled.

Madrigal and her bodyguards reached the car when they heard a shout coming from the door of the restaurant.

Then multiple shouts and screams.

Looking round, she was horrified to see Rickenby 3 or 4 metres behind, writhing in the air, legs kicking, as if seized and lifted by an unseen rope. He clasped the air around his head, trying to shred it with his fingers. His face looked sqwashed and crushed against glass as if a powerful force was trying to disarticulate his head from his neck.

"Shit," shouted Pearl racing from the Cruiser and lifting him further into the air. Members of the Wu security team were already out the door and tearing down the drive.

For a moment, Rickenby was levitated a metre in the air by the force, and then came crashing down on his back. Pearl, who was holding his suspended form, caught his shoulders as they almost slammed into the ground.

The Chinese were shouting "jellyfish!" in Mandarin. Madrigal's supreme composure ended. A deadly jellyfish lightCowl wrapping her apprentice's head.

"Dale," she shouted and leapt on Rickenby as he lay on the ground, shuddering. She could now feel the hard ball of congealed light around his head, suffocating him, preventing any air between his face, mouth and the skin of light. She could see the tiny glint of gold fleck, the power chip, in front of his right eye. Rickenby's eyes were starting to cloud with his impending death. She felt the coldness of the hood of light. Frozen down by some nearby boson enhancer, the photons clamped fast around the skull and face.

"You have the wrong guy!" she screamed at the fleck of gold, trying to tear off the bottom of the seal of light. It was just under his chin. "This is NOT Marko. Let him go."

The White Lady security people were beside her.

"Not too late, Lady Phipps," said one man in a suit. In his hurry, he shoulderRolled her aside, straddled Rickenby and pulled a stemtube from a pouch in his belt.

"Tracheotomy," said the White Lady man, who had a knife in his hand. The medic, for that was his role, ran a gentle fingertip along Rickenby's upturned neck and punctured the windpipe, plumb in the middle. "Breathing will depend whether they managed to freeze the light all the way down his throat. With luck, it was dark down there and will only have frozen across his mouth. Only a jellyfish kiss – not a swallow."

The Chinese security man slid the tube into an air passage and a horrible rasping ensued as Rickenby dragged air into his lungs, and exhaled as noisily, drops of pink blood and fluid fluming from the end of the tube.

"Good," said the Chinese man. "Slowly." However, it was unlikely Rickenby would have heard with the photons congealed in his ears. Madrigal nodded encouragingly, hoping he could see her.

He breathed in again. Then out. Light started to flare in her assistant's eyes again. He fought for every breath.

"Stabilising." Pearl applied an oxygen spritzer to the end of the tube, giving Rickenby some help.

They knelt round the young trainee Courier – Pearl, the 3 securitizors, including the field medik, and Madrigal. She held his hand tight. Chime, weapon in hand, was already scanning the woods through his visor, looking for a control team with a remote. LightBenders were very local unless the Brazilians had improved the technology. They also needed batterized.

Mebbe the Brazilhoz did have Andaman Marko's strokes. Mebbe they were now all over AuZgov platforms, stealing secret after secret. It was unthinkable. Madrigal assumed the Brazilhoz controllers were well out of the way because what they'd done was audacious. Mebbe they were still in Brazil, with a technology that could reach around the globe, aimed by anonymous operators. What a terrible thought that was. When they made light malleable, the government saw it as a force-Field for good, to protect homes from storms, but now there seemed a steady slide to using good technology for violence, yet again. She was disgusted.

Other White Lady men were running down the causeway and fanning into the woods beyond, diving into the undergrowth hunting for whoever had the control unit. The sky, which had gone the colour and texture of yellow muddy chalk, already swarmed with remote controlled bees.

"Let this man go," Madrigal again said to the chip. She knew the controllers could see and hear her. "This man is Courier Dale Rickenby, he is not your target. Your target is in Australia." She said it twice, in English, Mandarin, and Portuguese, the 3 linguas of the age. The Brazilhoz would have heard, but they didn't believe her and the hard jellyfish of light sat over Rickenby's head until the Chinese found an appropriate jammer to break the photon link.

Then the light dissolved amid furious apologies from her absent father's business partners.

*

The hum of passengers and tinkle of music interfered with the sound levels on her clamB.

"Coming to get you now, love," she said into her little screen. Todd smiled, highBeam. She could see relief in his eyes. Over the past few years she'd seen him smile more on a screen that in real life. This pattern of neglect was about to end.

"The Spokes is fun here, but I missed you," he said from far away.

"I missed you, too. But I'll meet you in Hobarttown tomorrow and we can go back to Perth together."

"So you really are coming home?"

"I have to help Dad. He's getting old now."

"Ok!" said Todd. For him, the news was getting better and better.

"I'll see you soon, sweetie." Madrigal clipped off and sat forward in the concourse bench seat, looking out at the rocket port.

She had a few hard truths for her dad, that's for sure. What was his game with the White Lady? Did he know about the Marko business? Hanging in Asia for half a year with his Phipps team screwing deals out of people and probably screwing around just generally. Mad old bastard. She had admired him, yes. But with caveats, including the effect his absences had on her mum.

Now she was furious.

She looked beyond the clouded glareProof windows of the RammPort at the 2 or 3 jjets parked on the launch strip, with their ominous sharklike shapes. One was for Brisbane. One probably aimed for Sao Paulo. Or Jo'Berg.

Their Ramm would probably track back over their far north gas shelf, which was now inoperable. No matter how much hardening of the platforms and mechanisation and submersion – it was all too dangerous. The company would have to pull back and maintain the southern tide/wind conglomerations. They may have to reopen some LandBased gas constellations too. She was thinking like Dad already.

And there was a lot to think about. Telling Wen she was beaten by circumstances – defeated by her birthright. Retreating home.

Dale Rickenby sat beside her, throat bandaged up, still looking haunted. Poor bugger.

Pearl and Chime were out checking the RramRamp. They'd already checked devices to detect possible lightBenders and drones.

"You sure you can catch this flight, Rickenby? 3G Ramm, after all that?"

"The sooner I am out of here, the better," he rasped in his damaged voice. "Fuck doctor's orders."

FINGAL WEN

THE 2 bargeCatamarans, filled with mourners, had tied up alongside the landing jetty and the processional was now moving down a beautiful timberFramed path and up the narrow flight of stairs. Around 200 peeps, mainly senior AuZgov administrators in their best suits and uniforms, were climbing the yellowed sandstone steps up the headland to the iron chapel at the top. They were silent & reverent. A row of lamps lit the way in the Hobarttown gloaming. A party of Slotters led the processional in half march. Muffled drums thumped at the front.

As the processional wended its way along the jetty that jutted into the river, 'Arald saw Madrigal Phipps halfway down the crowd, holding her little boy's hand. He was first taken with her simple elegance, then taken aback that she was not in formal uniform, but wearing a calfLength black dress frock with a warm velvet stole, leather boots to ward off the cold and a small sqware black hat. For a moment, his brows adopted a critical crease. No uniform at a formal interment? She was an AuZgov Courier for goodness' sake. Then he remembered. Dr Phipps was to move back west. To look after her father's business, she'd said. He halfSmiled. *Madrigal*, mused 'Arald, *was a rascal, a risk taker.* What a suitable outcome that she left the administration. Her nice little boy wore a dark purple teflite jacket and woollen cap.

As he watched Madrigal, 'Arald held Wen round the shoulders and they shuffled along with the crowd. Wen was a slumped presence. Despite being the tough nuggety administrative commander, dressed in full uniform, with blue jacket, braid loops, medals and cap, he was distraught and needed a help and a hand from his husband. Wen's face pointed down, at the smooth wooden jetty slats, and his cheeks were pale. So many people from the Spokes, from Canberra and Wellington were there. 'Arald nodded to familiar faces on Wen's behalf because Wen was somewhere else.

*

Earlier, when they were getting dressed at their Hobarttown house, with its panoramik view across the Derwent, Wen confessed that *apart from 'Arald,* the 2 dead men – Kingdom and Bluestone – had been the only people in his life he'd felt entirely comfortable with, and were the 2 people who had inspired him to his mercurial success in becoming the eminence of the security system.

Wen was removing his casual shirt and gazing at the dress uniform jacket on the end of the bed, pressed and ready.

"Kingdom, Bluestone and I ... we worked as a team in the Age of Purity. We had a clear singleMindedness. Could trust each other. Like brothers. We would sit around the tables of Canberra or down here in Hobarttown talking, smashing those ideas from one to the other like sqwash balls, getting the job done."

'Arald found this odd. While he'd liked Simon Bluestone's irascible wit and nimble intelligence, he was dubious about the other fellow, Kingdom. That bloke had gone completely rogue. Mad even. The man cut Fingal off years ago.

Normally 'Arald would have scoffed and begun a fullBlown, negative character assessment of Kingdom Allenby, poking fun at Wen, declaring him deluded. But under the circumstances, 'Arald bit his tongue. His husband had a bit of a blind spot. Kingdom Allenby was Wen's only weakness, and the man's messy death appeared to be a spear through his heart.

Wen had said, "With those bottled juve juices, we can escape the physical deterioration and aches and pains of old age, but the hard weight of experience and memory bears down on you like a rock," he sighed. "You might feel as young as 30, but these passing years still turn you into a maudlin old man, and the older you get, the harder ..."

"I know," said 'Arald.

Wen sat heavily on the end of the bed, still without his boots, ungroomed, like a man trying to move through glue.

"... the harder it is to look at the world and see it shine." He paused. "Have I told you about the time Kingdom rescued both Simon and I from being bashed in a pub on the Sydney waterfront? In a workers pub one evening when we had furlough? When we were studying?" Wen had smiled. His only smile of the day.

"If one punch had been thrown, that incident would have ended all of our careers. Kingdom Allenby waded in and saved us for glory."

"No, you haven't told me about your brawl," 'Arald had said. "You must do that tonite, but let's get dressed. The barge will be leaving soon."

A cruiserV limo was already waiting outside to whisk them to the ferry terminal, and they were hardly dressed.

"I tried to help Kingdom after the war," said Wen. "After he was damaged, I reached out."

"I know you did," said 'Arald.

"He couldn't come back then, but he's home now."

'Arald had never seen his husband in this state before. It was very unsettling.

*

Todd had never been to a funeral. Carefully, he asked his Mum, "Is that the chapel up there?"

"Yes, love – at the top of the steps. Those men in front take those silver boxes up the staircase and a celebrant will talk about my old boss, Simon Bluestone, & the other man, Kingdom Allenby, & then the boxes will be put in the catacomb with other people who have passed."

The waves chopped under the jetty as they walked. The crowd climbed up the stairs in silence, only the huffing and puffing of the unfit to be heard, and swishing of cloth. They reached the top lawns. Sullen clouds, like yellowed bruises, sat above Mt Wellington and there were drops of rain.

She scanned the huge horizontal windstacks, dull pewter armour across half the mountain, which powered the town and beyond, the never ending southern gusts cranking 1000s of rotors. Madrigal glanced back towards the Derwent & it was silvery charcoal in the dusk. She glimpsed one or 2 darker rings on the surface of the estuary like glittering donuts with their unlit centres filled with living protein – fish – tended by the floating farm communities. There were many more further down in Storm Bay and throughout the D'Entrecasteaux Channel, and she wondered how those people held on during the recent 'phoon. A precarious living.

The processional merged qwickly into the room they called the chapel – it was cool and the rain was increasing, and noone wanted to get their best clothes wet. The room was packed for Bluestone with his colleagues and family. Noone there to mourn Kingdom, she thought. Only Wen would remember Allenby as he was. And she and Chime were the only others who had seen Kingdom Allenby in the flesh, although it was in the Ville when he was dead on a gurney.

Now the remains of both Bluestone and Kingdom Allenby were in silver casqwes.

Madrigal was sad that young Flick was missing the interment of her father in the section of chapel wall that held members of the class of '58. But she'd probably never be told about his early years as an AuZgov officer. Or even where he would now rest. This was Sacred Administrator bizz.

She knew this wasn't Kingdom's real endpoint: a ceremonial interment with other passed Commanders and Couriers. His endpoint had been on a soggy median strip, protecting his daughter in a gunfight. And if the burning revenge of Baabi hadn't happened, Fate should really have found him dead in a bar, drinking lampjuice at the Nest, and buried in a muddy grave near his longDead wife.

Kingdom Allenby had rejected those early days, those pre weatherWar, Purity days, long ago. He was no longer of the world of formal pomp and oratory that now surrounded his mortal remains.

To Madrigal, it was wrong. Allenby's country was up in the Cape.

Now she, Madrigal, was also forced to leave that world, a lot more reluctantly. She smoothed her skirt, knowing out of uniform was a statement of fact she had resigned. She'd miss the eucalypt green teflite uniform with the collar of woollen trim. At least, in the sweltering Tassy heat, the black dress she wore was a darmsite cooler that a woolTrimmed uniform.

The crowds, the candles, the drum was Age of Purity pomp indeed. She knew this double funeral was more for the living Fingal Wen, than for the dead.

In the Chapel, the celebrant said words that were crisp, even momentous. Fingal Wen was shaking with grief. Mortality was closing in on him too. The first generation of people that were able to defy death, with stem cells and spartan health regimes, happily overspending their qwota of allocated heartbeats. Wen too would end lodged up there in the Wall of Remembrance underneath them, as would the P/EM, and sooner rather than later.

Madrigal observed it all from a few metres away. This was a liminal moment, she thought. The administrators of the Age of Purity, now passing, were either dead or too old to go on. Purity was passing, and a more volatile world was on the way.

"The deaths of these men were savage and untimely," intoned the celebrant, "and the perpetrators have been caught and punished. But the deaths of these 2 officers while grievous, is not an injustice on which we should dwell. Rather it is the efforts of these 2 officers over the many decades to keep harmony, keep peace, keep AuZtralia safe. They guided us through difficult times, through the joining of Asia and the northern AuZtralia as one entity, a homeland, without rancour. They brought us peace. Like no other generation in our history, we shall remember them."

"We shall remember them," intoned the crowd. "Lest we forget."

The Last Post was played.

The processional then made its way down the ancient spiral staircase into the bowels of the catacomb. Madrigal looked down the cylindrical steps and could just see the leaders with their white gloves holding the silver boxes, way down, on the third wind of the stairs. They were heading down to the 4th basement, the most prestigious ground. Portentous music was being played up ahead by a small group of musicians on drums and trumpets, and the sound welled up, thumped and magnified against the stone. Thick chords of mourning and dwelling.

The roughCut sandstone wall, a deep orange yellow in licks of light, was pitted with crevices in which many 100s of small boxes could be glimpsed. Silver flashes of the buttends of containers in their holes, like eyes winking. An old art gallery that the then Puritans of the Commonwealth had had reqwisitioned and then refurbished almost a century ago for their own funereal purposes. By now Madrigal and Todd were at the back of the crowd and she lifted her son onto her shoulders so he could see. The boy on her shoulders was still, and fascinated by the ceremony. She felt his warm little legs around her neck.

"Simon Bluestone rest in peace, your service done," intoned the celebrant. And the same words again for Kingdom Allenby. Because of the gloom, she couldn't qwite make out the Ceremonial Pivot, but he looked very much like Chime ... yes, it was Chime ... she could sense his distant presence, laying the 2 boxes to rest, side by side, sliding the cases into the holes in the wall.

"We are deep down underground," said Todd looking across the sea of heads at the men and women to the front where Slotters attended to the ceremonials. "Are we below the surface of the Derwent?"

"Not qwite," said Madrigal sqweezing his leg, and feeling his bum bones pressing into her shoulders. He was getting heavy. "Come down, and we'll find you a drink."

"In a minute, Mum. I'm still watching," he whispered, clamping her neck with his legs. She grimaced, but allowed him another few minutes perched like a cat.

While Madrigal had never met the goneRogue Kingdom in real life, and only heard bitter remonstrations about him from his daughter, she felt that down in these catacombs she owed it to Flick to be her proxy. Madrigal made an ulterior decision and vowed to scope Flick (if she could locate the young woman) and let her know her father had been "cared for" even if he hadn't been properly buried in the country he'd adopted.

Tho' she couldn't tell Flick where her Dad rested, a little information was the least she could do.

"Your Dad was buried in a simple ceremony. I was there," she'd lie, in a mollifying voice. It wouldn't do, but it was something.

But while she felt no sentiments for Kingdom, she was definitely upset about Bluestone's passing. Madrigal and Bluestone had worked hard together. He'd annoyed her immensely towards the end, with his born2rule airs and silly old fashioned words, but he'd been the best teacher. She remembered her panic early that morning in the Ville months ago, the hotel bellhop, the slumped corpse, the dried flecks of spit on the cheek. Bluestone had been a mentor. And they'd spent many hours together plotting, planning, talking and taking missions everywhichwhere. The more she thought of him, the more she could see his dry old face now, in front of her, looking kindly.

Tears trickled down her cheeks and she was glad Todd couldn't see them from his shoulder perch.

"Friends," intoned the celebrant, "that is the end of our ceremony. Our mourning here is done, but we can remember them, the efforts of these men in those troubled years, stewards who helped us peacefully pass from one world to the new. We will now return to the chapel for qwiet reflection & supper and before the barges return us to Hobarttown."

At the supper in the clifftop chapel, in flickering candlelight amongst a noisy crowd, Madrigal and Todd were surrounded by the Slotters she had trained and worked with. They didn't really care about the deceased – old men from the past– but were very concerned about Madrigal's departure – the exit of the living.

Wowz, she thought, *how good to they all look in their dress uniforms and Todd looked so tiny beside them.* The loss of her own uniform and status made her ache with regret.

All were there – Chime, Folly, Dante and Pearl and several others she'd worked with. All gave her farewell hugs as she and Todd were flying to Perth in the morning. She felt their steel-Hard physiqwes against her and thought, I'm one of them, I feel at home, so why do I walk out?

But there was no choice.

Ultimately, Pearl stood at the edge of the lawn with an arm round her shoulder. Inside, Todd circled the food on the banqwet table for the seventh time.

Madrigal was a little drunk from the wine.

"I'll miss you, ma'am."

"You can call me Maddy now, Pearl," said Madrigal looking down the river to the twinkling lights of the city where a hotel room and early morning jet to Perth awaited.

"Can't. You'll always be, ma'am," said Pearl. "Don't even think I'd call you anything else."

"So sorry I'm leaving," said Madrigal.

Pearl gave Madrigal's shoulder a sqweeze, and said in her deep contralto voice: "It's only fun 'til the shit gets real."

Madrigal snorted and stifled a laugh. "Bluestone used to say that."

"Yep ... I stole that one from Courier Bluestone." They gazed at one another for a moment.

"When's it going to get real for you, Pearl?"

"Hopefully, never," said the Slotter with a wry grin.

CASSIE

ANDAMAN Marko steps across the hopperPort at the Ville to stare at the wetlands to the east, the canal district, and the jumbled city everywhere else. Is it hotter than ever? Is he imagining the full force of the 49 degrees? No matter, it's just bearable. Any nonResident would have wilted after the first few steps in the outdoors. Not Andaman.

He walks to where a car waits for him, with driver. The chauffeur is Kiko – one of his usual blokes, and he is pleased to see him.

"Let's go, Kiko," he says slinging his large snailshellPack into the rear of the vehicle. The car is cool. The windows, tinted darkBlue, kill the glare.

"How'd we go this summer with the Cloud?" he asks his old driver. Kiko shrugs.

"Coupla big blows in Jan, Boss. Not as bad as the year before. But's been a warm one."

Andaman nods appreciatively.

He swings by the Swarbar, his old haunt, hoping for Flick, says hi to the staff and has a cool one. There is no rush. Kiko waits in the shade and smokes chopChop. Flick hasn't been seen round town for months. She could have headed off, all the way to the west – that was her threat, wasn't it? On the other hand, she might still be parked down at the northern marina. The povvo one. He'd chuck his bag at home and go look for her later. He'd find her – the only person he knew who made him feel calm, these days. Just even thinking of her helped. Now, head for home.

Pool would probably be rank & green. Did the milisi empty his frijjs? Probably carpeted by mould given the "warm one".

The car cruises up the back road through the forest 'til the rear of the hill and the top car park, where he pays Kiko with a couple of $New, much to the chauffeur's delight. "Good to have you back, Andy," he said. "Where'd you go?"

"South," says Andaman, not willing to elaborate, but "South" suffices. It means a welter of unpalatable issues for Kiko, a small Timorese guy, who grunts and delivers a mock salute as he drives off.

Andaman hauls his pack to one of the viewing platforms at the very top of the hill and stretches and looks down into the valley where the canals and river meander into the bay, like a net of light. Pallaranda Island out in the middle of the bay that had once been an airport until the rising ocean gorged on the salt plains to the north.

The city wraps around Mt Stuart and disappears in a haze of white up to the Harveys Range escarpment. It's very hot. The monsoon is retreating now and the storms are crumbling back to the permanent motherCloud between the fifteenth parallel and the eqwator. In the hi40s the humidity plucks at his skin.

He leans across the border of the platform and looks at the top of his house, halfway down along the road there, and sighs. The adventure is over. His style has been cramped. The pledge he has signed says he can no longer use his strokes, most of which he revealed to AuZgov. He'd held back on some of the modals around falsehoods and lies. The linguistic bits. But they'd work it out. They weren't that stupid.

Unfortunately, the very highest authority ruled that he was now officially in "limbo". The P/EM, Fingal Wen, someone.

Banned from the virtual, he could live off his substantial riches, but only through delegated investments approved by AuZgov. His wings were clipped.

Andaman grimaces. Life is going to be dull, stale, unenthralling. But then he has his house, his riches and he has his friends. And Flick. He'd find Flick. She'd been released from the barracks after the creepy woman had been captured and then turned to dust like a vampire. Flick, wherever she was, would be back on the boat, now preparing for the rest of her life too. She was fun. They could escape together.

Sighing, he lifts his pack and clamB pack and starts walking down the stairway and round the path to the back entrance of the bottlehouse. It's cooler on the shaded path between the rock and the rear of several of the houses clamped to the cliff face. Past the Waterburys, past John Maxwell's rear doors accessed by a small drawbridge. He keeps going round and could smell the cool water on the rock face. The path gets thinner and at last he's at his home. It's always a sqweeze, up the railed steps. To get through to his house entrance, he had to kick his pack along the walkway and go sideways. In doing so, he looks up and spots a package on one of the steel pylons that pinned his house to the rock. A small, sqware block of white, not meant to be there. He'd built the place. He looks up at the other pylon and sees a similar white package. He shudders in terror.

After the last couple of months, it isn't difficult to work out what the packages hold. He breathes deep, steps back slowly and pulls out the clamB, which dutifully searches for micro signals. There was one emanating from 30 metres away. A connection.

Andaman withdraws to have a think.

A bomb.

First thought: could be AuZgov, wanting him permanently stopped, but that is silly. After working with Madrigal and even

Wen, he knows they are utterly homicidophobic —couldn't kill. They lamely use Slotters as a very last resort.

On the other hand, the woman Baabi, he knows, had been fully vested in the task of killing him.

In fact, the great Dr Madrigal Phipps herself had told him after the killer's capture that Baabi hadn't said a thing from her arrest onwards, but had been cocksure, defiant. He now realises it was probably because she'd set up this one last shot at killing him. Somewhere in his house, on his door, somewhere, was a tripper – the signal he detects on his scan would be broken, the charges would go off, blowing the house down the rock, into the suburbs and forest verge, way down the bottom of the cliff.

Only explanation.

Wasn't White Lady. No. The White Lady syndicate were sorted. AuZgov had their written word, according to Dr Phipps. She said they'd been spoken to when she rang him with assurances. Only Baabi and her employers, the Brazilhoz, had still been determined to kill him. Him. Slot him out and off. Extinguished.

His skin prickles, and it isn't just from the copious sweat. There is nothing but darkness in these bombs on his beloved bottlehouse. A dark vengeance which he'd been running from for months and couldn't shake.

His whole life is poised on the brink. He could explode everything, fake his death, vamoose. Run with Flick. He could kill himself. But first he'd better scope Flick. Always back to thinking about Flick and that cinnamon kiss on his doorstep.

If he fakes his oblivion ... what about that. Just blow the place up and walk away.

Then he looks down between the houses at the 100s of roofs staked below where the cliff ended and the slope towards the sea began, and shudders again. What a thought that is! There are schoolkids ambling home, and a few food stalls, and a man way below making sandals out of a pile of rubber tyres. House roofs with unknown scores of people inside, almost directly below. He knows them all. They're his neighbours. What was he thinking? He could never do it.

Nothing could or would prompt him to detonate the charges with 100,000 litres of water in the poolCoolant area, not to mention the tonnes of structural steel keeping the house floating in the air. No. His house was a bomb, courtesy Baabi, and he wouldn't set it off. He ought to act.

Andaman Marko pulls his device from his belt and scopes Dante. Dante, who punched his number into his scope back in Hobarttown.

He hasn't got Madrigal's number. She's a cypher who comes and goes. So were the people at the barracks, and Fingal Wen. Only Dante spoke to him face on face about what he was and what he could become. And for his safety had left a number. The only one who left a number.

"Yeh?" Dante's voice.

"Dante, someone has placed bombs over my house in the Ville. I was coming through the back and saw them locked on the joists. If they explode, it'll be mayhem."

Dante is firm, but friendly. "Chook, walk away slowly – a team will be there in a nano."

"Any team has to make their way down the back path, the path I escaped along. If they go through the front, the white package things will detonate. I think it's rigged on a locational switch."

"Stay scoped, don't hang up," says Dante. His voice is authoritative. Reassuring. "I'll loop some other people." Looping noises clicked on the line.

There are kids down the slope. Dante would be somewhere far away. The Spokes. Wellington. Canberra. He could hear more voices on the scope, Dante explaining.

"Milisi will be with you shortly. You need to stay put. Go round the front and wait. Let noone near."

That meant walking down some steps, across the terrace, and back up to the road. Some way.

"Noone else should die."

"Noone will." Madrigal's voice was joined into the signal somehow. "Andy," her familiar voice says, and she really has the voice. "This is for sure Baabi's agency. She was tasked to kill you. And though she is gone, she's boobyTrapped your house through and through. The bombs on the exterior may only be the start. There may be poisons, all sorts of nasties inside."

"Ok," says Andaman miserably. His house is a death house.

He walks gingerly down the path again. The bombs must have been there a while, because Baabi had died already, courts denying her juveJuice. Died with the body burning up. Not anything like a stateSanctioned execution. So called natural causes took her, after she was denied the hormones and enzymes and stems. Time was well up, once the cocktail was taken away.

Down the last of pink granite stairways and onto the skyTrack road. He walks past the Armstrong's place, white and splendid, Johnny Zhong's fine house with its eyrie and his other neighbours. The road is thin. Everything is these days. Had to fit so many structures into the town to fit all the people. The sea is green. Storm season with its malevolent Cloud drawing back to the eqwator. It's some time since he'd been to the Ville, and once the bombs are gone, he can settle back in. Into his palace. God, what a break, seeing the packages. How'd he do that?

Madrigal's voice cuts in and he realises he was still pressing the device against his ear: "Andy. Milisi and forensiks are set to go through with a nit comb. She was out to get you. Didn't tell you but your pic appeared strong in the imagery from Baabi's limbic probe."

"Nit comb. Right. Will do."

From the corner of his eye, up near his front driveway, he sees a figure. He looks again and starts to run.

"No," he shouts. "Wait"

Cassie.

She must have heard through the Swarbar guys, the blabby guys at the Swarbar, that he was back. Had he given her a wand for his place? The day of the first disaster? Way back when, in the Northern Lights, and they picked glass out of each other? She must have lifted one from the wand rack and waited his return all these months. Cassie was another girl he owes heaps to. He starts to panic and sprints towards her, pumping his legs.

"No, Cassie," he barks. "Stop! Stop now!"

Waving.

She stands in a kneeLength sarong, Xshirt and a cascade of hair, and looks round and sees him. Waves wildly in his direction with a big, red lipstick smile and raises a triumphant arm, a bottle of champagne in hand. She points to the bottle and heads to the front door.

Too far up the skyTrack for her to hear, to see the fear in his face. She swipes the pad at his front door with the wand.

The blast is massive and deafening, like a crack of thunder inside his skull. Cassie is consumed in a fireball. The greasy flame and tremendous spray of water blow perpendicular to the cliff. The cloud contains beams, shattered panels, and other undefinable debris. Blast blows him to the ground, the heat horrific. While his house detonates and disintegrates, the floating houses on either side of his, come asunder from their pins, and slowly slide, like a pair of old drunks, down the wall of the cliff. He tries to regain his feet, and stumbles again as the skyTrack buckles and heaves, and he crashes against the steel and sees the water pour in a torrent 100s of metres down, sluicing through the suburb below, washing away people, buildings, cars, all the way down the hill with his poolwater, the rubble that had been his home. He gets to his knees and runs the few metres back to the hard rock granite staircase, reeling on the suspended steel roadway.

The scope tumbles from his hand, following the rubble, down, like an afterthought.

Baabi's legacy.

*

Somehow Andaman has clambered down rocks and pathways to the street. Groups of people are already teamed up to move rubble, hard glass and rocks, looking out for survivors in the crushed apartment buildings. Milisi are pouring out of trucks, fanning out with eqwipment and creating cordons.

The ground is sodden with rubble and mud from the coolant tanks of the houses that were dislodged and fell from the cliff. He can hear wailing, and is not sure whether the wails are sirens or human screams. It's the only sound that penetrates his blastClouded ears.

Further away from the ruins which rained down on his neighbourhood, he walks, staggers, through a reserve of trees that masks one of the stormSurge terraces. His mind is a jumble of images from the weeks and months prior. The back of the landV and the masked guys in the jungle; through the windows at the Spokes, the fish swimming in and out of vision, silver scales glistening in the artificial light of the recDeck; Lolah's soft face on a pillow, replaced by Dante's angry helmeted one; Madrigal Phipps looking at him qwizzically; Flick.

Flick steering *The Capricorn Sky,* back turned to him, with her sinewy arm on the wheel and the other bent against the wheelhouse window. The images swarm like the fish in the dark window.

He falls and curls up for a while under a fig tree in a bed of orangeFlowered Heliconia and tries to calm himself. Heliconia flowers are redYellow explosive bursts, in wax. Andaman groans, but he's hidden from HighEyes, amongst a cloud of leaves. Breathing in and out calmly only forces tears from his eyes, and he oscillates between anguish and fear and guilt. The guilt of bringing such destruction to so many people overwhelms him. He still hears the sirens, but wonders if they are in his mind.

Some hours on, coming across Warburton Terrace, he is almost KO'd by a jitney.

Andaman finds Flick. Finally finds her. It's taken him a day of struggle. She's on the verandah of the kiosk at the povvo marina. Perched on a seat, drinking an orange fizz looking at her boat. Looking sad. She's been crying. She must have seen the blast on the face of the cliff, because everyone would have, and thought him gone.

Gingerly, he walks up to her and she looks up in astonishment and leaps to her feet and says "Andy" in a strangled voice. There is light in her eyes. She grips him, face in his chest, like dear life. He holds her.

There is noone else around.

"Come on," she says cautiously to Andaman, leading him to her boat. He's wobbly on the cabin steps and she goes down first, then holds his elbow as he descends. The side of his face is seared with what look like second degree burns, and there are glass fragments in his arm, marked by patches of dried blood. But it's the look on his face that is most alarming to Flick. It's not something that can be solved by her little old first aid book. It's the look of a man who is utterly lost.

Still, she holds him tight.

His voice chokes. Noone has held him like that ever. He can't speak. He prises her off and finally looks at her, his mouth opening and shutting like a landed fish.

Manages to say, "Flick ... can you teach me how to disappear?"

ABOUT THE AUTHOR

Once, in Australia's deep North, Colly Campbell was a both a journalist and sometime playwright and musician. He moved to Canberra with his family and worked as a media and policy adviser in the Senate for Labor and latterly for the Minister for Defence. He was closely involved in many Senate inquiries, governance reform and multiple Federal election campaigns. He was also, for a time, Communications Director at the *Australian Institute of Criminology*.

Pacey crime and speculative fiction intersect in Colly's Venn diagram of imagineering, and having worked around Government and travelled all over Australia, the future holds an endless fascination and concern.

He is now a full-time writer.

The Capricorn Sky is his first published novel. The sequel, *The Kyoto Bell*, was published in 2021.

Find more about Colly Campbell at www.collycampbell.com.au